I0822440

UNTEMPERED

FATE UNTETHERED

BOOK ONE

ELISSE HAY

Copyright © 2024 Elisse Hay. All rights reserved.

No part of this book may be reproduced in any form or by any electronic or mechanical means, including by information storage and retrieval systems, without written permission by the author, except for the use of brief quotations for review purposes.

ISBN

Hardback: 978-1-923344-02-0

Paperback: 978-1-923344-03-7

Ebook: 978-1-923344-04-4

Editing and Formatting by Shelly McKewin | The Fiction Editor.

Proofreading by Samantha Pierce | Radiant Editorial.

Cover and chapter art by Gretchen Cobaugh | Lichen and Limestone.

Map by Elisse Hay.

OTHER TITLES BY ELISSE HAY

Something Wicked

An urban fantasy romance series about a burned-out social worker witch helping her clients, and defending her peace.

Foul is Fair

Villains by Necessity

Met by Moonlight

Thunder, Lightning, Rain

Fate Untethered

Untempered

Unchained (coming soon)

AUTHOR'S NOTE

This story has been developed on the lands of the Wadawurrung peoples of the Kulin Nation. I acknowledge their elders, past and present, and their living connection to this land.

Content Notes

This book explores themes of family violence, gendered violence, plague including illness relating to infant and mother death, and (unrelated) difficult premature birth of a healthy child. For full notes, see the end of the book or the author's website.

For me, because I deserve this space. You can have the next one.

Matri'sion Tribal Lands

The Steppes

Raider's Ban

La'Angi

Azashi

Arcanloc

Black Borough

Raa'shi

Wolfswail

The South

The Citadel

Ltona

PROLOGUE
ISOLDE

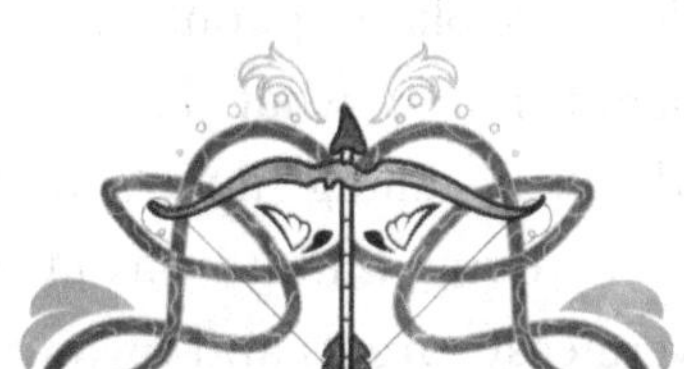

"The deadliest weapon is the shattered blade." ~ *Matri'sion proverb*

Go, they'd said.

She could disrupt fate's plans, they'd said.

Well, the girl wasn't even able to change her own slippers without triple-checking whether she should. Anxious, flighty, and obedient were traits I could name. Her only use was her malleability, and I didn't have time to craft her into the weapon we needed.

Her brown eyes were huge as she looked around the rooms we'd been shoved into as if she hadn't looked around them constantly since we'd arrived early yesterday.

When I'd first seen those eyes gleaming in the firelight, big and liquid, I'd thought they were animalistic. I'd hoped for a time that the soothsayer had been right, that she did have some deep, well-hidden streak of strength, some killer's instinct. A small, drab lump who looked younger than her eleven years, she slid into her chair before the plain table, eyes downcast.

She'd need strength *and* a killer's instinct if she were to truly be our salvation. And I'd seen naught of it.

Somehow, she'd stumbled through the festivities that should've marked the start of their wedding celebrations last night. When I thought of how that celebration was now postponed, I couldn't help but smile. Her gaze flickered up to me in alarm.

"Eat," I told her, impatiently.

Her fingers fumbled the plain spoon, and something about that graceless anxiety brought home what I'd managed to do for her yesterday when she'd been falling apart, and I'd convinced her betrothed she was far too young, and he was far too honorable to wed her now. Soft hearts were easy targets and my aim was true. The young fool had *wanted* me to convince him. I'd barely had to do anything except listen to him ramble about honor and love.

He was the scholarly son of a country lord, and he didn't even need to shave yet. What he knew about honor or love would make the shortest tale of time.

Whether or not this girl was who we needed, I'd saved her some pain and postponed her nuptials. All the lordling had to do now was break the news to the Butcher. Living through that task would also be useful for him, I supposed.

I watched dispassionately as the child pushed fruit around in her porridge. The province we were visiting was obviously not wealthy, but even so, the grains were thickened with milk and sweetened with honey. She could at least be grateful, even if she couldn't be fierce.

I opened my mouth to tell her to eat, not toy with it, but her head snapped up like a rabbit hearing the hunter. A split second later there was a knock at the door.

The way her face had drained of all color had the hairs standing up on the back of my neck.

Blood beat heavily in my veins, and that pre-fight rush of battle energy filled me with power and purpose. I strode to the door, flicking my cloak over my forearm as a makeshift shield as I went. In a rush I pulled it open and positioned myself in the gap between the child and the world, ready to defend.

There stood the Duke of La'Angi, the infamous Butcher of Wolfswail and stalwart defender of the locways that kept the poor in the gutters and the rich few on cushions. The Butcher barely glanced at me before his eyes latched onto his daughter. Every muscle in my body tightened as I dropped down into a curtsy. If they learned what I was, the possibility of me stealing this child away vanished.

I'd never been so close to a real monster.

Heat radiated off him, and my mouth was dry as the Steppes in summer. His hands were jarringly clean. They should've been blood red.

"Your grace," I said, giving way so he didn't walk over the top of me.

I was unarmed, unprepared—and he was undefeated.

His massive shoulders were hard beneath his plain woolen jacket as he walked past. Somehow, even his steps held rage.

I was a Matri'sion warrior. I did not cower before big, bad-tempered men just because they had collected titles and I did not recognize the locways of Arcanloc. If men came into our territory, they were prey, and the fatter the purse the richer the pelt. Steeling myself to inform him that the child hadn't yet eaten, I drew in a breath.

"Isolde," the girl said, the word quick, urgent, and making that breath stick in my chest. "Please go and—tell lord Luca I will meet with him later in the day. For that ride. I must speak with my father."

The man stopped to angle the top half of his body toward me, pinning me in his gaze as he waited for me to follow her instructions. His cheeks were ruddy, his lips now invisible.

There was fury in him.

The lordling had done it. Luca had done it. He'd postponed the wedding.

My feet were frozen to the ground as my heart raced. *What does it mean? What is he doing? Can I justify my attendance if—*

"Go," the girl said, the word as sharp as a cracking whip.

Shocked at the sudden change in her as much as the ring of command in that single word, I fell back. I was halfway through the door before I'd even stopped to think.

She'd known it was him.

She'd known it was him and she'd been scared.

There was violence in the man. Everyone knew what he was capable of, of course, but now it wasn't buried deep; it was just under the surface. It was in his eyes and mouth, fists and feet.

I turned, but the door was already closing in my face. A meaty arm dropped into my vision, another surprisingly clean hand splayed over the sturdy wood.

Ignoring the hard knot in my belly, I looked to the side, my body poised to defend. Two heavily armored men stood there in the black of the Duke's personal guard.

One, sure. But two? And then I'd have the Butcher to manage—without any tactical advantage.

"Move on," Mikus said, his eyes fixed on the curve of my breasts. He was known around the castle as the Butcher's Cleaver. It had taken me less time to identify him as a vicious beast, than it had to unpack my bags when I'd first arrived in the guise of handmaid to the lady.

The Duke's voice sounded from behind the door, full of frustration and disappointment.

I paused at that. A disappointed Butcher was probably not a deadly one. As I hesitated, Mikus' hand tightened on my shoulder. He was so close and tall that I had to look almost directly up. Pulling myself back, I resisted the urge to grab that hand and shatter every bone.

"Mind your manners, sir," I said stiffly, making a show of straightening my dress as I pulled away.

Mikus' answering smile was wide and hard. But it was Wade, on the other side, who said, "I'll mind more'n that if you linger." The leer was an entirely unnecessary addition to the threat in his words—and wild horses, how I would've *loved* to have my knives.

I felt suddenly naked without the weight of my war-belt and quiver in these unfamiliar skirts, so far away from my tribe. With all the dignity I could muster, I turned on my heel and went to find the little lordling.

Mayhap I'd be able to use whatever happened between the Butcher and the child as leverage.

The way her head had snapped up went through my mind. Her eyes locking onto the door. Her pupils tightening to pinpricks. She'd had no way of knowing who it was. The child must be terrified of life.

Enough time had passed before I tracked down the lordling that I was grateful to my cloak for staving off the cold. I found him in the deepest section of the keep's library, his nose in a book. He sat in a chair by the fireside like he owned the place—neat hair, velvet clothing, richly embossed belt, arrogant tilt to his chin. All the typical trappings of nobility.

I managed not to curl my lip when I said, "The lady will see you later this day."

He blinked, his eyes slowly focusing on me. "Oh. She still wishes to see me?"

That made me pause. Did she? More likely, it had been an excuse. "Why wouldn't she?" I asked, my mind whirring.

She'd looked me in the eye. She'd spoken to me with purpose and force. My belly twisted. It was the first time the possum of a child had spoken to me, and it had been a command to make me move.

"I postponed the wedding," he said, his book drooping in his hand, his brows drawing together. "The exact date is yet to be decided, but I'll accept nothing until she's a woman grown." He was putting aside the book and I set my teeth against the impossible formalities I hated but remembered so well.

She'd *ordered* me.

"Hasn't she been told?" he asked, standing. "I thought to tell her myself, but the Duke—"

Is telling her now. "Farewell, my lord," I said, cutting in over his apologies, before turning my back on him.

I didn't know what was going on, but I'd be damned if I was going to allow myself to remain ignorant.

I'd try her door first. If those two guards were there, mayhap I'd change my route. I'd scouted the area when we'd first arrived. I knew the way through the garden and access points over the curtain wall, so I could enter her room unseen by the window if I needed to.

"Isolde," Luca called. There it was again, the ring of command in a noble's voice. In comparison to that tiny, scared child, this lad sounded like a magework puppet, all show and flash. But that tone still served as a warning and a reminder. *Do as I say. I have the power.* That's what he meant.

What was it with nobility this day?

My pace quickened, causing my hair to bounce into my face. I tossed the blonde curls out of the way and didn't bother looking back.

There were no men wearing black tabards in front of her door when I returned. Probably best for all of us. With the hum of violence low in the back of my brain, it wouldn't have ended well if Wade had gotten lippy with me again. I inhaled deeply as I opened the door, half-hoping the Butcher would still be there.

He wasn't. There was no one there at all.

I held myself still, listening.

Silence.

My eyes tracked across the room, looking for anything out of place. My heart beat steadily and ice settled into my veins as I shoved the door closed, hard, to protect my back. There would be signs of what passed, information written on the ground.

I didn't see her at first. She'd almost completely vanished into the floor, or so it seemed. Pale as a ghost, she lay, helpless. I didn't go to her immediately, clearing the rest of the rooms to ensure there was no further threat before I folded myself down beside her.

Demanding my hands be steady, I pressed my fingers to her throat. She was warm, and I could feel the drum of her lifeblood, a slow, tortured rhythm. My lungs expanded, and I felt the press of my bodice against my upper body as I swelled with rage.

What an illustrious leader. What a brave warrior. What a peerless General.

He won a war against a child. He ought to be proud.

Working quickly, I ran my hands over her head and neck. She was banged up, but I could identify no serious bleeding. Her arms were whole. She hadn't tried to defend herself.

Of course she hadn't.

Fury pounded behind my eyes as I straightened her form and went to get a pitcher of water. She hadn't defended herself, but she'd known it was coming.

And she'd sent me away.

I heard a hitch in her breath as I knelt beside her again, flipping up my dress to tear one of my underskirts in a quick, vicious motion. Her eyelids fluttered. "Stay still," I told her impatiently. The naive child had tried to protect me and look where it had gotten her. "You've taken a few hits, haven't you?" It wasn't a real question. The answer was painfully obvious.

Her eyes, when she opened them, were the same pale liquid brown that I'd seen just an hour ago, but unfocused. Now, her breathing was shallow and reedy.

"I'm going to check for breaks," I told her, frustrated with my own poor judgment. I felt past the flimsy barriers of her clothing, searching for knots or irregularities in the rounded bones of her ribs. I left my investigation, feeling sick, after finding two.

"I need to get you up," I told her grimly. If those bones moved too much, they could puncture something important.

He'd made a bloody mess of her.

"Can't," she said, and the word was desperate and broken.

I remembered the way she'd ordered me out. The word bounced around my skull over and over. *Go. Go. Go.* The way her head had snapped up like a terrified rabbit.

"Won't," I corrected, ruthlessly.

She could take what I would give.

Her big eyes closed in pain. Her mouth was drawn, and I had no doubt she was in genuine agony. I stayed there, reliving every moment I'd shared with her, weighing it all up again, judging it in a new light.

What if she wasn't simply a coward? What if she was exactly what she needed to be to survive?

What would happen if she learned that she didn't need to be a wallflower, but a spearhead?

I leaned forward and rested my forehead gently against hers. "I'm going to get these injuries strapped," I told her.

There was pride in my chest, a hot, hard ball. I'd done wrong…but *she'd* done smart.

She'd done what she could. Now I'd match that.

"I'm going to help you, Audrey." Her eyes opened, unfocused and confused, but present enough to settle, briefly, on my face.

I smiled at Audrey, hard, with teeth. She met my gaze and a tear spilled down her cheek, her own expression one of hopelessness. I didn't wipe the tear away. She'd earned it, and more.

"I know you don't believe that's possible, but it is. More importantly, I'm going to help you help yourself." She continued to lay there, breathing those shallow breaths, and my heart roared with fury. Taking her forearm, I prepared to lever her up, quick and smooth. Gentleness wouldn't help her now. Steel would. Strength would.

I had plenty of both to share.

"First lesson, Audrey," I told her, feeling the strength of my own rage. "We are only conquered when we believe ourselves to be."

CHAPTER ONE
CHAY

"First, consider your approach, as it is critical you avoid startling them. Direct incursion from behind or the front will mark you as a threat and make taming your target either impossible or a very complex endeavor."
~ *How to Tame Your Brumby: A Collection of Raider's Ban Wisdom*

Ten years later

La'Angi was the birthplace of legends—and nightmares. It loomed over us between the limbs of the apple trees and their yellowing leaves like some sort of old, angry god. I was going to be within those walls soon, in the heartland of military prowess. I'd grown up hearing it spoken about with reverence.

I wasn't planning on birthing any legends or nightmares, myself. I had enough of both.

"Remind me again why we're here?" Callum complained, staring up at the foreboding keep in the distance.

Awe sat uncomfortably in the hollow in my guts, but Kadan

grinned, the expression charmingly crooked and full of fun. From the front, his father Darrius, Count of Raider's Ban and our liege lord, shot him a quick, amused look, anticipating the upcoming levity, before turning back to the road ahead of us and feigning dignity.

Kadan rolled his shoulders, settling the road-stained tunic better over his shoulders. He looked more like a merchant's son than the prophesized one. With his dirty blond hair flopping over the crown-like scar on his forehead, no one would guess his birth had been preceded by comet storms. His moment of birth had been marked by a solar eclipse, and then celebrated by every soothsayer and wise man in the lands. The scar he hid with a studied nonchalance was left by a lightning strike that, to hear his father speak of it, had been less godly and more terrifying. The real legends looked like everyday men and acted like them, too.

Kadan's smile vanished, and with eyes on where Callum sat scowling, he said, "You wanted to try your hand at seducing the lady of La'Angi before Luca claims her." The words were heavy with the ring of sincerity, driving home the ridiculousness of his statement.

Callum's lips twitched as he shifted in his saddle. "Don't wish that on me. Wild horses—the Butcher as a father-by-law! Luca's a braver man than I."

"Braver," Kadan repeated, pretending to consider the idea as we rode toward our destination and the Duke in question. "Less intelligent," he offered, with another glitter of fun in his eyes. "Besotted. More ambitious. Take your pick."

"Can we only choose one?" Callum sighed, giving in and going along with Kadan's jest, leaning forward in his saddle and absently running his fingers over the full quiver of arrows before him. He was nervous—and considering what we were *actually* up to, I didn't blame him.

The Butcher had the kingdom at sword point, and the King's advisor was stealing everything from us while we stood by, helpless.

At least, that was their intention. We weren't practiced at being helpless, though.

How brave or besotted Luca was, marrying the heir to the Butcher

—well, he did seem fond of her. He'd certainly visited La'Angi often enough over the past few years. Love or ambition? I'd always assumed the latter. You take La'Angi, you take the military, and then the country, you controlled the locways and every level of our society. "He told me La'Angi cider was almost as good as the expensive bottles of knappchs we import," I offered, to keep Callum from complaining again.

"Ah, see," Kadan agreed, with a nonchalant flick of one hand toward me, as if I'd just proved his point. His warhorse snorted and swung its head in my direction. "Noble women who don't know we're scoundrels, cider, our friend's wedding—and, of course, the famed La'Angi tourney. I'm confused as to why we didn't do this earlier."

He left out "the assassination of the Butcher". Yet more evidence he was wiser than people expected when they saw his carefully curated shit-eating grin.

Grim laughter rippled through the ranks of the men around us as though those unspoken words were heard. Even Callum's scowl crumbled before the statement.

We'd been looking for this opportunity for years.

I saw him open his mouth to respond, but I'd switched my attention to the north of the road, where the orchard was dim and leaves lay heavily on the ground, blanketing the roots of the trees ahead of the coming winter. Was that hooves? Was it one of ours? Surely—

A flash of movement was my only confirmation. Kadan reacted a moment before me, grabbing Callum's reins and urging both of their mounts out of harm's way. I reined in hard to avoid the path of a big chestnut horse bearing a young rider as a kite might bear a ribbon.

The chestnut whipped around, kicking and whinnying in fear, panicked to find itself in the center of our group. With my heart in my throat, I waited for the rider to give it directions as I tried to get Bliksem and myself further away, but they were either overwhelmed or clueless.

"Get clear!" Callum shouted unnecessarily as the beast reared up, snorting out a challenge as the rider scrambled to keep their balance.

"Lean in," Kadan told the rider, his voice carrying over the horse's commotion and the men's shouts of surprise.

Desperate to help, I found myself doing exactly that, following Kadan's instructions as if my own acquiescence would make a difference to the rider's struggle.

"Close to its—" The beast whirled and bucked, snapping at Kadan's own horse. The idea of this poor chestnut taking on a blooded Raider's Ban warhorse would've been funny if there hadn't been a lad on its back, one obviously untrained. The rider was wrestling with the reins, trying to drag the horse's head in close to their knee, holding on grimly as it fought him, and I couldn't do anything except stay out of the damned way.

Then bloody Kadan was out of his saddle and tossing his reins to Callum, offering an apple in an outstretched hand to the half-mad creature. "Only Kadan," someone muttered behind me even as the beast was rearing again. The wry calm of the statement was at odds with the life-and-death battle before us, jarring me from my own razor focus for a moment.

"Whoa, there," he was saying, his voice low and easy, but it was too little, too late. The rest of us knew it. Even, I suspected, the rider knew it. The horse's hooves struck the air, and I watched as if time had slowed as the beast went over further, then further again. My heart beat fiercely in my throat.

I knew people were going to die. We were coming to La'Angi, after all. But this was not a fortuitous beginning.

"Jump!" Kadan shouted, at the precise moment his father called out the exact same word.

Whether it was the two layers of wisdom or that the rider simply knew what was good for him, he leaped clear of the horse, rolling across his back on the ground and springing to his feet like a cat.

"Get him clear!" My liege lord commanded, but again it was an unnecessary order. I was out of my saddle, wrapping my arm around the lad and tossing him as far as I could from those deadly, flailing hooves. Kadan lunged for the reins at the same time, trying to save the horse, reacting on instinct.

I found myself stumbling as the youth latched onto my arm, spinning himself around and pulling me with him—and then my legs went out beneath me. My head was full of the smell of rich orchard and terrified beast. I drove my boot heel into the ground and shoved us both away from where I could feel the reverberations of its struggle. Everything was a blur around us as I put all my energy into getting away from the threat, my arms firmly locked around the youth. With the roar of my heart in my ears, I again planted my heel and shoved. I still felt hooves nearby. Kadan had the reins, though. If anyone could salvage this, it was him.

Now another body length away, I rolled over the youth, risking a glance to get the briefest idea of how close those deadly hooves were.

Or, I tried to, but the world spun. I was lifted and then landed on the ground again. My bones rattled with the force of impact, and the air rushed out of my lungs. Disoriented, I tried to make sense of how the youth's knees were squeezing my ribs and my right arm was pulled across his body at a strange angle, while also keeping track of our distance from the terrified horse.

Gray, smoky steel moved through my vision, but my mind didn't actually identify it until after I felt the cool edge of it against my skin. That sensation spoke to a deep part of my brain. I froze, and my focus snapped from the horse to the youth.

A bird sang nearby, a strange, unfamiliar call, and men spoke in rushed, hurried tones, but it was all background noise. My limbs felt overfull. Remaining still was agony.

I didn't try to swallow around that warm steel, but let out a very gentle breath.

Well, fuck.

"Hold," someone said nearby.

The horse made an irritated noise, and I realized quiet had settled over us. I almost preferred the chaos.

I knew the youth above me probably had more than a dozen bows bent in his direction right now. Kadan had talked our way out of the Ltonan prince's dungeons, into a peace treaty with the Red Hand, and away from a dozen hungry heiresses—but my faith in him hadn't stopped the roaring of my heart.

Killed at the hands of a boy who didn't even look where he was riding before we could even start this rebellion. The irony wasn't lost on me.

"The horse needs some time to calm, Sister," I heard Darrius say. His voice was as relaxed as if he were discussing the weather.

"Sister?" The question came from beyond the youth above me, and a quick laugh followed. "Well, if you're my brother then my old papa's got some serious explaining to do."

The words danced over me like dappled sunlight, barely felt and hardly a distraction. Most of my vision was taken up by a floppy brown hat and the curve of the youth's head beneath it. He wasn't big, but he seemed to weigh more than a dozen horses, and his hand on me was like a vice. The blade against my throat didn't shake. I could feel the strength in his thighs and the bite of his fingers. In another situation, I would've quite enjoyed it.

"We were just on the trail of a fox that's been killing my brother's chickens these past nights." The youth was listening intently, but I couldn't make myself focus. My mouth was a desert. A tickle on my neck made me wonder if I'd been cut or whether I was just anticipating the brief movement that would end my life. "Didn't mean harm. Guess we weren't watching as close as we ought, but we'll be on our way—gotta catch this fox before we lose the track."

Above me, the rider turned his face ever so slightly. His hand stayed steady, and he remained like a block of granite atop me, but I could see more than a sliver of his face for the first time.

He had pale brown, whiskey-colored eyes, and they were locked onto something beyond us—someone wielding a bow, I suspected. His jaw was square but smooth. The crinkle of leaves under a boot in the direction of that gaze confirmed my suspicions.

I'd never developed a taste for whiskey. People in my family liked it a little too much.

Resisting the urge to draw in a deep breath or try to hurry Darrius along, I stayed still, wondering who it was he was pinning with those eyes.

While I doubted, at this point, I was about to have my throat cut, I was very ready for us to be done here. The ground was cold and damp and aches had started to set in.

Suddenly, that gaze cut down and locked onto me. Trapped behind my ribs by a sudden, inexplicable tightness, my breath burned. Heat spread throughout my body, and my discomfort fell away as I became deeply aware of every point of contact between us. His thighs gripping my chest. His hand wrapped around my wrist. The crush of his weight pinning my arm between us. The heat of him. The strength. I flexed a little, pressing up into the resistance above me.

I wasn't in the hands of a young man, but a highly skilled woman.

"… never known a Matri'sion to lose a track."

The words came from the other side of a waterfall. They only registered at all because of the ripple I felt going through the woman above me.

I drew in a breath but held myself still. Some of her hair poked out from under the ugly cap, and it shone like the best chestnut, a deep brown with a red glow. I wanted that cap gone. And the knife, too.

Down, Chay, I thought, dimly.

In another situation, I could've happily drowned my sorrows in her. I could already feel the burn of that knowledge in my blood.

She started again and I thought, for a moment, I'd said that out loud. But she asked, "You're a knight?" And her eyes had narrowed in suspicion.

There were some freckles across the bridge of her nose, less than a dozen, and only faint. Her long mouth was a straight line of displeasure.

I didn't try to respond. I figured it best, given the knife at my throat.

Darrius' voice filtered through to me only faintly.

The blade at my throat was suddenly withdrawn. Distaste curved down the edge of her long mouth, and I didn't know whether Darrius had said the wrong thing, or whether she liked this situation less than I.

Her cap drooped slightly more to one side. It was a silly angle, not a jaunty one, but another lock of hair escaped, longer than the first, and kissed the edge of her jaw.

The bird sang nearby again, a long, beautiful call. The woman above me leaned back, sheathing her knife and casting her eyes about.

Without thinking, I started to reach up, wanting to brush away those wayward strands of hair.

She flinched like I'd tossed a viper at her, recoiling violently, steel back in her hand and swooping toward me. Another bird call, and she paused, the knife halfway between us, her eyes locked on me. Distrust was stamped clearly across her features.

My hand had already dropped away. I was way out of line. I was so far out of line that I'd need to pack provisions to get back there. "Apologies," I said, making sure my irritation with myself didn't come through in my voice.

She didn't respond, but settled back slowly, her limbs coiled tightly as if she expected me to strike.

"Hey, Chay," Kadan said nearby. "We've made new friends."

Friends. Somehow, Darrius had made friends with the person accompanying the woman. I realized one of my hands was still tangled up in her shirt, crushed between us, and I forced my fingers to unlock rather than press closer, shrugging off the wave of humiliation I felt at the sight of my own weakness. *You can worry about that when the candles burn low,* I thought.

She climbed off me without hesitation, her movements graceful in the way of a wild creature.

Of course she was tall—almost as tall as me—with strong shoulders. *Of course* she was. I'd blown my chances with the most attractive woman I'd seen in…a lot of seasons.

I climbed to my feet, stiff and awkward with annoyance at myself. I probably never had a chance anyway. For all I knew, her entire family had been hung and drawn by the last knight who'd crossed her path.

We were in La'Angi, after all.

I liked that reminder and let my frustration swell, directing it to the

Butcher, sitting in that squat, uninviting keep that was the topic of ballads and dirges, both.

"It's a shame this meeting never took place," I heard Darrius saying to an older woman dressed in trousers and a man's shirt, a quiver strapped to one strong thigh. She stood tall despite her average height, her blonde hair tightly plaited down her back. "I'm sure meeting you both would have been a delight. Best of luck in all your endeavors—and do feel free to introduce yourselves should we ever cross paths."

The woman beside me hunched her shoulders and dropped her eyes to the ground in a way that made my worry flare.

Why was she shrinking?

The older blonde woman tossed her horse's reins to my attacker, taking the still-skittish beast who was foaming and stressed for herself. Kadan had saved the horse. I hadn't even noticed that minor miracle.

I met Kadan's eyes, searching for guidance, but his expression was thoughtful and his only word of wisdom was, "Curious."

He strolled back to his mount with a loose-limbed walk that only made me feel stiffer in comparison. Trust Kadan to understate a situation so easily.

Callum punched me on the shoulder, grinning as he did so. "How's your throat there, Chay?" he asked, wiggling his brows. "Got a stiff neck?"

There was no way I could've managed a response, so I just brushed some dirt off my shirt and went to where Bliksem waited for me, climbing back into the saddle.

"What was—" someone began.

"Not yet," Darrius cut in, the words almost idle. He glanced into the trees as if expecting them to have ears.

Eventually, some blood must've returned to my brain, because I realized Darrius had mentioned Matri'sion.

The renegade Steppe nomads, who claimed and defended one of the richest parts of the Steppes, were half-myth, all women…and could not *possibly* exist in La'Angi.

Had the blonde been a Matri'sion? Surely not. What was she doing so far east?

My mind went to my attacker, and now that my brain was working, I realized the way she'd tied me up was reminiscent of what I'd heard from Darrius' stories. Darrius was the only man I'd ever known to travel across Matri'sion territory. It was part of his legend.

Not even the Matri'sion disliked Darrius.

Were they both Matri'sion? What were they doing in La'Angi? Unease gnawed at me. La'Angi was the key to the country. Everyone knew it. But Matri'sion weren't a political power. They weren't strong enough to take Arcanloc, and even if they were, they'd never expressed an interest in such a gambit before.

"If anyone recognizes either of those two, anywhere, you're to say nothing," Darrius said to the group as we moved through the orchard, his words firm. "You don't mention this encounter to anyone. Not to your drinking buddies, not to one of us, not to them if you see them again, and certainly not to anyone from La'Angi."

I blinked. This was all obvious, wasn't it? With the Butcher being who he was? It'd be a swift death to exist publicly in La'Angi as Matri'sion.

Kadan started whistling a merry tune, and Callum broke into song to cover any awkward silences. I took up the chorus, and voices rose around us.

Had they been fleeing?

I let out a long, slow breath, rolling my shoulders under the grimy shirt on my back. They ached where I'd struck the ground.

Then I caught my first glance of La'Angi, up close.

The keep stood atop the cliffs, dropping down to the bay beneath on one side. On the other, circular walls spread down the hillside like dark ripples. A lone patch of green marred one area, indistinct from this distance. Smoke filled the air in the lower levels, lingering around the thatched roofs.

I felt my belly tighten. A group of traders, their carts well-guarded, watched us warily, slowly heading toward the sad, squat city. Kadan lifted a hand, and we greeted them as if they didn't curl their noses like we were shit on their shoe.

At the gate, there was a short line to enter the city. Guards sporting the La'Angi crest of a sword and apple moved freely among the crowd. I wasn't sure how regulated the fees they took were, and didn't plan to find out, ignoring Darrius' conversation with them and studying the walls and gate as we slowly neared.

I hadn't expected the curtain walls to be *small*, but I still hadn't been prepared for the sheer height and depth of the fortifications. I'd been to Azashi and even laid eyes on the child-King. And these walls might've been taller than those around the King himself.

Which probably made sense, as the King's power came from his military, and the Duke controlled the lion's share of it.

One of the guard met my eyes. He stood beside the big wheel that was currently wound tight, holding the gate open. I ignored the hostility in his gaze.

We had the fastest horses in the country. But behind walls, fast horses couldn't do much.

"Two?" Callum asked, with a grin.

I nodded. It'd take two of us to raise one of those gates.

I saw Callum turn and murmur it to someone. Trusting the information would spread, I skimmed my eyes over the location and number of guards. They traveled in threes and held spears and shields. La'Angi favored crossbows, and I knew they'd be loaded and waiting out of sight and the weather. Off to the side, I saw a guard take a knife and slice open a sack, rummaging through it. Whatever he found he must've liked. Some went into his pocket. The man standing beside the donkey looked impassive as a second guard stood beside him, hand on his sword, staring at a nearby young woman who was trying to slip behind another cart.

"Twelve on," I told Callum as he leaned over toward me. "Twelve around." I forced my eyes away from the guards as we entered the lower level of the city. Those odds weren't insurmountable. It'd be how far away reinforcements were that'd make the difference. Given

La'Angi's reputation, I was going to assume we wouldn't get a lot of time.

I leaned forward and ran a hand along Bliksem's neck. Kadan glanced over, grinning that big, shit-eating grin, his blue eyes full of trouble. "Keep your eyes out for the red lamp district," he said, loud enough to be overheard. "I wouldn't mind sampling the local talent."

I nodded, playing along and making a show of looking around, though I knew he wouldn't be relaxing in the company of anyone he didn't know until we were free of this place. The street was wide and cobbled, but the side streets on this level were deep mud. This close to a main gate and along the main road, inns dominated. I had no doubt fleas did, too.

Fortunately, we hadn't come here to lie with dogs.

CHAPTER TWO
AUDREY

"Beware the man who smiles easily, because he either desires to trick you, or is being tricked, himself."
~ Barloc's Wisdom, compiled by F. Bergsoniir

The internal numbness was familiar. I scrubbed quickly in the cold water, my movements rough with urgency. Isolde didn't say anything. She didn't need to. We both knew the entire situation could've been avoided.

They were tourney competitors. I was going to be sharing feasts and dances with them.

Relying on the disguise had never been my plan. It was an added layer of protection, just like a quick dash across the stream to throw them off the scent.

Now, everything hinged on it.

I didn't ask her for reassurances. If any one of those men recognized us, we were in trouble. I had no lies handy. There was no way I could say, "No I didn't lose control of Vixen." She'd been white-eyed and lathered with panic when we'd brought her home. It'd taken me an eon to get the poor mare through the city. The stableboys had *remarked* on it. That my usual horse and old friend, Storm, had bit someone so hard he'd swore he'd never work with horses again…didn't help.

The guilt would be there, under the numbness.

"What dress are you wearing?" Isolde called.

My head swam. "I don't know." Those dresses and I mutually disliked each other. "The lilac." It was simpler than the others. It'd be fast to get into.

"For the first banquet?" she asked. "Your father will want the pink or the puce."

There was a scream in my throat. I dropped the brush and stood. I'd do. If there were any spots of dust, Isolde would sort me out. "Pink." Mayhap I'd get lucky, be struck by some sort of brief, socially acceptable illness, and not have to wear the puce.

A knock at the door made me cringe. *Luca*. I didn't have enough energy to deal with his exuberant positivity.

I pushed water off my body and scrambled for a comb, wishing I could just tap out of the entire affair. I knew Isolde was seriously considering hunting down the people we'd run into, and I wouldn't be surprised if they all had an arrow in their throat by morning. Especially that lump of a knight who'd grabbed me. The memory of having him between my thighs had yet to leave me.

Mayhap I'd help her.

The door opened and she entered, dress draped over her arm. I knew, from what she'd taught me, that the cloth could double as a protective shield in that position.

Somehow *she* smelled like a daisy. *And* she'd avoided getting her hair wet.

Viciously, I ripped the comb through mine.

She arched a brow. "Want a knife for that knot?"

"It'd be faster."

"He'll wait," she said, taking the comb firmly from my hand. I didn't know if she meant Luca, still at my door, or my father at the banquet. "You need to breathe."

I didn't tell her I *was* breathing, but it was a near thing. "I need to get through tonight," I corrected.

She yanked on the knot. "You'll get through tonight easier if you aren't flooded by battle energy," she said briskly. "We both know it." She stopped, then, and said, "I'm grounding you."

I closed my eyes, bit back the snarl of impatience, and stood still as she settled her hands on my shoulders.

The pressure was heavy. I felt it down my back, into my hips, through my knees, into my heels, and out through my toes. I breathed into it obediently, with slow, deep out-breaths. Beneath my feet, the rug was thick but cool. The blisters I'd earned from walking home burned.

Terror swirled, dark and thick, no longer held back by the rush of energy that danger brought. I missed the strength of the battle energy, not for the first time.

Why was I still here?

"Breathe," Isolde said, the word totally calm. "We're okay."

I did, drawing air deep and making her hands lift, then blowing it out slowly past lips that needed balm after my time in the wind. "I want to talk to you about leaving," I said quietly.

Her fingers tightened fractionally, then released. "As you will." She removed her hands, that tiny flex the only sign I'd spoken the words she'd wanted from me since I was eleven. "Later. When your betrothed isn't listening at keyholes."

Luca wasn't the type to listen at keyholes. He'd have his nose in one of my books or be setting up a game of chess. But I nodded all the same. There was no way we could plan our flight now. I was supposed to be in the banquet hall a half-hour ago.

"If it's because of those men," she said, the words as brisk as her movements as she raised the comb again, "I have their measure."

I wondered what it cost her to say that as she started in on the knots in my hair, her strokes a balance of speed and precision. Gentleness didn't come into it, with Isolde. But neither did false niceties.

My sudden need to escape *was* partially because of the roving band of unwashed, horse-scented louts we'd had the misfortune to run into who'd identified Isolde accurately as Matri'sion. But it was also because of the man who waited for me, his nose in a book, his head in the clouds.

I was supposed to marry him in less than a season.

I couldn't do it. And yet, I couldn't leave. The thought made my head feel too full, and my knees wanted to give way. But I had to do something.

Doing nothing was, in a way, a choice.

"We'll discuss it later," Isolde murmured, quieter. "We can leave tonight, though, if that's what you want."

The offer made the bottom drop out of my belly. I wriggled my toes in the rug to remind myself I was still attached to this world. "No." Not tonight. I couldn't. I wasn't ready. But soon. I knew it had to be soon.

She had her tribe to return to. She'd waited so long. I thought of Storm and Vixen, hopefully sleeping now, safe in their stalls. My heart ached with all of my mistakes.

I didn't tell Isolde that, though. I'd just be reprimanded for considering them such. "Too many people."

She made a noise I didn't try to decipher and said, "That'll do. Let's get you ready." Which, knowing Isolde, could've meant anything.

Luca's face lit up like a hound spotting its dinner when he saw me, and I hated that he made me feel even more tired.

"You've bright eyes today, Audrey," he said, offering me his arm with a small bow and kind smile. The velvet of his doublet was soft beneath my hand, and the stones cool beneath my aching feet. We were going to be late, but hopefully not later than my father.

"Have you heard of the trial they're running in one of the mining districts in the South?"

"Not as yet." I resisted the urge to glance around for listening ears, but couldn't help but drop my voice to a murmur. Trust Luca to talk openly about the South.

At least he followed my lead, dipping his head a little closer to mine. His steely eyes sparkled as if it were a game. "It's good news. They've built machines to draw the water out of mines, so there might be fewer cave-ins."

I smiled and squeezed his arm, keeping the motion light so I didn't hurt him. "How are they powered?" I asked, quietly, nodding in greeting to a visiting merchant I recognized but couldn't name and ignoring the unease coiling in my belly. As long as he didn't say the South again, we should be safe to discuss the topic.

"Steam," he said, smile widening as if I'd confirmed his suspicions. "And magework."

I frowned at this a little. "Don't they have to mine the coal to heat the water to make the steam?"

"They're starting with the coal mines," he agreed, still smiling. "They estimate that only thirty percent of the coal will be needed to fuel the furnaces to run the pumps."

"Efficient," Isolde said sweetly from her place behind me. "Think of all the lives that will be saved."

I shot her a warning look, knowing her honey-coated tones masked her sarcasm, even if Luca didn't. Magework was worth a lot more than coal, and that sort of design would be patented to the King. They'd be paying for the privilege of mining in slightly less dangerous conditions for decades, I had no doubt. "I'm sure it's one of many such changes," I said to Isolde, warningly.

Luca put his hand over mine, patting it comfortingly. "I'm sure, too," he agreed. "I hope we get some time to talk further tonight. I've missed you, my sweet."

Out of the corner of my eye I saw Isolde's smile widen even further, her eyes as flat as the drawings of the mythical sirens in the deep who lured men to their deaths.

Entirely unaware of the danger he was in, Luca chuckled knowingly beside me. "Just a few more weeks and you won't need to worry about anyone overhearing us speaking so."

I'm going to break his heart.

I pushed the thought aside as we reached the Great Hall. I had a role to play, and Luca would forgive my poor manners for tonight. After that…well, soon I wouldn't be his problem.

We didn't need to be guided to our seats, but we were anyway. My father's huge, throne-like chair was empty for now, and the relief that washed through me made my head spin. Still, the moment I'd sat down, the readiness hummed again in my flesh.

He would appear. I would manage his demands. Then I could leave.

That was how these things always went.

And so it did this time, too. I tried to look absorbed in my meal while beside us my father spoke about the borderwars with Luca, whose knowledge of military history was surprisingly good for a scholar. I waited, knowing I could be called upon at any time—either for not listening enough, or for listening too closely. The tension was familiar, the exhaustion unavoidable. I finally got away when the music started and the ballrooms opened. The physical distance didn't change the fear in the back of my brain. Much as I hated it, I knew I wasn't safe.

And it wouldn't change until my father was dead.

I breathed deeply of the perfumed air and smiled at people around me. I let them spin and myself drift, trying to not be dragged under by the sheer crush of sensation. Luca's arm was my anchor. *You can do this, Audrey.*

"I see Fiona's here, with Henry," Luca said as we made our way through the crowd, our pace leisurely. "He's competing in the sword."

Much like my wedding, I tried not to think of Fiona. She was my closest living relative—and she resembled my mother far too much for interaction with her to be safe. The less attention I paid her, the less my father paid her. As for Henry… "I hope he wins a purse," I admitted, quietly. "If he gets the mage academy up and running, it'll be a boon."

"Is that why he's competing?" Luca asked, frowning slightly at me.

I shrugged. "I can only assume."

We danced and talked. I tried to keep my focus on Luca, our companions, the groups we flitted between. Faces caught my attention, though. Familiar faces—families I knew, had learned the histories of, mostly, from the eastern side of the Aza Ranges, and others who'd traveled further, who I didn't always know. Trying to keep track of them made my brain feel like I was being kicked with spurs. I smiled. I breathed. It swam about me.

"Ah, and from the other side of the ranges," Luca was saying, turning us and lifting a hand in greeting. "Lady Audrey, this is lord Kadan."

I knew the name and the associated territory. I'd heard it whispered about my entire life. *Raider's Ban*. Home of the country's best horseflesh and cavalry—and despised by my father.

As the noise and smells of the room rushed forward, I let my eyes dance over his face just briefly.

My hold on Luca kept me upright.

"A pleasure," he was saying, with a bow. "May I, Luca?"

Luca was my anchor, and I clung. I couldn't breathe.

The men from the orchard.

Luca was looking at me with understanding, that soft sickly sweetness that made me want to break his smiling mouth or fall into a weeping ball. "The ill will is one sided," he told me, holding out his arm like he was handing over my reins to this lordling. My brain picked out odd details. The irregular pattern of sun-bleached streaks in lord Kadan's dark blonde hair, the strange scar across his forehead, the crinkles at the side of his eyes that spoke of humor. My heart skittered against my ribs.

Where was Isolde? My head spun. Was this an ambush?

Luca thought I was upset about the ongoing feud. He had no idea.

But he was irrelevant. Luca was almost always irrelevant. Mayhap that was the way of sweet people. I forced myself to look at the horse lord's face as my hand was placed in his.

"I'm glad to have a chance to meet you," Kadan said, and his eyes weren't flat like a siren's as he guided me into the dance. I trod on one of his feet, and he spun me the other way, hiding the misstep. "As Luca said, I'd rather our parents' arguments remain between them."

He wasn't decrying me. Did he recognize me?

A tiny bit of tension ebbed. It was enough that muscle memory could kick in, and my feet followed the right steps, finally. I let my eyes rest on the tip of one of his ears. He didn't smell like horse anymore. My skin crawled.

He was the 'Ban heir. That meant the man today had been a 'Ban knight.

I'd had a knight in my grips. The memory of the solid weight was the memory of a 'Ban knight. I'd *held steel* to the throat of a Raider's Ban knight.

"Everyone's staring," he murmured, his smile softening a little. "If you smile a little and laugh, they'll think we're getting on, and this is normal, and we've just met." He spun me away, and the music was pouring into my overfull brain agonizingly, competing to be soaked up alongside his words. I desperately focused on the movements as the words seeped into my mind. *Battle energy*. Isolde was always right, and I hated it. I couldn't figure out what to do like this, and the Wife herself couldn't have grounded while in the arms of the heir of Raider's Ban.

But he wasn't, this second, exposing me. I breathed out and focused on how my body was moving, the soft slide of the fabric against my legs, the comforting warmth of his hand on mine. His palms were calloused, and he didn't hold too loosely, or too tightly.

"I heard you'd had a riding accident this afternoon," he said in the middle of a pulsing, swirling crowd of people that made my head spin.

I couldn't find any words.

"I'm glad you're uninjured," he went on. "Mayhap, while we're here, we could go for a ride with you and Luca."

He absolutely knew who I was.

Was he trying to coerce me? My head buzzed as if it were full of bees, and I wanted to flee. "I'm sorry, my lord," I said, and somehow the words sounded relatively normal, but perhaps I couldn't hear even that properly. "The music is a little much for me."

Mayhap I could get out of here.

He didn't miss a beat. His smile had toned down, somewhat. "So I take it you like horses?" I hadn't responded before he went on, casually, "I've a beautiful piebald at home who I'm hoping to put to Bravura, my stallion. Neither of them are friendly, but they've got legs on 'em."

"That seems important," I agreed.

His grin was swift and somewhat wonky as we halted near the edge of the gardens, on the precipice of that manicured, gently lit area where people wandered and spoke in hushed tones, and the noisy, chaotic movement inside.

"Is that not a phrase you use here?" he asked, waving over a circulating servant and helping himself to a drink. He didn't pick one up for me, but looked across the top of his glass. "You look like you could use something."

The horse lord's words swam in my head. I glanced at the tray the servant held before him, eyes off to the side and expression as neutral as a statue. He was balancing it all perfectly.

How I wish I could do that.

Swallowing my misgivings, I reached out and took whatever was closest. "Thanking you."

Kadan nodded and propped one shoulder against the elaborately carved pillar, kicking a foot against it. Luca was so far away now, and the server left us with a bow. Kadan sipped as if he had nothing more important to do.

The drink in my hand was apple cordial and tasted like blood.

I was acutely aware of every moment that passed in silence. The need to do or say something that would shatter the peace was almost overwhelming.

But they stretched out, two, then three. The song changed in the ballroom, and two older nobles I couldn't focus on enough to identify wandered past. I was in a maelstrom of sensation and guilt and terror, and I could feel it chipping away at me, like it was ripping off my armor. And I could feel it, but I couldn't feel anything at the same time.

"I think I've got us a path back," Kadan mused but didn't

straighten. "If that's your preference. If we dance, we're less likely to need to talk to people on the way."

My head pounded. I had to respond. My mouth moved, and I said, "I'd love to dance." And I didn't bobble the glass as I sat it down, or trip over my feet. I wasn't properly connected to anything, but I had to be.

He talked about his piebald's last foal, how she'd labored overnight, how the mare was looking promising, how he'd only brought one horse with him and worried about the others. At one point he said, "Don't react, but your father's spotted us," and I felt like his hands had turned to coals against my skin. "Mine's distracting him. I'll get you back to Luca, then we'd best part ways for now."

For now?

His eyes were on my face when I glanced over. "The enemy of my enemy is my friend," he offered casually. "Don't you agree?"

He was trying to maneuver me. Well, he'd been successful so far. But I knew the enemy of my enemy was just another enemy.

CHAPTER THREE

CHAY

"A person who cannot acknowledge fault will never be trustworthy."
~ Raider's Ban proverb

She was the daughter of the Butcher.

I waited, stretched out beside the hearth in a chair that was somehow less comfortable than my saddle. Kadan's people—our friends—lingered, full of hushed talk we hadn't aired when she'd been spotted at the banquet.

The daughter of the Butcher.

We were all sworn to secrecy. We'd held the facade through our shock. But they needed to talk it out, and it bubbled around me, excitement, horror, and glee.

Interesting, wasn't it, that we were here to kill the Butcher, and we ran into his daughter?

Interesting, that she was riding with a Matri'sion, who stood for everything the Butcher hated?

Interesting, that *we* knew about them both the moment we set foot on his land, but *he* didn't know what was happening under his own nose?

Interesting, that she almost cut my throat?

So interesting.

I swirled the beer I wasn't drinking around the mug I didn't recall picking up. It was warm and golden. Her eyes had been, too, but more enticing by far than this swill.

I knew better than to touch liquor. I didn't have the head for it. Or the temperament. It drove men in my family to selfish, violent things. And damned if I was joining their ranks.

She'd been quick and sure with that knife, and fought on the ground like a Matri'sion.

She wasn't just nobility, she was the Duke's only child and heir.

I finally set aside the beer. That was exactly the reason Luca was marrying her. Take La'Angi, take the east, take Arcanloc's military.

Take everything.

Taking La'Angi was nigh impossible, of course, short of unlocking some sort of forgotten old magic to enable you to sell your eternal soul to some sort of ancient devil. Or a freak accident. Or marrying the heir.

She was the Butcher's *daughter.*

I'd always voted for the ancient devil, myself.

Kadan fell down beside me with a long sigh that spoke to my soul. "Wild horses," he groaned, and I realized we were finally alone. Before he could say anything else, a knock at the door drove me to my feet, and I scooped up my sword belt.

He didn't protest my habitual protection of him for once. He just kicked his boots off and stretched out his toes toward the flames, letting his head fall back. "Pretty sure I'm asleep," he told me. "Unless you think she's worth it."

I couldn't help but smile. I loved the man's humor—and his optimism. Opening the door, I found someone I was relatively confident Kadan didn't want in his bed. "Hi, Luca." Out of habit, I propped my shoulder against the door, using my body as a shield.

I wasn't officially his guard. No one paid me to protect his scrawny ass.

I just did it for kicks.

Luca gave me a nod of acknowledgment as if I'd just bowed to him. "Evening, Chay. Is Kadan still up?" he asked me, his eyes already skittering over my shoulder, though he kept his voice down.

"I'm pretty sure he's asleep," I told Luca, straight-faced.

"No, I'm not," Kadan said from behind me. "I was just resting a moment. Come in!" And I stepped back to see Kadan reach out with one bare foot and give a chair a nudge of invitation. "Saw you rubbing elbows with the Duke earlier. Didn't want to—" he arched his brows "—interrupt."

Luca, of course, hastened to tell Kadan that no one thought he was an annoyance. When, of course, the Butcher damned well did.

At that point I probably should have excused myself, because I knew well what these two were up to, and someone had to make sure they weren't overheard.

Did Luca know who he was marrying in a few weeks?

Did he appreciate her?

I scowled into the fire.

"I was grateful your father arrived when he did," Luca said, his sigh big and gusty. "Did you and Audrey put aside your differences? She didn't say much to me, but she's had a very long day and has a delicate disposition."

The memory of the knife against my throat and the strength in those hands sat ill against Luca's words.

"She did seem shaken," Kadan agreed, and once more the man's ability to bullshit amazed me. I'd seen him do it many a time, but the sincerity in those big blue eyes of his while he lied through his teeth always blew me away. "She mentioned a riding accident. We talked about horses. I think we're okay."

It was the floppy hair and the crooked grin. No one could imagine someone with such sweet, unassuming charm could be so devious. Even if his birth *had* been foretold.

"Well, that's good, then." Luca cleared his throat and settled in the chair I'd just vacated. "I was hoping you'd be awake still," he said, glancing politely at me as if I, too, were someone he wanted to see. If only it hadn't been so wooden, it would've seemed earnest. I wasn't offended, since the feeling was mutual. I just settled back into my new chair. "Audrey mentioned some changes to the scheduled festivities." He sent Kadan a loaded look. "Victor—the Duke—" he corrected swiftly "—changed the entertainment, and the large feast on the fourth day has been brought forward, with only informal meals being offered the following day." He was looking at Kadan as if this was critically important, but I recalled Kadan mentioning this possibility weeks ago. "Many anticipate leaving the morning after the melee."

"Yes, I'd heard," Kadan said with a dismissive flick of his fingers. "We've passed on the information. There isn't much more we can do, I suppose." He grinned at Luca and added, "It'll be done, one way or the other, won't it?"

I wondered what it'd be like to be the daughter of the Butcher of Wolfswail. I wondered if it'd be much different from the way I'd grown up, as the sixth grandson of the illustrious General Charles of Black Peak, with the legacy he'd left behind of terror and poverty. It would probably take a few generations for La'Angi's wealth to dry up. It had with us, anyway. The terror, though…that was a deep well.

I doubted she'd be mourning him.

Luca was wincing. "I wouldn't mind walking away from the whole thing, honestly." I kept my eyes on the fire as those words landed in my mind. *Might be too hard. Mayhap I ought to retire for a spell, revisit this when the situation is more agreeable.* That's what he meant. Kadan and I both knew it. Typical Luca.

"Don't wish too hard," Kadan advised, uncharacteristically serious, and my attention sharpened. "I'd rather you live to see your hair start to gray. Wheels are turning already. We need to steer them, or be crushed." And, bless his heart, he didn't say, *"As I warned you time and again."*

"It'll be gray before midwinter the way things are going," Luca muttered on a sigh.

Why Kadan liked Luca's company, I'd never understood. When I thought of the way the Butcher's daughter had sat at the high table, staring at her plate, barely visible she'd made herself so small… Luca's whole head would be full of grays if he gave a single shit.

She wasn't my problem. I was here to make sure everything went to plan, not to rescue anyone.

She had a Matri'sion maid. She was fine. Hells, mayhap the maid or the lady would do the job themselves if we gave them half an opportunity.

And yet, something dark coiled in my gut.

"Any extra information?" Kadan asked him, his eyes narrowed. "You can speak in front of Chay."

They sure could. I wasn't about to tell Luca to eat shit. He was the best option we had, aside from Kadan, who wasn't an option. I'd long since stopped grieving the reality of that.

"Not yet," Luca told him, with a shake of his head for added emphasis. "I'm worried about Audrey, but she'll be okay, I'm sure." Kadan made a hum of agreement and provided Luca with some quiet to fill. He sat there for a few moments in silence, before offering, "She takes ridiculous risks."

"Oh?" Kadan asked, his face the picture of mild surprise. "Surely such a mild-mannered thing cannot be such a source of worry."

It almost made me uncomfortable to watch him playing Luca.

Luca cocked a brow at Kadan. "Says an unbetrothed man." And he grinned as if it were a joke. When we didn't laugh, the grin faded and he drew a deep breath, lowering his voice. "She's—in a difficult spot. I'm doing what I can to help, of course, but I keep coming up against Victor."

My heart squeezed in my chest. *Good.* That was good, wasn't it, that she had someone devoted to her? Shouldn't we all have that? I reached down and grabbed a log, tossing it onto coals that didn't need more fuel, and grabbed a poker to rearrange it.

"How so?" Kadan asked, sounding concerned. Knowing him, he'd be genuinely worried about Luca's well-being. Luca was our friend, more or less. He'd been around us for a long time, anyway.

And he was about to wear the crown, if we had anything to do with it.

Because he was going to marry her. Take her father's army. And take the country.

I poked the log too hard, and sparks tumbled everywhere.

"Victor's a brute," Luca said, his voice uncharacteristically harsh, his words unusually forthright. "I told you what the Duke did the last time the wedding was postponed."

Kadan frowned, straightening a little in his chair. I recalled the conversation vividly. Kadan had played it cool at the time to better support Luca, but he'd been shaken. Add to that the history between Kadan's father and Audrey's mother, it was possible Kadan was especially concerned about the lady.

Or mayhap he was just lucky that shit still shocked him.

"Are you thinking of postponing it again?" Kadan asked him, all nonchalance gone.

"No. No. Even if I wanted to—which I don't—it'd be too risky. He could kill her. He almost did," he added, standing and pacing to the bottle of knappchs sitting on the empty table, pouring us all a short glass. What remained of the bottle, with its pretty little apple design on the label, revealed that none of us had been quick to drink the La'Angi spirits. "During the last tourney, I came to stay. She's been keeping me away," he told us, the words tight, the pauses long. "She didn't say as much, but I can tell. She's trying to protect me."

Those hands had been strong and sure, that knife faster than I could've anticipated. She'd be able to protect him if it came to it. And something about that made me ache.

In my mind's eye, I pictured how she'd shrank.

"From?" Kadan asked, his eyes slightly narrowed.

But the answer was in my own memory, and I felt the weight of it in my belly as flames danced over the logs in front of me. Physical capabilities didn't protect you from the way your soul could be eroded.

"Victor. She doesn't know what's being planned," he explained quickly, passing me a short glass I didn't want and hadn't asked for, and carrying the second to Kadan, who took it in silence. "But she has an inkling of what he's like." An *inkling?* Luca's earnest statement made me swing my gaze to him in shock. Did he think she was living the coddled life of a Duchess-to-be?

She was the *daughter* of the *Butcher.*

Glancing down, I saw my own fist, white-knuckled on the poker, and forced my grip to ease. I set down the delicate glass of clear liquid.

"But I came anyway, last year."

"I recall hearing word of it," Kadan acknowledged, when Luca's pause extended even longer, and he picked up his own glass.

The way Luca took a mouthful of liquor as if it were a health tonic and then reached for the bottle again made raw memories rumble, so I turned back to the fire. "I brought her a chess set," he told Kadan.

Chess. She was a strategist. I shifted a coal fractionally, feeling like someone had scooped out all my guts. She probably had to be, didn't she?

"She likes chess?"

"I don't know. But she's got a good head for analysis." The words, given so matter-of-factly, confirmed what I would've guessed myself. "I only got to play one game with her. Victor came. He found me in her rooms, and he—" he broke off, his mouth twisted as if the rest of the sentence was too foul to touch his tongue.

There was ice in my chest. The poker weighed heavy in my hand. I knew how that sentence ended. I could feel it.

"I tried to take responsibility, of course—since it was my idea. There wasn't much I could do with a dozen guardsmen throwing me out, though."

I resisted the urge to glance up and look around the room. Were her chambers the size of this? As the heir to Raider's Ban, Kadan got the second-best of just about everything…still, even if her rooms were significantly larger, I doubted a dozen guardsmen would be able to get in, much less swing a sword in those quarters. And anyway, you held the door, not the center of the room.

She'd know that. She, and her Matri'sion maid. So if they hadn't defended…why?

"My sources tell me she wasn't seen for weeks," he finished, the words both furious and desperate.

I straightened and returned the poker where it belonged. What did she benefit, staying here?

Kadan took a deep breath. "Well, it doesn't really change what we're doing, does it?" I trusted Kadan on that front and stretched out my hips. Was she unable to make it to the tribes with her maid? Was the maid unable to return? Was her heart so tangled up in her hopes and beliefs that she couldn't see the stars in the sky spelling her destined doom?

"What does she think you should do?" Kadan asked, leaning forward intently, hands clasped lightly between his knees. He was the picture of a concerned friend.

I stilled and turned my attention to Luca. He opened his mouth, paused, closed it again, and frowned as if puzzled.

He hasn't asked her. The hot ball of fury took me off guard.

Nope. Butcher's daughter. I struggled to rein myself in.

"I haven't asked her. She doesn't understand the situation."

I was committing treason for this man.

No, you're committing treason so Kadan doesn't end up where Luca's sitting. Kadan wasn't going to be forced into marriage, and he wasn't going to pick up a crown. Because he didn't want what his stars spelled out. He didn't want the *cost* of that destiny.

With that reminder, it was easier to hate the Butcher and the small group of advisors who manipulated the child-King, allowing others' bodies to form the bridge to Velkyn so they might sit beside the One himself. Luca was just an ignorant man I'd always been friendly with and never considered a friend. But I still had to stop my hand from forming a fist.

"You just said she was good at analysis," Kadan pointed out, his tone holding polite interest. Wild horses, I admired that man. Where he found his patience, I would never know. He didn't follow the statement up with anything, just letting the quiet sit, waiting for comment.

I struggled with my own temper, reminding myself of the complexities of the situation. People had to do things, sometimes, to survive. Dark and horrible things. I sat with that rage and shame, letting it ebb. There *were* situations where people couldn't be trusted with everything. But still, you trusted them with as much as you could, and you damned well thought about it first, so you knew *why* you were making your choices.

Or you were like Luca—as useful as tits on a stallion.

"I...She doesn't know court," he said, scrambling to justify himself. "She doesn't understand the powers at play. The lady's wonderful, don't get me wrong, and I'm confident given time she'll be an amazing asset, but she's young, yet, and inexperienced." I stared into the fire. He just kept on charging, didn't he? "Frosts, Kadan, she almost broke her neck this afternoon—and she'd slipped her guards! If Victor knew she rode unaccompanied, *he'd* break it!"

My heart ached for the woman whose whiskey eyes burned, then dropped to the ground as she shrank.

"Strikes me that a person old enough to reproduce ought to be trusted to have a say in actions taken to protect her life," Kadan drawled, and my admiration for his patience only grew. "She's the expert after all, isn't she?" Before Luca could respond, he grinned and said, "So, she rides without a guard, hey? She'd do well in our lands."

And not too many other places. The Butcher's men were in charge of training the militias across our country. Every year, we had to work hard to undo the damage their beliefs and processes did to Raider's Ban. Most didn't bother to watch the Watch.

Luca's words died in his throat, and a smile touched his mouth, as if there were anything good about this entire mess. I resented his happiness, and I had no damned right to.

"She would love Raider's Ban." His smile was misty, and Kadan smiled along, too. I didn't, but fortunately they didn't expect me to. "I was with her the first time she slipped her guards, years ago now—she would've been eleven, mayhap. We went for a ride, and a storm blew in, driving us into an inn beside one of the watchtowers that guard the roads. The man running the inn was obviously known to the guards. Well, the men got roaring drunk and spent all their coin dicing with the innkeep. The next day—" his smile widened at the memory, and I was glad that my resentment didn't "—she stopped off, had a cordial and biscuits. As soon as they got comfortable, she was telling them she'd be back soon, no need for them to stir themselves."

Kadan grinned at the tale. The look he sent me was swift and unreadable. "And you spoke sense, of course."

"I tried," he said, frowning. "But she…well." His frown deepened, and he took a sip of the spirits. "She insisted I could protect her."

Kadan's brows rose, his grin still intact. "Oh-ho. Careful who you tell that tale to. Riding unchaperoned through an orchard with a Duchess-to-be? That belongs in a ballad, friend!"

It wasn't like Kadan to make those sorts of comments, especially about someone so young. I hid my surprise poorly, judging from the look he sent me that clearly said *play along*, his charmingly crooked smile fixed as he flashed it in my direction.

"We were chaperoned, of course," Luca said, shooting him a quick, quelling look. "Audrey's maid is never far from her side, and that woman is sharper than any knife I own." I glanced at Luca, but there was no undercurrent or inference in the statement. He didn't know the depth of truth in his words. "But the point, which you're missing entirely, is that Audrey takes risks of her own that complicate things."

How dare she live her life. I turned back to the fire, mentally running through the other candidates we could put forth in Luca's place.

But Kadan was the one they wanted. And he refused.

Kadan, making a bit of a show of how little he cared—with some shrugging, sinking back in his chair, and a voice both mildly disinterested and cheerful—said, "To me, she sounds like a woman of many resources."

"She is," Luca agreed on a sigh. "Just enough to get her into trouble. No one needs to experience Victor's wrath twice."

Silence descended between us in the wake of those words. Personally, I'd never seen the Butcher at work, but I'd seen his ilk. Unlike Kadan, shit didn't shock me.

"Once you're wed…your claim will be all the stronger," Kadan said quietly.

His claim would *exist* based entirely on hers. I didn't say that. We all knew it. By himself, Luca was the second son with little to inherit of his father's tiny, poor holding.

Luca sighed and ran his hands through his hair. I didn't look at him, hunched over his knappchs, anxious and completely misinterpreting the situation. He didn't see how she'd been molded by violence into someone with finely tuned survival instincts. He'd never understand the cost, or the benefit, of those skills or help her use them in a way that allowed her to reclaim herself. To him, she was a conveniently appealing stop on the journey to taking power.

She was wasted on Luca.

Kadan flashed him another grin. "If that doesn't make you happy, I do have a lot of very fast horses, friend. You could spend your wedding night in a different type of saddle." I thought of the woman who'd been ready to cut my throat only hours ago. If he attempted to pressure her into the marriage bed, he'd be eviscerated. Mayhap we needed a secondary strategy. I didn't want that for her.

Before Luca could get too pissy about the very mild reference to the wedding bed, Kadan said, mild as fresh mare's milk, "I take it Audrey can ride."

I deliberately didn't look up. She might be passable with a knife. Perhaps even better than passable. But she needed some help handling her horse.

At least the question shut Luca up for a moment, though. "She's adequate and would adapt fine from side-saddle," he said slowly. "I don't know, Kadan. It would be a big risk."

"Doubtless," Kadan agreed with a shrug. "I won't press you to take it. But if it feels like the best chance…"

Luca offered his hand, and Kadan clasped it in his own. I tried not to think of her missing opportunities to manage her horse or the reverberations of those deadly hooves on the ground so close to us.

"You always did talk me into things I'd never consider myself," Luca half-laughed, shaking his head. "Mayhap that's why I love your company."

"Could be my golden good looks," Kadan suggested, ruffling his fingers through his hair comically. "My charm. The way my farts smell like daphne."

"That all helps, without question," Luca agreed dryly, enjoying the joke, though it was an old one, as he held out his hand to me. "It's good to know I have people I can trust." He looked between us as if he wanted to remind us—*me*—not to speak to anyone, but wasn't quite sure how to say it.

I sat there in silence and waited, wondering at what point in my life I'd become a man who didn't give a shit about treason.

"We'll say nothing of this," Kadan assured him, standing. "And Chay barely says boo."

"I wasn't questioning—"

Of course he'd been questioning. And, more out of love for Kadan than Luca, I said, "You know my family. You know my history. If you need a friend—" *or if she does* "—you know I'll support you."

His frown smoothed a little at this reminder. He clasped my hand again, firmer this time, bowing his head over it in acknowledgment.

Farewells done, I walked Luca to the door, shut it firmly behind him, and made sure it wouldn't open again accidentally.

"Luca's got no idea," Kadan breathed softly.

I said nothing, setting the glasses aside with finality. I had nothing to say.

"Ah, shit," Kadan said on a mocking laugh. "I'm done. That's it for me." He ran one hand through his sandy hair, this time in a motion that was thoughtlessly artless—pure, unselfconscious habit. It settled charmingly around his face. "Are you okay?" he asked me, eyes swinging in my direction.

I felt the warmth of the man's genuine concern and didn't try to smile or wave it off. He'd know. "It's different here than where I grew up," I said by way of answer. He kept looking at me, though, waiting for the explanation. I shrugged. "It's there. The reminders of yesterday, things I thought I'd forgotten. But they aren't right on top of me, you know?"

"I don't know," he admitted. "It doesn't sound like the best place, nor the worst."

I remembered the way the Duke had walked into the room, and quiet had rippled out around him. People had shuffled aside, lifting their drinks like shields, their eyes on him. I hadn't had a drink and would never use one as a shield. "Given the circumstances," I said, my mind skimming to his daughter and how she'd shrunk, "I'm doing damned well, 'Dan."

His hand on my arm was warm and firm. The encouraging smile on his lips paired with that worried expression better than the cider had gone with the meal tonight. "You don't have to, though," he reminded me. "If you need to step out, someone else will keep my guts on the inside of my belly."

I snorted. "Not as well as I can."

"We're in the real world, brother," Kadan said, his grin widening and some of the worry lifting. My heart sat a little lighter at this return to normalcy. "There's no bonus points for technique, just dead or alive. I take it you'll sleep in here somewhere?"

I shrugged, glancing over at the couch. It wouldn't fit me. "Might go get my bedroll."

"Good. I'm planning on snoring, just so you know."

"You always snore," I told him, hoping he might tonight, to jar me from the nightmares I was sure I'd have. "Just so you know."

CHAPTER FOUR
AUDREY

"The clouds broke and ravens gathered. Across the battlefield, the silence of a thousand men was heard. And into the silence the Son said, 'The simplicity of faith is this: everything the One says is true, and disbelief is impiety. These truths are known as the locways.' The ravens' beaks opened, and the message reached all ears, and all understood. Those who ignored the truth became food for the Son's ravens."
~ The Book of Bread and Salt

The day of the tourney dawned bright and clear, but the wind had the bite of the coming winter. It crept in through the windows while we sat together on the stone meditating, and cooled our skin while we drilled as the day's color bled into the sky. My head ached like I'd drunk too much knappchs as Isolde strapped me into the first in a series of day dresses I hadn't chosen and didn't allow myself to care about. And I hadn't found the words to tell her I'd been identified by the knights yesterday. It seemed both unimportant and too big to put into words.

I didn't trust the 'Ban heir. But I also didn't think he was an immediate threat.

The La'Angi tourney was the biggest on the circuit for anyone interested in the sword or melee. I heard the purse for the joust and archery was pathetic—not worth the trip unless the competitors had other business here. But our melee was the best.

"There isn't a single Kingsguard since Barloc had conquered The Countries That Were who hasn't won a La'Angi tourney!" I'd grown up hearing. "And everyone who comes is vying for your father's favor."

But no one ever said the rest of it. They wanted *his* favor, but they asked for *mine*. Because it was the same thing. I was an item, owned by him, without rights of my own. Interest in me was interest in him. Flattery of me was flattery of him. So said the locways, the rules that formed the very foundations of our society.

I reached up and ran my fingers over the ripples of the ribbon coiled around my hair, ready to be given as a favor. Isolde bustled around me.

He didn't own me. But he didn't know it.

If my autonomy went unacknowledged, was it even real?

"Have you a timeline?" Isolde asked me, going back over the laces of my dress with sure fingers, resettling and smoothing them.

A lump formed in my throat. "Regarding leaving?" I asked her, just to be sure. Not to delay, of course.

Her answer was the quick, unimpressed flicker of her attention to my face in the looking glass before us, and a slight tightening of her lips.

Time was running out.

"What do you think is best?" I asked her, hoping she'd take the query for pragmatism rather than avoiding choice. "Should we hide in the tourney crowd as they leave?" That would give me three days to brace myself.

She paused for just a moment, and this time her eyes didn't cut up to me. "Are you sure you want this?" she asked, quietly. "Once you go..."

I didn't want to let go. I knew what La'Angi was like. I knew my father, the long moons of being completely ignored, the flurry of attention I had to try to manage, then the violence when I inevitably failed, then the long moons of being ignored. I knew how to get through all of that.

"I know."

She nodded and continued with my laces. "Then I'll make preparations. With the outflux of traffic we ought to have luck, if we leave ahead of the crowd. The celebrations on the last night are rowdy. We won't be missed."

Of course she could make it work.

I looked at myself in the mirror, seeing my tired, puffy eyes and the sad curve of my mouth, and wondered why I'd thought it could ever be different.

~

Eventually we made it to our seats at the tourney ground, nestled deep in the canopied and cushioned nobles' area. Above us, my father shared his box with Phillip von Rhea, the old King's advisor and the young King's representative this tourney. He already had Luca perched on a chair, too, as if he were a student to the finest tutors.

"Don't you dare feel bad for him," Isolde said so quietly I could barely hear the words. "He could've dissolved the betrothal entirely." She swept her skirts around her feet with the precision of a razor against a throat. "He opted to postpone it."

But I just felt sick. He'd been young, barely sixteen to my eleven, when we were supposed to wed. I hadn't understood, then, why I was supposed to marry Luca.

There was a lot you could get a sixteen-year-old boy to believe in before he formed his own opinions. And my father liked things just so.

"He did what he could," I said, but I didn't know if the protest made it to her ears. The cowardly part of me hoped it didn't. I was tired of defending him.

I was tired of him needing to be defended.

My dress flexed as I drew in a deep breath, making my ribs expand. The back of my neck itched where I felt my father's eyes on me as competitors filled the grounds, then the sensation lifted as I heard Luca's voice rise and fall.

My eyes wandered over the competitors and the shields they bore. The man I'd knocked over just yesterday in the orchard was down there, his hair black as night. I couldn't see from here the dark blue of his eyes or whether he'd removed the stubble from his chin, and I didn't care. The relevant things were his colors and his name. He was Chay Shieldbreaker of West Grenvele, but, unusually, he boasted the Raider's Ban field. That, paired with the Barloc-given combat surname, suggested his family had been important when Barloc crafted our nation. Raider's Ban colors indicated he was *still* important in 'Ban.

I sat there, a lump in my throat, watching the big, black-haired knight who had hit the ground like a felled tree. What did one have to do to earn the approval of the Count of Raider's Ban?

The stands far to my right was where the 'Ban family and entourage sat, down near the rail. They'd been positioned in the worst seats, but there was a crowd around them, and the area felt…jovial.

Beneath me, Chay had his hands on his hips as he guided them in big, lazy circles while he listened to whatever was being said in the group before him. There weren't any other 'Ban bannermen I could see—at least, none with Darrius' colors. The knight hadn't been wearing those colors when I'd pinned him under me. The gold of the 'Ban wheat wouldn't do justice to the blue of his eyes.

"'Tis an interesting array of competitors," Isolde said from beside me, and I ripped my gaze away from those rolling hips, feeling nauseous.

I'd been staring. Of course I had. I'd done the exact same gentle exercise this morning while I woke up, before drilling with Isolde. The trickle of awareness was a normal response to seeing someone engaging in the same activity I enjoyed. It must be.

"I wonder how Mikus is doing today," Isolde said, her expression pleasant, her tone friendly, but the words a reminder of how deadly this tourney could be. "Mayhap this year he'll win your favor?" she asked me, arching her brows, but she didn't wait for my response. She knew how I felt about him.

The first round eventually began as spectators were still settling in. The grounds were full of competitors and stewards shouting for fighters, directing them to arenas marked on the ground with chalk. Yasmine, a longtime companion who I swapped seeds and letters with, arrived with a big smile and a quick curtsey.

I did a double-take when I saw her dress. "Excellent color choice," I said, trying to identify what it was about the outfit that made her glow. Yasmine's skin was deeper brown than most. It seemed like there were all types and shades of skin, and all textures of hair, found at all levels of our society, but deep brown or very pale were unusual everywhere.

"Thanking you." She resettled her overdress, clearly pleased. "We've a new tailor. And I've had success with a new strain of lupin. You're going to love me, Audrey."

"More than I do now?" I asked her, wondering if it might be joy, not her clothing, that lit her face.

She made a noise of agreement, and I listened with half an ear whilst watching the comings and goings on the field beneath us.

Our conversation paused whilst Mikus took apart a knight from the west of the Aza Ranges.

An unfamiliar chap with a crest declaring he was a borderlands knight came up to the edge of the stands and looked up at me. I avoided his gaze, and he was wise enough to take the rejection for what it was and turned away graciously. He was heckled on his return.

Once, I'd dreamed of having a knight jump the rail, charge up to me, draw his sword, and challenge my father to combat. Public combat would, of course, gain him enough respect that we'd live on in La'Angi in peace.

The dream had then shifted to my knight pledging himself to my service and training me in the sword. And public combat, were I involved, would of course make everyone respect *me*. *She's as powerful as any man. As her father*. It would make me the first woman to own land since Barloc conquered The Lands that Were.

But weapons took years to become proficient with, and I didn't have years.

There were ways around it. I could've put an arrow in my father's eye a million times over. But, as I'd told Isolde, the language of La'Angi was the sword.

Why I felt like I'd lost someone dear to me, I had no idea. The dreams of childhood lit no lamps, and I glanced over to check that Yasmine hadn't noticed my wandering attention. Her eyes were still locked on the group of men tormenting the one brave enough to seek my favor earlier, and polite enough to accept rejection with dignity.

"As if you wouldn't do the same for every one of them," she said, seeing my attention following her own, her lips curved in displeasure. "It makes them feel big, though, to risk naught and mock those who do."

I hummed in agreement and moved my eyes to the field, breathing through the sudden rush of grief that sat across me like a wet cloak.

Perhaps it wasn't so unusual that I'd wanted to learn the language my father spoke.

Perhaps it wasn't so unusual that I wanted him to stare up at me from the ground, his eyes wide and shocked.

Perhaps it wasn't so unusual that I wanted him to know I was better than him.

But I wasn't a child anymore, and it was a lot safer to disappear into obscurity. Anyway, the bitter, pragmatic part of me knew he'd die before he acknowledged me as aught but a failed investment.

"I'll win this tourney for you, lady Audrey!" shouted a mediocre knight in front of me.

I smiled and it felt as warm as congealed porridge. "Good luck, sir." I nodded politely, then deliberately swung my eyes away.

It was part of the dance, and I'd done it often enough they all knew my steps.

Isolde leaned over and murmured, "Henry's up against Mikus next round."

I glanced over at where the shields were displayed, my stomach sinking. If I'd thought it'd make a difference, I'd have given Henry my favor in a heartbeat. The best I could hope was that he lost without injury.

Chay's fight wasn't much to see. He danced around, got his opponent to overextend, then used the opening decisively. "Hmm," Isolde said from beside me, and I knew she watched, too. Since she was, I didn't try to disguise my interest and turned to study him as he walked off the field.

From this distance, I couldn't see how deep and blue his eyes were, or whether he had horsehair stuck to his shirt. But I could see the strength in his legs as they ate up the distance.

Yasmine leaned over beside me. "He's new," she murmured. I withdrew, embarrassed, and she gave me a nudge, her eyes sparkling. "You ought to see if he can dance tonight. If he doesn't fight Mikus."

I felt ill again. Before I could respond, Isolde nudged me lightly. "Knight from Pia," she murmured.

I glanced over as he fumbled a block and frowned. "Really?"

She shrugged and didn't say anything. She didn't have to. I felt her interest turn to disdain as she, too, witnessed his error.

Yasmine smiled over our heads, waving to someone in the crowd. "I'll tell you about the lupin later," she murmured, under the rise and fall of talk around us. "When you're…less distracted." And the look she sent me was veiled mischief before she stood. "This evening? *After* dances."

"Yes. Please. And apologies."

Her smile widened, flashing dimples. "Never." Then, skirts in hand, she squeezed past us.

Guilt gnawed at me, sitting alongside fascination as I watched the displays of combat. Yasmine's seat was barely cold before Luca came and settled beside me. "What do you think of Craaig from Pia?" he asked us, rubbing his hands together.

"Passable," I replied, assuming it was the fumbling knight. One mistake was probably one too many. But, since he was here… "What of him?" I asked, lifting my eyes in Chay's direction as he walked onto the field again.

Luca shot me a fast grin. "You've got a good eye, my lady. I've put a fair sum on Chay." He lowered his voice a little more and said, "He's a friend." Then, at normal volume, "I've seen him move, some. Not bad in the joust, either. You'd love his horse."

I doubted it.

Again, Chay won in much the same fashion—skirting the fight, waiting for an opening, then taking it. It wasn't how most of these men fought. Some of his movements reminded me of the Matri'sion fighting Isolde had taught me.

I felt the unease simmer in my veins and reached for anger instead. I should be able to say that. But I couldn't. Because Matri'sion were treated like some far-fetched rumor a sly merchant had made up to sell his spices from the north. How could there be a tribe of women, after all? How could they have babies, and who would look after them?

I had no defensive anger, though, just an aching hollowness as my head filled with the shouts of the crowd and the sounds of the competition. Resisting the urge to glance and check if my father's attention was on me, I turned instead to Luca.

He glanced at me, his smile small and a little concerned. "Are you well?" he asked softly.

For a moment, I wasn't surrounded by the crowd. I was back in his keep, eleven years old, alone, and terrified. And he was kneeling before me, offering his bleeding hand.

My mouth went dry at the memory. I hadn't asked him for a Blood Oath. I'd only heard them whispered about when I was that age. Terrible, unbreakable things full of old magic that no one understood anymore, and only the King and his General could employ.

"Audrey?" he asked, his gray eyes like heavy clouds. "Should I fetch us a cool drink?"

He'd committed treason by swearing a Blood Oath to a scared child that night.

I wouldn't have trusted any less, and somehow, he'd known that.

"No." I tried to smile and failed, so I glanced away, wishing I could tuck my hand into his. "Memories took me," I admitted quietly, knowing the words should be safe enough to share with him.

He asked nothing more, just rested his hand on mine. His sweetness made that lump in my throat burn again.

He'd come to meet me, that day, and, in the face of my fear, offered me a lifetime of magically reinforced loyalty, punishable by death. He'd given me a small string of weighted coins to hold—to anchor me to this realm when I felt I might just spin away. And then he'd left and demanded our wedding be postponed. Somehow, he'd made it happen. And for that, I was eternally in his debt.

Even if Isolde did want to hang him from a tree with his own guts as a noose most of the time. And I'd be lying if I said the thought hadn't appealed to me occasionally, too.

Luca cocked his head and, seeing his attention was on his friend, I offered, "Fran's form isn't the best." I injected just enough surprise into my tone that Luca took it with a worried frown, as if Fran wasn't a limp-wristed fop.

"No," he mused. "It isn't."

One of my father's bannermen came up to us and bowed deeply to me, angling himself so the display could also have been toward my father.

"I will win this tourney for you, my lady!"

Low odds of that. "Good luck, lord Gregory," I said with a nod, turning back to Luca. "There's a good turnout this year from the west, isn't there?"

He murmured his agreement, picking up his end of the small talk while Gregory left. He didn't get offended when it petered out once the man was gone. And when Mikus strode out to meet Henry, he squeezed my hand beneath the cover of my skirt as I felt my heart start to race.

I drew in a deep breath, my thoughts with Henry's wife, Fiona, and the opportunities their mage academy would bring.

"Luca," my father called, as Mikus attacked in a flurry of violence that instantly overwhelmed Henry.

"Coming, your grace," Luca replied mildly, squeezing my hand once more as he stood, hiding the affection with his body. "He'll be okay," he murmured.

I used to love Luca's sweet lies.

Sometimes, I still did.

CHAPTER FIVE
AUDREY

"The Wife is the mother to us all. She makes the world a softer, more welcoming place. As did the Mother, so should we, her daughters, blessed with softness and welcome, share our gifts." ~ *Etiquette in Arcanloc*

I had one memory of Fiona and my mother sitting in Mother's drawing room, sipping mulled cider. It was just a moment, frozen in time, with no context attached, but it felt peaceful. Fiona had been young. Was she nervous? Had it been before she'd married Henry, or when she was pregnant? I didn't know. But something in me said *she's good*.

I wasn't in the habit of following every instinct, but I liked to know what was happening around me. Fiona had trained as a Magework Healer—no small expense for such a backwater fief—and had attempted to set up a school to train others away from the central mage wing of the palace. She'd petitioned the King no fewer than four times, making four separate trips across the country to do so.

To stop her, they'd put a hugely expensive hurdle between her and the ability to train others—a purpose-built mage academy.

Beneath me, Henry stumbled back from Mikus, his feet somehow finding the one uneven patch of ground on the beaten area. My heart ached for him. But it was also kind of sweet, that he signed up to be humiliated at best, just for the chance to help Fiona with her dream.

The chair beside me seemed unusually empty.

Henry's shield took a blow, and with my head buzzing, I looked to Isolde. Her classically beautiful face was framed by a few wayward curls. Her lips tipped up a little at the corners as if in amusement, and her eyes were hard as stone, fixed on the field below.

"Your father's watching you," she murmured, the words barely making her lips move.

I swallowed down the bad taste in my mouth, breathed deeply, and found the core of calm in myself, and turned my gaze forward again.

My eyes were on the field, but I focused all my energy on my breathing, the flow of the cool air into my lungs, and the way it spread through my chest. I focused on the cushion beneath me, protecting me from the hard wood of the chair, and the strand of hair that was pulled slightly tighter than its fellows.

The crowd roared. They'd been given blood.

Isolde nudged me gently, and I saw Mikus approaching the edge of the stand, his blunt sword red, looking up at me.

A hysterical laugh bubbled in my chest. I didn't dare let it out, just turned my attention away into a far-off corner of the field where two squires were talking. I'd never given Mikus my favor, and I never would. I had some hard boundaries, and publicly supporting a brutal killer was, I felt, a sensible one. The crowd blurred into the distance, a ravenous wave.

They'd eat us all alive.

"He's gone," Isolde murmured. "The wind would be a kindness for those in a gambeson," Isolde mused, a little louder, flicking her blonde curls out of her eyes as the breeze made them dance.

She was providing me with cover and, pitifully grateful, I took it. "Better than the rain last year," I agreed, seeing Fiona disappearing in the direction of the Healer's tent, her skirts in her hands and tears on her cheeks.

I assumed my father didn't want them getting a mage academy, then.

Grimly, I turned my eyes to the remaining competitors. Someone called for my favor, and I barely heard them.

"That man of yours is causing problems, Victor," I heard the King's ambassador say, as if this was an entirely new concept.

"Mikus doesn't know his own strength," my father responded dismissively. "Accidents happen in these settings."

"They happen more to some than others," pointed out the ambassador.

Isolde shot me a fast, surprised look that I was too shocked to return. Someone had spoken—albeit subtly—against my father?

"Luck's a fortune." The statement drifted down to where we sat, and I believed it. "Smart men know luck's always a factor. You have to plan for it, plan for it all to dry up."

I heard Luca make a polite response and tuned out my father's lectures. I'd heard that one before and would be able to cobble together a response should he call on me.

Somehow, the competition continued as if a man hadn't just been carried off on a stretcher. I watched, filling my brain with the movement and noise.

Winners after the second round started more aggressively vying for my favor. I lifted a hand, nodded acknowledgment, sometimes offered them luck, and kept my ribbon to myself. I hadn't decided on anything. I was struggling not to wonder if Henry had been alive when Fiona made it to his side…or if he was alive now, still.

This time, Chay didn't fight until the lineup was almost done. My eyes kept going back to him.

I hadn't noticed his horse the other day. I wondered if it was a piebald, like the one Kadan had chattered about. I wondered if they were close friends.

As if he knew I was thinking of him, he glanced up at me as he strode onto the field and met my gaze.

Even from a distance I felt the warmth of recognition, and my belly did a slow roll. Perhaps I imagined it, but it felt like there was a hush across the stands for a moment, then a flurry of whispers behind hands.

My father would be furious if I gave Chay my favor.

In my mind, unbidden, rose an image of Chay vaulting the rail as if I needed rescuing, and I felt the pace of my heart increase. I drew in a deep breath and exhaled the childish hope that would see me waiting helplessly for a rescuer who could only ever be a different type of jailer. Before me, Chay studied and deconstructed his opponent's strategy, and at the end of the fight he strode off without so much as looking up at me, leaving me with the familiar, bittersweet feeling of being unseen.

"Hmm." Isolde's eyes narrowed as she watched him go.

The speculation in her look made me wonder if he was actually a contender for something other than jogging my childish dreams.

Another round passed, then two. How he actually fought was a mystery—what he did was lure opponents into making mistakes. He had stamina and patience. His footwork was excellent. The way he used his shield wasn't ideal, but mayhap he just hadn't needed it yet.

Still, something about that little oversight niggled at me. Mikus had the crowd screaming for blood twice more in those two rounds, and I ran through the various possible outcomes in my head, watching as the shields on the competitor's wall dwindled.

"Mikus is in fine form," Isolde noted, as the knight pumped his sword in the air and another poor bastard was carried off. "There's a reason 'Ban bannermen don't usually compete." She remarked on it the way she'd notice a vaguely interesting cloud pattern in the sky.

My eyes went to Chay, the only 'Ban bannerman in question.

He was going to end up fighting Mikus. I wondered if they'd skew it so it would happen, even if he didn't earn it, just so Mikus could break him, too.

It wasn't a comfortable idea. I thought again of his loose shield and may as well have been able to see the future—dead or deeply injured 'Ban bannerman, smug Mikus.

He'd tried to help me yesterday. Even if he'd done it all wrong.

And mayhap Kadan would be upset if he was injured, which was a risk to me. Certainly, I wouldn't mind the opportunity to stick it to Mikus. It wasn't sensible to stop and drive a knife into his gut myself before I left, and I probably couldn't, anyway. But I would take pleasure from seeing him beaten on the tourney field.

And by a Raider's Ban bannerman? I chewed on my lip and thought of how infuriating that would be, trying not to laugh at the thought.

I needed to get that knight to tighten up his sloppy shield work, though. Since I could've cut his throat yesterday and had opted not to, there was a chance he'd put some stock in my advice if I could just make him aware of his simple mistake.

All I had to do was get him to pledge his victory to me so I could get close enough and tell him what he needed to do. Decided on my course of action, I waited with impatience simmering under my skin, and the fights slipped by in much the same way as time went on. Knights jostled for my favor more aggressively as the field narrowed, but I barely saw them. In the sixth round, my target walked to a ring right beneath me. But he didn't look at me for approval. Not even once.

He was the one damned person who didn't want my attention.

I couldn't help it. No—no, I could've, but I didn't want to. I leaned forward and called, "Sir Chay of West Grenvele, I am in need of a champion." He looked up, and I couldn't read his expression, though I was close enough to see he had shaved away the stubble on his jaw. That didn't matter. I just wanted him for his swordsmanship.

Like wind through the leaves, the whispers around me grew and caught the attention of the crowd. I crushed the rush of dread in my veins and ignored the way Isolde's hands flexed in her lap.

"Will you win this for me, sir?"

He offered me a deep bow. “No, my lady,” he called up with a friendly smile. “I fight for my own honor.”

Fury burned deep in my chest. I was trying to help him, and he just threw it back in my face. Worse, that he was claiming the thing I’d wanted myself for so long.

How many of us ever got to fight for ourselves?

CHAPTER SIX
CHAY

"Cornered dogs bite." ~ La'Angi saying

My lungs burned from the fight I'd just won when Mikus strode up to the edge of the stands. The crowd was still screaming for him, and the Duke looked on with quiet approval from above. But Audrey just continued to look through him, utterly unaffected as he did everything except demand her favor.

Why had she offered it to me?

The way she'd danced with Kadan like she was hewn from granite yesterday made me doubt she wanted the attention of a man just to upset her father, and while I knew she'd been watching me, it wasn't with warmth.

I rolled my shoulders and didn't stare at the spectacle Mikus was making or look at what Kadan was up to, instead heading toward the boy with the water and drinking ladles. Callum and the crew had Kadan for today. And if they didn't, that flimsy railing wouldn't keep me from him.

"Apologies, Your Grace," I heard Mikus call up past my whiskey-eyed onlooker with her bored expression. "My momentum carried me through. Trust I'll make amends with…" he paused for a moment, "…the knight's family."

I'd heard the poor bastard's knee shatter from across the field. That was the strength of a charging bull, sure, but it was being inflicted against specific targets with surgical precision.

I doubted he was truly so callous to have shattered the knee of a knight he didn't know. He was aware of whose life he was forever changing. He just made it *look* like he was a mindless beast.

I'd tried to talk myself out of competing. We were here for Luca—and I for Kadan. I shouldn't have entered. I knew I shouldn't. Luca had told me. Callum had told me. Even Kadan had looked surprised.

But, curse it, I'd always dreamt of taking out the La'Angi sword, or mayhap even the melee. There was no higher honor…and I didn't have so much I could leave an opportunity like that behind. Not since my grandfather had anyone in my family been worth anything. I'd grown up hearing the stories about him and staring up at the medal he'd won.

It had sat above the mantle in our hall for years, beside his cloven shield and broken helm. And I remembered when my pa had tossed that medal at a debt collector to pay for the lifestyle he couldn't afford.

I assumed the helm and shield were still there. Even melted down, they wouldn't be worth much.

A hand on my arm dragged me back to the present, and I looked at the steward's painfully neutral expression.

"Yes?"

I followed his gaze past where Mikus had been standing and saw her, skirts in her hands and eyes on me as she danced down the steps to the edge.

I considered smiling, waving, and walking away.

I wanted that medal for *me*, this time. I didn't need her approval. I didn't need anyone's.

But one ribbon wouldn't undo that, either, I told myself. And a small part of me trusted her. She'd never know we were forged in the same manner, tempered to a sharp but brittle edge. I'd been re-forged. Had she?

My feet were already moving toward her before I'd finished my thought. I felt like the eyes of every single person in La'Angi were on us, and I didn't like the sensation. I was comfortable in the shadows of those more used to weathering the attention. But I heard Luca's dismissal of her and remembered my own thoughts of her survival skills.

She knew separating herself from the herd made her weak, but she did it, anyway. Why?

"I'd like you to win for me," she said, before I was close enough to see the freckles I knew dusted her strong nose. She didn't wait for an answer, one of her hands reaching up to the ribbon tradition dictated she give to one of us, along with her blessing.

It felt like a moment since we'd been this close, but I could remember the weight of her still. Mayhap this was why it was called a favor.

She needs a champion.

It was a tourney. It didn't mean anything. I was sworn to Kadan, and even if I weren't, he'd saved my life. More, he'd saved my soul. I wasn't for hire.

In the stands behind her, the watching faces peered at us like crows waiting for an injured cow to still. Soon, they'd pick over our corpses.

Somehow, I remembered to bow. Her hair tumbled free in waves where it still wanted to adhere to the pattern it had been held in, gleaming red where it drank in the sun's warmth. She untangled her ribbon impatiently where it caught in her hair. I kept my face impassive as I thought about how long she'd be spending brushing those snarls out later. Or whether fingers might work…and what it might feel like to tangle myself in it.

She was pale under the flush splashing over her cheeks. I watched her shake the snarled ribbon, her strong hands white-knuckled. Though it was just a small movement, it spoke of a world of irritation and not a lot of forethought.

The woman wasn't tempered, but not in the way the circling crows believed.

"Can I help you, Embers?" I asked, bracing a hand against the rail so I didn't reach for her.

If she heard me, she didn't respond. The ribbon finally flew free, and she shook hair out of her face. A tiny bit stuck to her bottom lip, and I resisted the urge to ease it away. "Mikus'll fight dirty," she murmured as she leaned in close with the ribbon, her hair whipping around us. I felt it tickle my face and struggled not to react. "Dirt. Elbows."

I'd figured that out already. The bigger question was why she was telling me any of this. I drew in the smell of her, something light and floral, as she wrapped the ribbon around my shield arm with brisk movements.

Was she *worried* about me?

"He keeps a knife in his shield, and he's slipped with it before," she went on, her eyes firmly on my arm where she was tying the ribbon. "He won't stop once the fight's done. Don't turn your back."

I resisted the urge to look up and assess the Butcher's reaction to me being so close that his daughter's hair tickled my mouth, too.

"He's your father's man," I said, cutting over the bubbling words. "Don't get involved." She should know that by now. "I don't need your concern."

Even if Luca was right about her taking unnecessary risks, she did it due to the relatable drive to escape those watchful eyes and the ever-present threat.

She tied the knot harder than she needed and something about that show of temper made me feel better. The pressure bit through my gambeson. Her too-hasty fingers dug to rectify her mistake. "I'm already involved," she returned. "Your shield work is sloppy, and he'll have seen it. He'll go up and under. Move forward, not back, if he does."

She didn't know about the rebellion. Luca had all but said it. How was she involved? My mouth was a desert. "Are you safe, Embers?"

I regretted the words as soon as I gave them to her, but couldn't take them back.

Her breath shook, and her fingers slipped again. I stood impassive and resisted the urge to soothe her.

"No one goes toe to toe with Mikus," she said, the words tumbling over each other. "He won't expect it."

No one went toe to toe with the Butcher, either.

I wasn't saying I wanted to, but I wasn't saying I wouldn't.

"I'll look after me. You look after you."

She stepped back with a curtsey. "May you seize victory, sir Chay."

Once more, I didn't look up to where the Butcher reigned on high.

Seizing victory was the goal, yes.

CHAPTER SEVEN
AUDREY

"Once the seed is planted, do not jostle the soil around it for half a moon cycle, except to remove the weeds in its immediate vicinity with caution."
~ Growing Greatness: Common Garden Plants in Arcanloc

Last year, I'd given my favor to a Ltonan. I hadn't been allowed out of my rooms until I'd sewn a flag for every holding in Arcanloc. Every. Single. Holding. It had been mid-spring when I was done. My fingers hadn't healed from it until summer.

But I'd been right, damn it. The Ltonan, a second son of a baron from somewhere east of the Citadel, had damn near had Mikus, until Mikus had tripped him over in an illegal move that no one bothered to correct. The La'Angi crowd liked La'Angi fighters…and blood.

"Your big heart'll get you killed," Isolde said two rounds later, as the lists dwindled dramatically. "His shield is tighter."

It was, and the fact didn't please me. He could've played on it and lured Mikus into an attack. That was his strategy, wasn't it? Anticipate, then overcome. Still, if this was what he did when he was concentrating, I wasn't overly impressed.

"It's not my big heart," I told her, wanting credit given where it was due. "I want to see their faces when Mikus is beaten by a 'Ban knight."

Isolde snorted. "If he lives, it'll be by your grace," she said bluntly. "Again."

That was an angle I didn't dislike. And the memory of him lying helpless beneath me was one I was comfortable with.

He was against a borderlands rapier-wielder when I saw him caught up and unable to lure his opponent. In the extended exchange, his bladework was exquisite, his speed excellent, and his footwork more than good. But he used the shield like it was there only to block when he was threatened. Not that I could've done better, but I'd *seen* better. I'd grown up playing on the castle walls while the guardsmen drilled shield walls and spear work. I knew what it was *supposed* to look like.

How irritating to have chosen a champion who was middling. Still, he'd listened to me, and wasn't that a nice change?

He walked off the victor of that bout, and I sipped my cider without tasting it.

By the time Chay and Mikus met for the final, I'd predicted a half-dozen rounds prior, my head was pounding, and my eyes felt like they'd been rolling around in a hearth. I was entirely finished with the noise and the movement, with trying to keep track of faces and competitors, and also not fidgeting.

When he got through to the final, I wished I hadn't drunk anything at all, so knotted was my belly. I still wanted Mikus to lose, but mostly, I wanted it to be quick. I knew better than to twist my hands or stand and cheer. Plenty of others did, even those in the stands. They cawed like crows.

Mikus had reach, strength, experience and, I was grimly confident, the blessing from my father to do as much damage as he could. My hands ached from holding them so still. If I could just have scrubbed at my poor eyes, mayhap it would be less agonizing. Mikus' mouth was moving, and I knew he wasn't murmuring poetry, but if Chay cared, I couldn't tell. My champion kept him moving, evading swing after lunge, returning only a fraction of the man's attacks.

"He's looking for patterns," Isolde murmured to me, the words low beneath the roar of the crowd.

I could see that much. "Is he finding them?" I asked her, unable to pick any out myself. I just didn't know enough. I hadn't practiced enough. The frustration prickled under my skin. Of all the combat skills I'd wanted, it was the one I'd never been able to learn. Isolde was an archer. She'd taught me some knife and grappling, and I knew how to throw a punch now, as well as take one.

In a blur of movement, I saw Mikus get up and under Chay's shield, and I saw it get shoved away. Chay moved in, and a fragile bubble of pride formed in my chest as I watched him drop his shoulder and avoid that attack. He was in range of the knife I knew Mikus kept in his shield.

I'd seen him use it a time or two. Not always on the field, either.

Chay attacked, but Mikus evaded, and they broke apart, neither with the upper hand. "You made use of your time," Isolde noted, sipping her juice. "Good advice."

Pride burned painfully bright in my chest, and I couldn't help but resettle my weight to shift the way it sat behind my ribs, uncomfortable with its pressure. The pattern resumed—Chay testing, Mikus responding, Chay avoiding. My heart didn't slow to a normal rhythm, though. I didn't try to respond to Isolde. The roaring had faded around me, or my focus had narrowed. I could see the drips of sweat on their faces, the strength behind those sword swings.

Once, Mikus let his shield drop a little, feigning exhaustion. But Chay didn't fall for it—if anything, it made him more wary. And when Mikus toed up dirt Chay just backed up until they weren't near that place anymore.

Isolde glanced down at her juice as she swirled it in her cup. "Did you?" she asked, idly.

She didn't care if he lived or died. "Yes." My tone matched hers almost perfectly. I'd warned him. And I was glad, too. I was glad to see the extended show of skill, swordsmanship, and raw physical prowess. And I quite enjoyed seeing Mikus having to work for his victory.

Mikus' words had become shouts. Foul things about Chay's parentage, about sex acts with his horse, about his intelligence and body and honor and heart.

None of it seemed to faze Chay. I wondered what one could say if they wanted to spur his temper. We all had something. Apparently, Chay's something didn't include public, high-volume discussions of how much of his horse's ejaculate he enjoyed slathering on his face.

His bladework never faltered. There was a grace to the sword I'd always appreciated. Even knowing it was ridiculous, I felt my lungs burn with Chay, and my legs ache. I could feel the ground beneath my feet, the weight of the shield, and the stifling heat of the padded gambeson sticking to my back. It made sitting still so much harder. I wanted to move with them as they clashed together, hilt to hilt. Chay almost had him but was pushed back by pure brute force, and Mikus maneuvered him into a position that made my gut twist.

Rather than evade, Chay engaged and took a blow to his shield. The force of it echoed in my head, the crash of metal against wood, the head-splitting crack of sound as the wood gave way. Trying to draw in calm breaths, I questioned whether it was possible that my ears were right. The shield *seemed* whole. I was getting lost in the give-and-take.

Urgency drummed in my veins, my heart was in my throat, but I stayed still as the crowd erupted around me.

Mikus' leg collapsed and he went down hard on one knee.

Isolde let out a snort, but the cider in my belly rose. I swallowed both it and my heart as Chay leapt forward and Mikus lunged—not exhausted, but luring Chay in close.

My eyes didn't close, though my mind skipped ahead to frozen memories of other times Mikus had lured people in.

The glistening spill of intestines. The puff of dust as bodies fell.

But Chay knocked aside the attack and moved inside of Mikus' guard.

The burst of pride was so huge and sudden it made my eyes water. I locked my jaw as he tagged Mikus.

He was *my* damned champion. *Mine.*

Everyone saw it. Everyone knew.

The crowd roared, of course. They always did. They preferred blood to skill, but they'd take anything they could get.

My heart seized in my chest as Mikus got up under Chay's shield, dropped his sword to grab Chay's arm, and drove his knee into my champion's chest.

I was on my feet, a scream locked in my throat, hands fisted helplessly in my skirts.

Chay's elbow snapped up and out, smashing Mikus in the jaw with enough force to make him stagger back. The scream in my throat blocked my airways. Noise surrounded me, a world of shifting, indecipherable fury and hunger.

I sucked in air and fought the battle with that hot ball of feelings, letting myself rock, just twice, foot to foot, before I sat, hunched over that agonizing lump inside of me. Stewards came forward, their steps hesitant, glancing between one another, Mikus, Chay, and my father. The crowd was screaming for more.

I couldn't take any more.

It was over. Mikus couldn't go back in and blame it on momentum or not knowing his own strength—Chay was, very clearly, waiting for him to make another pass, regardless of how obvious it would be.

As I watched, Chay kicked Mikus' blunted sword behind him.

"Well," Isolde mused. The word came from far away.

Mikus spat a wad of blood, turned on his heel, and stormed off the field. Only then did Chay let the steward take his arm and raise it.

My head swam. The noise was a physical assault, and I was already flayed raw. I closed my eyes and wished it really was done. The banquets, the dancing, the stress, and socializing.

I'd won. Now I just wanted my bed.

Isolde leaned into me, our hips touching. Her presence was

anchoring, and I breathed into her, moving the energy slowly through my body.

I opened my eyes to the brightness of the day, the fashionable clothes attached to fashionable bodies, the movement of the crowd, and the reflection off jewelry. It was all too much.

"Eyes straight," Isolde murmured.

My body was heavy. I kept my eyes forward and drew from her strength, desperate.

Chay was crossing the field. I recognized the way he held himself, the tight line of his jaw, and the way his mouth had opened to suck in small bits of air. I recognized it all too well, and it made me feel hollow.

"Congratulations on your win, sir Chay of West Grenvale," my father said, and the crowd fell silent, waiting like dogs beside their master for scraps. "Your prowess today is a great honor to my daughter."

My stomach rolled. Chay's eyes cut to me, momentarily. The world seemed far away.

I waited for him to refuse, but he didn't. He just bowed low to me despite the ribs I was sure were cracked, the movement stiff, his face set and pale. I felt the agony in my own chest and wanted to weep.

"Thanking you, Your Grace, my lady."

But there was no gratitude in the words.

CHAPTER EIGHT
AUDREY

"Do not engage in unwinnable battles."
~ Barloc's Wisdom, compiled by F. Bergsoniir

Luca grabbed me before I made it into my chambers. I was exhausted all the way to my soul, and when I looked into his stormy gray eyes I just wanted to cry. All I wanted was what he offered, the gossamer dreams he spun. *Dreams. Not reality. Not truth.*

"Audrey," he said, horrified. His arms went around me, and I just couldn't return the embrace. I didn't have any warmth in me. Not for him. Not for anyone. Hollow, I shut my eyes. "You warned him, didn't you, that Mikus fights dirty?" He held me to him, rocked me. And despite myself, I relaxed slightly. He offered me everything neither of us could have, and so help me, I loved the hope he spun. But none of it was real. "He's got a couple of broken ribs, but he's alive. Thanking you."

"Did you win much?" Isolde asked him, the words acidic as she forced herself between us. His fingers clung in fleeting protest, making my dress rake agonizingly against my flesh as it twisted. "Did you figure how much it'd cost her?"

I didn't have the heart or the head for Isolde's blame or Luca's dreams. "Not now," I said, but the words were small and weak.

"You don't know," he began, then shook his head, reaching for me. "Change is coming, Audrey. You won't have to be afraid soon—"

His hands were slapped away. Isolde planted a shove square in his chest and drove him back. "How dare you," she spat, furious. Then I heard familiar staccato steps, the creak of leather, and the chime of metal.

Ice ran through my veins.

Isolde pulled me further behind her and spoke over whatever Luca was about to say. "The lady has had a long day," she said loudly. "You may of course send word, and we can arrange a time—"

My father rounded the corner, and I felt the world sway. Time seemed unusually slow, and the scene around him was blurry, but I could have replicated the simple, bold pattern edging his cloak and counted the studs in his belt.

The moment Luca saw him, I could tell. I watched from the corner of my eye as the color drained from his face like a jug of cider at a table full of knights. His cheeks went from red to pink and then almost gray. The transition took an eon. He fell back a step, eyes almost as wild as Vixen's had been when we'd chanced upon that pocket of 'Ban bannermen.

My father's lips moved, that long mouth that was so often a slash of displeasure in his square face imparting information I needed to hear but couldn't. Out of time with his moving mouth I heard words erupt.

"Wise as ever, mistress Isolde. Escort lord Luca to his rooms, Wade. He has a banquet tonight."

Before the words were done, Luca was being forced out of the corridor away from the family wing toward his rooms. He looked at me over Wade's shoulder, his eyes full of sorrow and guilt. I felt nothing at all as I was swept along into the room with the fire burning and the piles of books Luca had lent me.

My father smelt of the oils used on his boots and scabbard. I noticed the familiar scents from far away. He opened his mouth. Words tumbled out, beaded and ran off my mind like I'd waxed and weatherproofed it.

I sat, because his hand gesture said, "*sit.*"

Neither of his black-clad personal guard—the La'Angi family guard—were Mikus. Isolde stalked in, her expression calm but her eyes stormy. My heart felt like a stone in my chest. It kept me from drifting out through the ceiling and getting lost in the clouds. She stood with her back to the fire. The poker was a finger's breath from her hand.

In a few days I'd be in a saddle, headed east. We'd make a new home somewhere else. Adventures would ensue, of course.

"...with Luca to support a liegeman of Raider's Ban," my father said, the words cool. "But I don't think you're that gullible or foolhardy."

I didn't want adventures elsewhere, though. I wanted my home.

I needed to listen. I looked down at my hands. They were lying one atop the other in my lap, steady and calm. My heart beat slow, heavy, rhythmic. It felt like it belonged to a drummer deep in the city. Outside of me. Away. "No, Your Grace," I said. My lips, my tongue, didn't feel like mine. They were cold, thick, and squashy. Not mine. Not me.

"Are you going to tell me," he began, the words precise and full of anger, "that you were just playing your little game—identify the winner?"

Of course he knew the game. Or had guessed. We'd made no real secret of it. Why should we? And it was the perfect excuse. "Yes, Your Grace."

"As long as the winner isn't one of our own," he continued, dark, low, and slow.

My mind, unencumbered by the weight of my body and fear, flew. I saw every breath he took and the smallest shift of expression, studying them all. "Your Grace," I began, the words as crisp as his own, "you and I both know Mikus is the best. He's the best fighter *and* the best brawler. If I picked Mikus every year, where would the challenge be?

My game isn't to identify the winner, Your Grace. My game is to identify the person who will fight Mikus."

His lips were still thin, his eyes narrow, but there was a slight softening in his shoulders, the smallest tilt of his head, that told me I'd made progress.

"Did it occur to you how that would look?"

I sighed. "Not really, Your Grace. Mayhap I spend too little time considering people's talk." I stood and went to where a jug and cups had been laid out and poured my father a drink. Spiced juice.

He was silent while I served him, swimming gracefully through the tension in the air. It wasn't really my grace, though. They weren't really my limbs. "You spin a good tale," he said, taking the cup without sampling the contents. "You get that from your mother." From above, I saw the softness in his shoulders, the line of regret between his brows, and I knew I'd misspoken. "But I have no patience for games, girl."

And wasn't it fortunate I wasn't in my own skin right now? I should've stayed seated and compliant. I didn't look at Isolde, with the makeshift weapon right by her hand. If it came to it, could we take out all three of them?

"Your Grace, I—"

His hand shot out, but not toward me. Isolde's hair was in his fist, and a knife was at her throat. She was pulled back and off balance. My feet carried me a step away. The room was gray around the edges, but she was so clear. They were so clear. My father's level eyes, long, neutral lips, square jaw. Isolde's curls in his hands. Her jaw tight with pain. Her neck arched, her legs at awkward angles, her hands splayed in the air, poised. The knife was the same gray as Luca's eyes. He'd used it to carve venison last night. There was no sign of the thick gravy that the meat had swam in, though. Not on the blade, or smeared over Isolde's throat.

Father's mouth was moving, but the words came slowly, like rocks thrown into a pond.

"Sullivan."

I was grabbed. No, no, my clothes were grabbed. It all felt the same. Pressure. Pulling. Flesh and cloth were the same. Neither was me.

"Help my—"

Ripping. Biting. Cold air against my back. I tried to spin, tried to struggle. My dress had been torn, the bodice pulled down over my arms, tangling me.

"—daughter—"

Before I could move I was shoved forwards, belly over the arm of the couch, face down.

"—understand—"

My skirts went up. The cold was a piece of information that didn't apply to my own skin. I knew he wouldn't kill me. I knew Sullivan was the dog with the most control, too.

"—what—"

I lifted, twisted. Hands bit into my hair, forcing my face down into the cushions. Air. There was no air.

"—Raider's Ban—"

Heat, pressure. A body behind me. A hand. It bunched and tore the fabric at my hip. No. No, the flesh. That was flesh. At least some of that was my flesh.

"—men—"

I tried to turn my head, tried to breathe. I couldn't see. Couldn't draw more than a sliver of air. It was hot. It had come from my own body.

"—do."

The weight of him was crushing. Endlessly crushing.

And then he was gone. One moment, there. The next, gone. But Isolde's hands were on me. I'd know those hands anywhere. Anytime. I was levered up. Hair was brushed from my face impatiently.

They'd left. Why couldn't I remember them leaving? Father would've spoken, before he left. I needed to remember what it was he said, so I could avoid it next time. I wouldn't pour the juice. I'd sit and be compliant.

She put her forehead against mine. Her hands on my arms. She spoke but I didn't need to hear the words to know they were reassurances. I drifted, somewhere above, somewhere beyond. Her hands squeezed, firmly. Slow, for a while. Fast, for a while. Moderate, for a while. Left, right, left, right. I matched my breathing to hers. My skirts were bunched, and my backside felt strange with only my drawers between me and the world, so I resettled the fabric. Next time, I'd know what to do.

At the first trickle of terror, I opened my eyes and lifted my hands. I held on.

"I've got you," she said grimly. "I've got you, Audrey."

My heart was beating. Hard. I breathed. I couldn't match her pace. A wave of horror came up and swept me away.

The agony of it was everything. Everywhere. A sob was ripped from my chest. Her hands squeezed. Rhythmic. Faster, slower, faster, moderate, slower. Left, right. I wept. Her forehead bit into mine, and I felt it. It was mine. And my body hurt. My hip. My shoulders. Where the fabric had pulled and torn with so much force. My neck where I'd been forced face-down and held. I coiled my hands around her skull and cradled her, shaking so hard I don't know how our heads didn't rattle and knock. My chest was heaving. He could've killed her. He'd never kill me, but he could've killed her. He would've. Without hesitation or concern.

One blue-eyed swordsman could never be worth Isolde's life.

"I'm so sorry," I managed between sobs. "I'm so sorry."

"Yeah, you screwed up," she said ruthlessly. "But who treated a person like a thing, Audrey?"

The speed at which he'd grabbed her. Horror. Terror. It had me by the throat. By the hair. I wept, clenching my teeth, refusing to wail. It wouldn't matter. There was so much pain. "I shouldn't have—"

"Who held the knife?" she asked, her hands biting as they squeezed. Left, right, left, right.

He had the same eyes as me, golden brown. The same jaw as me, square and strong. The same mouth as me. The tears seared my throat.

My knees collapsed, and I couldn't, wouldn't, stop them. She went with me, holding me.

"Father," I said eventually. The Duke. Victor. The Butcher of Wolfswail. The General of Arcanloc.

"Did you hold the knife?" she demanded.

Those eyes. Pain ripped my chest. It vibrated through me. It consumed me. "No."

"Say it."

I sucked in air and felt the pain ripping through me. "I did the best I could."

She nodded. Her head bumped mine. I sobbed, rocking. "Again."

"I did the best I could." And the words hurt, still. But they wouldn't. Not for long. Because they were true. Because they were right. And if anyone could show me that, Isolde could.

"Who overruled your autonomy?" she demanded, fury in her words.

I tried to pull away, and she just went with me, squeezing. My hands went to my face. Tears. Snot. I curled up and crushed myself down. My face into my skirts. I couldn't breathe. It hurt so much I couldn't breathe. Her grip adjusted, then the squeezing continued. Slow, slow, fast, slow, moderate, moderate, fast. I didn't fight. I couldn't have. I cried and rocked, but it didn't empty that well of agony.

"Who pushed you down, Audrey?" she asked, when the tears began to run dry.

I wiped away some of the wet mess on my face. "Sullivan."

"Did you do it?"

"No."

"Did you survive?"

"Yes."

Her voice had softened. "Who should be ashamed, Audrey?"

I shuddered. It was there, in my breast, in the marrow of my bones. Dark. Tacky. Hungry. "Sullivan. Victor." I breathed with her, almost. "I did the best I could." And it still hurt, but it was a dull ache. I struggled up and pushed my hair back with wet fingers. "I need a bath," I said, and the words shook. Though he'd only touched me through my clothes, I still needed to scrub myself clean.

"You do," she agreed, unconcerned. "And the Butcher needs an arrow through his throat. Both can wait. Work with me a bit more, Audrey."

So I nodded and breathed. I felt the irregularly rhythmic squeezes on my arms. I let my mind circle, let my heart hurt. And it eased, eventually. The words, mayhap. The movements, perhaps. I rested while she rang for a bath, keeping the rhythm myself with my feet. We breathed, together.

The ball and banquet happened without us. We talked about what we needed to do. When we needed to do it. Next steps. Survive the archery tomorrow. Keep our heads down. Minimal presence at the feasting and dancing, and avoid Raider's Ban riders at all costs. Tell Luca we didn't want company. That was all we needed to do tomorrow. We could do that.

I fell asleep curled up in my bed with Isolde stroking my hair. Safe. Loved.

CHAPTER NINE
ISOLDE

"And then Hruudwulf looked upon the moon with new eyes, at once ensorcelled and free." ~ *Southern lore*

Power flooded my limbs, and I was upright and moving before my brain clearly identified the sounds of combat. Thumps, grunts, ripping clothes, rapid breathing, something falling with a pretty twinkling sound. *Audrey's accessories.*

It took me one heartbeat to be in her room. The glow of the fire showed a writhing pile of limbs, but I couldn't make out enough to safely intervene. The next heartbeat, I was ripping the shutters open and letting moonlight flood the room. The crack of a breaking bone made my teeth ache, and I saw Audrey, then, beneath her spindly assailant, their arm stretched out and now bending the wrong way.

The attacker was still struggling, but I had a clear shot and I took it, kicking out.

Their head snapped to the side, and they went slack in her arms.

I found a fallen knife and scooped it up, assessing the damage to my charge as best I could in the low light.

Fast breath, pale cheeks, eyes puffy from crying. Whole.

But how close had we come? *Twice in one day.* That was two times too many that I'd almost lost her.

I swallowed down the rage born of fear and looked closer at Audrey as she straightened. There was blood on her, but it wasn't the mess that a mortal wound would've left. Still… "That isn't a scratch you've got there."

She looked down at herself, the movement making her unconscious assailant slide further onto the rug and out of the grip of her legs. "It's fine," she said dismissively.

Ungently, I yanked the blanket they'd been tangled up in from beneath the assailant, making their head bounce against the rug. Their face turned to a better angle for me to see the silver loops in their eyebrow, connected to a silver chain that went to their ear. *Worg.*

A chill went up my spine as I gave the blanket a stiff flick, then folded it neatly. "Keep pressure on," I told Audrey. We needed light.

Twice, I'd almost failed her.

I needed to figure out what we were going to do.

"It's fine," Audrey protested again, but she sat up and pressed the blanket to her wound. "I don't know what woke me."

I didn't either, but I'd bet that chest wound would've been a throat wound if she'd been in a deeper slumber.

"I kicked the blanket at them." Audrey looked down at the scrawny form at her feet, her breathing still quick. "They were surprised."

I was surprised, too. I'd tucked it in firmly.

"You did well," I said, lighting a few candles. I didn't need to inspect the knife in my hand to know it'd be Southern make. I could already feel the excellent balance. Long, wide, double-edged, straight. This weapon was designed to cut people, not dinner. It wasn't curved like I favored, and it was longer than what was used locally, and wider. The steel was good. Excellent, in fact.

There was only one place I knew you'd get better steel than

La'Angi. And that was at the source, in the hands of the people used to strip those resources from below the mountains.

I turned the knife over in my hand, trying to calm my too-quick heart. Audrey was fine. She was staring down at the slumped would-be assassin, her expression blank.

She was as fine as she'd be while we existed in this glorified torture room.

The attacker was Southern. There were no markings on the knife to identify them further, and I wasn't keen to explore their silver too closely. I could've woken them up and made them talk, but I didn't need to. I knew why they were here.

Luca had talked plenty.

Judging by the dull look settling over Audrey's face, though, she wouldn't have put two and two together yet. But she needed to be involved in deciding what we did next, so I needed her to know the context. Anything less was unjust.

"Luca sent an assassin after you," I said, enunciating the words slowly and clearly.

She looked up, shocked. "No, he'd never..." she trailed off.

He wouldn't do it *deliberately*. But I could imagine a lot of ways he'd do it *accidentally*. From Audrey's silence, I knew she was figuring that out. And if he was allied with the Worgs...

It really wasn't hard to imagine that, given the opportunity, a group of rebels would act to ensure the sins of the father wouldn't be revisited by the heir.

She let out a long breath. "He wouldn't send an assassin after me, Isolde."

We didn't have time for this. "He doesn't love you. He doesn't even know you."

The only sign of the damage I'd done was a brief flicker of her eyelids and the frown that smoothed away, leaving her looking peaceful.

I wanted to swear.

I wanted to apologize.

"You hide the best of you," I offered, sensibly. "Because if you didn't, they'd take it, and they'd break it." Her expression was flat. I waited as she breathed, watching the way she elongated the exhales and drew the air in deeply with grim pride. "Audrey—"

"He swore me a Blood Oath," she said, cutting over me. "Something went wrong, or his blood would've boiled in his veins when he attempted to plan this."

I waved that away. "He doesn't attempt harm *any* time he interacts with you, yet he has done plenty of damage. He's ignorant, and *you pay for it.*" She didn't argue with me, at least, though I knew getting her to agree out loud would be like drawing hen's teeth. With a sigh, I offered my palm for the blanket she was using on her wound. "Let me see the damage. We may as well wait in case the others have better luck." I doubted they would. That boy couldn't organize a successful rush to the privy.

"The others?" I could see the meaning sink in after she'd spoken the words.

She sat with that thought for a moment. I turned with my borrowed knife to cut a strip off our guests' cloak, then started trussing them up.

I was halfway done when Audrey said, the words so soft I could barely hear them, "He always did promise he'd look after me."

Ah, yes, Luca and his big promises. "Present circumstances bear testament to his dedication," I agreed sweetly and, just for emphasis, ripped another strip of cloth free.

She didn't flinch. *Good girl*, I thought grimly, stripping the unconscious assassin of their other knives and tossing them behind me.

Anyway, we all knew Luca would do better to kill Audrey *after* they were wed. He didn't even have to do it deliberately. The childbed worked same as a knife to the throat, and a babe increased his hold on La'Angi.

The crack of her door being thrown wide made alarm flood my veins, but I didn't react. I'd trained too long and too hard for that.

Audrey didn't, either.

The Butcher strode in a moment later, sleeves rolled up and shirt open at the throat in a surprisingly informal moment that was only emphasized by the spray of blood on his boots and his hair still military neat.

Audrey had stood, taking pressure off her wound to curtsey. His eyes took in her injury and the attacker beneath me in a moment.

"Send for a Healer," he snapped, and behind him, I saw Sullivan's about-face.

"I—Your Grace, I—"

One flick of his fingers, and Audrey fell silent. I watched, ice cold, as he took one of the knives where they'd been thrown. His eyes were on the silver the would-be assassin wore as she lay slumped at my feet.

"Keep the pressure on it," he told Audrey, without looking.

Audrey's eyes danced to me, then away, as she returned the blanket to where I'd instructed she hold it.

I wasn't getting the jump on him now. But I could take him to the ground, if I had to.

He didn't question us, though, just directed a curt nod in my direction with a brusque "Well done."

Of course he'd never assume it was his daughter who'd bested the assailant. But still, I should've dropped a jug or something, so I could've claimed I'd smashed it over her head.

Regardless, he was distracted, and I'd take the reprieves I could get. "Needs must, Your Grace."

"It would seem so." He turned over the assassin with one booted foot. We all gazed down at her form. I didn't mention he'd rolled her onto her broken arm. She was probably Audrey's age but as finely built as a bird.

He reached into the collar of their shirt and pulled out heavy silver loops, letting them fall onto their thin chest. The slow rise and fall of her breathing made the metal glitter in the silence of the room. I stood back, watching the Butcher's face.

He knew what it meant. And, from the way he was looking at that necklace, he knew this Worg's importance.

Audrey had no idea. She stood, hands clasped before her, eyes on the rug somewhere to the side of the unconscious attacker. Ignorance, for her, was safest right now.

Heavy, unhurried steps warned us of Mikus' approach long before he arrived with the jangle of metal and the creak of leather, stinking of beer and sweat. He'd obviously thrown his black tabard over top of whatever he'd worn to drown his sorrows. I wouldn't have bet on him having been in his cups too long. He was too stable for that. But I was interested to see half his face was swollen beyond recognition. Mayhap the 'Ban rider had done a better job than I'd thought, or mayhap Mikus had gone looking for a way to vent.

"Forget something, Mikus?" the Butcher asked, his words almost idle as he straightened.

Every single one of us in the room, except the unconscious rebel, felt the implicit threat in that calm.

Mikus bowed deeply. "Your Grace, after the tourney—"

"After you disgraced me," the Butcher corrected, coldly.

They were doing this right here, and I wasn't going to show my thoughts. We'd had two close calls today. We just needed to get through this one.

"Sullivan should've been on the door, Your Grace," Mikus said firmly. "The Watch was set."

"Funny," my father said without any trace of humor. "That isn't what I've heard."

Mikus' jaw worked. He dropped his eyes to the assassin, but I could feel the fury in him.

"Von Rhea is dead," my father said, straightening. "My daughter could be. Who should pay the price for that?"

"The men not at their post," Mikus replied. "Your Grace."

"If I didn't set the Watch on La'Angi and the duchy was overrun, I think I'd be at fault."

The urge to move toward Audrey was physically painful to resist. The Butcher stepped up close to Mikus. I recognized the pose and the power in the older man's limbs, and the impotent rage in Mikus. Dread beat somewhere in the vicinity of my belly.

If this became lethal, we were far too close.

"Next time you fail me will be the last. Are we clear, soldier?"

Mikus' head bobbed once, hard, and relief trickled through me.

"Good. Sullivan is new First Blackguard." Color flared in Mikus' cheeks and that relief turned to ice at his expression. "Bring the woman. I do like to have political prisoners before we even declare war." Then he walked through Mikus, forcing the big man to fall back to make space as the Butcher left.

I didn't move as Mikus strode over. He, too, paused for a moment at the sight of all that silver. And then he was picking up the assassin like they weighed no more than a ham. His eyes settled on Audrey as he did, and a chill washed through my bones at the sheer menace in that look.

All the air seemed to have been sucked out of the room. There had been real threat in that brute. He spun, and the woman's boots hit the door on the way out. A flake of mud fluttered to the stone floor.

Alone again, I circled the area, sticking to the shadows and moving quickly toward the door. "Von Rhea," Audrey said, horrified. The King's representative. A poor target. Better that they'd sent all the assassins at the Butcher. I closed the door firmly. "War. He said war, Isolde." There wasn't shock. She was just stating facts. "It'd be against the Southern rebels. Surely, this is the start of a rebellion." Now she sounded puzzled, and I turned to her, watching as she turned it over in her head. What she said made sense. "If there is war, he'll go South. He broke Wolfswail once. He can do it again."

Any further commentary she held until after the Healer arrived, and I wondered if I ought to count the Butcher's attendance as the third time Audrey had escaped death this day. Luca had told us there would be change.

Which meant Luca was part of this rebellion.

Which meant Audrey was betrothed to a problem.

She should've known that part, although the political implications were, I had to admit, not as predictable. Who'd have thought the dreamer would actually *do* something?

Of course he'd done it wrong, but mayhap I ought to have credited him for doing it at all.

CHAPTER TEN
CHAY

"Only the guilty shudder at the Worg's howl." ~ *Southern saying*

The hunched figure straightened as soon as I'd closed the door behind him, throwing back the threadbare scarf and pulling the lightly faded woolen hat from his head. A fine layer of gray hairs the same length as Luca's own went with it. I'd seen his disguises before. They were subtle and effective. Not a skill I anticipated a new King would need, but certainly helpful when it came to killing the old one. Wordlessly, I accepted the walking stick he passed over.

I hadn't seen Audrey today in the stands. Her chairs had been decorated with the colors of a different house. No one had batted an eyelash at her sudden disappearance. My gut had been tight all day at the aura of forced calm emanating from the staff. But I held onto the questions I had no right to voice.

"I was worried you hadn't received my message," Kadan said, waving him toward a chair before the fire.

"My rooms are being guarded," Luca said shortly. "It took me time to get past them."

Kadan's expression was already as grim as I'd seen it, but I saw his eyes flicker toward the door I stood in front of, and I took pleasure from the way he saw me and relaxed back, a little of the tension in his shoulders unraveling.

I'd worked hard for that trust. He'd worked hard to earn it. And the pride I felt for both of us grabbed me by the throat, filling my chest with a warmth so sweet it hurt.

"I wasn't followed," Luca said confidently, pouring himself a cup of spiced juice. "What news?"

"They took one of the assassins alive."

Luca froze.

"The Duke has paid for a Magework Healer's services throughout the entire day, and another for tonight," Kadan went on.

It wasn't new information to me. I'd been with Kadan when the update had been murmured in his ear, in the aftermath of the joust that had been an abysmal showing, bar our own riders. Even *I* would've placed, a fact that had been declared a number of times by my amused friends, all crowing their glee.

As much as I'd tried to stop myself, I hadn't been able to hold my fears at bay. I was, after all, her champion. Surely, I had a right to know what state the lady of the keep was in? But I'd waited, and reminded myself she was the Butcher's daughter, first and foremost.

Then the waterboy, who supplemented his wage by charging for interesting tidbits he learned whilst doing his rounds, had visited us.

"I wondered," Luca said, the words harsh. "I expected him to either publicly eviscerate us, or to have my throat cut in my sleep and for my death to remain an unsolved mystery that didn't even make the footnotes of a history book."

That was a highly specific option. I glanced over at Kadan to find a grin spreading across his face. "Look at us, finding a third option like the bred-in-the-bone troublemakers we are."

Luca lifted his cup in toast, rubbing a hand over his jaw and leaning back against the stone hearth. "There were *seven* of them, 'Dan. *Seven* Worgs. He took out *four himself.* And no one heard a *thing.*"

People who were close enough to the Butcher would know when to keep their mouths shut. I'd expected to hear bells tolling, people running in the halls, and general distress. If the assassins had managed to take out more than just the King's advisor, mayhap there would've been chaos. Instead, life had continued as usual.

There was something eerie about that level of violence not creating even a ripple in the day-to-day running of the keep, and it was sickeningly familiar. I should've known we wouldn't hear any news. And I didn't love that Luca had anticipated this reaction, at least somewhat, but I was caught off guard. I knew better.

"Do you know which of them remains alive?" Luca asked, his voice a monotone.

"The one who went after your bride," Kadan drawled.

I felt like the entire keep had come down on me.

I'd suspected the Duke, angered by the assassination attempt, might have harmed Audrey.

But to have assassins go after her? Why hadn't anyone *told* me?

Because she's nothing to you, and you're nothing to her. I sucked in a deep breath and ignored the quick look Kadan sent me as I held the air safely behind my ribs until my mind started to work again.

Matri'sion weren't known for their mercy, but the Duke even less so. If his daughter had been killed, would the assassin still breathe? Surely, someone would have told me if she was *gone.* After all, Luca's entire plan hinged on her. They'd been healing one person. *Surely,* that one person was Audrey.

I should've known this was where we'd end up; another failed attempt on the Duke's life and the child-King's crown, suffocated by the threatening silence. I was glad I'd had so much space that I'd forgotten the steps to this dance. And I refused to learn them again.

"They were targeting Victor and Von Rhea," Luca objected. "That was the agreement."

"Well, mayhap they understood the terms differently," Kadan

drawled. "I have it on excellent authority that an assassin left Audrey's rooms in the company of one of the Butcher's Blackguard and in poor condition, and there's been a change in the hierarchy of his people."

I tightened my jaw to hold back the demand for information.

"He suspects them?" Luca asked, like a hound distracted by a butterfly while the quarry grazed nearby.

He didn't suspect his men, though. Not really. But he'd be looking to lay blame. I looked at the plain walking stick Luca had found. It had authentic dings in it where it'd fallen, the base of it worn smooth and compacted from long use. I hoped whoever he'd got it from could afford an upgrade for what Luca had paid. If he'd stolen it, I'd be disgusted.

A knock on the door came, and Luca fell silent, removing himself from sight immediately. I cracked it open, ignoring the stab of pain in my chest the movement earned. Whilst I had the excuses that came with the late hour at the ready, I didn't need them. Darrius stood there, his linen shirt rolled up to mid-forearm, his sandy hair only slightly neater than his son's unruly mop. I shifted to let him in.

"How're you, Chay?" he asked, stepping in. "I've barely had a chance to see you these last few days. There was a lovely horse blanket that would look fabulous on Bliksem in the market today, but I was sidetracked before I could pick it up. I sent Toby for it, but he got one with too much purple."

"I'm sure it's lovely," I assured him. "But I have blankets."

He snorted, but didn't engage in the argument, shutting the door firmly behind him. I knew damned well it'd be among my gear next time I went to saddle Bliksem. "If Luca isn't here, we need to consider how the hells to get him here," Darrius said to his son, pouring himself a tall juice. "Gates don't open until dawn, and trying to force our way would be too obvious, so we've a few hours to hide him and figure out a plan."

Luca reappeared from Kadan's room. "What's wrong?" he asked, looking between the two of them.

Darrius, without any sign of surprise, said, "Victor has one of your assassins."

"They aren't *mine,* per se," Luca said. "'Dan was just telling me. My chambers are being guarded, and I was followed today, but it's all unobtrusive. It might even be security."

Kadan snorted, his head falling back. "The assassin knows you, Luca," he said.

"I wore a disguise," he objected.

"You know who the Worgs are," Darrius said, serious where Kadan was irreverent. "That's why you chose them. I'd bet your life that they know exactly who you are."

This made Luca pause.

I realized that as he hadn't asked if Audrey was hurt either of the times the surviving assassin had been mentioned, and hadn't commented on her absence, he probably had reason. I wasn't accustomed to putting my trust in Luca, but I needed to practice.

"Who did they catch?" he asked, then shook his head. "It doesn't matter. They sent only their best. Even if they *do* know who I am—and that's probably likely, you're right—they'd only hurt their own people if I were exposed."

"They took Ylva Wuurgard." Darrius said the name with a heaviness that made me check Kadan's expression, and I saw his eyes flutter briefly closed, his brow knitted. He wasn't a pious man; when his lips formed words, they were an expletive.

The Butcher had gotten lucky, and we had not, then.

"She won't talk," Luca said shortly. "That woman's made of steel. They don't survive the South if they aren't."

For just a moment, I was a child in a body as big as most adults, behind a full tavern, my head ringing from a blow to my skull and mud between my fingers. "*How's he still up?*" The disembodied voice came from somewhere behind me. "*How's he still up?*" But deep in my bones, I had the sure knowledge that if I went down and they took the coin I had, then I'd never get out of that mud. And the desperation that flooded my veins was molten steel.

"Victor breaks everyone," Darrius said softly while I kept my breathing measured, waiting for the rush of feelings to cool. "*Everyone,*

Luca. There is no steel that cannot be shattered, and the tougher the alloy, the more brittle the product."

I flexed my hands to feel the lack of mud between my fingers. I'd never had this lecture from Darrius, not about myself. I'd never needed it. I'd seen the proof of once-sharp, twice-broken people everywhere I'd looked in life.

"Steel is an analogy," Luca told him dismissively. "She isn't too brittle, and even if she *wasn't* tough, how would it serve her now? The point isn't your excellent and, I'm sure, very wise lesson about strength, Darrius. What I wanted to communicate was that the Wuurgard heir won't talk. It would cost her too much."

Heir. He'd said heir. He'd sent a Southern heir to their long, painful death at the Butcher's hands. And, at the same time I was struggling with that thought, the man's disregard for softness was worming its way into my mind.

Neither realization felt any better than that mud between my fingers.

"I doubt much will serve her now," Darrius said, grief in his voice. "I'm seeing if I can get someone in to give her mercy, but I expect he'll be prepared for that. She *will* talk, Luca. There is nothing Victor will not do in pursuit of his goals, and if that means re-starting her heart a dozen times, he already has a mage prepared to do that."

The depths of that level of control made my belly knot, and I could feel my blood drum faster. I forced myself to hold my hands relaxed and didn't allow my breath to hasten.

At least death had always been an escape option for me. The Butcher didn't even allow that. Not until it was on his terms.

I thought, again, of the woman who'd taken me to the ground, the clarity of her whiskey gaze, the way she'd impatiently shaken the ribbon from her hair under the guise of naming me her champion, all so she could pass on a warning I should never have needed. My mouth was a desert.

She was safe. That's why they weren't discussing her. The knowledge settled in my belly and brought me a measure of peace.

Around me, discussion had turned to escape. Kadan used the information we'd gathered on our way into the city to outline what we'd need to force our way free, but we all knew it wasn't really an option. Luca's family holdings were on this side of the Aza Ranges. If the South knew their heir was being tortured, it would be a race to see who'd reach Luca first—forces from La'Angi, or assassins from the South.

While we shared the common goal of hating the King, the harmful monopolies that hamstrung hard-working people, and the laws that kept us all silent and subservient, our small rebellion had little in common with the South, and we all knew it. They were the poor cousin none of us really wanted to deal with, so far in debt you'd invite them over to break bread and feel obligated to send them home with half your larder. I'd been that cousin. I'd bit the hand that fed me, not understanding it wouldn't also punish, thinking only of short-term survival. I got why Luca had entered into an agreement with the South, and I also understood why no one was entirely comfortable with having them at the table. One cousin you could help. A region of them, though, that had once been a nation?

"I'll send word to the Worgs," Luca said heavily. "They might be able to help the woman. At least they'll appreciate hearing it from us."

The woman. I wondered if she'd been the only assassin who hadn't been a man, and why they'd sent her after Audrey. I wondered how she'd lived and how the Matri'sion had faired. And while they discussed how they could reduce the harm to the relationship between our group and the Southern rebels, I felt the walls closing in on me.

Someone was going to need to get Luca out of this place alive. Kadan was going to volunteer, of course, but he was highly visible. The less movement around his quarters, the better. Callum was a better bowman than I and arguably a better horseman, too. But I was here, and in close quarters, I'd do Luca more good than Callum.

Darrius was patiently listening to Luca insist the Southern heir had more to lose if she spoke than if she didn't, but Kadan met my eyes over Luca's head. At my silent summons, he quietly stood and slipped around the outside of their conversation without disturbing them, his stockinged feet padding quietly on the stone.

"I'll get Callum to accompany us," I murmured. "Want me to see Luca home?"

Kadan shook his head. "He's got his own men," he murmured. "Ready their horses, and yours, and Cals, for a dawn rush. Just get them out, unless you're spotted. You're in the melee, friend. Use it as an excuse to be in the city if you need. I can always meet you at the tourney ground."

I didn't like the idea of being so far away from Kadan, but if things got hairy, it was a better alternative than outright fleeing.

"There's a limit to how long you can hold onto yourself, son," Darrius was saying. "Victor, he's made a career knowing exactly where that limit is."

My belly twisted. I put my hand on the door. "I'll let Cal know," I told Kadan, and he nodded his agreement. Briefly, his hand rested on my shoulder. His eyes didn't smile as he met my gaze. But he didn't stop me or ask how I was faring.

He knew I wasn't going down into that mud.

CHAPTER ELEVEN
ISOLDE

"When unexpectedly coming across someone you know, it is permissible to apologize for your lack of preparation, but ensure your chagrin does not override your joy to greet them. Make it clear you are always happy to see your acquaintances."
~ Etiquette in Arcanloc

I'd *known* I should've pushed Ettie to leave before the tourney. Now the city was flooded, and sneaking her out would take more bribes. Worse, with the whisper of war and the failed assassination attempts, everyone was walking on eggshells. Ettie's hands hadn't stopped shaking, and the bruises around her throat might need a little more coin to help people forget. I'd need to pay for her to travel as a guest, at least for a while, to give her time to recover. I'd budgeted on her working as she traveled.

But the worst was that she still wasn't ready to leave.

Balancing the tray of apple turnovers and breakfast foods that had been my excuse to visit Ettie in the kitchens away from her husband and children, I moved quickly along cold hallways. Behind me, I could hear the servants stirring, going around to light the braziers in preparation for the well-to-do who wouldn't be eating for hours. Out the window, the mist hid most of the city, and I could almost imagine I was back in my forest, the stone wall to one side of the mountain, the pillars and hip-height safety railing, the trees and brush.

If I could get Ettie to the safety of those woods, so much the better. And if she needed to take her children with her, they'd be more than welcome there, too. I could deal with the added cost and inconvenience. And with the failed assassination attempts—and the one success—they'd be looking for Southerners. Not short, flour-dusted women with an infant on the hip and another on the breast.

The trick was making her realize it wasn't actually *her* fault that she was married to a fair-weather fiend.

I didn't hesitate when I saw Wade at the post before Audrey's door, with a member of the guard on the other side. But unease twisted in my gut.

They didn't usually change shifts this time of day. It was possible Rulff had been pulled away on another matter, but after the upheaval of the last few days, I felt my focus narrow and my blood quicken in my veins.

There was nothing unusual about Wade's appearance, except for his timing. The guardsman's presence wasn't unusual either, except that he'd also switched, and that I didn't recognize him, which meant he wasn't a regular within the keep. My options stretched out before me, and I quickly discarded most. They stood between Audrey and I. And she *would* open the door, if they knocked.

I was, undoubtably, overly cautious. But that's why I was alive.

I approached the archway leading to her room without altering my pace. As usual, I flicked Wade a glance that made my disgust for him crystal clear, cutting from his clean-shaven face to his pristine boots, the hallmarks of La'Angi brutes. Behind his boots I noticed a bottle with the unmistakable stamp of magework on the broken deep green sealing wax.

Battle energy flooded my body, and I dropped my weight, whirling the tray at the guard I didn't know. He went down in a tumble of pastry, porridge, and pottery. I went to grab for his spear but was brought up short, an arm under my breasts and a hand slapping a cloth painfully across my mouth.

I tasted blood and felt my ribs groan under the force of his hold. The smell of metal, oil, and herbs hit my nose and made my head swim. I held my breath and went to drive my head back into Wade, but he avoided the strike and grabbed my right hand, pinning it against my side. His breath was hot. I flexed, making myself as big as I could, and felt the laughter he expelled across my cheek like a toxic cloud.

Then I relaxed.

Slipping out of his hold, the world spun drunkenly around me. Free, I grabbed for the spear from the fallen guard, but it wasn't where it should've been. My fingertips jammed into the wood, jarring my joints. *Poison?* The bottle. Wade scrabbled for me, and I drove my fist into the side of his knee. I didn't have the leverage to break it, but he collapsed like a play fort made by children regardless. I was already to the other side of the archway, kicking over the bottle and hearing the glass smash. *Not on my watch.*

There was something deeply satisfying about hearing things break.

My hand tightened on the door to Audrey's room, my hand ready to turn the knob, when I heard boots on stone. "Finally," I heard Wade say.

I ducked my head, but he grabbed my other arm and drove me into the door, twisting my arm up hard behind my back.

He shoved the cloth toward my face, but I turned and sank my teeth into his hand. My lips were still open as he covered my nose this time. The grain of the wood bit into the side of my face, and the world spun, black and pulsing, around me. I struggled, not caring about the pain in my arm. I'd had it dislocated before. There were worse things.

I'd had them before, too. All the worse things. And as I stomped on his booted feet with all the strength I had left and clawed for his eyes, I was falling into darkness. In my chest, my heart beat too fast, terrified.

"There, now," he murmured in my ear. "There you are." My skin nearly crawled from my flesh. If I vomited, I'd choke on it. I knew I would. But still, my stomach roiled.

Voices, behind us. The rise and fall of conversation. The booted feet weren't coming to protect us. I'd never expected them to, but there was no bitter tonic like being right. My arm was released. It flopped uselessly by my side. I was dragged deeper into thc darkness but fought to hold on to the sensation in my limbs. The pain, the burning in my chest, the bite of the roughly woven cloth against my mouth, the pinch of nausea. The sensation of his hand moving across my belt and dipping into the pouch at my waist.

The key to Audrey's room.

Please, have heard. I felt him withdraw it, lifting it to the door I could no longer see with my eyes but could picture in my head. I heard the tiny sounds of metal bumping against metal, loud in my mind.

And, with the last of my strength, I drove my body forward, jarring his hand, bending that key, and, hopefully, making enough noise to wake my charge.

CHAPTER TWELVE
THOMAS

"Then the traitors were given a swift death and burned alongside our enemies."
~ *The Fall of Wolfswail*

My hand shook as I splashed water over my face. It ran down my chin, warm by the time it reached my neck, carrying cold sweat as it went. The dream wasn't as easily cleansed from my mind. My heart still hammering in my chest, I took a deep breath, then another. The house was quiet. The rest of La'Angi was as quiet as it ever was.

No shadows moved in my peripheral vision. But I waited, seconds stretching into eons. I couldn't shake the feeling there was something wrong. It hadn't just been the normal nightmares this time. The threat was real. Immediate.

Soft sounds came from the next room, and energy rushed through my body. I straightened away from the basin, grabbing my sword belt on the way out of the room, my feet finding their way in the dark, urgency clawing at my throat and locking my fingers over my weapon's grip. My chest expanded as I drew air in deeply, bracing myself as I took hold of the sheath of my sword with one hand, better to draw it when it wasn't at my waist.

Light from the moon slanted in the open shutter on the window. Even as the horror of that filled me—that shutter had been closed when I'd checked on the girls before bed—I saw the cat sitting there, paused in the act of licking a paw to pin me with an arch look.

It had nudged the shutter open. Fury flashed through me, chasing away the fear.

The cat.

Again.

I forced myself to take a deep breath, squeezing my eyes shut. There was no burst of pain, no noise, no movement. The cat hadn't woken me. I couldn't blame it. Not for that, at least. For being a constant source of discomfort and annoyance, yes. It was just the dream. Again. And I'd let it get me by the balls. Again.

The dream, and Gerad's late-night visit. The dream, and my wonderful wife's treason. The dream, and my role in covering up Rose's crimes.

As if hearing my internal struggle to be charitable toward it, the cat leapt back down and stepped lightly through the girls to unerringly locate Sandra among her sisters. It curled up in the hollow behind her knees and happy purrs filled the room. I couldn't help but tense up at the noise. Would it cover approaching feet, the sigh of a blade being unsheathed?

At the foot of the bed, Beatie struggled to pull the blanket up to account for the precious, stolen warmth, her childish face showing deep disapproval and then smoothing a split second later. Whether she had enough covers to be happy or whether they were unnecessary for her comfort, I didn't know, but I felt the fist of panic release my heart fractionally at the sight of the peaceful scene. *My girls*.

Quietly, I readied and let myself out into the morning, kissing my Rose gently and leaving the still peaceful house behind me. They were safe, for now. I had to believe it.

Open a gate. That's what I'd been told to do.

My gut twisted, and the sweat on my body wasn't due to a nightmare this time.

The familiar cobblestones gave my boots good purchase. There was a light mist, barely discernible, and a hint of purple in the sky. The weight of my shield over my shoulder dragged on me. It was covered by my inside-out tabard. I wasn't on duty yet. But I was, of course, always. It was all I'd ever known. All I would ever know. I'd thought that was glorious, once. I'd loved that I was a solid link in a bright shield wall.

And then I'd survived the war in the South.

And then I'd fought at Wolfswail.

And now I had to pay for my wife's crimes with favors to bad people.

Swallowing down bile, I passed through streets unchanged since my youth, into the guard tower over the Outer West Gate. I pulled on my tabard, revealing my shield. I tried not to see the other two men who arrived and took the wall either side of me.

Had Mikus' men come to all of us in the night?

Had they been struck down by their dreams, too? Or by their fears, and turned, like so many did, to the whispered Old Ways, trying to find hope?

I didn't want to know.

"Two hours to dawn and all's well!" came the call from deeper in the city.

I listened to it spread, the peaceful ripple of voices. When it reached me, I joined the chorus, standing beside the wheel that would raise the gate. The words didn't stick in my throat. I wasn't green enough for that.

Hooves on cobblestones, the stomp of boots. I looked resolutely out into the darkness, running through the orders I'd been given in the depths of the night. *Swap your watch. Raise the gate.* That was it. That was all I'd been told.

But I knew who Mikus' men were. And I knew the one person Mikus would flee.

Gerad's hand had spread across the scarred wood of my table, the same one Rose had served me meals on since we were wed all those years ago. The same one Sandra had hit her head on when she was but a babe and racing around the room, before I'd known better than to join in with the frivolity. My girl still bore a scar from that table, from my poor, if well-intentioned decisions.

Not today, though. She'd not get another today. I had two orders. I planned to fulfill both.

The Duke would kill me, but Mikus would kill my whole family.

"Raise the gate," I heard Mikus call from below.

I went over to the wheel. My Rose, she hadn't meant anything by what she'd done. She was heavy with child and anxious, was all. Natural, even for a woman who'd been through it all before. And with her keeping me up half the night weeping after Gerad's visit, it was no surprise my nightmares had been so vicious. But I didn't blame Rose.

The wood was cold beneath my fingers, worn smooth by years of use. I could picture the tree my lovely Rose had visited yesterday, as plenty still did. Oh, it was outlawed, but it was a source of hope, too. Outlawing hope was a difficult thing. And she'd just been scared. She'd asked for a blessing of the old tree.

I hope it brought her peace for the coming birth, whatever happened. I hoped she didn't carry the guilt with her. It wasn't hers, not really. Dropping a few chicken bones under some roots…what did it hurt?

The whole family would hang if it were known. And Mikus would make it known.

I glanced up as I put my shoulder behind it, and my eyes danced over the mounted figures of Mikus and Wade, the guards down there wearing the same tabard I was. The Duke's tabard.

Here we were, though.

I heard a muffled noise, female, distressed. "If that damned maid hadn't fought so hard—" Mikus hissed, the words loud in the darkness.

An arrow punched through my chest and sent my heart into the stone wall behind me. I looked down, agony in every breath, in every fiber of my being. There was nothing there. No shaft. No wound. But I could feel it still.

"She's worth it," Wade said, dark delight in his words. "Yours might turn you into a duke, but that bitch on my cock is going to turn me into a king, my friend."

"Well, your damned queen used up too much of the tonic," Mikus said, raising a boot and kicking the struggling lady in the shoulder. "Shut up, bitch, or I'll shut you up."

I'd known he'd be going against the Duke. But by taking *the lady*?

The lady. The lady was there, thrown over the saddle of Mikus. The lady was there, tied, but struggling. Her maid was there, tied, but still, her hair matted with blood. Not struggling.

My hands were stuck on the wood. I felt my heart still beating spans behind me, the pump of my own lifeblood.

I couldn't do this. Not again.

I shoved Rose from my mind. Eyes were turning toward me now. "Come on, old man." The speaker was young. He shifted his weight anxiously. Who did he have to lose? "Raise the gate."

I stood, frozen. I was a dead man. I was a walking dead man already. But I'd been a dead man for decades. I heard the howl of snow, the far-off baying of a pack of wolves on the prowl, felt the bite of cold so fierce it made my toes burn.

The young chap swore, glanced around, walked toward me, and put out his hands for the wheel to lift the gate.

I shoved my shield into his mouth. His teeth shattered. His head hit the stone wall behind us, leaving a bloody mark. I spun, unsheathing my sword. I was a dead man. I'd been dead since the last time I'd stood by. *Wind, snow, a woman's grunts of pain.* The man to the other side of me ran at me. My body answered when my brain couldn't. Steel rang like funeral bells. Running steps. *Weeping. Snow.*

"Thomas, what are you doing?" Disbelieving, furious snarls. His swing cracked my shield. I threw it at him, charging. My feet found purchase on the stone walkway. Why was it dry? Where was the snow? I felt my sword bite fabric, flesh, and bone. I planted a foot on his chest, ripping it free. I was as strong as an ox. He fell, blood spurting from his leg the way it was spurting from my chest. The snow should've been red. There was no snow.

I turned and saw a familiar face red from the effort of turning the wheel. The wheel I'd walked away from. Defended.

"Don't stop!" Mikus' words. Not for me. For the familiar man backing up, baring steel. I was a dead man. I lifted my sword, and he fell back a step. Beside the familiar solider was the boy whose face I'd smashed, sitting in a rapidly widening pool of his own blood. Stepping past him, I raised my sword, and the familiar solider raised his shield.

I thrust my weapon deep into the chain, jamming the gate only a fraction open. The scream of steel on steel, the grind of the mechanism thwarted, echoed through the quiet city. It was just open enough that the pressure from the weight of the gate would make that a time-consuming job to undo.

More time-consuming than killing me.

Something in my heart eased at that sight. I looked up at the man wearing the same tabard as I, and wished I'd kissed my wife before I'd left this morning.

He stared at me in utter disbelief for a moment, then another. "What's—" but Mikus fell silent. Hooves on cobblestones—at a hard pace. The man before me lost attention for a moment. I charged. Dry stone. Power. He hit the wall. Smashed my head with the inside of his shield. His sword clattered on the stone below. Should've been softened by snow. I drove my forehead into his face, felt the gush of blood from his nose. Shoved him over, ripping my tabard out of his hands as he overbalanced.

"Get the damned gate open!" Wade was shouting. Boots. Running. *Snow. Wolves.* I glanced down. Wade had the maid, threw her over his saddle. She moved with the liquid quality of the unconscious. He anchored her with a hand possessively on her rump.

A gale was screaming in my head, wailing. I ran. Good, dry stone. My heart pumped behind me where it stayed, lodged in the stones. The top of the stairs. Spears.

I grabbed one. Lighter than usual. The wood was cold in my palm. Damp. No ice. I was dead already but still breathing. Then a big man, his hair dark and shoulders wide, burst into view on a huge fuck-you horse, a tourney lance in his hand with its gaudy red and black paint and no real tip. He rushed past Wade and sent him sprawling back. He hit an unsuspecting Mikus with the lance. It shattered into a million pieces, and his beast trumpeted in fury.

"Oh, shit," someone breathed, from the stairs, as the big knight's horse struck the air with its hooves, majestic and terrifying in the pre-dawn gray.

The knight was down on his feet. The lady was struggling to hers. He grabbed her like a sack of potatoes and threw her up onto the horse. My heart pumped blood onto the stones. I felt the hot spurt of it, the splash of where it misted over my boots. I didn't look down. There was no hole in my chest. Not that was visible. Wade was coming at the lady from behind, his eyes full of fury. Mikus was drawing his sword.

"Get the cursed gate!" someone shouted from the stairs.

My spear snapped forward. Snow screamed as my attention narrowed. The clamor of combat came from below. A woman's shouts. Ahead of me, the men dodged, bringing up their own shields. Time. I was a dead man. But I could buy time. I fell into the flow of combat. High, low. Faces, thighs. Avoiding shields, searching for gaps, keeping them down on the stairs where they couldn't flank me. Someone shoved forward from behind in their fury to progress. I opened the man at the front's thigh up as his shield was raised too high. He fell back. Flurries of snow swirled around me as I moved. I could feel it kissing my skin. Those shields, that staircase, those men, were my world. Someone came at me with their sword. Tried to knock aside the spear. I changed my grips. Let the spear dip. Deflected the sword. Freed a hand. I grabbed my knife. Stepped forward, sliced down. He screamed. Staggered back. Clatter of sword on ground. My spear leapt as he fell. Stabbed. Short, sharp. *Keep the head free*. Air, into my lungs. Icy.

"Enough!"

The word cut through the storm, the snow, made the men before me halt. I didn't look away from them. I knew, deep in my guts, whose voice that was. My knees went weak. I didn't blink.

"Kill them," I heard him order.

I was a dead man. The men before me fell. Crossbow bolts punctured shields, helms, chests, guts. They fell, bags of bone and betrayal. I could smell the pine forest, the snow, the freshly emptied bowels.

They were dead. The spear shook in my grasp, suddenly as heavy as the stone wall itself. I stood to attention. The wood bit into my hand as I tried to stop my spear from clattering in my shaking grip.

Below me I saw the Duke nod. Sullivan stepped forward. Mikus turned to run, trying to dive beneath the cracked gate. Sullivan came up from behind him as he crawled on his belly in the mud. They'd fought together for more than a decade. Sullivan brought a mace up, over his head, and down on Mikus' spine.

Beyond the twitching limbs of Mikus, the little lady was standing, her hands still tied, covered in blood. Her maid stood in front of her, swaying on her feet but with a knife in her hand. Wade was on the ground. He only had one eye now, his face still and lifeless.

"As the two of you may know," the Duke said, his words crisp, "There has been some unrest as of late. This is a poor time for me to be two knights short."

The little lady swayed. I watched her, struggling to understand what the Duke meant or who he spoke to.

A curled finger. Crossbow bolts were replaced around him, the sound echoing in the silence. I was one of the two he was talking to. Everyone else was dead or with him. I tried to swallow, but my mouth was a desert. A glacial desert.

"Don't," the little lady gasped. "Please, Your Grace. Spare them."

"Sir Chay of West Grenvale. Thomas. You both seem to be useful men to have about. How do you feel about continuing to defend this duchy as you have this morn?"

I tried to speak, but it just came out as a croak. The crossbows were trained on us. The knight with the big horse and long name, and me.

The maid staggered, but was grabbed by the little lady. The bloody knife skittered across the cobbles. The Duke waited with outward calm I knew wasn't to be trusted. I cleared my throat, and managed, "I will gladly serve."

"Good. Come here."

There was no refusing him. My feet found their own way down the steps, though my legs threatened to go out with every step. I slipped on the blood or the snow, once. I couldn't tell which.

"I've a liege lord already," the knight said, his words like gravel. The crossbows all turned, now, on him. Sullivan did, too. The mace in his hand was dripping. Mikus wasn't twitching any longer. I looked away as the boy's hands fisted hopelessly at his sides. "I'm sworn to Raider's Ban."

I waited for the sounds of his death, not tarrying. It didn't matter what the Duke asked of me. I'd do it.

I always had.

"A Blood Oath will override whatever you've sworn to others," the Duke said. Confused for a moment, I wondered who he thought I'd sworn to, then realized he was speaking to the big knight. "And I'm in a mood to ensure loyalty."

I made it down to the road. My legs kept going. Good legs, they were. Great, even. I watched as Chay, standing like he'd had a spear shoved up his ass, took his sword. There was no threat in the movement. He'd have had rocks in his head to try anything, then, with half the garrison's crossbows pointed at him. His horse stamped its feet impatiently behind him as I approached.

Blood Oaths were binding. I wasn't scared of that. There was no magic, old or new, that would take my soul from my wife, and he already owned the rest of me.

I didn't stand too close to the big knight, though. Because I didn't know if he'd figured it out, yet.

Even as I thought that, he let out a breath between his teeth and ran his palm across the edge of his sword. He knelt. He offered his sword.

But he didn't offer it to the Duke.

"I swear," he said to the lady, the words full of piss and vinegar, "to serve you every day as I have this day, until my heart no longer beats."

The Duke's eyes narrowed. I saw Sullivan heft his mace. The lady's attention flickered to her father, her cheeks white as death.

She was splattered in blood already. I'd seen her splattered with more, but never in her nightclothes, her eyes puffy with tears. She was taller than my Sandra, and older. She had no scar on her head, because her pa had never chased her around the dining table, laughing.

But he'd make sure none of those crossbow bolts ended up in her gut when the knight was executed.

Rather than give the order, though, I saw the Duke's lips curve, as if he were amused. "Accept it," he told the lady.

"I accept your pledge," she said, the words so fast they tumbled over one another. The hand that she closed over his was still tied. "Stand, sir Chay, and serve long and well."

Eyes swung toward me. I looked between the daughter and the father, disoriented. "Your Grace—"

"My daughter deserves the best, most loyal men, don't you think, sir Thomas?" the Duke asked me.

I fell down on my knees before her, gracelessly. I wasn't a knight. Or I hadn't been.

My hand wrapped around the spearhead. It sliced into my hand, but most of the blood wasn't mine. "I swear to protect you," I told the girl. Her feet were bare. It made tears rise in my eyes. "Until my last breath."

"I accept your pledge." Her hand was icy as it wrapped over mine. Icy, but surprisingly strong. "Stand, sir Thomas, and serve long and well."

CHAPTER THIRTEEN
ISOLDE

"You must forgive yourself before you can ask others for forgiveness"
~ Matri'sion proverb

My head still pounded like a war drum. Audrey had gotten us out of the Blackguard's hands, straight back onto the Butcher's block. We were being moved to the central spire, where her mother had lived—and died.

I took the washcloth and dipped it into the water, breathing in deeply the healing herbs that were steeping. Audrey crouched down to where I was kneeling, taking the cloth from my shaking fingers. The room pulsed and distorted around me with the drumming of the blood in my veins.

"Beatrice—I'm sorry, I know you've so much to do, but, please, if we could have some juice. Whatever those dogs used on Isolde still hasn't left her system. She needs to drink."

I saw the wary look thrown our way by the 'Ban knight—by *her* knight—from behind a dresser he was carrying. I met it, stare for stare. Drugged and sore-headed or not, I'd wear his guts for garters.

Audrey's hand was firm as she pressed the cloth against the throbbing back of my head, where someone had hit me *after* drugging me. I felt the water trickling down the throat of my dress. My skin was ready to crawl off my flesh, but I stayed locked in position. People moved to and fro, carrying out large dust cloths, bringing in chests of Audrey's books and belongings. Most weren't allowed over the threshold —only Millie, Beatrice and Grahame were permitted past the guards.

The Duke didn't like his daughter being threatened.

The increased security didn't matter. If he was heading off to war, delaying our leave-taking for a few weeks would only help us. There had been no time to discuss it, but I knew what Audrey was like. She'd need time to process all these new angles. And he'd be further away when she felt comfortable to take up the reins. I hadn't looked at the maps, yet, but winter would be upon us soon. The Brannough wouldn't freeze, even in winter, but the storms would make crossing it difficult and dangerous. We could wait until winter, and Audrey could process what she needed.

I watched as she withdrew the cloth and wrung it out. Blood bloomed in the water. Mine, from the blow I'd taken to my head, not hers, and that brought me a measure of peace. I'd played my role. She'd been able to look after herself. She'd have been fine, even if that big lout hadn't stepped in.

He'd never believe that, I suspected, but he sure regretted his actions. Bloodsworn to Audrey. If my head hadn't been pounding so hard, I'd have laughed myself sick.

I tipped my fuzzy, furiously aching head to one side as she cleaned my wound. My eyes fell closed as I listened to them moving around us. Occasionally, someone would stop and ask Audrey where she'd like something, and she'd give directions merrily.

At some point the spiced apple juice arrived, and she pressed a glass of it into my hand, then helped me move onto a divan that was half covered in writing implements. The folded cloth was held against my head. "Sit still," she told me, kindly. "I'll be back. I just need to help Millie."

I drank the juice like a tonic, then crushed the rebellion my stomach attempted to stage. I let the noise of my surroundings wash over me, a back-and-forth conversation about getting something up the stairs, a knock at the fortified door, the scratch of bristles on stone.

It wasn't until I heard steps coming in my direction that I cracked open an eye. The young guard with the beautiful horse and no idea how to use a shield.

He took the cup from my fingers, topped it off, and returned it, stiffly. "We haven't really met properly," he said, kneeling as if he were about to lay the fire. "I'm Chay." I lifted the glass to my mouth and sipped without responding. "And Audrey needs you."

I withdrew the cloth from my head and set down the juice. I didn't trust him as far as I could throw him, but he was bloodsworn to her. He couldn't harm her if he tried. The tribes wouldn't allow him into the Matri'sion when we left, but he could make his own way. As long as she was safe, he'd done his duty.

He understood his role and didn't follow me, his eyes locked on the ground and his jaw stiff.

If he knew I could care for Audrey by myself, so much the better.

I kept one hand on the cold stone wall, just in case. With each step my head ached with a fierce pressure, but I climbed every damned stair to the second level. As painful as it was, the knight was right. She was best served by me.

When I got there, I found Grahame on one end of a bed held on its side, with the person on the other end hidden from my view. Grahame's face was red and covered in dust as he tried to maneuver the massive wooden thing into the room.

I blinked at it. How had they gotten it down the spiral staircase? But I turned away, my eyes searching.

Audrey was there, on her knees, scrubbing at the floor beside Millie.

"Feeling better?" she asked me, brightly. "We're just getting rid of that old bed. It's far too large for me anyway."

I looked back at the bed. It didn't look like they were getting rid of it. It looked like they were blocking off the staircase with it.

Without bothering to tell her that, I turned my eyes pointedly at the sudsy brush in her hand. Millie sent me a guilty look. I paid her no mind because I had none to spare. "What're you doing?"

Audrey looked at me, surprised. "It's been more than a decade since this tower's been used. We've chased out mice and all sorts, haven't we, Millie?" Millie nodded her agreement, but stayed silent. "Best to start fresh."

She wasn't cleaning, she was pushing water around. Before I could muster up some sort of response, there was a grating noise, and both Grahame and the bed came into the room in a rush.

"There is no way that's getting down those stairs," I told Audrey. She waved away my statement and shot a sunny smile at Thomas, who'd emerged from the other side of it. One of the cuts on her face left from where they'd attempted to use her face to mop up the tonic I'd shattered—picking up mostly glass—broke open. A single bead of blood appeared below her lips. His eyes skittered away.

The bed was her mother's. The realization hit me like lightning. She wanted to get rid of it because it was her mother's. Everything in here was.

I went up the stairs to the upper level of the tower, the pain pushed further away by necessity. The cleaning hadn't begun here—there was a bird's nest in the rafters, dust cloths waiting, and some aged fabric piled to the side.

I knew Arabella had died. The official story was that she'd died at the hands of a fanatic assassin. She, and everyone in the tower. There'd been no survivors. The locals didn't talk about it often, and never at length.

I walked through the circular room. The light was excellent, with privacy and temperature safeguarded by expensive colored glass panels in the windows. There wasn't much furniture, now the bed had gone, just a big, opulent dresser, clearly the bed's pair. I walked over to it. The dust cloth had kept it in reasonable condition, and the tower hadn't leaked—the wood was glossy. I ran my eyes over the tracks left from moving the bed, the boot prints and drag marks in the thick dust that had settled over the exposed floor of the tower's upper level in the almost two decades it had sat untouched.

There was something unusual about the stones where the bed had sat. I walked over, keeping away from the tracks out of habit. My head swam and throbbed, but I narrowed my eyes, forcing myself to focus. Audrey had never spoken about what happened here. I assumed she didn't know, either. She'd been an infant, barely old enough to walk, still not talking, if the stories held true.

I studied the flooring. It was definitely a different color here. And when I looked closely—the change wasn't abrupt. It bled along the hairline joints between the stones. It looked neat, too, as if the stone had faded beneath the bed, which was impossible. Curious, I went over and shoved the dresser, which went all the way to the floor. It would be impossible to clean under it without moving it.

Footfalls, quick and sure, made me look over toward the stairs. Moving my head at that angle made my head throb and the world go gray around the edges. I turned my body to match the direction I faced, and some of the sickness eased.

Chay appeared at the top of the stairs, an axe in his hand. He gave me a nod and turned his gaze to the lone piece of furniture. "She might do better on the lower level." His words were icy. "This probably isn't going to be quiet."

Warily, I positioned myself better to defend against a cut from the tool. "What isn't?"

He lifted the axe, wordlessly, pointing it toward the dresser I'd just shoved.

I glanced at it. I wasn't one for furniture, but I saw no reason to smash this one.

"Look inside it," he said, annoyance in his tone.

I narrowed my eyes at him. His oath to Audrey didn't extend to me, the same way Mikus' oath to Victor hadn't extended to Audrey.

I'd deal with him, later. For now, I gave the door of the dresser a nudge. I watched his shadow as I glanced in, keeping track of his movements even as I saw the completely empty hutch. Empty, except for a tiny brown handprint on the side of the door where a child had pulled it closed.

The bottom dropped out of my belly. I threw it open. Some streaks here, on the ground. Dragging. Small feet, pushing away from the door, into the hiding place. Another handprint on the bottom of the cabinet. Coming or going, she'd needed purchase.

She'd been here. She'd seen it.

I drew back, staring at the floor, disgusted with myself.

The stones beneath the bed and dresser weren't faded. The others were stained.

My stomach churned. *No survivors.* It was the mantra, the warning, when the locals were bold enough to speak. And yet there was one. Why hide that?

The whole assassin tale never sounded right to me. Not when I'd seen the violence that man turned against his own daughter. The world spun around me, making my stomach lurch uncomfortably.

Chay said nothing, watching me with impatience.

Disgusted, I realized he'd seen it long before I had. But the oath was doing its job if he was getting me to defend her against old demons. I didn't care how grudging he was. I cared about the final victory.

"Give me time to get her downstairs," I told him, resisting the urge to hold my skull.

Lips thin, he nodded, waiting as I left.

Audrey was standing with her hands on her hips, looking at the bed like it was a vase that didn't quite match the décor of the room. "Well, it's too big, it can't stay here."

She wasn't going to sleep up in the top room, not with the ghosts that lived there. And she was right, the bed was too big for any of the three little rooms on this level.

"Leave it here," I told them. Her knees were wet from the water. Had she seen the brown of old blood seeped into the stones here, too? Had she recognized it for what it was? "After all, why not?" I asked her, at her surprised look. "Look. A spot for a bath." I pointed to one of the side rooms. "For me." Point. "For your clothing." Point. "It'll be warm, protected, and central. We can use the downstairs space for entertaining, and the upstairs space isn't really needed. It'll be cold up there, too." And a perfect empty space to train together. I went over to where the bed was propped on one side against the ground. "Unless it isn't to your tastes?"

She looked around and chewed her lip. "I suppose here would work. I was thinking—"

"Oh, but the sunlight here, milady," Beatrice said, rallying. "Those small chambers, they're fine, but look—look here." She threw open the shutters and showed Audrey a view of the gardens. "Imagine waking to that, milady." There was a smile in her voice. "Mistress Isolde, she knows what's good for you."

The woman didn't know how right she was. Audrey met my eyes, relief in her shoulders and in the sheen of tears in her eyes. She nodded once, sighing. "It seems excessive, but if it just won't fit…"

"The downstairs, that was for the guards, back in the day," Thomas said, as he lifted his end of the bed without too much difficulty. I made note of that, grimly. A soft belly didn't rule out strong arms. "But there's only two of us. We hardly need it. There are two bunk rooms—we'll use one as a sitting room."

Audrey was about to argue, but I had Chay's warning ringing in my ears. "Let's go look," I suggested brightly, looping my arm in hers and tugging her toward the staircase just vacated by the bed as Grahame and Thomas settled it in the center of the room.

Behind us, I heard the crash and splinter of Chay's demolition. Audrey flinched. Her smile widened. "There's a lovely window," she said brightly, her feet skimming down the steps, "that overlooks all the baileys. I'm glad you're feeling better now to look at it, because you'll love it. Back when La'Angi was the capital, in The Country That Was, this was where royalty lived. Look. Don't we need a window seat here?" She swept over to the wide window, with its curling, beautiful prison bars.

I had no interest in a window seat. I skimmed my eyes over the space. "Put your desk there," I told her. "It has the best light." It had the only real light on this level, with the other side all reinforced stone and steel. She needed the light with the hours she spent lost in reports and scrolls.

"Well, I suppose I have no window seat to put here," she said sadly. "I do like to think of you here, watching."

She was right. It was, strategically, an excellent position. It was also a vulnerable one, if they had a sharp bowman. It wasn't so much one window as three, with tall pillars of stone placed between to allow watchful eyes to track people's movements. "You ought to sit back a little, with that desk," I said as she began to shove the heavy thing over, her body held to protect her muscles and maximize their power. "You don't need the wind and rain on your books." Or to make herself an easy target in case our assassin's friends came to visit.

She nodded her agreement, stopping somewhat back from the windows. There were no sharp bowmen I knew around these parts. The greatest threat to Audrey came from the man who had unrestricted access to everything in this city. Still, the small layer of protection that distance and angle afforded her made me feel better.

Audrey reassembled her desk. Tapestries were hung, and the fire was stoked. I stood, leaning against the wall, exhausted and sick. She was hurting. She was hurting and scared, and there was no time or safe place for her to process that. I let her go because this busyness was a way of coping. It gave her a measure of control.

In the back of my mind, I was storing away information for when my head ached less. Doors that could be barred from both sides. Barred windows. Tight, defensible staircase, favoring the upper levels. This place could be either a refuge or a trap.

Over the walls and buildings of the city, I could see all the way to the tourney grounds where flags were flying. In La'Angi, not even the death of the King's right-hand man could stop the tourney.

A knock at the door made Audrey straighten from her broom, but Thomas moved past us at a fast pace.

Beatrice hesitated beside me, the smile on her lips sad. "It'll take us time to get used to these new rules," she said, looking at where Audrey stood, watching Thomas the way a rabbit stares at a rustle in a bush. "Such a brave girl," she said fervently. "After this morning, to be so kind still!"

I smiled. It felt like someone else's skin moving on my face. Kind? Brave? This was learned and perfected through a lifetime of torment. I didn't have tears left in my soul. They were ashes.

Only when Thomas returned alone did Audrey relax.

She had Grahame and Millie fooled—Beatrice, too, and Thomas. She was bubbly, her words coming fast, her hands full of chores. I watched as the three men brought in my own bed, hating that intimacy. Millie was already making up Audrey's. But my eyes stuck to Chay. Of all of them, he was the threat.

I hated the whole situation. That he'd spotted those handprints before me, that he'd seen through Audrey's act, that we were stuck with him.

If only she'd cut his throat in the orchard, we'd be in a very different position right now.

He was fetching and carrying when Millie, coming down from above with an arm full of fabric, crashed into him, though he stepped back to avoid her. An impersonal hand under her arm steadied her. She went beet red, but he didn't seem to notice, stepping out of the way so she could continue on.

He'd make excellent fertilizer.

Audrey began unpacking in earnest, and all I could do was be there beside her until her bath was drawn. When it flooded the room with the stink of too much lavender, I took the books from her hand and herded her toward it.

"I should be looking after *you*." Her protest was strident, and I could see pushing her harder would complicate the situation, so I let her help me wash Wade's touch from my body, knowing it would take time for it to fade from my soul. The bath wasn't relaxing, with work continuing in the tower, but it served its purpose.

The water was still warm when I finally got her in and sitting down. I dressed swiftly and then leaned on the door. Ignoring the bumps and scrapes of what was happening outside, I sat in front of it and held the world back.

At first, she scrubbed herself briskly. "I'm not done yet. I should be bathing later, once it's all sorted. I'll just get dusty again." I didn't argue. I watched as she scrubbed off the dried blood and lathered her hair. At about that point, I could see her begin to calm. It was a small change, initially—she'd pause to look at the water trickling from her hair before going back to scrubbing. She'd let out a long breath. But gradually, these pauses grew longer and closer together, until I judged she'd come back into herself. As much as she'd be able to, anyway.

The comb I'd been using on my own wet curls, I turned on her hair. She shut her eyes and let me—a testament to her exhaustion and trust.

"Want to talk about it?" I asked, unsure if I could do a good job of this conversation, but understanding the necessity.

"What a day." She sounded achingly sad.

"You did well." Nothing but the truth for her. "You protected yourself until you had an opening. You did exactly right."

The breath she let out was long and shook a little. "I killed a man."

"You did." My memory of it was blurry, but I remembered taking the knife from her fingers. "You won free from the best swordsman in the land."

"Chay's the best swordsman," she said quietly.

"Well." I worked a snarl in her hair free, slowly and gently. "You saved him. Does that make you the best?"

"Doubtless." But the word was sarcastic.

I wondered what played more on her mind—today, or her yesterdays. "Will you be able to sleep in your mother's bed?"

"I'd sleep in an apple tree," she said wryly. I hadn't asked that, but I let the attempt at misdirection go and kept working on the snarl. "I remember curling up with her in that bed." Her words were as thin as the few tendrils of steam coming off the water. "When it was dark and cold. I remember how she'd wrap me in with her and kiss my head. It felt safe."

Safety was an illusion that discouraged people from seeking change. I didn't need to tell her that. She'd seen it herself.

The snarls eventually unraveled, and I sat, my shoulder against the bath, and met her eyes. Simultaneously older than she ought to have been and younger than I expected, she didn't offer me any false smiles or reassurances.

"I never thought he'd put me here." Her eyes were on the ceiling.

"Why?"

"Because it's still hers," she said slowly, as if she were figuring out the answers even as we spoke. "He can't even say her name."

I couldn't read the emotion in her voice. "What was it like, between them?"

She frowned. "I don't remember a lot. I remember him coming by during the day, taking her upstairs. I remember one night when I went to get in bed with her, he was there. He was more terrifying than whatever dream I'd been running from. I remember she told me…" she trailed off, breathing deeply. "She told me to be very quiet when he was near. She told me—" she smiled, a little, "—to never cry when she was hurt. 'He wants us to be his, and we are not.'"

I whistled, long and low. "He wouldn't have liked that at all."

"He killed her," she whispered, the words floating like an admission of guilt into the gathering shadows, lurking there.

"I know." I gripped her arm and watched the tears crawling down her face. I had nothing to give her, no way to alleviate the decades of pain and loss. "And that isn't your responsibility. You survived. That's exactly what you should've done."

She sank lower in the water, breathing in deep, her face carved in lines of old, unhealed pain. She said nothing, but her hand wrapped around my forearm, a strong, anchoring grip. She shook. She wept. I sat with her, my heart a desert.

Her mother had thought they were safe here. And mayhap she had no options—mayhap they couldn't have fled successfully. Look at what had happened, though, when she hadn't taken that risk. Would the Butcher have killed his own daughter had she not hidden so well? The thought made fury kindle deep in my belly, made my head pound harder. I rested my forehead against hers and felt her shudder.

"He will not have you," I promised her from the depths of my soul.

CHAPTER FOURTEEN

CHAY

"Horses are very responsive to tone. Be consistent."
~ *How to Tame Your Brumby: A Collection of Raider's Ban Wisdom*

My back ached, my still-healing ribs were in agony from spending the day moving chests, and my shoulders were tight from the stress that hadn't unraveled since last night. *Victor breaks everyone.* And here I was, firmly in his grasp.

"People're returning from the tourney." I glanced out the window, wondering if I'd spot Kadan, following Thomas' gaze. There was proper glass in the huge opening. There was a film of dust on it for now, but I had no doubt that was temporary.

Two days ago, that tourney had been my life's ambition. Now, all I could think about were my friends, and whether Luca had made it out alive.

"The Duke'll arrive soon."

The Butcher of La'Angi. Fury pulsed at my temples. I forced my hands to unlock from where they'd gone to my sword hilt.

"Keep your mouth shut," Thomas advised me, quietly. "Your shoulders straight, and your eyes ahead."

Words to survive by.

I could feel the mud between my fingers.

"He'll open the door with a crash when he comes in," Thomas went on, stretching out his back. "Expect it. Don't preempt what he wants unless you're very sure. He tolerates questions better than failure."

All good, even wise, information. It swam in my head. Embers knew her way around a knife. She'd held off Wade and landed a blow to Mikus' knee that had meant the brute hadn't totally outpaced me, with my broken ribs and my naive heart in my throat.

But no one had mentioned it. You'd think after the bungled assassination attempts and Mikus' betrayal, that the Butcher would be crowing about his daughter's prowess. Instead, there was silence.

Had no one seen?

How?

I followed Thomas back downstairs in time to see her emerge from the room I'd rolled the half-cask into that morning. Wet, her hair looked almost black. The bubbly good cheer had faded, and her tawny eyes looked old and sad.

I almost ran into the wall and took a sharp turn to redirect my body down the stairs. I'd come to her rescue, unnecessarily, and now look where that had gotten us.

Would I be allowed to farewell Kadan?

I took hold of another chest of clothes from where it had been dropped off right outside of Audrey's tower. Its weight was nothing beside the power of my anger. My shoulders ached from holding myself out of that mud.

There were a number of servants coming and going out here, and they all looked a lot less confident than they had earlier in the day.

The reason for their worry loomed, larger than life, as he turned the corner. The Butcher. Servants dropped down into deep curtsies or bows and cast their eyes down. I remembered what Thomas said, but I was holding a chest and wasn't going to pretend to care for his rules. I'd sworn myself to *her*.

Mayhap I should've let him fill me with crossbow bolts. My spirit could've watched over the ensuing civil war as Darrius sought an apology, and Victor refused to give it. The straw that broke the donkey's back.

Audrey had the Butcher's jaw, his long mouth, and his eyes, too.

"Come on." He swept past us, and Thomas jerked his head at me as if I were supposed to understand what that meant. The two men in the black tabard of the Duke's own guard settled outside the door. I really hoped they didn't expect me to do that all day while Audrey pottered around in here.

He opened the inner door with an almighty crash that echoed through the tower. Past him, I saw Audrey in a dress that was too tight across her strong shoulders. And despite it, she looked every bit as powerful as her father.

Unease plucked at my heart, and for a moment, I was a child again, looking to hide behind a woman's skirts.

"Close that, sir Thomas," the Duke said, coming to a halt before the fire. Behind us, Thomas closed the door obediently. "The situation has changed," he said to Audrey. I kept my face straight and held the child within me close, away from the Butcher's searching eyes. "After the assassination attempt by the Southern rebels," he said to Thomas and I, "and given the changing situation—" a polite euphemism for *I've realized I can't trust my own men*, I assumed "—I am increasing the security around my daughter."

The way he said *my daughter* was the way most men would say *my sword* or *my saddle*. She was a thing to him. But at least she was a precious thing. I was just a tool. I breathed around that knowledge and straightened my shoulders, better to protect the boy in my heart.

"Aside from the four of you, there are three servants permitted to enter this tower who you have already met. Anyone else who wishes entry must be accompanied by one or the other of you." The man's gaze made the contents of my stomach turn to liquid. "Whilst my daughter is within this tower, you may organize a roster between yourselves as to who is in attendance and when. I expect one of you to always be present. Mistress Isolde, if there is a man present, I expect you to be in attendance regardless of whether it is one of the trusted men or not."

"Of course, Your Grace." Isolde's brows were raised as if he'd just issued her an insult. Unease crept up my spine, and respect. She played a close game. And here I was, just hoping he didn't look too closely.

He acknowledged her words with a brief nod and a modicum of respect I hadn't anticipated. "If Mistress Isolde is indisposed, the door to my daughter's chambers remains barred. If my daughter leaves this tower, I expect all of you in attendance. Nineteen years ago, a man gained entry to this tower through deception. He was a Southern rebel." His eyes rested on me for a moment. I felt the tension in the air like a living creature. "He killed the Duchess and more than half the guard before being dealt with. The guards whose errors cost me so dearly were executed. Not a single person survived that. When I tell you to go with every single man, I expect it to happen."

"Yes, Your Grace," Thomas said, his words gravelly.

"Sir Chay, if my daughter visits the infirmary, where will you be?"

I was still scrambling to sort through the history he'd just tossed at us as I tried to sift truth from lie from misdirection. "I'll be in the infirmary, too, Your Grace," I told him. "In attendance."

"Sir Thomas, if King James visits, where will you be?"

"If we're in the tower, Your Grace, I'll be in attendance," he said. "Or sir Chay will be, depending on our roster. If he visits out of the tower, I'll be in attendance."

"He'd better be out of the tower." The threat hung in the air. "You know your job well, woman," he told Isolde. "Do not flag. Anyone's failure will mean everyone's death. I expect your presence tonight, child. You two," his eyes rested on Thomas and I, "see you're cleaned up. You'll be in attendance. You are dismissed."

He swept out, and I allowed myself to fall in behind Thomas once more as he let himself back into the entry chamber. "We'll get the last of these chests in," he said brusquely. "Then I'll go, get us both a black tabard." He eyed me critically. "Your boots could use a polish, son."

I looked down at said boots. They were a bit dusty and a bit worn, but they were fine. Was that actually the most pressing thing he'd taken from that tirade? Disoriented, I fell in behind him. And when we returned to the half-assembled room, Audrey, still pale, stood. "While I have you both, this level has traditionally been for guards' use. It was going to be for me, as they've turned the second bunkroom into a sitting room. However, I don't need all the space, and I like company. This is a shared area."

Thomas somehow managed a bow around the chest he held. I didn't bother trying. My ribs weren't that much better than they had been, and I couldn't save her damned life if I couldn't breathe.

In a bid to get the reins back in my hands, I asked Audrey, "Are we going to the banquet tonight?"

Beside me, Thomas shot me a look so shocked that my attention was dragged fully onto him.

"Sir," he said, his expression become shuttered, "I'm not sure what you're talking about, but, for the sake of the lady, I ought to let you know that the Duke—"

There it was. I cut in, hard, impatient. "My oath isn't to the Duke. It's to Audrey." I wasn't ending up in that mud.

The blood drained from his face. "They're one and the same, sir."

The feral gleam in Isolde's eyes, the way she shifted ever so slightly to put herself between the door and where Thomas stood, made unease slide under my skin. But my mind was trying to put it all together. Was the Duke the same as Audrey? Was ending up in the mud the same as ending up serving Audrey—who was, herself, either in it already or a hair's breadth from going down?

I wasn't keen to mess with a Matri'sion. Even a wounded one. So, erring on the side of caution, I said, "Here was me thinking that we were owned by a grown woman with her own opinions and desires." And the One help me if the daughter was anything like her father.

Thomas' mouth opened, closed. Wide-eyed, he looked to Audrey for support. "I don't own you," she said, clasping her hands together with enough force her knuckles went white. "And I won't ask you to split your loyalty, Thomas."

Split? Mine had been severed and was actively hemorrhaging, and Thomas' needed to be amputated.

"You're here," I told him, viciously. "Because you swore the same oath I did."

"If you think undermining the Duke's influence is a good way to protect the lady—"

For a moment I heard my mother in my head, her words lost to time, just the urgent downward motion of her hand at her side telling me to be silent. "Fuck the Butcher," I said, but kept the anger from my voice. Despite my dismissive tone, Thomas paled. "My only priority now is listening to the woman I'm bloodsworn to." But I hadn't sworn to be sweet and nice and let her bullshit us all. I'd never visited my mother's grave. I wondered, now, if I should've. "Our loyalty is to her above all others, without question." The words tasted like stale beer. My head throbbed.

"My lady," he said stiffly to Audrey. "I apologize for my companion. He doesn't understand how things are done in La'Angi."

"Understanding and accepting are different things," Isolde drawled, almost idly. "And here was me thinking we were going to discuss schedules and setting the Watch."

"My lady, with all due respect, it wasn't a quarter-hour ago your father was in here reminding us of what happened to your mother." Thomas looked at me, at Audrey, then to Isolde, pleading, now. "We need to keep you safe, milady," he added. "You know that means respecting your father's wishes."

"I don't—" she shook her head, those whiskey eyes big and soft and round. "I never intended for—"

"Intention is irrelevant," Isolde said, and I folded my arms. The message hit home, and Audrey's eyes dipped to the ground. It should've pleased me that she felt some responsibility over the situation, but instead, irritation gnawed at me. "Look, Audrey, things are moving fast." She eyed Thomas speculatively. I remembered, clearly, how her eyes had skimmed over the prints in the dust earlier. I hadn't seen her in action, but when I did, I didn't want to be on the receiving end. I resisted the urge to step away from Thomas. "If you hear things that go against the Duke's bidding and don't help to keep those secrets, you are breaking your oath. You *know* he'll harm her."

Frustration rumbled. I'd gotten myself up and out of the mud. The alternative was a gravestone.

"Stop!" Audrey said, aghast. "Stop, Isolde. Please. We have a banquet to attend, and Thomas' whole world has been turned around already. Let him be. Have you a wife, sir?"

The word "sir" made him jerk like he'd been branded. "I—I do. And girls. Six of them. One on the way. Probably. My lady."

Audrey stepped closer, resting a hand on his arm. With eyes big and soft as a doe, she murmured, "I won't ask you to put yourself in danger. I *will* ask that you keep my secrets, unless they are too heavy. If you cannot carry them, I can arrange for you to stay at…" her eyes skipped over to Isolde, who shrugged in answer to her silent question. "At your new lands."

And yet here I was, trapped. Did I need to knock someone up to get some kindness?

His eyes closed. The lines were carved deep into his face. "I—I should go and get us both a tabard. We need to polish up."

"Of course."

"Is it your wish to attend tonight's banquet?" I asked her again.

She sent me a cool look that made me want to snarl. "It is," she said firmly. "And it is my wish that I follow all of my father's requirements, as closely as I can, particularly in public. So please, Thomas. Go. And send a runner to your wife, let her know you'll be home once the meal is done. I won't be staying to socialize."

He bowed to her and walked out. He had to walk around Isolde, who didn't step aside as he left, watching him with unblinking eyes. I heard her drop the bar after him and didn't move from my spot opposite Audrey.

I deserved to know what he was too much of a coward to hear. It wasn't like I was allowed to betray her. I could hardly do my job if I didn't know what I was doing.

She ran her fingers through her wet hair, shaking it out, color creeping up her cheeks. And when Isolde came back, I said, "So, tell me what it is you're not telling him." And I waited for tales of how they smuggled out injured women and terrified children for a fresh start elsewhere and sent those who were bloodthirsty back to the Matri'sion tribes.

She just arched her brows and looked me over in assessment. It was probably supposed to be terrifying, but she'd already taken my measure, and we both knew it. She'd at least kill me quickly. "What do you know?"

Bitterness was on the tip of my tongue. I didn't like its taste. I knew that sometimes to kill the King, first you'd have to kiss the ring. I knew to get out from under the boot, you sometimes needed to press a kiss to it.

I knew I wasn't going to drown in the mud.

"I know you've been lying to Luca." Who was *also* bloodsworn to her. I wanted to laugh at the thought, but it wasn't with mirth. She was gathering a collection of us. "That you're Matri'sion," I said of Isolde, and then turned to the woman who held my life in her hands. "And *you're* Matri'sion trained."

Something flickered over Audrey's face. Worry, warmth. Something like that. Something more. I didn't want her cursed *warmth.*

"You're his friend. Luca's."

If that was the most important thing she took from our interactions so far, no wonder we were here now, lambs to the slaughter.

Isolde tilted her head a little, as if I amused her. "You've traveled in the Steppes. You know of the prophecy."

My heart twisted. "The Sweeping Stallion."

She hummed in agreement. "First, he'll unite the tribes. Then, he'll take the known world."

Except he didn't give a cuss about the known world or uniting the tribes. He'd figured out pretty quickly the cost of unification was life, and the cost of peace was individuality. He'd opted out.

That didn't stop the assassins, though. And neither could I, from here.

"He's not interested," I said. It was no secret. He'd ensured it. "He says there are enough jokers in power."

Amusement sparked in Audrey's eyes. "And you believe him?"

I didn't laugh with her. "Why wouldn't I?" The humor in her gaze died a brutal death. *Good.* She wasn't allowed to laugh at him. And with that thought, I looked deliberately at Isolde. "You'd know he rode north five years ago, and came home without claiming any of the gifts or fealty offered. This isn't about Kadan. You've secrets," I acknowledged. "I sure won't be telling the Butcher." The repercussions on the woman I was forever linked to would probably kill me…or her father would. "So, what's the rest?"

"Victor is a monster," Audrey said, the words cautious, as if this was some dire secret we didn't all know. "Personally, and as General for Arcanloc."

I waited for her to go on. She looked at me from those golden eyes, her face unreadable. "And?"

She glanced at Isolde for guidance.

Audrey had no idea. She was just doing what she was told. And, for a moment, I saw myself again, as a boy, looking to my mother.

I made a noise of disgust before I could stop myself, turning away. "Let me know what I'm actually doing once you figure it out."

"Don't speak to her like that," Isolde said icily.

I shook my head more aggressively than I should've. "Before you threaten someone," I told her, going to polish my boots like the good puppy I was, "you need a way to hurt them. And I've got nothing left, my lady."

CHAPTER FIFTEEN

CHAY

"It was a fallacy that Wolfswail was invulnerable. It had not been overrun in many generations, but Southerners have less lore than us, so they still whispered about the death of a mythical magic-wielder. The General, in his wisdom, heard these whispers, and used them." ~ The Fall of Wolfswail

The unfamiliar man stripped off his black tabard, laying it crisply across a bunk in preparation for our return, and stared at me as if I were shit on his shoe. As first meetings with mentors went, I'd probably had worse.

I set my teeth and followed.

Thomas watched us go, his face impassive. I heard him drop the bar over the door behind us.

"When the Duke leaves, it'll be the three of us," the man told me, leading me into the belly of the keep without hesitation.

The long look he shot me made me wonder if I was about to be ambushed. I resisted the urge to loosen my sword in its scabbard, mostly because the quarters were too tight for it.

"Eat during your breaks. If you're on overnight." He shot me another of those veiled looks, and I knew damned well I was going to be drawing the worst shifts for some time. "Well, make sure you're prepared to be awake."

That didn't make sense to me. I could nap in the side rooms that winged out from that entry chamber, and no one need know. There was a giant *bar* on the giant *door.*

He hadn't told me why he was my mentor, or how long he'd be here for. I didn't even know his name. There was nothing unique about him. He had the same short hair, clean jaw, and shiny boots as the rest of them.

I guess that was the world I lived in now.

"Shame you didn't get to compete in the melee," he said, turning down a wider, busier corridor, then grabbing my arm and yanking me to the side before a delicately built woman fell before me.

We both bowed as she swept by, lost in her conversation and not even realizing the close call.

The other guard sneered at me. "You need a lot of training, Horse Fucker."

I remembered Audrey's ribbon around my arm, biting into the fabric and reminding me to tighten my shield up, and my stomach writhed.

"We could've started yesterday," he said threateningly.

I resisted the urge to respond to the guard's transparent attempts to draw me in. I knew something had happened in the melee. I'd heard the whispers cut off when I came near and saw the looks I was thrown. No one spoke to me about it, though. Clearly, this lump knew what had happened, and he was keen to use it as a weapon.

If Kadan was dead, I'd've heard. There would've been fighting in the corridors. And lots of other people would probably do that for Luca, too.

Did I want to know what had happened? Yes.

Was I giving this lout confirmation of the chink in my armor? No.

"It'll be the last time the Horse Fucker heir ever rides here," he said smugly, and shot me an expectant look as he shoved his way into the mess hall.

My heart ached. *Kadan*. I didn't respond.

"But you'll see that tonight," he went on, without needing my invitation. "You'll have to stand behind the lady and maintain the perimeter. If you see the Raa'shi heir, you're to hold him."

Unease crept up my spine. Had the Wuurgard survivor talked? Kadan and I wouldn't be implicated, as the deal with the South had been driven entirely by Luca. What other reason could the Duke possibly have to hold him?

"You're a cold bastard, aren't you?"

I scratched my jaw. Thomas had told me I had to shave and cut my hair, but damned if I knew when I was supposed to have done that or how it would matter. Anyway, Audrey hadn't seemed to care, and she held my reins until I figured out how to get the bit between my teeth.

"You obviously want to tell me something," I said, aiming for indifference and hitting it neatly as we wandered in. "I don't feel like dancing, so if you want to use your words, you go ahead. Otherwise." I glanced around and identified where the line for food began. "I hear I eat while I can." And mayhap I'd carry something back for Thomas. If I was going to be stuck with him for the rest of our lives, I may as well get on with the relic.

My temporary mentor stood beside me in the line, and I realized his face was flushed with temper. Mayhap he'd had a hard-on for Mikus.

But I hadn't killed him. I would've. But I hadn't.

Be okay, Kadan.

Around me, uniformed servants and off-duty guards looked back with varying levels of subtlety and hostility. Irritation prickled between my shoulder blades, but I resisted the urge to resettle my shirt.

"Your kind aren't welcome here," he whispered.

I was a lot more capable of looking after myself now than the last time that'd been true. It didn't matter if I had no skirts to shelter behind. I had friends, and I had myself. *Kadan will be fine. I'd've heard if he wasn't.*

I sent the guard an unimpressed look. "Obviously," I drawled. "Since I'm bloodsworn to defend the Duke's most precious possession."

He didn't like that truth any more than I did. I moved forward in the line, ignoring the looks we were getting.

"You were a bannerman for the Horse Fuckers."

Was I the horse fucker, or Kadan? All of us? Consistency was too much to ask for. I'd need to check on Bliksem. They could say what they wanted to me, but I'd be damned if they'd hurt my old friend. For now, I let my gaze drift over the heads of the people in front of us and ignored the looks directed my way.

This was the rest of my life. When the line moved forward, I could barely lift my feet, they had become so heavy.

"Shame you weren't there," he said again. "Hey, Barth, how's the stew?"

The young man nearby grinned up from his bowl, and I didn't miss the cruelty in his look. "Fanciest horse I've eaten. Tastes like all the others."

Bullshit. I moved along with the line, ignoring the cawing laughter.

"Who knows, mayhap if you'd been there to kiss that fancy pony better, it wouldn't be dead," my mentor said with a grin.

"I hear my kisses are pretty amazing," I agreed blandly. "Don't know anyone's said I could raise the dead, but sure." I'd been tormented by people who knew every flaw in my armor. This guy was a fly buzzing around shit. We shuffled up so we were next in line, and I took a plate for me and one for Thomas. He, at least, hadn't come for me.

"He'll never walk again," my mentor breathed in my ear. "They're going to take his legs."

The blood roared in my ears, and I fought not to react as it came my turn to step in front of the cook. "Extra stew for me," my mentor said with a nod. "I hear it's something special tonight."

The cook gave him a beady eye, then turned his suspicion on me.

Kadan.

I couldn't hear the words from the cook's mouth, but I knew what I was being asked. "The same," I said, and knew I'd have to eat it.

There was no way they'd had time to butcher Bravura, much less cook that tough bastard down into anything resembling food.

But there was a way that Kadan could've been sorely injured without it inciting rioting in the streets.

I didn't bother to sit. Anywhere I chose, my mentor wouldn't approve. Instead, I just took a spoon and started eating as I waited. It'd been a long day, and it didn't matter that I was sick to my stomach. I needed the food.

I wondered if the blood would boil in my veins if I neglected to look after myself and became a liability that way.

My mentor's amusement had drained somewhat. "You'll learn," he said. And I was pretty sure he was right about that.

CHAPTER SIXTEEN
THOMAS

"The right gates shall be opened and the wrong ones closed through your faith in the One." ~ The Book of Bread and Salt

At the knock, I settled my shield more firmly on my arm and opened the door to the familiar face of Joseph, who'd been a boy when Rose and I had moved into our home right beside him. At his feet was a basket of coal. "Heard this was needed," he said, rocking back on his heels. "Congratulations, sir."

Sir. I was already reaching for the basket before I realized that was my title now. "Thanking you," I said without thought. "I believe there's enough for a three-day, with this." Not that I knew how high the lady burned her fire.

"That's good, then." He cleared his throat. "Mary, she sent for Master Fitzherbert to attend your Rose, I hear."

The world slowed around me, and my attention narrowed to his familiar expression. The lines worn into his skin over the decades had gathered in folds of worry between his brows and around his lips.

"We knew you'd make the payments work," Joseph went on, hands in his pockets. "And you'd want to come home to Rose. You've always said so. You said she was worth everything."

She was. And Fitzherbert's rates might just cost me that. "Is she okay?"

He shuffled back a step. "I'm guessin' so. Not much that mage can't heal."

I'd seen things mages couldn't heal, but those who were willing to pay for a mage to attend the childbed rarely lost the mother or the babe. Whether it was because of the magic, or because the only ones who could afford a mage could also afford to feed the family…

I looked down at the basket of coal in my arms, having forgotten it was there, unsure of what to do with it.

I needed this watch to finish so I could get home to Rose.

"Mary, she's probably taken the little ones," he went on, taking another step back. "I expect they'll do well to wait with us tonight. Unless you've rooms, now, in the castle?"

Rooms? I thought of the little home we'd been lucky enough to find for ourselves, on the first floor, no less. The world didn't quite make sense when I thought of leaving that home. "Oh. I don't know." I'd been knighted, but all I understood of it was the roles I needed to perform.

"Good timing, though. Mary, she was terrified of the cost of a Healer. She'll rest easy now, knowing you're," he waved a hand at me, taking yet another step back, his smile brittle. "I'm glad for you, Tom. You've earned it."

Mayhap he meant for that to be a good thing, but mayhap not. We all knew how people earned positions under the Duke.

But he was too far away, and I was too smart to correct him, so I just nodded and hefted the basket, closing the door after myself, my blood howling through my veins.

Rose would be fine, even if we were beggared. And mayhap we wouldn't be. Mayhap there was some way it would all be okay.

Whatever happened, I knew we'd be well with Rose still alive with us.

I knocked and quietly deposited the coal in its cubbyhole, my hands clumsy from the cold that had seeped into me when I wasn't paying attention. I was about to let myself out again when Isolde swept down the stairs. She'd have been a beautiful woman, if she didn't look like she was always sucking on a lemon. My Rose was older, and her clothes less fashionable, but she always had a smile. Surely, she'd have a smile this night, too.

Chay was late, and the ladies looked ready for the night's meal. The One knew I was ready to have the day done with.

They were headed for me, and I realized I was going to need to tell them they couldn't leave yet when heavy knocks sounded on the door. I opened it and found Chay and Mortemon both there, with their tabards.

With the women behind me and the men before me, I stepped to the side and let them all figure out the situation, no conversation needed. *Keep it simple, sweetheart,* Rose would've said approvingly. My heart ached.

I missed her. I hadn't realized how much day there'd been until I thought of her, at home, alone. But there had been so many new adjustments and small things to follow up. There was no *first day of Blackguard* training the way there'd been with the Watch, when we'd all been taken on in a group and run through what we needed to know, but Mortemon had done his best. Chay still looked scruffy, but considering he'd been sworn in only hours ago, I hoped the Duke would give him some grace.

I fell in behind the ladies as Mortemon took the lead, which would've pleased him plenty. As the Blackguard went, he was the runt of the litter and had been treated as such. It'd made him mean, and judging from the tension between he and Chay, they'd already had a run in. Chay hadn't cleaned his boots yet, but his tabard was neat beneath his belt, and his mouth was blessedly closed. Whatever had happened, they were keeping it between them.

Given how little my young shieldman knew, he did well to escort the lady to her seat at the table. I made sure my feet were in the right spot, and my shield was forward, then focused on breathing as the hall filled before us, people moving willy-nilly. My own girls would have already eaten and be helping Mary with the cleanup. Someone would be with my Rose. Whatever had happened, she was okay. They would've given her some honey water and clean linens. If she could stand, she'd've bathed. If she couldn't, they'd help her soon enough. I hadn't been there, but she knew she was in my heart, and I in hers. And she'd left that offering, too. Those little things, they made you feel stronger. If she'd wavered, she'd recall them. It would've kept her going until the mage arrived.

Sandra's birth had terrified me, but I'd been a much younger man, then. I'd never managed to feel confident in the process, but I knew how much a body could take, and I had faith in the mage knowing he'd only get paid if he did the work to save the patient.

Mayhap, with my new role, I'd be able to pay him and still keep all our bellies full.

The Duke swept in, deep in conversation with two men who I recognized but couldn't name. One of them usually held a chalkboard, as the dust on his sleeves bore testament.

Everything settled into place as the Duke moved forward. I didn't have to like his methods to respect his results. The lady served him calmly, unruffled by the long day she'd put in. People turned back to their meals, and talk leveled out. Everything was how it should've been, with the Duke paying no attention to my unkempt young counterpart.

I'd never once stood so close to the Duke. Even when he'd ridden past me that day in Wolfswail, he'd been on his horse and felt like he was on the other side of the country.

Servants laid out the meal, and I watched in silence as they ate. None of us met each other's eyes, or the eyes of those we served. I didn't dare shift throughout the entire meal. I could see the floor was dry. I listened to the folks walking across it. But I could feel the blood in my boots. My bones ached, but if I moved, my feet would squelch, and then the Duke'd look at me.

I was a dead man breathing, but I had babes at home who needed me to keep on bringing in the coins.

The rewards for the tourney were given out—the medallions, not the purses. The Duke wouldn't be so crass.

Escorting the lady back to her room was physically painful, but I fought not to limp. I just had to get home to Rose. It wasn't so far, now.

Mortemon didn't come into the tower with us, and I was relieved to close the heavy wooden barrier between his watchful eyes and the outside world.

The lady was already gone from the defensive chamber into the inner room, and Chay had wasted no time dropping the iron bar over the door that kept her locked safely inside. I assumed her handmaid would do the same from the other way.

"I know I'm on now," Chay said, looking up at me, one hand on his side like he was injured. His eyes shone overbright, but I doubted it was from the wound. "But I need you to cover for me."

I thought of the creases in Joseph's brow. *Rose.* "I need to get home."

"You don't know me," Chay said quietly, his voice shaking just a little in a way that unsettled me. "You'll learn I don't ask for much, but my friends are leaving tonight, Thomas. I may never see them again."

He didn't have a family, or mayhap those people *were* his family.

They'd sent for a mage. Rose would be fine. If she wasn't…if a mage couldn't hold her, nothing could. But the mage wouldn't take on hopeless work. I'd be naming another little girl tonight.

I had a family.

His blue eyes glistened. He didn't hide it.

"I'll cover for you for a half-hour." I hadn't been ready with a name. The babe wasn't due until winter, and we'd not yet agreed on anything. I could think on the name now. It wasn't wasted time. Really, 'twas sensible. The lad would focus on his role better.

He was gone before I could finish my warning about staying out of sight, and I sighed, closing the door behind him.

If he was caught by the Duke, I'd be on duty all night and for a lot more besides. Because he'd be dead.

CHAPTER SEVENTEEN
CHAY

"Skinny dogs gotta make fast friends." ~ La'Angi saying

My hand was shaking, but it didn't stop me hammering on his door. With every flutter of my heart in my chest I expected to see a black-clad member of the Butcher's guard spot me and drag me back. But the door gave way, and Callum's ashen face made my heart sink.

I was grabbed in a fierce hug and pulled inside. "We didn't know if you'd make it," he said in the hushed tones of a sickroom. The stink of magework—burned metal and incense—hung in the air. "The One, Chay," he whispered, still clinging. "I wish you'd been there."

I fought to not throw him off me and demand answers, returning his hug. The smell of horse and salt clung to him beneath the reek of mage, and my eyes burned. I just wanted my friend.

"He'll live," Callum said, the words an expulsion of emotion, half-sob and half-declaration. "Kadan will live, Chay."

My jaw ached from the questions I didn't ask.

"Let him up, now, Cal," Darrius said, and I was allowed enough space to see the sitting room was as full as I'd anticipated with the men I'd ridden with for the best part of my life.

The black tabard on my chest weighed as much as the keep itself.

Darrius put his hand on my back, and they made way for me. "I don't know what you know," the older man said, his tone hushed, too, his face long, lines of exhaustion carved deep into his weathered skin. "Luca's long gone. They didn't even know until the melee was underway, what with the attack on lady La'Angi."

From somewhere far away, I knew that was good. Luca stood between Kadan and the fate he refused to follow. If Luca lived, so did Kadan's dreams of a normal, happy life.

The room was softly lit. Flowers already adorned the bedside, and an empty jug with some cups. I stared at my friend, laid out on the bed, his skin sallow, his eyes sunken. His hair must've been washed, because it had been combed back to show the scar his birthing storm had left across his forehead. The soothsayers had called it a diadem mark. Our people called it a crown. He called it an excuse to avoid frequent haircuts.

The blanket started mid-chest, revealing the scar on his right shoulder where he'd been struck down in a skirmish years ago. The arrow had been fouled. Callum and I had taken turns carrying his scrawny ass what felt like halfway across the Steppes as he got sicker and sicker, looking for someone to fix what had been broken.

And we'd been successful, too.

"They dragged him from the saddle," Darrius said quietly. "Henry almost died."

I should've been there.

I could hear the waves against the shore. In my mind, Kadan and Callum were beside me. We were young, and they passed the beer back and forth, picking their way along the beach, talking about the adventures they wanted to go on. And I dreamed, too, of all the things that had become possible, beside 'Dan.

"He'll live." Darrius spoke with the calm of a man accustomed to passing on difficult news. "They've saved his foot, for now, but the mage didn't do more than stabilize him before he was called away."

Called away. There weren't many men who could call anyone away from Count Darrius of Raider's Ban, and only one person in the city with us who had that power.

Impotent rage flashed through my veins, and I felt the burn of it matching so sickeningly with the tears that prickled behind my eyes.

I hate him. The childish sentiment was entirely fair, totally justified, and I let it sit like a coal in my chest.

Kadan would live, despite the Butcher's best efforts. Despite me charging away from where I'd been needed, stupidly chasing a wrong I could, and did, right.

"I hear you're bloodsworn," Darrius said, and his smile was tired. "Arabella would've loved it. And you."

I shook my head, the words making no sense. "I didn't have a choice."

"Sounded to me like you found one," he said, and the smile settled a little more convincingly. His hand on my back rubbed a slow circle. "He's going to miss you. I'll figure out how to get news to you once we're home."

He didn't make promises. I'd always respected that about Darrius. When he said he'd do a thing, he did. Kadan took after his father in that way.

It's one of the reasons they were safe.

But, right then, I wanted promises. I wanted to know if this *obvious* attack on Kadan, and by extension Raider's Ban, was enough to summon Darrius' bannermen. I wanted to know they'd be rallying around Luca, and the Butcher's head would be on a pike and rotted before the midwinter freeze.

"Chay," he said quietly. "I don't know what tomorrow holds. But I'm proud of you."

It didn't make sense. I didn't know if that was because I couldn't, right then, imagine anyone being proud of me for anything, or if it was because I truly didn't deserve that regard for the choices I'd made to get here.

I thrust it all aside. "Luca escaped. Did the Wuurgard heir talk?"

"Not yet," Darrius said, his eyes turning back to Kadan. "I don't know how they're going to feel about this."

I didn't ask who the mysterious *they* was. I knew some of them, I could guess at others, but now…now I wore the crest of the enemy. "The faster Luca marries her, the better." I scrubbed my hand across my mouth to rub the bitterness away, my stomach writhing at the thought of crushing her into the mud so I could stand. "Wild horses, Darrius. I just said that."

"I supported it," he agreed grimly. "I'll be waiting to hear from you. And not just for personal reasons. Knowing she's Matri'sion trained might change everything. For all we know, she's fully initiated, but leaves off the circlet for safety." He was looking at a point somewhere out over the horizon. "Her mother was a force to be reckoned with."

Kadan's breath hitched. My attention zeroed in on his still form as his lungs worked and his shoulders shook, but he quickly settled.

"Collapsed lung. Mage fixed it, mostly." He shook his head a little, as if trying to unstick a thought that niggled at him. I waited, but he didn't say anything else.

I hadn't been there because of my own stupidity.

The memory of the way Audrey had taken the knife I'd passed her, the way she'd gone for Mikus' back like a cornered animal, sat alongside the reality of my friend, grievously wounded, nigh-dead.

"What do you need to know?" I asked Darrius, the question flat.

He shook his head. "Whether she'd cut Luca's throat, for a start. Whether she might be a power in and of herself. If the wedding isn't needed, if we could just take out Victor and trust *her* to hold the city…"

"Women can't hold property," I reminded him, my mind turning slowly.

He shrugged. "If she was an ally, she could *choose* her husband, at least. And free Luca to choose a wife."

"You could change the rules," I reminded him, knowing it was pointless.

"I could. Eventually."

And how many other people's friends would end up as Kadan was?

I wanted to sit beside 'Dan, hold his hand. I wanted to see his lashes flutter open and watch him try on his shit-eating grin.

"Victor's going to respond to the assassination attempt," Darrius told me quietly. "My best information says he's going to strike back at the South."

As if what he was doing to the captive wasn't punishment enough. As if the eternity of poverty they were restrained by wasn't punishment enough. "Why?"

"They killed Von Rhea. It's a publicity thing. And war is good for business." I felt sick. The horrific image of marching alongside the same men who'd almost killed my friend filled my mind. Following my thoughts, Darrius said, "You saved yourself a pew at the front of that service by getting yourself sworn to the lady. He won't bring her. Especially now the wedding's off. If she were married, it might've been tempting to see an heir faster."

"I'm glad I'm the nobody son of a backwater fief," I said, my body holding as much rage and hurt as it could. "I want to puke just talking about all this."

Darrius pulled me closer, and I stooped so he could press a kiss to my head. "Anyone who believes that is the true nobody," he told me, giving my back another rub. "Because you're my son, regardless of whose seed sprouted you." It wasn't the first time I'd heard it. But it still made me feel like I couldn't quite breathe right. "Would you rather not know the rest, Chay?"

I considered it for a moment as Kadan lay peacefully and entirely unresponsive. I wasn't going to get to say goodbye to him. So, I'd better figure out how I could get to say hello again. "Tell me what our new plan is," I said, and drew in a deep breath. The boy inside of me rested comfortably, trusting Darrius, and the rage ebbed, leaving sadness in its wake. "But tell me fast, not polite. I've a post to return to."

CHAPTER EIGHTEEN
THOMAS

"The greatest riches are the ones we love." ~ *Raider's Ban proverb*

When Chay finally returned, my feet still ached, but my heart was sitting lighter in my chest, and I was more than ready to go home.

"Thanking you," he said as he entered, his shoulders straight, the words thick.

There were tears on his cheeks, and I looked away, pretending not to notice as I busied myself removing my tabard. Borrowed embarrassment and compassion sat ill against thoughts of Rose. "I'll be by in the morning," I told him, hanging my tabard in the side room set up as a small sitting room for us. "I don't know when Mortemon will attend."

"Sure," he said, waving a hand. "Farewell."

I opted not to hear how heavy that word was or how he got all choked up, waving myself off and shutting the door behind me.

Had they been lovers? Had I misjudged it? I stood on the castle side of that thick door, staring at the reinforced wood, and second-guessed my choice to leave. Should I cover for the whole night, allowing them to have their last moments together?

The sound of the iron bar settling into place in the brackets on the other side of the door broke me from my reverie. He'd asked for a half-hour, I'd given it. He'd be risking too much to go back and linger with that crowd while he was supposed to be watching the lady.

I walked alone the entire way home, and while I was glad I could control my pace, I didn't like feeling so disconnected after the day I'd had.

The shadows weren't too long by the time I reached my little door, easing it open around the spot where it stuck, lifting my feet over the step to get in.

The smell of blood and sweat hit me like a mace, and I left the door wide open, fear rolling through me.

They'd called the Magework Healer, like I'd always said they ought. Healers liked money too much to let their clients die. I'd make the payments, and I'd keep my Rose. It was that simple. I'd find the coin.

But there was no sound from inside my home, and the fear had me by the balls.

I shut the door to keep out the chill in the air and went into our room, forcing my hand to uncoil on the strap of my shield as I set it aside.

Rose lay, almost exactly as I'd pictured her, hair in sweaty ropes, cheeks pale, and dark circles beneath her eyes. Unlike how I'd pictured her, though, tears streaked her face. Her body was curved around a tiny bundle at her side. She was naked beneath the layers of blankets artfully arranged and then pushed away to allow her access to the little one. Linen was piled in the corner, and I couldn't help but assess the amount of crimson on those sheets.

They'd called the mage. She and the babe were alive. That was what mattered.

The fear shifted to the cost I knew was going to hit us. The cost of fuel to run the fire, and the mouths I'd need to feed. The tinctures for winter ailments, and boots that would keep toes attached to feet.

Pushing it away, I knelt beside the bed, careful not to jostle it and interrupt her sleep. Her eyes drifted open all the same, and a smile touched her mouth. But tears were in her eyes, too, and fear. "I'm so sorry, Tom," she whispered, the words thick. A single tear spilled over her cheek, following tracks of those that had gone before.

My heart froze. "Why?" I asked her, around the knot in my throat.

"He didn't work well with me, our son," she said, the words slow and thick. "He had his own plan, and it was so daft. So daft." She turned her head, looking down at the sleeping babe. For the first time, I paid attention to the tiny form, so small that I instantly felt like a giant. "I've cost us so much," she said, the words tired and full of grief. "He took everything. The mage." My heart skittered. They'd given him a down payment, then. Of course they had. He wouldn't have believed we could pay at all if they hadn't. "We'll lose the house. We can't afford a mage, Tom. You'll lose us all. It cost too much for the mage. You should've gone to the Bonetree."

"The tree has done enough." A boy. I didn't quite know what to do with a boy, after so many girls. My thoughts rushed about like children through market day traffic. I didn't know what to do about a boy, or bills I couldn't even fathom. But I knew what to do with my Rose. Taking her hand, I rubbed my cheek against it. "You could never cost me too much, my dear. Not ever. We'll worry about it all another day. For today, we have everything we need." I'd make it so.

Her eyes fluttered closed, but tears spilled anew over her cheeks. "You always say that," she objected, but I could see she was ready to sleep.

"Because I always mean it," I promised her. "As long as we have each other, we'll be okay."

She made a soft noise of agreement, settling deeper into the fall of the bed. I expected her to slide into sleep, but instead she looked up at me, her eyes too bright in their sunken hollows. "We need to leave an offering."

"Rose." I struggled against the wave of frustration. "No, we don't need to do any such thing. A *mage* healed you. We'll pay him, and that's offering enough."

Her lashes fluttered closed. "Please."

I glanced down at the boy held at her breast, his little lips an absent *O*, so tired was he that he'd come unstuck from my wife's breast mid-feed.

"Thomas."

No good came from that cursed tree and superstitious beliefs. But all I wanted was for her to rest.

"Of course," I lied, pressing my lips to her forehead. In the protection of her body, my son's little mouth made a few half-hearted sucking motions. I watched the lines in her face smooth as she let herself rest, a little color back in her lips. Even exhausted and scared, she was still the most beautiful woman I'd ever laid eyes on, and with nothing else that needed my attention this moment, I let myself sit and drink in the sight of her, filling my heart and ignoring the dark, sickly coil of shame. I didn't deserve that trust. I'd crossed, then double-crossed, too many people today alone. I'd done too many things I wasn't proud of.

He owned me now. I was the Duke's. And that meant she was, and our girls, and this tiny little boy who might be so fine the sun shone straight through him.

"Tom."

The word was breathy. I hefted myself to my exhausted feet, ignoring the creaking of my bones. "I'm going. I'll see you soon." I looked down at the boy, so safely snuggled in with his mother. He'd have to leave her side one day. But, for now, I ran the pad of my thumb over his tiny cheek, marveling at the fine down that covered his body. *Stay warm, and eat well.* It was the best I could wish for the little fellow.

I knew where Rose kept the offerings she put aside. There were bundles of dirty feathers wrapped in moss, of rosemary stems stripped of leaves, and fish bones so thin and sharp they were dangerous to handle hastily, of thistle stems and broken bits of straw she came across throughout the day. I grabbed one from the small pile of such bundles hidden behind the wooden bread bin. It was easily disguised in my hand, so small and finely made it was.

Outside, the sky was dark and the streets cold. I folded my hands up under my arms, dropped my head, and went toward the gardens.

After the day I'd had, what was a little more treason if it helped my Rose sleep?

CHAPTER NINETEEN
AUDREY

"If you lose your quarry's track, remember it has not vanished. Retrace your steps, retry your strategies." ~ Matri'sion lesson

At the top of the spire, my mother's old room had been cleaned but left completely bare.

We sat, my first morning there in perhaps two decades. Just Isolde and I, breathing in unison, emptying our minds, sitting in the chill of early morning and sharing the quiet. Mayhap I should've felt some sort of connection with my mother, but it was just a big, empty room. I listened for her, but she wasn't here.

Instead, it was Isolde's breath I heard.

When my mentor stood, we trained. Stretching, strengthening, drilling hand-to-hand combat skills. We were silent, not out of need now, but out of long habit born of secrecy. She'd taught me to make my fighting stance my everyday stance, and I saw no need to break that now. Better to keep the habit of minimizing noise. It might be critical, one day.

By the time we went down for breakfast Chay had been replaced by Thomas. Isolde left to gather information, and I settled in with my books.

When Isolde returned, it was to tell me that Luca was gone. She knew more. I could *see* she did.

"What else?" I asked as she paced across the worn rug.

"Too much is happening," she said, frowning. "We *could* get out in the darkness and get lost in the chaos." The idea made terror rush through me like the cold winter wind, and I shuddered in on myself. "But waiting until your father is over the Brannough is a fair option."

Before I could question further, a knock at the door interrupted us. Mortemon walked in with a crisp bow. "My lady, I've come to accompany you to care for your horse. I understand you usually do this later in the day, but it suits to do it now."

It suits *whom?* But I smiled at him, hearing Chay come jangling up behind him. A lump formed in my throat at the sound of the knight's belt loops and scabbard.

Everything about this was unnatural. The setting. The company. The way this was unfolding around us. It wasn't how it was supposed to happen.

I was accompanied to the stables not by just two, but *three* Blackguard. When I went to Storm's stall, I saw Chay veer toward his horse, only to be stopped by Mortemon's hard hand on his shoulder and a, "You have one job when you're in the tabard." Isolde lifted a brow.

Chay was being taught the ropes, and not, I noticed, by Thomas. It made sense because Thomas was new to the station, but it still seemed strange to see the man with more gray than brown in his hair deferring to the younger, whipcord-lean Mortemon.

Restless, I tried to focus on Storm, but didn't get the pleasure I usually would from her company. I drew the weighted coins Luca had given me and rolled them around in my palm, but they didn't change the feeling of too many eyes on me. I went from the stables to the library, not caring that I was covered in horse hair, and took out a pile of tomes on the South. All were written by Arcanloc scholars, of course.

Anything else would have been censored or just burned. It was something, though, and it gave me a purpose while Isolde vanished to find out whatever it was she needed to know.

While I read the one-sided information about past uprisings and rolled the weighted coins in my fingers, all I could think of was the ferocity of the woman I'd fought.

They knew what they were up against. They knew the price. And yet they still tried.

I hoped, for their sakes, that their resourcefulness matched their courage.

When Chay came in that evening, he brought with him the smell of the autumn orchards and a small, folded note from Luca. He waved it at me, tossed it onto the chessboard, and walked out.

He'd seen me. I'd felt it in the orchard, but I hadn't really trusted it. But in the city, when the world had been whirling, and my heart had been racing, he'd pressed the knife into my hand. And he'd seen me. Just for a moment. I was sure of it. He'd seen me the way no one else had, and still, he didn't care about me. Not beyond his oath. *He doesn't have to.*

No one had to give a single Wife-paling cuss about another person.

But, if I desired his care, was that so strange?

The letter held no real information except confirmation that Luca was thinking of me. How was I supposed to feel? How should I respond? The parchment in my hand felt flimsy, the indentation of Luca's pointless words light on its surface. The night we'd met, he'd had me stand on his feet to save me the humiliation of not knowing the dance steps, and the gratitude I'd felt hadn't faded in the decade that had passed. That was Luca. Kind, thoughtful. Willing to help me within the locways but not willing to challenge them.

The parchment balled in my hands. I didn't know what my future held, but I wasn't sitting around waiting for him to contact me.

"I want to roll," I told Isolde, standing, book falling from my lap. Impatiently, I picked up the book, setting it aside.

Her brows arched. "Let's roll, then."

It was that simple because she made it so, and I did, too. I went up the half-remembered steps of the tower that had been my mother's, anger simmering in my belly, in my bones, to combat the helplessness, that childish gratitude that Luca evoked.

He hadn't refused to dance. Hadn't pointed out it was unfair. No, he'd smiled and whispered about secrets we could share. And that was Luca. That was all I could expect from anyone. All I could hope for.

I tossed my skirts aside. They just got in the way. The woolen tights and the shirt held snug by the war belt at my waist were protection enough against the cold.

Isolde didn't ask why. Her feral smile was full of glee, shared challenge, and frustration. She offered me her empty hand, her bare feet perfectly balanced on the stone.

I tapped her hand. *Fight, begin.* And I didn't waste time circling, looking for openings. I launched myself at her, held that anger in check as I'd been taught. A power source, yes, but not a guide. My legs locked around her waist, and she held us both up, fighting to get one of my knees free. I locked my arms around her, and in response, she took me down, hard. The anger in my bones rattled and roared. I clamped down on it and on her when she tried to make some space. I took a chance and bridged, sending her tumbling. Before I could follow up and press the advantage my weight and height gave me, I felt her grab my foot and instead was forced to defend against her ankle lock.

We struggled together silently. Our limbs were pieces in a game, our joints and muscles and sinews the board, our sweat the reward. And when she caught me in a hold I couldn't avoid or break, I tapped, blowing hair from my eyes. "Again."

She obliged me. Some of the edges of my frustration eased during the next bout—by the time we'd finished the third we were sheened with sweat, and I was feeling in control. Luca would do what Luca would do. That didn't have to be my problem.

“What didn’t you tell me about Luca?” I asked her, breathless still, feeling the healthy drum of blood in my veins.

“He’s no longer betrothed to you,” she answered bluntly.

A spurt of terror went through me, but I ignored it. It was the wailing ghost of useless dreams. "Why?"

"He fled. The day of the melee. While you were being kidnapped." She poured me a drink. "I suspect it's coincidence, not deliberate. He isn't that organized."

I thought of his warm smile and gently encouraging hands. The way he'd lean in and murmur some interesting fact. The way he'd listen as I told him about the way the city's layout had been modified, and he'd match it against the history of the time, and we could fit the puzzle pieces together.

"He'll be a better friend than husband," I said.

She grunted. "They nearly killed the 'Ban heir, too. In the melee. Sullivan dragged him from his saddle. The Duke's blocking access to mages, so they've ridden out, too."

My heart twisted like a weathered rope. I remembered the way Chay had walked in, face shuttered. How his disinterest had felt *personal.*

Well, at least I'd read that correctly, then.

Isolde passed me a drink, wiping sweat off her forehead with her inner wrist. "We need to make that guard of yours work."

I paused, cup halfway to my mouth. "Right now? After his friend was almost killed?"

She held up a finger as she downed the whole cup in one breath, and I took the break in conversation as an opportunity to drink, too.

"He knows how to use the sword." And with this statement, she tossed back her water.

I choked on mine, managing not to splutter all over her. She wasn't really suggesting what I thought she was? "Yes. Yes, Chay does. Not a shield, though."

Isolde nodded. "Thomas does, I'm sure. He was holding a spear the other day, and that's a fine weapon to become proficient with, but you've a hunger for the sword." She sniffed, topping off my water before setting the jug down on the bare stone floor, and I just watched, feeling like my head was stuffed with down. "He can't squeal to your father. It'd breach his oath. We won't let him teach you shieldwork, but his bladework and footwork is good."

Considering how rarely I'd heard Isolde say *anything* complimentary about *anyone*, I worked hard to manage my dual feelings of shock and jealousy. "What, just take his sword and say, 'Sir, how should I best use this to run my father through?'"

She frowned. "No need to tell him your plans. Just make it clear it'll put your life in peril if he doesn't teach you, which will trigger the Blood Oath, and off you go."

Isolde vanished before I'd finished running those conversations through. How could I trigger the Blood Oath *without* telling the truth? How did I know if the Blood Oath was active? Would *he* know about it? Even if I could make everything work…was this sort of abuse of power how my father had started a slow decline into a monster?

Chay was no longer my enemy, if he'd *ever* been. When he'd walked forward to collect his winner's medallion last night at the feast, my heart had damn near shattered for him.

His whole life was gone.

I heard the sound of him approaching, the jangle of his scabbard as it rubbed against his belt, the clink of his shield's strap. As if summoned by my thoughts, he appeared in the doorway, and I started at this intrusion in what felt like the heart of our space. But Isolde was directly behind him, her face still flushed.

The ground vanished from beneath me as he met my eyes. There was no warmth there, not like there had been in the orchard when I'd held a knife to his throat. And I suddenly felt like I might just vomit up all the water I'd drunk.

"You need me?" he asked, the words hard as steel.

I hadn't figured out what I was going to say yet, and even if I had, I doubted the thoughts would've survived the brutality in that question.

Did the ends justify the means?

"You had something to tell Chay, didn't you, Audrey?" Isolde prompted, and I realized she hadn't put her skirts back on.

He already knew she was Matri'sion. I'd been told to tell no one, ever, and yet here we were.

His chin lifted, his lips a hard line. The lump in his throat was still, and I didn't know what that meant.

My father had almost killed the man Chay had called friend just a day ago. He was here because he'd tried to help me.

"Audrey needs to learn the sword," Isolde said, the words brisk. "If she doesn't, her life will be in danger."

He was looking at me like a pile of horse shit in the middle of his path. "I suppose I'll have to keep you alive."

Isolde snorted, and I felt like I was about to fall through the cracks in the stones. "That's not how this works. You have a student."

"I'm no one's mentor."

I saw Isolde get in close behind him, her face turned to his ear. My eyes were on her feet, though, visible in the gap between his dusty boots. The patches she'd darned into the toes of her hose stood out as a different shade of gray. The arches of her feet were as graceful as the rest of her as her toes held all of her weight. She was stretching herself to her full height, and still her mouth only barely topped his shoulder.

"You were so full of yourself when you were telling me how to deal with your father's man at the tourney," he said, and the words were directed at me, not Isolde. "Why do you need me?"

All the reasons jumbled up in my head, and they didn't make sense to me, either, because we were fleeing, weren't we? When the majority of the army filed out to put down the rebellion? When it would take longer for whoever was left behind to come after me, because they'd first want to check with my father, halfway to the South?

I don't need you, I wanted to say. But I didn't know if that was true, and even if I'd been confident, the words were stuck in my gullet.

Suddenly, fleeing seemed like the *best* option.

"No," he said flatly, shrugging Isolde away. "I'm charged with keeping you whole. Putting a sword in the hands of someone who can't use it and expecting them to fight? That's the *opposite* of my job."

I couldn't breathe. He turned away, and everything that held me frozen melted. My legs shook, and I had to prop my hands on my thighs to hold myself up as the room whirled around me.

Mayhap, I thought dimly, it was because so much was changing. So many hopes and dreams budding, only to wither before I saw the bloom.

"Tell him, Audrey," Isolde said, her voice level. Only the impatient flick of her fingers gave away how agitated she was.

But I couldn't. All the ideas and the things I could say were tangled up and there were tears in my throat that I hated. They were choking me.

I was okay with no one coming to my rescue. I understood no one wanted to challenge my father. I didn't like it, but I could understand it.

But if *I* didn't do it, no one would, and I'd live in hiding for the rest of my life.

There were worse things, of course. I knew it. And to live alongside women like Isolde would be another, different type of dream. But even as I reminded myself of these truths, it didn't help the loss I felt at this brutal death to the hope I'd clung to for so long.

A cup of water was pushed into my hands. Isolde sat with me, our backs to the wall, and I tried to match her breathing.

He was gone.

"Tell me about your tribe," I managed, eventually. "Who is your best friend?"

She propped her shoulder against mine. "Katarina. She's the main blacksmith for my people. You'll love her. She has a laugh that you feel to the soles of your feet."

I tried to imagine a woman with such a big laugh and couldn't. Would they like me? Would I be welcome? I'd have a job, surely, as a hunter or gardener. But would they give me a job in their social structure?

I didn't want to go. I knew Isolde wanted to return, and it sounded so wonderful, but not for *me*. How much of that disconnect was the death throes of childish hopes of a happier tomorrow, and how much of it was the fear of the unknown, I couldn't be sure.

I didn't want to plot to kill my father. I didn't want to flee.

I just wanted to have a normal, quiet life. To live.

The tears clogged up my nose, and I knew if I sniffed, Isolde would be on me, but I hated the feel of it.

If wishes were threads, I'd hold a fine tapestry.

"He'll come around," Isolde told me softly. "He's taken the attack on his previous lord personally, I gather."

It took me a moment to realize she was referring to Chay, not my father.

The Duke of La'Angi came around for nothing and no one.

I looked up, finding Isolde's familiar face cut in lines of disapproval as she considered Chay's loyalty to his previous liege lord. Unbidden, the memory of the Raider's Ban heir pausing on the edge of the dancing and letting me just stand like a lump while I tried not to fall apart came to mind.

He'd told me he was my friend.

I still didn't believe it, but I did believe he was Chay's. And if someone had nearly killed Isolde, then their child asked me for a favor, I'd be less than receptive, too.

She nudged my cup at me. "Drink. You've sweated enough you need to replenish the moisture." I drank obediently. "His horse survived," Isolde told me, the words emotionless. "I understand they saved his leg, but that may be temporary. Still, he's rich as the Son. He'll be fine."

My heart broke. "Were there fatalities?"

"Not to my knowledge." She shrugged. "Chay's angry, but he'll learn you're not your father's daughter."

Mayhap he would. Mayhap he wouldn't. But I was glad, in that moment, I hadn't forced him to yield again.

CHAPTER TWENTY
CHAY

"A horse cannot be forced to trust."
~ *How to Tame Your Brumby: A Collection of Raider's Ban Wisdom*

I woke to my first morning as a La'Angi knight feeling like I'd just ridden halfway across the Steppes and been dragged the other half—gritty, aching, and tired. I dragged myself up and straightened the covers on the bed. It wasn't as narrow as some I'd seen. I couldn't remember if it was comfortable.

A quiet knock made me rise to admit one of the servants whose name I couldn't remember. Her eyes stuck on my bare chest and color rose in her cheeks.

As I stepped back, I wondered what joy she found in this keep, run by the Butcher. I remembered my sister picking flowers, wishing upon them, and tossing them into the wind that carried the reek of the failing sewage system. She'd laughed like it was the most fun she'd ever had. The flowers hadn't even flown well.

I couldn't recall if I was supposed to follow the servant. I stood inside the inner door, and she didn't seem to notice me as she readied a large, cold breakfast on a low table, laying out cutlery carefully. While I watched, she checked the water beneath a posy of flowers and moved to open the shutters, her movements slow and cautious.

I withdrew to the long, narrow room that made the bunkhouse for this tomb. There was a huge single door that was more solid than the main gate of plenty of fiefs I'd seen. A small entryway made a bottleneck, with my bunkhouse on one side and our repurposed sitting room on the other side. A large, solid stone wall between the entryway and the start of Audrey's chambers made the whole thing feel very secure.

I lived in a tiny little space between the Butcher and his captive.

I was the air between Audrey and the mud.

The bunk wasn't comfortable for me to lie in and wait for time to pass, but I didn't have a lot of options, so it was where I went. But it wasn't the wood above me that I saw. It was Kadan's face as Darrius outlined their plan with merciful precision, including the coup they'd been prepared to stage if the Butcher had merely been *injured* by the assassins. That hadn't happened, so we were regrouping for another charge.

That happened to be where Raider's Ban cavalry shone. Anyone with a pony and a stick could charge. Few could regroup well. Fewer still could do it time and again, with ruthless precision, the way we could. And while he wasn't talking cavalry charges, Darrius brought that competency into everything he did. According to him, there were four courses of action from here that their Council would choose from.

Have someone else marry Audrey, take La'Angi, swear it to Luca.

Have Luca marry Audrey against the Duke's orders, and hope it was viewed as binding in the eyes of the One...and the Council.

Have me hide Audrey away while they razed La'Angi to the ground.

Ignore La'Angi and the west, and instead, try the same strategy they'd attempted with La'Angi's mirror province in the east. Marry into the family at Black Borough, kill the Duke, and take the eastern arm of the military stationed at Black Borough.

None of the options included forcing Kadan to step into a role he was so sure would crush him. It was the best I could say of their plans.

Mayhap we hadn't given the Butcher enough credit. He'd known how to shut down Luca's plans and had already done so, neatly severing any chance of our rebellion rallying behind him. And he'd known Kadan wouldn't be so easily thwarted.

He'd gone for Kadan's throat, and I hadn't been there to defend it. I'd been carrying chests and smashing unwanted furniture.

I wasn't arrogant enough to think I could have single-handedly saved Kadan. But I'd've damned well tried.

I got up and let myself into Audrey's chambers. Whitehoof take their rules. I didn't care for Victor's dictatorship or living in two tiny rooms on either side of a chokepoint for the rest of my life.

In the gray of dawn, I spent time looking over the tapestries on the walls, but they were the same styles and settings I'd seen all over the castle. I suspected most had been repurposed from elsewhere—they didn't feel like her. The long, low chairs, the rugs on the ground, all felt like they'd been pulled from elsewhere, too.

Why hadn't she been in this area before? Too expensive to staff? Were there no guards he trusted?

Old Gods and the One, how I hated that *I* was more trusted than his own men.

Why had she wanted me to teach her the sword?

I looked up the curling staircase to the next level, where the servant hadn't gone and dawn hadn't intruded yet. The staircase was empty, of course, and the tower silent bar the cheerful crackle of the fire in the grate chasing away the worst of the autumn chill.

But Isolde was right there, motionless, on those stairs.

She was totally still—but somehow, she looked like she was coming out of the stone all the same. My feet were like hunks of granite as she started to move, and my brain tried to make me move in response. Every part of me screamed *get out of her way.*

That level of stealth was inhuman.

Her feet were bare and silent as she moved down the stairs. Her eyes didn't leave mine, and the air was caught behind my ribs. I was put in the mind of one of the big lions I'd seen stalking prey in the Steppes. Except Isolde didn't bother trying to disguise herself.

Wordlessly, she walked past me. I stood frozen, my feet like blocks of stone. She moved with the sinuous grace of a predator, and I was the unsuspecting prey, separated from my herd. Staring at me, her blue eyes looked utterly soulless. She curled her fingers around the tray's edges the way I'd grasp a hilt, with purpose and some expectation of violence or force. Clammy sweat prickled under my arms as she straightened and stalked away, moving past me so closely I held my breath rather than draw her ire. Her skirts brushed against the tops of my boots.

She hadn't made a single sound. Not a one.

I didn't breathe properly until I was back in my little airlock, the door barred behind me.

It was one thing to know the woman was Matri'sion. It was another to see it.

I rested my forehead against the wood and wished, with everything inside of me, I could go and tell Kadan about the horror I'd just seen.

Instead, I took the coward's way out and hid.

Thomas eventually arrived. He talked through the necessary information that Mortemon didn't want to give me. Apparently, knowing where the bathhouse was located sat lower on the list of importance than having my hair cut. We agreed I'd do nights, at least for the next few weeks, and he'd come by after training in the morning to take the shift during the day.

Leaving the tower, even armed with thorough instructions, made anxiety claw at my throat in a way it hadn't for years. I skimmed my hand over the hilt of my sword and found comfort in the weight of my shield as I moved through the unfamiliar corridors.

I kept half-turning to check on Kadan out of habit. Finding nothing but gray La'Angi stonework, unfriendly faces, and shadows alive with my own demons, kept my hand close to my sword.

Everything was wrong.

Even back in the tower I had to endure the silence with Thomas as we both stood around, doing nothing, saying nothing. It gave me far too long to compare my current living situation with the one I'd endured as a child.

Later in the afternoon I went to train. In the courts I was pointed silently away from the group of guardsmen who looked to be the equivalent of infantry in the Butcher's standing army. They met my eyes, sized me up, and then directly me wordlessly toward a much smaller group of men who looked to be finishing up. This area was attended by a woman holding a bucket and scoop. The tide was low in the bucket, her eyes flat and tired as she looked at me.

I saw those tired eyes, not the men in front of me, though they greeted me with big grins and open arms, though they swiped away sweat and jostled for position. I barely even saw the dulled blade I was given.

I'd done it. I'd come full circle. But this time, I wouldn't let that cycle repeat again.

CHAPTER TWENTY-ONE
AUDREY

"Ideas are only as useful as the actions they cause." ~ *Matri'sion lesson*

It took my father only a moon to prepare. The books said it should've taken him longer. No one would say why he'd had an army all but ready to march, and it wasn't because I didn't ask.

The King's own advisor had been assassinated. That was a fact. But something felt amiss.

I stood on the battlements of the keep wall, watching them march through the city. The autumn wind tugged at my hair. It held the bite of winter in it, the threat of darkness yet to come. Men marched below us, leaving for war. They marched abreast, their feet rising and falling in perfect time. Their steel-shod boots struck the cobbles so perfectly the sound echoed through the whole city. It made my head ache to hear it. Those reverberations had settled into my bones. I feared I'd hear them even when I lay down to sleep.

Carrion birds circled over us, and I saw Isolde glance up toward them, her expression hard. "Good omen," I offered, grateful for the distraction. "The One must be smiling on the Duke."

"They aren't over the Duke," she said, and I saw behind her Thomas' expression shutter.

I shifted, uncomfortable. Because they were, in fact, circling over us. Or the bailey, but there was little of import in the eastern bailey. "Well, as long as they don't make a mess," I offered, hoping she'd laugh at the idea of us up here, pretending to be dignified, secretly attempting to count the regiments.

She didn't laugh, though. "There's five birds up there, Audrey," she murmured. "The Woman in the Wood is watching."

Thomas cleared his throat loudly.

Isolde shot him an amused look from the tips of his boots to the end of his nose, and I didn't like how swiftly she dismissed him. It felt… unfair. "Change is coming," she said firmly, turning back to the men marching out of the city. Not a single gap had appeared in their ranks all day. I didn't expect to find one now. It made counting simpler.

I resisted the urge to sigh. Of course change was coming. That was what happened when people took up arms.

As I moved to follow, I saw Chay's expression, somewhere between amusement and derision, as he glanced up at the birds. I was sure at some point I'd heard him mutter a curse or prayer that hadn't been of the One, but even if he'd been devout, I suspected I could follow his thought well enough. Five birds didn't tell us any more or less than the stomp of those boots on cobbles below.

In some strange way, it was nice to feel that I'd followed his thoughts. For the first time since the tourney, we agreed. Neither of us spoke, though. I regretted not sighing when Isolde had made that mock-wise comment. Mayhap she'd correctly interpreted it, and some god was sending birds to warn us of dire things to come, or mayhap there was a tasty treat nearby. Whatever the reason, I'd let that first opportunity to actually have a half-friendly interaction with Chay vanish before I'd even known it was there.

I was suddenly aware of how he stood only a spear's length away, on the far side of the parapet. My hair kept whipping around, hiding him from even my peripheral view, but he was right there, as always. He did exactly what he'd been bloodsworn to do, and not a thing more.

That I respected his ability to walk that line irritated me a little, but that was likely just envy. I resisted the urge to glance over to see if his uniform was all in place. He had a habit of not lacing the throat of his shirt that Thomas regularly had to remind him to fix.

Drawing in a deep breath, I put aside the rumbling discontent at the reminder of what I wanted being so close, but utterly out of my reach. A tutor in the sword now seemed like nothing more than a naïve dream to replace the fantasy of a rescuer wielding a sword.

Isolde's lips moved every now and then as she murmured numbers to herself. My eyes wandered over the small eastern bailey instead. When word came they'd crossed the Brannough, we'd be able to leave. That was what Isolde said. By the time we knew they'd crossed, a week would've passed if updates were sent by pigeon, three if it came by horse. By the time they knew we were gone, the river would be rough, the road a dangerous slurry, and we'd be over the Aza Ranges and skirting the grassy fields of 'Ban lands, headed for the Steppes.

The thought was so abstract it didn't seem real. The way Isolde stated everything with such confidence, as if she were willing it to come true…it made me think she didn't believe it was real, either. Like this plan, this wonderful escape, was just another lie.

"You're looking wishful," she said, glancing over at me. "Want to put on some boots and go adventuring with some soldiers?"

In my peripheral, Thomas' eyelids flickered, and he recoiled subtly.

Isolde knew he'd done that march on Wolfswail. It was cruel of her to rub it in his face.

"I'm wondering how La'Angi will change between now and the solstice," I told her, partially because it was true and partially to stop her from needling Thomas.

"Leaves will fall," she said, the smile no longer on her face, her expression intent. "But they'll regrow unless you remove branches."

"Winter's a fair time to prune," I offered.

Her eyes narrowed. “Have you shears?”

I did. They were standing behind me, silent and unusable. So I blew out a long breath. “Mayhap I’ll learn to craft some. I’ve time to learn.”

She didn’t state her disagreement. That, from Isolde, meant there were no counterarguments to be had.

I didn’t know which prospect was more terrifying—preparing to flee, or trying to find another way to usurp my father’s power. But while she couldn’t disagree that I had a little time, I’d had plenty previously, and never solved the issue. I dipped a hand into a pouch at my belt and felt the weighted coins Luca had gifted me so long ago. They were warm, and smooth. I eased them into my palm one handed, and the weight of them was comforting.

“Change *is* coming,” Isolde said again, grudgingly. “She works in twisted ways, our Wood Woman.”

Over us, the carrion birds cawed, and unease skittered down my spine.

“My lady.” Thomas cleared his throat, and I glanced over. “The birds…your father feeds them. They’re a sign of approval from the One.”

“The Lady in the Woods would like a word with your One,” Isolde muttered, but she didn’t say it so loud that he’d need to respond. “And the bastards who twist her messengers.”

“They’ll follow the Duke, my lady,” Thomas said.

It was all a ruse. I looked up again, feeling hollow, wondering how many similar signs my father created to give himself credibility. He didn’t feed them because it was a pious thing to do; he fed them because, seeing them, people would look and wonder. And when they moved with him, those wonderings would move, too.

Hopelessness sat heavily, but I drew in a deep breath and let it go. Change *was* coming, and it wasn’t going to be as fragile as the illusions created by my father. The change I wanted was like those boots striking the ground in unison—obvious, undeniable, and unsubtle.

CHAPTER TWENTY-TWO
THOMAS

"The South came to Barloc needing a loan. Barloc, in his kindness, agreed, offering them generous terms allowing them to pay back this debt in the form of metals they were well able to mine, over the course of generations. They accepted these terms, and an agreement was struck." ~ *The Fall of Wolfswail*

"I hear they fished another body out of the river," Rose said to me, carrying over a refreshed pot of tea to our old table where I'd placed the documentation I'd been able to find, babe cradled in her other arm.

I wasn't used to that table being surrounded by the Duke's stone walls in a series of rooms that were mine now. It looked smaller here.

I took the babe from her, and she stretched out her back with a pleasant sigh. I watched from the corner of my eye as her plain dress tugged tight across her breasts. "They're always fishing bodies out of the river." I cooed down at my youngest, rocking him as he scrunched his face unhappily. "Aren't they, Vincent?"

Rose made a noise of dissent around the mouthful of watery tea she'd taken from her own cup. She always drank the dregs. I told her not to. "Not like this," she said, shaking her head, her mouth now empty. "'Twas all thin-skinned and black-veined, I hear."

"The water isn't kind to bodies," I warned her. "And there's no point putting stock in such talk." I'd heard it, too, and ignored it. But it was easier for me, I supposed. My primary companionship was Chay and the few guardsmen who still spoke to me.

She settled herself, and I took the pot to top off her cup. The smell of her herbal mix and a little sweetness from the apple peel she always added filled the air with comforting, homey smells. But this place wasn't comfortable or homey.

"Blueberries?" Rose asked, staring at the papers spread out before her on the table as I rocked Vincent.

"Blueberries," I confirmed, seeing a flicker of movement from the corner of my eye. A Beatrice-sized lump was standing behind one of the tapestries on the wall. The trappings might've changed, but the girls hadn't. "I do hope none of the little ones are still awake," I said for their benefit. "They may miss out on an excellent morning meal if they sleep late."

Rose's brows arched, and a smile folded itself into the corner of her lips. "Oh, they wouldn't dare," she assured me, playing along. "We already have so much to catch up on. They know if they stay up late and sleep late, it'll reflect badly on us all. Fetch me my new eyeglasses, Tom, so I can read this properly. And mayhap another candle."

I went to fetch the glasses, giving Beatrice enough time to return to her bed, rocking Vincent as I shuffled along slowly.

The eyeglasses were nigh useless, having been given to us by the mage as a patronage gift after he realized I'd been knighted. They weren't spelled to Rose's eyes, and we didn't know if we had the means to do so because information on Cammhinge, my holdings, was hard to come by. Wade hadn't been overly interested in the day-to-day running of it, from what I could tell.

"What does this mean?" Rose asked, shuffling through the papers.

I looked at the columns and numbers, the headings and notes. "It's information about profit. And cost."

She gave a long-suffering sigh. "You don't know either, do you?"

I didn't like that she smiled at me the way she'd smiled earlier at Sandra, while the girl was trying to learn how to style her hair like landed women did—with ribbons woven into the plaits and coils of it atop her head.

There wasn't anyone I could ask, was there? I could go to a merchant who'd take my coin, or to a noble who'd probably do the same.

"I've looked at it," I disagreed, because I had. "The province makes money, there's no two ways about it. But I think we won't really be able to figure out how much, or whether this information is accurate unless we're there." And the mage was being cagey about how much I owed. No one had insisted he write it down when he attended Rose for Vincent's birth. I'd started to suspect he'd taken the job only to get away from the keep, because there had been pressure from the nobility to attend either the Duke, or the Raider's Ban lord.

I'd gone from being a scavenger to the fatted calf. At least I'd grown up a scavenger. I knew how to pick a carcass clean.

"But you're tied up here," she pointed out, quite sensibly.

"I am." Vincent was calm, now, in my arms, his tiny fists balled up to his face, his hands wrapped to prevent scratches. "You could go, though. Take a carriage ride with the girls. Children. Spend the winter away from the frozen muck of the city."

She frowned. "Alone?"

My heart ached at that small change in her expression, and I held Vincent closer against the sudden gust of icy wind. My logic was sound. I wasn't making big decisions without thinking them through. It had nothing to do with the fact that there was yet another war against the South, and the Duke was marching on Wolfswail.

The candle didn't flicker. It should've flickered, given how cold the wind was.

"You'd have Sandra's help," I reminded her.

But Rose was shaking her head. "No. No, I cannot do that to her, Tom." Vincent fussed, and I turned my gaze on him, rocking him slowly, holding him tight, but not too tight. Never too tight. "She's going to be expected to manage a fief or holding one day. She needs to be here, learning how to do that."

The thought of returning every night to Sandra's bright eyes and expectations made something inside of me wither. "I think we'd do better if she had some space from the lads expecting to fuck their way into our fortune," I said bluntly, to end the conversation.

"You assume I can stop that from happening?" Rose asked me, those brows arching with such dignity it hurt me to behold it.

She was right. I hated that she was right. "Who will help you, then?"

"I think sending me away is a poor choice," she said primly. "We do better together, Tom. You know that. You've told me every day since you got back."

The wind screamed, and I forced myself to cross to her, picking my way carefully over the rug that crunched like snow beneath the leather of my boots. "Rose," I said, sitting opposite her, willing her to understand.

But I couldn't find the words. Or the reasons. I just sat there, staring at her, chilled to the bone.

And mayhap that's all I needed to do, because that haughty expression thawed, and she looked on me with compassion. "We're just useless links, alone," she told me, reaching out to cup my face in the palm of her hand. "But together, we've made a strong chain."

I closed my eyes and searched my heart for any way to explain it to her. But all I could find was, "They're marching on Wolfswail, Rosie."

"I know, Tom." She stroked my cheek, and her touch was so warm on my chilled skin, but I didn't dare turn into it. "I know. Those blueberries, they'll grow without me being near them. Our children won't grow without you."

They would, though. I'd seen so many other men's children grow just fine, though their pa's bones remained in piles in the South, sitting atop ground too frozen to dig. The scavengers had been well fed. They only took the sweetmeats by the end. Not like us. We'd cracked open every bone we'd ever found.

"Please, Rose." She looked at me, so sweetly compassionate, so kind. So ready to tell me *no.* "You don't understand. Bad things happen near the Duke when he goes South," I managed to say, and somehow, my teeth didn't chatter.

Seeing that *no* thawing and the tears springing into her eyes brought me no pleasure. But we both knew what I said was true.

CHAPTER TWENTY-THREE

AUDREY

"Only the rich can afford to be kind." ~ La'Angi saying

Isolde stood in the doorway to the steward's archives, angled to catch a beam of sunshine as if she needed it for the panel she was embroidering. From the corner of my eye, I saw her hold the hoop up in her hand, turning it slightly. She paused, lifting my attention from the columns of numbers that hadn't revealed any secrets to me yet.

Chay shifted, too. I couldn't see him, but I heard the clinking chains on his belt and scabbard. I knew what I'd see if I did glance over. His hand wouldn't be on his sword hilt. That was part of why it made such a racket. One of his thumbs would instead be looped in his belt. His fingers were long and strong. They'd hang, half-coiled as if in anticipation, from his belt.

Swordsmen always had strong forearms. I stared at the columns on the parchment before me and wondered if his hands might be equally as strong. They were wide, that much, I'd seen. But when he moved things between his fingers absently, or when he whittled, he did it with the care of someone who knew his size.

I shifted in my chair. Last night, he'd been whittling. He'd held up a piece of wood and traced the dips and curves with his fingers, his eyes mostly closed, an expression of intense concentration on his face.

I was jarred from my thoughts by another distracting jangle of his belt, so close yet so far from those hands, and I shifted, easing my cloak away from my suddenly too-warm body. Beyond his distracting clamor I heard quickly approaching steps of hard-soled boots against the rug that offered little buffer between feet and stone.

It had been almost a moon since my father left, but I doubted I'd ever hear steel-shod boots on stone without that small spurt of fear.

One of the steward's assistants hurried past me, and out of habit, I put out a second hand to stop the pages beside me from fluttering to the ground as his cloak caught the stack. I kept my eyes on the columns before me rather than risk anyone seeing the disapproval stamped across my face.

"Steward Daniel is busy, guardsman," the assistant was saying. "Tell me the problem, and I'll see it's dealt with."

"No, I need to talk to him *myself*," the impatient guard demanded, and I risked a glance up at the unusual force in the words. His face was semi-familiar, but I had no name for him. "He's been ignoring us for a week, Billy. You know he has."

Whatever the assistant said was too quiet for me to hear because Chay shifted again, and his belt made the *jangle*.

I blew out a slow, calming breath and turned back to the numbers. Before I'd even found my place on the page again, I heard, "People are dying!"

Isolde's body was somehow more central in the doorway than it had been a moment ago, though she barely moved. I wondered when I'd learn that trick. I'd asked her a few years ago, and she'd just looked at me like she had no idea what I meant.

"Sicknesses are normal," the assistant said, his tone soothing. "I know they're distressing, but they're also to be expected as the weather turns."

The sound of a door opening preceded Steward Daniel's predictable, "What's this?"

"There's more sick, Master Steward." Impatient Guard bobbed a bow from the glimpses between Isolde and where Thomas stood to one side of the wood-framed doorway. "Five more. I've got them in the small west hall, but—"

"There's a mother," the assistant cut in. "And a few little ones. We know children always get sick, don't we?"

My head spun at their casual dismissal, and I stood.

Steward Daniel glanced over at me, his smile fixed to his face. "We will of course assist this woman," the Master Steward assured Impatient Guard, returning his attention to them.

"Your assistance isn't working," the guardsman said, continuing to earn the nickname I'd given him. "That's Mick's wife, Master Steward. You said he'd be the last we'd bury."

I halted behind Isolde. Her needle kept moving steadily through the fabric. She didn't miss a single stitch.

"What's this about a sickness?" I asked, and Isolde angled herself slightly, though Thomas, on the other side, didn't move. Like a bridge being lowered temporarily, they were allowed partial access to me.

"It's nothing for you to worry on, my lady," the Master Steward told me. "It's under control. We'll help Mick's wife, guardsman. Thanking you for bringing this to us."

Steward Daniel turned to leave, but Impatient Guard's hand shot out. It was pale against the forest green velvet the Master Steward was wearing, and shock skimmed across my skin.

Isolde was, once again, in front of me. And now Thomas had allowed the tip of his spear to droop over the doorway, barring passage to both of us. And trapping us inside.

When Isolde did it, it felt safe. When *Thomas* did it…

"Please, Master Steward," Impatient Guard said, releasing the fistful of scrunched fabric almost instantly. "We need to do more."

"None can do more," Steward Daniel told him, lips thin. "Go. I'll see to them."

I watched as the guardsman, his face as pale as his hand, turned smartly and left. His steps weren't hurried now, but the measured rhythm of the La'Angi-trained.

"A word, please, Master Steward," I said, but Steward Daniel just gave me a brief bow, gestured to his assistant, and vanished. I stood, incredulous, as the assistant vanished in the other direction.

As if they'd done this a thousand times already.

"What is going on?" I breathed.

Isolde settled her needle through the threads and lowered the hoop. "There's been a strange illness," she told me. "I thought nothing of it." Her expression clearly said that had changed.

"'Tis just the normal, my lady," Thomas assured me. "And if it isn't, best you let others manage it."

"You're no Healer," Isolde agreed.

Mayhap not, but I did have *some* power, as my father's heir. It was possible that if I kicked up enough of a fuss, the Master Steward might be forced to take more action than…whatever he was doing.

"What *is* he doing?" I asked them.

Silence met my question.

My head felt fuzzy at that complete non-answer. Then Isolde met my eyes, and the world stopped for a moment.

There was nothing good happening here. Nothing at all. And I'd been completely unaware?

The guard had said they were in the small west hall. I already had inconvenienced my watchdogs to get information, hoping it might be useful. I may as well follow up.

So I set out for said hall, and they damned well had to fall in around me.

"Curse it, Audrey," Isolde hissed. "Even if there *is* an illness, what is the point in *us* getting it?"

"We'll take precautions," I assured her. "They aren't going to just *tell* us, Isolde, you saw the Master Steward! What other choice do I have?"

"I could ask a hundred other people," Isolde told me, clearly frustrated.

They'd been shown to the hall. That wasn't where you'd place someone highly contagious, but nor was it somewhere to settle a sick family to administer aid. I turned it around in my head, ignoring Isolde as she strode along beside me. How did someone saturate every movement with disapproval, and how did I learn to replicate this?

By the Wife, how I wanted Steward Daniel to know the depths of my disgust for him.

I didn't know what was happening, but I despised all of it. And I knew damned well some of that disgust should've been for me, too, because I'd been sitting in my tower counting down days and ignoring everything else.

Thomas stepped ahead of us to open the door to the hall. I saw his eyes go over Isolde's head, and he shared a loaded look with Chay, jangling along behind us.

The deep, centering breaths I took were in time with Isolde's. I shortened my strides as we stepped into the warmly lit hall. There was a woman sitting by the big fireplace, but aside from her and the children I suspected had come with her, the hall was empty.

The hay on the floor crinkled beneath my feet, and I cast my eyes over the tables. In the place of chairs, long benches sat. In the Great Hall, we had magework lamps that didn't smoke or flicker. Here, the walls were blackened above the brackets holding torches, which had at least been mostly lit. I knew I'd been *in* this hall, but I couldn't remember when.

Two children had paused in their game of jacks and were climbing to their feet, flanking the woman rocking gently by the fireside, an infant at her breast, a toddler against her legs.

I was close enough to see their clothes were plain but good quality, though they hadn't recently been cared for. The tallest boy turned to face us squarely. His gaze made me stop dead in my tracks, terror running up my spine and sinking claws into my brain. Whatever color his eyes had been, they were now almost completely black, and something so deeply unnatural about it made a large part of my mind demand—*run.*

Thomas continued forward, passing me by. He gave the boy a small bow, deference to the new master of the house, but the child hadn't looked away from me. Some part of me, some dark, cowardly part, wondered if he'd spring if I turned to flee.

Isolde's hand on my arm silently recommended caution.

"Chay," I said. The word sounded painfully indifferent.

What did they have?

"Yes, my lady?"

I barely even noticed the disdain in his words. I didn't care about his feelings at this moment, nor my own embarrassment. "Find me a Healer," I told him quietly. "A mage."

Thomas turned to object, but Chay was already following my instructions, his cloak swirling behind him and his equipment clinking as he moved with haste I appreciated.

Thomas' objections were written on his face, but before he could unnecessarily remind me of my father's arbitrary rules—which we'd probably already breached by being here, and which *would* be contrary to his wishes, even though he hadn't explicitly said "don't visit people with deadly illnesses"—I tried to remember what had been said about this family.

Mick's wife. *Who is Mick?* "I understand you're Mick's oldest," I said, hoping I had the name correct.

"Why did he run off?" the boy asked, jerking his head after Chay.

And what could I say? *I think you're dying?* How about *I've never seen an illness that makes a person's eyes as black as an inkpot.* A split second passed while I searched for words. "I sent him to find a Magework Healer," I told him, hoping that honesty would be enough to pay for my brief hesitation.

The woman made a noise of pain low in her throat. "We've no coin to pay," she said, the words full of grief.

"Then it's a good thing I do." I took them all in, looking at eyes where I could. The boys playing jacks were the only ones who did not seem to have one foot in the grave. The mother's skin was white as chalk, her veins showing up as gray tracks up her neck and in her cheeks.

I had no idea the cost of a mage. I'd never needed to. If I'd required a mage, I'd had one. I knew I had a lot of wealth at my fingertips. I'd get Isolde to check standard fees so I wasn't bled dry for future interactions, and I'd do what I could for this family.

I turned to the boy again, ignoring the rush of guilt at the idea of leaving in just a few days and never needing to worry about future interactions with *any* of these people. "How do you feel?" I asked him, because that was what mattered right now.

"Fine," he said so furiously I knew it to be a lie.

"Hurts," whimpered the toddler on the woman's lap. "It hurts."

"Shh," the woman murmured, smoothing the child's hair. Her hand was bone white, her nails blackened. Her veins were dark threads under her skin. "The warm is nice, isn't it?"

A knife twisted in my heart. There was nothing else I could do to help.

"I'm sorry it hurts," I told them, but the words sounded awkward to my ears. The graceless sentiment came from the bottom of my soul. "I'll do everything I can."

"Have you had something to eat?" Thomas asked the boy.

"Not hungry," he said forcefully.

But the two playing jacks looked up. "I am," one of them said hesitantly.

Isolde smiled at them. "We'll fetch you something to eat, then. Come now, my lady, you can help me carry."

She took my arm and steered me away. Once we were clear of them, Thomas said, "My lady," like a plea. I met his eyes, and found in them both desperation and terrifyingly, trust. He knew, too. He knew they were doomed.

In the hallway, Isolde's hand settled on my arm above my elbow. She didn't quite pull me along, but she came damned close. "Do not touch them," Isolde said in a tone that brooked no argument. She looked first at me, then at Thomas. "Or I'll cut off whichever body part it is that might…might have *that*."

"How many?" I asked them, letting Isolde steer me.

"I've heard of seven or eight deaths," Isolde said, glancing at Thomas. "I assumed it was a regular illness, exaggerated."

The thought of those black eyes made something deep inside of me shy away. It was no wonder Steward Daniel didn't want to face the reality of it. There was something terrifying about those eyes. I didn't know what, and I hoped I never would, but it was there, very real and ancient.

"Thomas?" I asked, because he just walked in silence.

He ducked from my gaze, watching a servant bustling past, doing her best to be unobtrusive. But he said, slowly, "I haven't been tallying the deaths." That there might be enough to *need* tallying hadn't even occurred to me. "It was mostly in the lower quarter, though." Something about that acknowledgment sat ill with me, but before I could question him, he said, "I heard a body was fished out of the river, and the fishermen got sick after."

"How close were they?" Isolde asked, the words sharp. I could just about see her assessing the risks. *Get close, get sick. Audrey is at risk. Keep her away.*

"You need to be awfully close to pull a *body* from a *river*," I told her, irritated. "I'm not planning on pulling their bodies from the hall. There should be no issue."

"You need to be close to deliver soup, too," she replied sharply. "And we have no idea how close is *too* close."

A girl with a damp apron saw us coming and held the door, dropping down in a curtsey. I knew I was about to be forbidden from attending by Isolde, and while it made sense, I had no way to explain how much I hated the idea.

I'd been helpless for so long. I should've been used to it.

Knowing damned well what I was doing, I followed Isolde to gather a basket and leaned in, murmuring, "Mayhap we ought to leave a day or two earlier."

She made a thoughtful noise, blasting the cook with a smile as the woman did a double-take at seeing me present. "Sorry to disturb you," Isolde said. "The lady and I were just popping in quickly. Your dough is looking excellent, Bernadette."

I hung back until a basket with small, still-warm sourdough rolls was thrust into my hands. Isolde carried the soup, bowls stacked neatly atop the tureen. The smile on her lips was genuine as she guided me back out. I hated how swiftly it faded.

I knew it wasn't my fault she was unhappy. She'd made choices for herself, and there wasn't a force known to the One, the Wife, or the Son that could make Isolde do a thing she didn't want to do. But still, it twisted up my gut and made me want to make my excuses and hasten back to the quiet of my tower.

"I don't like this," Isolde said unnecessarily, but the words were directed at a grim-faced Thomas. "She needs to stay back."

"Understood, and agreed, mistress," he said stiffly. "I can take it from here, if it pleases the lady."

It pleased my cowardly, shame-soaked heart. And mayhap that was why I couldn't let myself consider the wisdom of my choices as I saw a servant hastening out of the hall, an empty coal cart pushed before her.

Isolde gave me a gentle nudge and jerked her chin toward the servant, frowning. I followed her gaze, not seeing why she'd drawn my attention. "What?" I asked quietly, as Thomas held the door for us.

"Unusual to see coal carts around in the afternoon, isn't it?" she murmured. "Come now, we'll leave the family to eat their soup while sir Chay fetches the Healer. They can find you once it's done."

I followed her in, and we set the food down on the table at the mother's back.

I stood back as Isolde set out the bowls. The mother nudged the child on her knee toward the food, but he wouldn't stand. I watched, unsure if I should offer to take the infant, but Thomas was already stepping forward, his expression one of kindness. Freed from the necessity of action, I glanced down at the toddler leaning against his mother's legs as the jack-playing boys took soup and bread to the side.

Thomas had frozen, his arms half-outstretched, bent at the middle with his shield at his feet.

The toddler's head lolled to one side, awkwardly.

The mother's wail made time freeze. The raw agony of her scream held a pain that made tears spring to my eyes and stole the air from my lungs. I fell back a step, the high-pitched, primal noise of grief making the world spin. She rocked aggressively, her arm scooping the limp toddler to her legs as the infant was clutched to her breast.

Isolde's hand went again to my arm, though I hadn't seen her get there. She pulled me back a little further, and—the Wife help me—I let her.

But only for one step.

Thomas was no longer frozen. He stripped his cloak from his shoulders and was easing the infant from the mother's arms. I couldn't hear his murmured reassurances, but I could see the movement of his lips and the shine of tears in his eyes.

Isolde's hand bit into my arm as she tugged on me, and I pulled free.

Thomas glanced up at me, the babe bundled in his sturdy cloak, but it was to the oldest boy that he carried it.

The boy, barely seven winters old, dropped his spoon with a clatter. His mouth, hanging agape, snapped shut, and he took the infant with hands that seemed too small to carry such a burden. But he didn't fumble it, just held the child close. The little one waved a hand at their brother, and I told myself I couldn't see it properly not because the infants skin was so pale it was transparent, but because my eyes blurred with tears.

"I'm sorry," I said, but those words were drowned in the mother's wails, and I was glad. What good did my regret do?

The door opened, and Chay's familiar face, carved in painful neutrality, blurred until I blinked away tears. The mage entered behind him, an unfamiliar man who glanced around warily, his gaze lingering on me.

"He's a Magework Healer," Thomas said to the older boy. "He'll help."

The mage shot him a look of caution, putting down his toolbox on the table with a thump. The woman was weeping now, and I didn't know if I should look at her or not.

"I've not seen this," he told me matter-of-factly. "How long have you been unwell for?" he asked the older boy. The mage's fingers were long and marked with scars and burns as he undid the catches on his toolbox, and it sprang open. Cogs whirred, and an elaborate selection of metal and crystal implements were displayed. Tiny cases formed miniature staircases up and down the display, and the whirring, clicking sound of a mage's work hummed in the background.

"I'm not unwell," the boy snapped.

"How long have their eyes looked odd?" he asked the brother, setting out three ceramic basins in a triangle around the eldest.

"Three days," said the boy opposite him.

The older brother scowled. "Their eyes are *fine.*"

"No, it's been four days," said the other, shaking his head. Unconcerned, the mage snapped on his metal-framed eyeglasses, flicking through the crystal lenses, frowning and cycling back, until he found what he wanted. "Ma got it the day we got eggs, remember?"

The eldest brother's scowl deepened. His cheeks took on a strange gray hue, but before there could be an argument, the mage snapped his fingers, and fire ignited in the bowl, making the boy flinch. "Have you had a runny nose, felt hot or cold?" asked the mage. The boys shook their heads. "Do you think your ma has?"

They hesitated, the older one holding the infant closer than I thought was perhaps wise. The last few tendrils of steam curled off the soup before him, forgotten. "Ma, she was strange. Not hot, but ice cold. Used up a week's wood in one night."

The mage accepted this silently, measuring out oils into the bowls. Sparks crackled where the liquid met the flame. The familiar smell of fragrant oils and metal made some of the tension ease out of me. Would he be able to offer me information on the sickness once he'd healed them? "I'll see what I can do for this one," he told me, his movements brisk as he tightened the seal on the jar of oil.

Thomas had known what to do for the mother when she'd been mourning. *That* was what I needed to do, not flee but help where I could. I didn't know what to do, but I had to do something, didn't I? Wasn't that my role?

"Do what you can, please," I said, relieved to have someone who got straight to the point and wasn't going to make me justify, explain, or finagle. The hum of magic contained within the mage's box made the quiet of the room seem heavier.

He nodded, taking the infant from the arms of the older brother with not a gentle word to soften any of it. He just took a few deep breaths and then went curiously still.

Isolde was looking at me again, and I knew she wanted me to run. But I wasn't running.

I looked to the woman, sitting in a puddle on the ground, her arms around the body of the small child. She wasn't wailing *or* weeping. She was perfectly, utterly still, her eyes staring toward my left shoulder. The world started to spin around me.

"Breathe," Isolde said softly, and I did.

The woman's eyes were deep, dark black, veins beneath her skin like ink-stained cracks. Even in death she clutched the child to her breast.

I was standing in a hall with two now-dead people who'd had a mystery illness that made them look like evil itself had infected them. And I had not a clue what to do.

Isolde's hand was on my upper arm again, and this time, I wasn't breaking free. I looked up, jolted from the shock to see the mage's skin was deathly pale. Even as I tried to recall the exact shade of brown of his skin when he'd arrived, the veins in his neck became clearer. I watched the darkness spread, like he was cracking and crumbling before us. There was something hypnotic about it. The fires in the bowls flared, sparks spluttered dramatically, and then were snuffed out.

I found myself unable to look away until man and child slowly melted to the floor, a lifeless pile of flesh. Did people always look boneless in death? Had the illness changed something that meant they moved so slowly? What sort of illness could spread through the mage's spells?

"Audrey," Isolde said quietly, "You need to leave."

I couldn't breathe. I couldn't make sense of it. That wasn't how magic worked.

"Ma?" asked one of the children who had been eating.

"Go, Audrey," Isolde said, releasing me. "Now."

Even with the ring of command in her voice, my feet were rooted to the floor, and it was lucky they were, or I'd've flown to the rafters and become wedged there. I couldn't move. I couldn't speak, either, to tell her. The cogs of the mage's box were silent.

The younger brother stood, his soup tumbling off to the side. The metal bowl bounced away with a noise that felt like a knife to my skull. Opposite him, his older brother stood, looking from the mage and infant to his mother's fallen form.

Isolde's hand bit into my arm so hard it was a wonder it didn't make me weep from the pain, but I couldn't feel it. She was pulling me backward, but my feet weren't working properly. I watched them, the two young children. I couldn't tell what their faces meant. I didn't know.

I tripped on my skirt, but Isolde held me up until I could recover to the sound of ripping fabric as my skirt gave way.

The younger brother screamed—rage and terror and grief all blurring into a blood-chilling war cry—as he launched himself toward me. A split second later, the older brother's wail, thick with tears, joined in.

He was scrambling over the table. He was furious.

I'd been trying to help.

I'd just wanted to *help.*

"Don't let them touch her," Isolde ordered, her voice cracking like a whip as she shoved me behind her.

Thomas grabbed the oldest by his shirt and pulled him down off the table, but he scrambled under. Isolde planted her foot squarely in the youngest's face, kicking him away. Black blood oozed out of his nose as he staggered.

My heart was as dead as the mage. I put my hand to my own face, tasting the blood, feeling the hot, burning agony. Through my tears, I saw Chay grab the eldest around the waist as he lunged at me.

Tiny arms clawed at the air. Tiny feet flailed. He'd clambered through the spilled soup. Some of it was on his breeches.

Stop, I wanted to say, but the words got all tangled up in my throat. *We want to help.*

"You killed my da! You killed my ma!" the younger brother shouted at us, sobbing, blood dribbling slowly down his chin.

Either the child in Chay's arms broke free, or he let him go. He came toward me, and Isolde shoved him back, too, her kick hitting him in the chest and making him sprawl into his younger, bloodied brother.

I took a step back, away from the horror almost involuntarily. I couldn't breathe around the sobs, screams, or useless regret tangled up in selfish terror.

The eldest boy gathered himself for another leap, and the world was spinning around me, tilting, crashing down. Isolde's hand on my arm wasn't there to keep me up. The straw didn't soften my fall as my knees hit the ground. The eldest, who'd accepted his tiny sibling, who'd amused his little brothers, who would hold *me* responsible. My hand crushed my mouth, tried to hold my own agony in. It didn't belong here.

I didn't belong here.

He jumped at me, and Chay stepped between us, sword drawn. He said something, a warning. I couldn't look away as the child speared himself on the blade.

Thomas stood, shaking, frozen in place, but Isolde stepped in front of me and settled into a stance I knew was defensive.

The younger child was running at me. I heard Isolde shout, heard my own wail as if from far away. At the last moment, some instinct kicked in, and I tried to scramble to my feet through the tears. There was violence around me. So much. I couldn't make sense of it, of the lurching, spinning world or the words tumbling around the air nearby.

And then it was quiet, finally. And the last child's head had been separated from his body.

Chay dropped his sword like it burned and turned his eyes on me, disgust in every line of his face.

I couldn't make sense of that much hatred. I couldn't carry it.

So I didn't try.

But I shed tears for him, anyway. He, and the other innocents.

CHAPTER TWENTY-FOUR

ISOLDE

"Allow no good deed to pass without consequence." ~ La'Angi saying

I held my tongue until Thomas dropped the bar on the external tower door, locking the whole city out and separating us from what had happened in that hall, and then I rounded on them. Fury pounded through my veins. "How are you still alive?" I demanded, going straight for the throat. "How have your oaths not burned you both to a crisp for taking so long to act?"

Thomas looked at me like he wasn't really there, but Chay offered me his sword, the blood thick and still gleaming black. "I suppose this doesn't need cleaning, then."

Audrey stepped forward. "I'll—"

I stepped between her and that fouled blade even as Chay twitched it away. Rage poured through me, barely held within the banks of my will. "No, you will *not.*" I thrust a pointed finger toward her rooms without thinking, and the stubborn child dug her heels in, her long mouth thin with displeasure.

I didn't try to fight her on it now. "*You,*" I said, turning that finger on Thomas and shoving it in his chest, blood roaring in my head. "You just *stood there.*"

"Isolde," Audrey began.

"She's right," Thomas acknowledged, bowing low to Audrey. "I'm sorry, my lady. I don't know how it is I survived such poor service, but, oath or not, I'll not put you in that position again."

Before she could accept his woodenly offered words, I heard the knocker on the wood right behind Thomas' back.

Silently, Audrey slipped out, and the two knights moved to allow access to the door, revealing the Captain of the guard and a handful of well-armed men.

"Sir Chay," the Captain said, stepping into the gap so the door couldn't be closed to bar him out. "We will be holding you prisoner until your case is viewed by law, acting by Son-given rights of the One, for the violent deaths of at least one child on this day."

Suspicion coiled in my belly. The Captain had been swifter to punish than he'd been to help, due, in no small part, to Chay's previous liege lord.

I watched, unimpressed, as he tossed his sword on the ground and sent me a quick glance that was full of accusation, as if this had been *my* fault.

And it was, partly. I'd known the situation in the hall was trouble. I hadn't realized how much, though, or how swiftly it would find us.

They didn't shackle him, but they did strip his tabard and weapons from him. I had no doubt he'd feel their disapproval for his last liege lord before he made it to his cell, and while that knowledge didn't make me happy, I had bigger issues.

Once he was gone, I turned to Thomas. "You should change your clothes, too." I looked at Chay's bloody sword with distaste. "We all ought to bathe, post haste."

"If it's in the city…"

It'd be in the bathhouse. I didn't overly care if Thomas lived or died. As far as I was concerned, he was useless. Still, if he got sick, he'd bring it too close to Audrey. "Ring for it to be sent to your rooms." He opened his mouth to object, and I said, "No one will come in or out. I'll go fetch Audrey's water myself, immediately."

He obviously didn't like it. "The Duke's orders were very clear."

"You catch that, we're all dead," I said bluntly. "You could die, either way. But you know what's more likely to kill your family, don't you?"

He did. He'd just witnessed it.

Limbs stiff and feet unsure, he walked away and left me finally, blessedly alone with Audrey.

She was going to be furious if she knew what they'd done to Chay, so I just said, "I'm going to get water. We all need to bathe; I've seen to it. There's no one on the door, so ignore any knocks."

"He killed children, Isolde," she said, and the words were hollow. "For me."

I pushed away the memory of that scream and screams like it. "Yes," I agreed. And I left her to reflect on that, going to the cubby and ringing the bell, then waiting and schooling myself to patience.

The children had the illness. From all accounts, they would've died anyway. Instead, she'd stuck her damned nose in where it wasn't wanted or needed. Things became complicated when inexperienced people made their way in.

The rope was tugged as it accepted the weight of the bucket, and I began to pull the thickly plaited fabric, lifting the water from the kitchens far below. I knew it would've been hot when it went in. It was still steaming when I got it up and poured it into her bath, then returned the bucket to its loop. The weight of it the next time made it clear they didn't know who'd rung for this bath. I put my back into it, grimly wondering what in the worlds Audrey had hoped to accomplish with that stunt in the hall. Truly, it was evidence of my restraint that I hadn't asked.

The repetitive task was soothing, and by the time the cask was loaded I was sweating from the exertion, but calmer. I sent the last of the buckets back, sprinkled just a touch of her favorite herbs into the water, and went to find the young fool. She wouldn't bathe quickly. We'd need to sit with her grief and disillusionment. But mayhap she'd see the wisdom in fleeing tonight.

I'd had the thought so many times before that it didn't come with a spark of hope, just weariness.

There were always reasons to stay, and she always found them.

In the common room of the tower, she sat in front of the fire, dirty cloth in one hand and Chay's sword in her other.

Horror burned like bile at the back of my throat. I snatched the rag from her hand, then the sword. Tears were on her cheeks.

She didn't fight me. "His oath won't harm him, will it?"

The blood didn't smell right. I couldn't put my finger on what it *did* smell like, but it didn't smell right. "What?"

"Chay's." She stood, dusting off her skirts. "If he leaves, that isn't harming me, correct?"

That proper tone in a voice thick from crying made my rage spike. "I suppose it depends on how he interprets his own actions." As far as I could tell, oaths to protect were based entirely on *perceived* impact, rather than *actual* impact. It was the only possible way Luca wasn't dead. "He hasn't fled, Audrey."

I regretted the words as soon as I saw hope light her eyes. She drew in a deep breath, and just as swiftly it was extinguished. "He should," she said, the words like rocks falling into a well. "I know he should."

She wasn't wrong. "He'll get his chance." If they let him out. "Come on. I'll clean this." She'd made a mess of it, but she would've gotten there.

"Where is he?" she asked, taking the steps ahead of me. "With the tabard on the ground, and his sword discarded…"

"No one fleeing would willingly leave behind their primary weapon," I pointed out, but she froze ahead of me, and I knew as soon as she figured out what must've happened. "You need to wash, Audrey. You can't get what that family had." She opened her mouth to object, and I put myself in the center of the narrow, curling stairwell designed to defend or entrap. "*No.*"

Her resistance collapsed, and fresh tears filled her eyes. She lifted her skirts and hastened to the tub.

I was shocked when she didn't slam the door behind her. All the same, the fouled blade and I stayed out. And when the damned thing was clean, I tossed the cloth in the fire and kept the sword, hiding it beside my bed. It was too long for me and too heavy, but Audrey's arms were longer than mine, and she'd always wanted to learn to use one.

Mayhap she'd get the chance.

That night, as I half-expected, she needed time to cry herself out and adjust her worldview to include illness that took babies and guards who'd slay children. She sat with me as I told her tales of the women I remembered, who might be dead or alive, and left her to sleep with swollen eyes and a raw nose, still clutching the sodden handkerchief.

Before dawn was more than a suggestion on the horizon, I was up and letting myself out on silent feet past a lightly dozing Thomas. He was easier to slip past than Chay, who would go to bed but lowered the bar over the door. Thomas had attempted to stay up and hadn't locked the door.

The castle was equally as simple for me to navigate. I kept to the main halls, as at this time of day, only servants were likely to be stirring. From my basket, I took my wig, slipped it on with a practiced flick, and gave it a quick one-handed fluff before settling my cloak to cover most of it. I encountered no one. One of the small, lesser-used gates was already open, with kitchen maids yawning as they walked into the darkness. I stepped in their shadows. Even before they commenced their work, they smelled of yeast and spices. One of them flicked a big-eyed glance at a guard who gave her a very proper nod and a very improper, long, lingering look as she walked out of his view. I didn't impede his line of sight, though it left a sour taste on my tongue. Quickly, I peeled away from the servants to make my way to the meeting spot in the stables of a semi-reputable inn that was one of my favorite locations to use.

It was, as ever, busy enough that my entry wasn't noteworthy, but not so busy that I risked extra attention. The woman I'd come to meet was there, a young, freckle-faced thing with the solid build of a woman who'd worked for her living. I recognized her from the awkward way she stood in the third stall, brushing the horse inexpertly.

I waved her out and saw her double-check the brooch on my cloak, a pretty pink flower with a few gold thorns on the stem. Her caution pleased me. She'd need it, from what I heard.

I rattled around in my head trying to bring up this one's name, but it slipped away. Young, lower-class, married to a young, middle-class chap —unhappily. His parents controlled everything. She had no horse in any race and was tired of it.

From the way her hand hovered occasionally over her abdomen, she might not simply be thinking of her own future.

"You'll work on the road," I told her, my voice low. I knew she'd been told this already, but reminders never hurt. "Cooking, cleaning, mending. The merchant will take you to Ange's Pass. From there, you'll need to hunt out the Blue Bower."

"And find Vanessa," she said briskly. "Who will help me with the next leg."

I nodded and reached into my basket, taking out a small pouch and passing it to her before we left the shelter of the stable. "For Vanessa—or to get you out of trouble, if you need it."

She took it without thanks, tucking it away as we made our way onto the road. Her eyes got stuck on the cobblestones. We walked in silence until we reached the east edge of the market, where one of the merchants I'd worked with for some time was—but so were the La'Angi guard.

I slowed my pace somewhat and curled my shoulders, but the additional tweaks to my disguise weren't necessary. They paid me no mind and were gone before I'd delivered my charge. The merchant scowled after them. I gathered from his expression this wasn't a standard bribe-collection trip.

"Morning," he said to us, still scowling. "Been regretting waiting," he told me gruffly, hitching his pants. "House down the road from where I was staying was set alight two nights ago. Sickness, they say." He nodded to the woman. "Good time to be getting out, lass."

Sickness. The image of those children came as if called by that word. A fist squeezed my chest. Sickness was a foe I couldn't fight.

But that was a problem for later. I reached into my basket, took out a preserves jar, and passed it over to the merchant, holding it so the gold inside didn't chime. It was heavy this time—she wasn't the only woman going with him, just the last to be ready.

"Ah," he sighed, smiling at me as if I was giving him his favorite marmalade. "Thanking you, my dear."

Pleasantries died on my tongue. I nodded. The guards had stopped not far into the market and were having some sort of animated discussion. Every now and then a hand would wave this way. "Safe travels," I murmured, stepping back into the shadows.

It started to rain, soft, slow, and soaking. The merchant and his carts left, not needing to worry whether they'd leave prints in the mud or how long before they washed away.

I glanced back to the woman to check—but, yes, she'd been equipped with a good, fur-lined, oiled cloak. Of course she had. I had a tight, conscientious organization. I waited to make sure the others I knew were scheduled for today were there, too, before it was too late. Sure enough, a young woman, round with child and doing her best to conceal it, walked beside the second cart, a sack over her shoulder and her jaw hard. Behind her, another woman kept looking back from her healing black eyes. My heart squeezed for her. One of the caravan's guards gestured her on gently with his hand. If he saw the tears on her cheeks, he gave no sign of it.

Go, I thought to her, aching. *Go, and start anew.*

The rain set in as I turned to return to the keep. I'd stood for longer than I'd meant to but would still make it before sunup.

I'd thought that it would hurt less as time went on. I'd thought that being able to help free others would make my own captivity less horrible. But time wasn't making it easier.

My feet felt heavy against the cobblestones. I refused to let them drag, though. Audrey had lived this long in this hellhole. I'd undone as much of the conditioning as I could and would continue to support her so she didn't fall back into the poisonous locways. The big, squat castle atop the cliffs sat like a bloated king on a crumbling throne and, oh, how the black hatred pumped through me.

We could set it afire. Or, better, we could murder the leaders in their sleep, and the city could wake to streets awash with blood. The knowledge pulsed within me. We could do it.

The power locked in my limbs and the hard beat of my heart made me want to charge ahead, when I saw a knot of guardsmen on the side of the road, clearly arguing with one another. A hand cart stood nearby.

I could cut their throats and have them in the cart. I'd still be back in time for no one to miss me.

"…you should do it," one of them was saying furiously. "You're the strongest."

"Yeah, which means I can beat you to a pulp, which means *you* should do it," a guard responded.

"Hey," another said, hope in his words. "Why don't we get someone else to?"

I lowered my head in the rain. The hot ball of hatred in my soul had its own pulse. I felt eyes on me and deliberately kept my steps short. "What, her?" someone scoffed. "Sure. Let's get nana to carry half a dozen dead people out here," he mocked. I heard a short scuffle, a few dull thuds, a muttered curse. "Go. Hurry up."

The advice wasn't meant for me, but nonetheless, I followed it, ducking out of sight and picking a winding path back to the castle, my heart beating quickly.

A dozen dead people that the La'Angi guard *weren't* directly responsible for was a truly shocking turn of events.

The alleys and backstreets were known to me after so long in this godless place. I kept my head down, and my feet flew over the ground.

How many were dead?

We needed to leave tonight or we needed information, and I knew which it was going to be. How was the illness spreading, what treatments had been tried? I flexed my fingers in my gloves and felt the bite of the cold, wet leather. Bad weather for a sickness. If it snowed this year, travel would be hard. The ground would already be hard to turn. If many graves were needed, they'd be in trouble.

Thomas started when I came in, waking with a half-choked snore and blinking tired eyes in the dark hollows of his face. As I looked up from the handle of the door, I realized my wig was still partly visible in the basket on my arm. Furious with myself, I flicked my cloak back over my shoulders and exaggerated the arch of my back so that like magework, his eyes dropped to my breasts. He wouldn't notice how wet the rest of me was. I swept past him with a toss of curls and a smirk none of them ever understood.

Some guard he was.

Audrey was stirring when I got in. I laid out my wet cloak and boots, then threw another log on the fire. We were ready to flee at a moment's notice, but we'd been that way for years. I had three caches of weapons, clothing, and coin.

I wondered, as I drew back the curtains with a ruthless flick, what her bloodsworn guards would do if we left.

Simplest to silence them.

She half-rolled, half-fell out of bed, her grace stripped from her by the nightmares stalking her sleep. I went to my own room and swapped out my plain dress, then took a scarf to try to contain my hair, at least for a time. I met her in the training room. The space wasn't fancy, but we weren't fancy people.

We didn't need to be fancy to take down the Butcher. We needed to be strong.

We sat together in silence, hands on our bellies. I breathed deeply and turned my attention inward to the feel of the coldness of the air on my nostrils, the strength in my stomach as it forced my hands up, the deflation as the air left me. I ran my mind slowly over my body as it took over the deep, healing breaths. I assessed the strength of every joint, every muscle. My feet were cold, but strong—my calves a little tight today. My knees might stick when I stand, but my thighs would carry me forever. When I was done with my assessment, when my mind was firmly on my own flesh and blood, anchored to this reality, I let myself belong, for a time, in that space of calm. And when I had to break the calm, I did so gently and respectfully. To have come so far and done so much, my body deserved no less. I stretched those trustworthy sinews and muscles out patiently, preparing them for training.

Audrey took longer than usual to do the same today. It didn't surprise me. While waiting for her, I went on to strengthening exercises I could do myself. Once she was ready, we started with basic combat drills that we could both do in our sleep. I watched her move, the way she shifted her weight, the angle of her fist, the set of her shoulders. We broke apart silently. I held out a hand, and she tapped it gently. *Fight, begin.*

I leaped at her, and she caught me, gripping me hard so I couldn't overwhelm her. We grappled together, a friendly but earnest competition. We sparred, rested, and sparred again. We fought on our feet, with quick strikes that never hit hard. We fought on the ground, using limbs as levers and joints as locks.

"Drink," I said after we broke apart, wiping the sweat off my brow with my arm.

We rested for a time. She returned with the staffs we often practiced with, and we ran through drills for a time. The monotony of it let my brain relax even as my body hummed with strength awoken. We could've pushed harder, but this was a marathon, not a sprint. We took our time.

Our routine eventually carried us back out of the training room, though I'd have preferred to stay there, in that place where problems and time seemed suspended. I took a seat before the fire while we broke our fast together, listening to its happy crackle absently as I watched Audrey.

She was clearly deep in thought. There was no point waiting, but still, I held what I knew a little longer than I could have, letting her finish her meal before explaining what I'd seen.

It didn't take her long to make the same links I made. If guardsmen began to refuse to deal with bodies, it would mean they'd sit on the street. The illness would spread. And, just as deadly, if they refused orders, they then were marked as dissident and had no cause to follow any orders.

She paced, digesting the information. We didn't discuss it at length. I saw her glance at the window—at the length of shadows. "Passable day to visit the market."

She hadn't asked what I'd been doing. There was nothing to discuss. We both understood that.

"Do you need to see it yourself?" I asked her, holding the sting of hurt at bay until I knew it was warranted. It wasn't like Audrey to interrogate the truth of my words. Not like this.

"I do if I'm going to take it to Steward Daniel," she said, the words laden with the promise of conflict.

So, she wanted to go to the top. I wondered if that was because she didn't know the power of the people. "The market would be risky. We'd be better to ride. We could tour the orchards with the guards." If I could convince her to flee, mayhap I could kill her guards and hide them in barrels of apples or some such.

I was pondering how much effort it would be to dispose of Mortemon and Thomas when Audrey said crisply, "I'll need Chay to go far."

"Why?" I asked, suspecting she'd be happier to feed the La'Angi men to the fish.

She just sent me a level look. I paused, assessing the darkness under her eyes, remembering how her bed had creaked and groaned as she tossed last night, and wondered how close to a lie I could ride this omission.

The words to deflect her died on my tongue, though. I couldn't do it. I hated that I couldn't, because I knew what would come next. Aside from anything else, I knew she wouldn't forgive me for it.

"I assume you'd need to order the Captain to arrange his attendance." They wouldn't have executed him yet.

Her mouth popped open, horrified. I was glad to see fury, not tears, in her eyes. Even tears would've been okay. Fury *and* tears meant the day would be useless.

"They *held* him?" she demanded.

"I should have told you," I admitted. "You assumed, and I let you."

"Isolde," she said slowly, as if she picked out every single syllable with deliberation, "no one else will ever hold your place in my heart. But my heart has space to hold others."

The knife hit home. She lifted her skirts and climbed the steps rapidly. I remained behind, teeth gritted against the pain.

I wasn't jealous of those louts. I knew how little they had to offer and what a burden they'd be, but I wasn't jealous.

It was easier for her to assume the worst of me than to acknowledge she was going to put us all in danger by delaying further.

I caught the cloak she tossed at me and threw it over my shoulders, but I stopped her before she could storm off. "People are dying," I reminded her. "They died on his sword yesterday, but they also died at the hands of a mage trained to heal, and from the sickness. It's spreading. We don't know how fast. We could already have it."

"Then we'd best stay where people are motivated to find a cure," she said, her tone as steely as my own. "My father will be gone for *years,* Isolde. You said it yourself. The winter will make the roads harder for our pursuers, but it'll make them harder for us, too. We decided against cutting through Ange's Pass this late in the season, so there's *nothing* to be gained for leaving tonight instead of in two moons' time."

Nothing? "Distance from sickness is not nothing," I hissed. "Freedom is not *nothing*!"

She pressed her fist to her chest, her long mouth twisted in a bitter line. "Freedom is *here,* Isolde. That's what you taught me. They can't take it from us until they bleed us dry."

The knife twisted. I heard her go, and for once I wasn't a half-step ahead.

My future stretched out before me, bleak. Heavy stone walls, rules that ate at our souls, petty, meaningless battles that would never be enough to disrupt the locways.

Chilled to my bones, I looked out the window at the patch of blue in the sky, but the wind hastened it out of sight, to be replaced by heavy clouds.

I wasn't wrong about her. I knew what she could do.

I just wanted her to do it.

CHAPTER TWENTY-FIVE
CHAY

"To be born ignorant is common, to remain ignorant is noble." ~ *Southern saying*

Their steps echoed down the dungeon's corridor. It was a group of them, this time, not the pair who'd gone down the hall and tormented the heir a few cells down.

Either they were coming to kill me or haul me back up to keep on serving.

Staring up at where the dark ceiling surely was, I couldn't figure out which I'd prefer. And didn't that just say everything there was to say about this whole situation?

I'd never gone to visit my mother's grave. I'd visited her while she was alive after I became a squire, then again after I was knighted and had my own land, and later, when I'd heard my sister, Caitie, was back home widowed, with three little ones. Three times in total since I'd somehow gotten away with my life and enough of my soul intact that I'd been able to heal.

They'd never left. Ma had passed the winter before last.

Consumption. Caitie was still there, best as I knew, smoothing over our old man's bad temper and trying to shush her children so they didn't attract attention. Her eldest would be almost old enough to take as a squire.

I'd planned on going back in a few years and seeing if he'd want to come on with me. But I'd never gone back to farewell my ma.

Every time I'd seen her, I'd said goodbye. Every time since I'd watched his hands lock around her throat until she went blue.

The keys rattled against the door, and I saw through the gap the flicker of light on a man's irritated looking face.

Well, they weren't here for my death, then.

The door swung open with an almighty groan, and I looked over despite myself, sick of my own company.

I didn't know what the collar pin meant on the shirt of the man who held the keys, but I *was* surprised to see Her Ladyship Herself tight-lipped behind him. For just a moment, I remembered her as she'd been in the orchard—hard as steel and just as deadly.

She hadn't left.

She ought to.

"Sir Chay," Collar-Pin said stiffly. "You're returning to your post immediately."

The lady clasped her hands before her, looking at the guard expectantly. She'd had that same expression when she'd asked me to be her champion. My heart twisted in my chest at the memory.

"The guard apologizes for the misunderstanding," Collar-Pin went on, color in his cheeks, the torch in his hand wobbling.

So I suited her better alive than dead.

Who else would slay a child for her?

Sick to my stomach, I hauled myself up. "You're out without your proper escort," I noticed, throwing salt on wounds. Whose, I wasn't sure.

"The dungeons were closer than my tower after I'd been to see the Captain," she said primly. "And Mortemon cannot be raised."

She'd set that up. I was tempted to point out that Audrey had sent me after a mage while she trotted all over the castle just yesterday, and she hadn't been kidnapped then. But I could see the way they were already looking at me and realized I hadn't bowed or given her the title she'd been born with.

Too late now. I scrubbed a hand over my face and shuffled into the crowded corridor. Where Audrey went, so did Isolde and Thomas, of course, one old hound with trusting eyes and another ready to defend the hand that fed it.

Audrey looked me up and down so carefully that I wondered if she wanted me to lift a foot to inspect my shoes.

"I see you're injured, sir."

I didn't look at the guardsman. I hadn't started it, and I hadn't finished it, either. But I knew I wasn't the only one aching all the same.

"Sir?"

"Apologies, my lady. I didn't know that was a question."

"It wasn't," she agreed. "It was a polite conversation starter. The response is generally a similar comment on the same topic."

"I'm not trained in politeness, my lady." Behind her, Thomas' eyes flickered closed briefly. I could almost hear the man's prayers.

He was going to need them.

"I respect that, sir," she said, and her smile was small and kind. "That's why I explained it to you. Come, now."

I saw red. She turned, and I was forced to fall into the crowd around her, ignoring the smug looks the guardsmen were sending me.

I'd been thrown in the cursed dungeons for killing innocent children to defend *her* neck, when *she* was too stupid to leave her own pretty prison, and she had the arrogance to take a shot at *me?*

Something heavy hit a locked dungeon door on the way out. Long, thin, dirty fingers wrapped around the metal a second later, and big eyes peered through the bars.

Thomas and Isolde both had pushed Audrey behind them. The torches in the group bobbed. "I thought you must've come to ask me to eat your pussy," the woman said, her eyes fixed on Audrey. "Since we didn't get to finish last time."

Beside me, Audrey looked at Collar-Pin in accusation.

The prisoner's whole arm looped out through the bars now, pushing up her sleeve. I figured, after what I'd heard, the odds of the darkness on her skin being shadow or dirt was low. I remembered Darrius' words about a mage restarting her heart, his confidence in her breaking.

"I'd do it better'n them, and we all know it," she said with a grin, big green eyes sharp as shattered glass. "You're in my dreams, woman. Let me be in yours."

I scratched at my jaw again. I didn't hate that line, but by the Son, talk about a strange time to proposition someone.

But what an excellent time to get someone's attention.

"I'm going to be sending Isolde to check on her well-being regularly," Audrey said to Collar-Pin. "If I see any fresh bruises, I'm also seeing fresh heads on pikes. Are we clear?"

She didn't see the patronizing look Collar-Pin sent at her back, but I did, and I didn't love it. She was an arrogant shit who hadn't learned when to cut her losses, but she was right. Whoever the hell that prisoner was to the South, and whether or not she ate cunt like a champion, she didn't deserve what she was getting.

"Sir Chay," Audrey said, two steps ahead of me on the stairs, the red in her hair drinking in the glow from the torches. I followed at the edge of her light, keen to get out of the dungeons. "Sir Thomas. Traditionally, executions are done in La'Angi with an axe. Are either of you proficient?"

I didn't look at Isolde. I knew damned well what weapons the Matri'sion used, and how well. I wouldn't have been surprised if the lady herself had been trained in the axe, even if she *was* useless in a crisis. Thomas mumbled something about preferring the spear.

"I'm only passable," I offered in solidarity with the woman left in the dark. "If it's just the occasional need, I can assist in cleaning up the mess. But if it may be a regular occurrence, I ought to increase my training."

"Splendid. We'll visit the armory."

I recognized the noble *we* there; the collective that did not, in fact, apply to her.

I didn't tell her the thought made my belly roll because it didn't matter. I'd already become her executioner. I may as well be outfitted for the job.

CHAPTER TWENTY-SIX
ISOLDE

"Hruudwulf looked upon his followers with hunger and fear as the moon crept over the mountain. 'I do not wish to be like this,' he whispered to Gaelena. 'But this curse is beyond my control.'" ~ *Southern lore*

I'd been glad the would-be assassin had slipped her mind for so long. As soon as that woman had thrown herself at the cell door, though, I'd known Audrey would get involved.

"I'm to take the messages to the pigeons, and use the birds matching the colored wax," he repeated, looking down at the tubes in his hands that held the urgent requests for information Audrey had spent hours penning. "Then you want me to go to the prisoner. You want me to see if she needs clothing, food, or healing?" Thomas repeated, frowning. "But you *actually* want me to learn her name, how she's being treated, and who seems to feel strongly about her. Is that correct, my lady?"

"Yes," Audrey confirmed.

He nodded, his brow furrowed. "And, my lady, you'll remain here? To receive my report?"

He was worried she'd again ignore the Butcher's orders. Mortemon had been found coming out of an extensively joyful time with a few women and a lot of knappchs, but he wasn't up to his job yet.

I breathed in the tisane as it steeped and let her settle Thomas' ruffled feathers. She did a passable job of it, but he was only just leaving as Chay was returning, freshly bathed and tightening the sword belt around his waist. Impatience gnawed at me as I saw her eyes lingering on his hands on his belt. She was distracted by the knight, and not in a productive way.

"Would you like a brew?" Audrey asked him.

"No." He didn't ask for permission before he stretched out in her reading chair beside the hearth. He didn't put his boots up on the table and kick off her latest pile of reports, at least.

She perched on the edge of her seat, her expression earnest. "I'm sorry about those children, and I'm sorry you were held in the dungeons and mistreated. Can I do anything now to help?"

I sipped the drink and warmed my behind on the coals while he pondered that.

"Don't put yourself in stupid positions," he decided, finally.

Audrey nodded, no doubt putting far more weight in those words than they deserved. She *should* have been able to attend an unwell family without anticipating the *children* trying to attack her. And yes, I'd seen it coming, but that was my role. It was his, too, and *he* hadn't prevented the situation. So we'd all been stuck having to react to it instead.

"Is there anything specifically you'd like to advise on?" she asked him. "That's a genuine question."

He touched his fingertips to the black eye that didn't look too sore. "Whatever you're planning to help that woman in the dungeons, send her." He jerked his chin at me.

Another larger mouthful was uncomfortably hot against my tongue. I resisted the urge to sigh. There went my last hope of convincing her to do exactly that.

"Why is that?" Audrey asked, frowning.

"Because she's Matri'sion," the knight said, the words inflectionless. "And they won't see her coming."

"Her name is Isolde," Audrey said coolly. "You think stealth is required for a successful entry?"

I cleared my throat. "I'd advise we wait for Thomas' report," I jumped in before Chay could dig us any deeper and mention that *of course* the guards wouldn't suspect a *woman*.

I'd seen the grab marks on her arms. I didn't know if Audrey had, though.

"Do I get a battle axe now?" he asked her. "Or are you content with my sword?"

She made a noise of annoyance. "That talk was bluff."

It didn't need to be, though. I thought of the rumblings I'd heard about the Captain disagreeing with Steward Daniel's decisions. A well-placed arrow and just the tip of a knife at the right time, in the right place?

She couldn't keep the city, but she could bring it down.

"So I won't be executing anyone else?" he asked. "Well, that's even better than asking to not be in charge of killing children. You have my gratitude."

I watched the way her eyes darkened and the rapid pulse in her neck. Her hands didn't shake as she set down the cup, but adrenaline coiled in me. "I know you're mocking me," she said quietly, "because you're hurting."

He snorted, shutting his eyes. "Astute."

With his eyes closed, he missed the genuine grief in her expression. But I saw it. I saw it, and hurt for her, and hurt for myself because I was beyond feeling bad for every little bump and bruise on an innocent party.

"I swear to you, Chay," she said, the words heavy, "I'll never ask you to take a life in my name again."

"Don't recall you asked," he said, the relaxed pose looking forced. "I was ordered."

Color in her cheeks, she picked up her cup. "Not by me."

"Your actions dictate mine, *my lady.*" He stopped feigning nonchalance, sitting up. "You ought to be the safest woman in the whole country, protected by all this wealth *and* a secret Matri'sion warrior. You could just waltz on out of here any time you liked and live a long, *happy* life somewhere that bottom-feeder could never find you. And yet, you've needed *me* to save your skin twice this moon?"

"Don't think you're special," I recommended, my temper spiking but my words remaining cool. "You just happened to be in the right place and holding a sharp object."

"Which *you* weren't," he snarled at me.

"Funny, because I recall I held them off plenty forcefully, considering I *had* no steel."

"No steel?" he repeated, incredulous. "Are you a Matri'sion or a mouse?"

I drew breath to hit back, but Audrey, to my shock, laughed at him. I turned, stunned, to see her, hand pressed to her mouth trying to hold the mirth in, tears forming in her eyes as she gasped for breath. "I'm sorry," she managed, standing. "Oh, I'm sorry." She grabbed me with her spare hand, and I couldn't help but smile at that overflow of amusement. "By the One, sir," she said breathlessly, turning away from him, "I don't know what sort of mice you get in the west, but I doubt you want to see Isolde with steel in her hands." And without ever looking back, she vanished up the stairs.

He sat in her chair, deflated, staring after her. I couldn't read his expression, but there was some confusion in there, like he'd expected she'd collapse at his feet.

I didn't tell him that she'd been trained to take a lot of hits, but wouldn't stand to see others take them. He'd figure that out, or not. If he came for me a few more times, it wouldn't be too hard to convince her all her guards were merely burdens.

Still, the small twinge of compassion I felt for the big lump surprised me.

He *had* been short-changed. There was no denying it. But she'd never once asked more of him than he'd already been forced to give. He didn't know that when she said she'd never ask him to take a life, she'd meant it.

And now his uses had yet another limitation.

It felt like she'd stolen all the joy from the room when she left. I was glad she'd helped herself to it. "Be careful," I told him, gathering up her cup and brew. "We've no room for more enemies."

"Are you threatening me?" he asked, the words low and dangerous.

I rolled my eyes, and the compassion died brutally. As if I'd expend energy to *give up* an advantage? A friendly reminder was wasted on this man. "Mayhap you ought to do a lap of the battlements," I suggested. "Cool off." And mayhap we'd get lucky, and the north wall would crumble under the weight of his ego, sending him for a nice dip.

Upstairs, Audrey was brushing out her hair. She paused to take a sip. "What do you plan to do about the would-be assassin?"

Her expression became determined, and I sent a moment of prayer to my gods for patience. "We could take her with us."

It wasn't a question, but the tone she used, the lift of her voice at the end, and the way she lingered undermined the strength of her statement.

She'd gone toe-to-toe with the Captain of the guard without losing her cool, though. That had been a drawn-out exercise in "how to out-polite a man furious he's backed himself into a corner". The poor child deserved some gentleness.

There wasn't much to be had in La'Angi, and I had little to spare. But I said, "Audrey, you know that's a bad idea."

"She wants to hurt my father," Audrey pointed out, sensibly. "I want to hurt my father. We're practically sworn allies, Isolde."

"A lot of people want to hurt your father," I reminded her. "For good reason. That doesn't mean they'll be your friend. People can dislike the Butcher *and* not give a tinker's cuss about you." This one had also already attempted to murder Audrey, but I figured that could go without saying. "If you're curious about having her in your bed, I can introduce you to some lovely women who might strike your fancy and not your jugular." Color flared in her cheeks, but I didn't know if that was because she was uncomfortable with the topic, or with the accuracy of my guess. "Or if it's just a fleeting experience you'd prefer, you're best to pay for quality services from a professional."

She cleared her throat. "That wasn't my intention. I assumed what she said was simply a ploy to catch my attention."

It had worked, too. "If you take her out, she'll attempt to kill you, then flee."

"I think you're right." She sighed in regret, setting down her comb gracelessly to nurse her tisane. "Why didn't he kill her?"

Playing "let's predict the Butcher" was one of the games I enjoyed less than others. "Leverage. Amusement. Control. Evidence." I shrugged. "Why should he? It isn't like she can escape and cause him harm, and feeding one more mouth is no strain."

"Do you think she's important?" Audrey mused. "To the Southerners?"

I sighed. "If she is, what does it change?" She was stuck in another rut, and I could just see where we were going. "If I agree to free her, we could escape in her wake. Use her like a distraction."

"Divide their attention," Audrey agreed, clearly thinking she could talk me into fleeing *with* the woman rather than *away from her.* "I like it, Isolde."

I did, too, if she'd agree to actually get out of here. But when I looked into my charge's eyes, I didn't believe it.

She was dug in. This was her home. It was on the tip of my tongue to acknowledge it, but she turned away, finishing her drink in one hearty mouthful, breaking the moment. I held in another sigh, feeling it nestle up under my ribs.

It had been a long time since my encounter with the soothsayer's prophetic vision. The burning need I'd had to end the control the locways had on the lives of so many, to disrupt our predetermined destinies, had settled over time. Whenever I recalled where we were and how long we'd been here, I had to struggle against a sense of failure.

But mayhap we were exactly where we needed to be to untether fate from its moorings. It was possible my charge was the agent of change. She'd driven plenty of it so far. And if she wasn't, well, she'd likely be another lesson. So I left Audrey to find joy in her hope a little longer.

CHAPTER TWENTY-SEVEN

ISOLDE

"Before the growth goes the fire." ~ *Raider's Ban proverb*

I hesitated in the shadows as the guardsmen trekked tiredly toward their mess, leaving the odd spot of mud behind them.

"…the Captain gone, surely?"

"He'll put Smythesson in, for sure. I bet the asslicker'll forget the coin he owes me the minute he chooses my damned patrols."

"Smythesson is greener than the orchard in spring," the first guard disagreed. "Who cares if his cousin is a noble?"

"Steward Daniel does," the second guard told him, glumly. "I don't like this. My Mara, she's worried, too."

"We can't just shut our doors," the first one said. "Lock it all out."

The second guard fell silent, and I listened to their steps as they retreated. They'd cleared one corner too many for me to understand the next question the first guardsman asked, but I didn't chase after them.

I wondered what a guard from the main gates might report. Increased traffic, as people took long-overdue visits to family in the country, or relocated to better climes as they'd spoken about their whole lives?

And where were these people going?

Thomas was on the door when I returned, looking the exact same as he did every day. I couldn't imagine the energy that sort of uniformity took. I doubted he could imagine anything else.

"Mistress," he said, meeting my eyes. "I understand the lady wishes to visit the prisoner in the dungeons."

She did, because we needed enough of an in with this would-be assassin that she didn't kill us on sight, or refuse our aid and complicate the whole situation. And in typical Audrey fashion, she'd also decided this woman's well-being was at least partially her responsibility.

"I was in the city this morning," he went on, stiffly. "It appears the illness is spreading rapidly. Everywhere."

I paused, considering his wooden expression and how much it must've cost him just to utter those words to me, breaking his unblinking guardsman's pose. "Go on."

He glanced toward my hand on the door. "Reports are coming from local provinces. Even over the bay. I thought mayhap you might express these concerns."

"You don't want her to go out."

"I don't want her to get sick, mistress."

I didn't, either. Accepting the information with a nod, I returned to the rooms and found Chay waiting beside the fire, surrounded by flecks of wood from his whittling. He was lousy at it, but at least he cleaned up after himself and didn't say much.

Past him, sitting in silence at her desk, was Audrey. Her quill swirled over the surface of a messy page to one side. She glanced up at me, the thumb that had been flipping a parchment up and down stilling.

"What was said?" she asked me, and I felt her attention like a deer felt a hunter's eyes.

Appreciation and pride swelled in my chest. I closed the door firmly behind me.

"No one could answer my question. On the way back, I *did* hear, the Captain is unwell."

Her hand stilled. "He's got it?"

I shrugged. There were more illnesses than the one we'd come across, including self-induced ones from too much revelry. The Captain wasn't known for such things, but when the Duke was away, the guards would play. Mortemon was proof of that.

Audrey's expression was caught in the middle distance. I let her mind whir, going to the window to look over the city.

She'd figure out the situation with the assassin. I was more worried about the possibility of them locking down the keep. As if to underscore this concern, my eye was drawn to the thin ribbons of smoke rising from the lower city levels.

It was only a matter of time, really. The Master Steward would know that by now. An incurable, deadly illness seemed like just the thing to lock out.

Except the harvest wasn't in.

Before I could ask Audrey what supplies the keep had, which would help me figure out how long we would have some small freedom, a knock came from the outer door. Chay rolled to his feet, hurriedly sweeping the worst of the shavings into the fire and striding out. Audrey shuffled her papers, putting a page on top that looked equally as dull as whatever she'd hidden.

As soon as I saw Steward Daniel's heavy keys of office and patronizingly worried expression, energy rushed through my body.

We were going to have to go over the wall if they locked us in, through a sickened city. Or wait it out, knowing the castle was already compromised, and lose more of our precious lifespans to this prison.

"Unfortunately, my lady, I come to you under dire circumstances." He eased himself down into the chair opposite hers at her desk, uninvited. Thomas and Chay marched around the back of her and took up their stations much like they did whilst she ate in the great hall.

Trusting Audrey to have this wasted seed's measure, I opted to take the door.

I wondered if Audrey would see the opportunity here.

Chay was already known to kill infected people who approached her, after all. One more on that list would be plenty believable. Chay didn't even need to do it himself. She hadn't sworn another death would ever be *attributed* to him, had she?

"It would appear the plague has spread across the city with frightening speed," he said, leaning forward, and that word made me pause. Was it a plague, now? "As you saw yourself some days ago, it is also in these walls."

Interesting that he could acknowledge both facts. Most La'Angi men only saw the information that best suited them.

"We have our best working on developing cures," he said. "Please, don't be alarmed."

Audrey's brows rose fractionally.

"But you *do* need to take this seriously." He took a folded piece of paper magically from somewhere and offered it to her. I wished I'd been able to see that move. Paper was easier to hide than knives, but if it were actually a slight of hand trick with some skill, he'd bear watching closer than I thought.

"This is a list of symptoms, as closely as we can identify them. I knew you'd want to know them. And my lady…it may just save you if you do."

Audrey took the paper and set it before her. "What is your current strategy?"

"We're pouring as much support into the harvest as we can," he told her, and that sickly-sweet patronization faded. "Captain Xavier is setting up a field hospital in the lower marketplace."

"Why not the more central marketplace?" she asked, frowning.

His smile was paternalistic. "Because, my lady, the poor have a harder time carrying their sick than the rich do."

Her eyes narrowed slightly, but before she could question him, he was resting a hand on her desk. "I need to ask something of you, my lady. Something that will help."

Unease crept up my spine at the urgency in his tone. I saw Chay shift slightly. Thomas may as well have been hewn of wood.

"Ask," Audrey said. And I hated that her eyes were no longer narrowed.

"I need to quarantine you, my lady." She opened her mouth to object, and I watched with no surprise as he held up a hand to silence her. "You are the bastion of hope for our people. If they know you are still well, they will continue to work."

"How—"

"The plague may take some of us, or many of us, my lady, but the winter will take us all without provisions." The patronization was gone and his second hand was on her desk, the aged, ink-stained fingers laced together. "I need you to be safe so you can continue to encourage the people. I know you've a soft heart. The Duke, may the One smile on him, disapproves of that, but it's your strength."

She was looking at me, now, fury and hunger in her gaze, in the thin line of her lips and the razor set of her shoulders. "For how long?" she asked.

"I've no way of knowing—"

"Draw your battle line, Master Steward," she said, and the words were so cold I felt a chill wash over me, encasing the heat of pride in my chest. "I will not agree to indefinite terms on such an arrangement."

He sighed with regret, as if he actually cared, and I didn't even laugh. "Would you give us until the end of winter, my lady? For La'Angi?"

She scoffed, and I admired the derision she managed in that one small, ladylike sound. "Over a season of being cooped up inside?"

"As we often are anyway," he agreed. "We face hard times in the city, but 'tis the perfect season to be securely inside, if there must be such a time. Please, my lady. Remain where it is safe. For the good of your people."

Whatever argument she'd been having with him paused instantly. "I'll do it," she told him. "If I see you write my father asking for aid."

I resisted the urge to laugh at the myriad of emotions that flickered over Steward Daniel's face at this simple but effective way to ensure the his honesty.

"The trip out of the tower might put you at risk."

"Then allow me to witness," I offered, and Audrey nodded firmly.

He shook his head. "With respect, mistress, your movements put the lady at risk every bit as much as her own movements do. If you are to catch sick, surely she will follow."

He was right, and that irritated me.

Audrey turned and looked at her guards. Chay stood stony-faced. Thomas glanced hesitantly between us all.

Somehow, I managed to keep the glee from my tone as I requested, "May Thomas be the lady's representative in the castle?"

The Master Steward, when pressed, had no real right to refuse. He had to be the one to ask for aid, but Audrey would stay out from under his feet. He didn't realize how excellent a deal he'd made. She could do a *lot* of damage if left unattended.

Things were shifting. She could see it, too. It was in the thoughtful set of her mouth as she watched Steward Daniel leave with Thomas at his side, in the crease between her brows, and in the light in her eyes.

People were going to die. Nothing that was important was ever easy, and the locways meant too much to these people to trust their participation.

I didn't gloat. But I did cross to where she stood and press my hand to her shoulder, holding firmly. She wasn't the type to solve everything with a stroke of the knife. Perhaps that was best.

"He's scared," she breathed.

"As well he should be." I squeezed her shoulder. "Come. Train."

She shook her head a little as if to dispel the shock, then settled her gaze on me, firmed her shoulders, and followed where I led.

CHAPTER TWENTY-EIGHT
AUDREY

"The ultimate power is not needing to care." ~ Matri'sion lesson

He always stood a little back from the window. Even with his bred-in-the-bone rebellious streak, Chay respected that it'd be viewed unkindly if he was seen in *my* space.

That didn't stop him from invading it, of course. It just meant he took some steps to reduce the chance anyone externally would notice. And I, of course, couldn't do much about it, short of ordering him out.

I seriously considered doing just that for the third time since dawn as I flicked a wood shaving off the arm of my reading chair. And we'd only been officially trapped together for two days.

"Something strange is going on," he said, angling his head as if hoping it might help him understand better. His belt jangled. I thought of those thumbs, hooked into his belt, and shifted in my seat. "Even for La'Angi."

"What sort of strange?" I asked, then shook myself. He wasn't my friend, and he didn't want to be. That was fine. He had no reason at all to want to be here, speaking to me. "Is it related to the plague?" I asked, hoping he hadn't heard the first enquiry.

"I don't think so." He glanced over at me. "But I'm no expert. Mayhap *you* ought to have a look, *my lady*."

The way he said *my lady* made it sound like a curse spat out by the Old Gods. Rather than irritate him and go look, I stayed where I was seated. "If there are any unwell or dead, let me know," I said, turning back to historical reports on metal use, trying to figure out what might be normal.

Certainly not his jangling.

"Caring about people after they're dead *would* set you apart from your father," he mused. "A wise choice as ever, Audrey."

"My father cares about the dead," I said, keeping it light. "They spread disease. I hear it's harder to dispose of a man than it is to kill him. Especially in large numbers." I smiled at him brightly. Of course those big hands of his were hooked in his belt, his hip cocked. "If you really disliked me so much, I'm sure you could find an accurate way to insult me."

His eyes narrowed. "You're saying you're like the Butcher of Wolfswail and then saying *I'm* not insulting you, right? Do you think being like that man is a compliment?"

Don't engage, Audrey. But it was right there. "Are you defending that poor attempt to hurt my feelings, sir? Of all the similarities to have with the Butcher of Wolfswail—" I paused, unsure if I'd ever spoken that moniker before, but it didn't taste ill on my tongue, so I went on, "—being pragmatic is one I will claim."

He looked at the scroll in my hand. "Ah, yes. So pragmatic of you to lock yourself inside and read poetry for days whilst others die."

"You believe I'm so powerful I could make a difference if I left?" I asked, raising my brows. "My mere presence may somehow lift a plague?" I clicked my tongue and settled in. "You flatter me, sir."

"Would if I could," he muttered, and heat washed through me, hot on the heels of confusion. Then I untangled the wordplay. Not *compliment*, but *flatter*.

Feeling my cheeks burning, I pretended not to hear at all, in case he'd meant something entirely different. But though my eyes skimmed over the letters, I couldn't help but wonder what sorts of things Chay may compliment a person on…and whether he truly did only see my father when he looked at me.

Eventually, Chay moved from the window and took up his whittling. By the time I judged he'd been there long enough for it to be obvious I was avoiding him, the light was fading, and Isolde was curled in the chair nearby, napping. I stretched my aching back and set the letters I'd received aside.

The plague was everywhere. No one had found a curse. Any mage who attempted to interact with it died instantly.

There was no cure.

I walked over to the big window, looking out over the city. There were no new smoke plumes from when I'd looked that morning, at least none thick enough to identify in the dying light. The gates would be closing soon enough. I wondered how long it would be before they'd be letting the prisoner in the dungeons out. How long would it take her to reach her people? What would she tell them?

It was probably strange that I wanted to have a conversation with my would-be killer. It wasn't because her suggestion had been tempting. It wasn't.

But who *spoke* like that?

And how did they behave?

I rolled my shoulders in another attempt to dismiss the tightness, glancing across the bailey below in time to see Steward Daniel ride out. Surely not. He'd have time to clear the city, but not to return. In his wake, a handful of others rode, some with horses on a lead.

"Isolde," I said, ignoring the way my heart had begun to hammer.

She was there in an instant, wide awake, but only witnessed the last rider and his train of two horses. "What?" she asked me, the question holding no accusation.

I had to swallow the knot in my throat. Words crowded my head, and when she looked at me, I forced myself to say, "I think Steward Daniel is fleeing."

"What?" she repeated, this time incredulously. "He wouldn't dare. What did you see?"

But the words were all stuck, now, filling my brain so much that my mouth couldn't empty them. Because if the Master Steward left, who was in charge? What steps had he *really* put in place to help people? Was the Captain actually dying, and if he did, and the Master Steward was gone, who would remain?

Had he planned this? To lock me in, and then run away?

"That'd explain it," Chay drawled from where he sat near the chessboard.

"Explain what?" Isolde demanded.

I watched as, along the walls, guards began to light torches. "The cart loads of stuff I saw earlier. I said it was strange."

He had.

Below us, a glow came from behind some shutters left ajar. Were they being lit too, or was it just more obvious as the light bled from the sky? And would everyone bleed from the city, too, in the wake of Steward Daniel? Would they go like cider from a cracked jug, rushing anywhere they could? Or was the jug not yet so badly cracked that it was inevitable? Could I still right that jug?

A lethal smile was creeping over Isolde's face. "There's no one he could've possibly named," she said, the words low and full of threat, "who could hold the keep together."

The Captain was dying. The Master Steward had put forth a young man, loyal to my father, to take his place. He would've left his assistant in charge. He'd tucked me away, safe. He was tucking himself away, too.

The harvest wasn't coming in fast enough, or the plague was spreading too quickly.

He was going to let them all die.

Isolde stepped in front of me, but she was still smiling. My eyes fell on the bow of her lips as she spoke to me, but the words were too much, and I felt the tears spilling over.

This wasn't how it was supposed to go. It wasn't supposed to get this bad.

I needed to be present. I needed to stand behind whoever was managing the field hospital and the relief efforts.

We have to stay. The words wouldn't come out. They filled my head like caltrops, cutting me up no matter what I tried to think or do. This was my place. This had to be my place. I couldn't give voice to the words to explain that I couldn't leave like this, like a rat off a sinking ship. I *could* do something here.

"Audrey," Isolde said, and pre-empting her heartache, I held the weight of her disappointment. I was being crushed.

But I couldn't afford to break.

"We should leave, too, but we can't," Chay said mockingly. "First, we must attempt to rescue the poor, lowly people. Our intentions are good, so what does the impact matter?"

"Go cry into your bunk," Isolde snapped. "And hope that mayhap one day you'll have the courage to try."

He made a noise of disgust. "How *pragmatic* of you," he said, and the barb stung. "You don't know me, Matri'sion, and you never will." His eyes raked over me, though, not Isolde, disappointment in the tight line of his downturned lips.

I reeled, wishing he'd simply struck me instead.

"Promises, promises," Isolde muttered, pressing a handkerchief into my hand.

He was right. I was as likely to lead them all to ruin as they were to make their way there by themselves. I thought of those children, of their rage-filled cries that reverberated in my bones, and the way their black blood had oozed.

I'd gotten them a mage. It was all I could've done, and it hadn't worked.

Rather than retreat to my bed to cry, I snatched up my cloak and left the tower.

The stables were warm and peaceful. Isolde followed me, setting a torch in a bracket silently. I went straight to Storm, who nickered at me and came to snuffle my hair.

I drew in a deep breath, feeling the ground beneath me, just as she did, just as Isolde had taught me. I ran my hand down her smooth muzzle, smelling the hay and horse scents that spoke of safety. She searched me for treats half-heartedly, and I drew from her strength.

"What can she hear?" Isolde asked me, the question patient.

I listened, moving around her to run my hands down her neck. The sounds of the city were different than usual, but not in a way I could put my finger on. Not alarming, just unsettling. In the foreground I heard Vixen in the stall next to her snuffling, and Chay's horse chewing his cud. And then the creak of the door, the torch fluttered threateningly in its bracket with the gust of wind. The jangle of Chay's approach.

I expected more barbs. Bracing myself, I waited, staring at Storm's long, strong neck and the silver, neatly trimmed mane that teased my fingertips.

Instead, I heard the slosh and clatter of a bucket of water, the rattle of brushes, the happy equine snuffles that had once seemed so odd coming from an infamous Raider's Ban warhorse.

Isolde didn't prompt any more questions, just brought me Storm's grooming items, and moved over to her mare.

The three of us worked without speech, and I was lulled by the rhythmic motions. Storm leaned into the brush, and I felt the gentle pressure of her gratitude from the palms of my hands all the way to the soles of my feet.

I'd done what I could. It hadn't been enough that day. Mayhap next time it would be if I tried to learn more and do better. If I didn't forget.

In the aftermath of the emotions, the tiredness crept in. I packed up slowly, loathe to leave Storm but knowing I needed sleep.

Next time, we'll ride, I promised her silently. And a small part of me imagined riding into the sunset, tracking the evening shadows down to the Matri'sion lands. I could imagine the wind buffeting my face and the feel of her strength beneath me, connecting me to this world.

I'd ride, instead, through the apple trees. Because while a part of me wanted to leave, another part of me needed to stay.

As I waited for Isolde to finish, my eyes fell on where Chay was leaning up against his gelding. His expression was one of pain, and whilst the ground threatened to swallow me to see it, I could also see the peace he was drawing from his friend, much as I had with Storm. Demanding he leave would've been so easy. Expected, even. Instead, I turned away quietly to give him what privacy I could. But the image, once seen, was not easy to forget. The furrow in his brows that raised a little in the middle and turned down at the edges, as if in hopelessness. The downward curve at the corner of his lips, the slump in his shoulders, the way his hands had rubbed slow, deep circles in his friend's shoulder in a way that made me ache.

He was angry with me, and that was fair. I'd known he was hurting. It shouldn't have made a difference that I'd seen the evidence of it.

Drawing in a deep breath, I told myself that his horse, at least, could comfort him. Even if I couldn't.

CHAPTER TWENTY-NINE
AUDREY

"Gaelena said, 'What is a curse if not walking the path you are destined for, but did not choose?' But Hruudwulf, in his grief, only heard the words she said and not the magic she wove in the background. Staring at his loved ones, his fangs grew."
~ Southern lore

He stood broodingly beside the fire. I'd given him space last night and this morning, too. He didn't want to talk, and I didn't know that I really did, either. But I would've been able to focus better on my own tasks if he didn't glower quite so much.

"So, we're leaving the tower," Chay said, settling himself beside the fire, his hand on the mantle white-knuckled. The throat of his shirt was open, and the planes of his chest were as tanned as the rest of him. "Anything I ought to know?"

I pulled my eyes away from his chest, and fury pulsed in my head. "There are many things you ought to know. I don't believe it's my role to explain them to you, sir."

"Ah, and *now* you want me to tug my forelock and kneel? I see. And what am I booked in for this afternoon, my lady? Am I a co-conspirator or a yes-man?"

I reminded myself I'd stolen him from his life and forced him to take the lives of others. And I still couldn't stop myself from saying, "I think it's safe if you book yourself in as an unsufferable lump for the remainder of your service, sir. We can decide on details as they arise."

"Today is a fiery day. Noted." He shifted his sword, making a show of loosening it in its scabbard. "At your service, my lady. Since I've no choice."

"I wonder which one of us regrets that more," I muttered, wishing I could get comfortable and dive back into the columns I'd been deciphering. But comfort would mean creasing skirts, and I needed every starched scrap of credibility I could shroud myself in.

"I don't." There was real bitterness in his words as he turned away from me, and despite the way he jangled and the entirely just anger he held onto, my heart twinged for him.

He wasn't likely to forgive me any time soon, and I could live with that. But I didn't have to live with being his jousting dummy, either. I sat there, staring at the page in front of me, running through the different conversations I could have that would explain all fault tracked back to my father.

But it didn't. Those children had died to Chay's sword specifically because *I'd* chosen to be there. I'd wanted to do better than everyone else.

His service, and the strict nature of it, were not my responsibility. That he'd come after me that night to rescue me was *entirely* his decision. I would've been fine, probably.

My skin crawled as I remembered the whirling darkness, nausea, and Mikus' hands.

All of that was not my fault. But I had to bear the weight of those tiny lives. I had to learn from them, and ensure I never made such a mistake again. But that wasn't something I could promise to do. It was something I'd have to live.

Which guided me back to today's itinerary.

Isolde swept in, Thomas behind her, face pale, waiting to one side.

It was early, but the sun was up, and if Steward Daniel's assistant was abed late today, I'd be shocked.

I didn't tell Thomas or Chay our goal. Bees buzzed in my head as we set off, Isolde setting a quick pace beside me. Her eyes raked shadows and darted around corners. Her steps never faltered.

One day, I'd be like that. People would look at me and say, "*She's as reliable as the moon.*"

I quickly identified the stand-in Master Steward, not because I could see the pins of office, but by the pile of papers in his arms, his frustrated expression, and the two haggard guardsmen in front of him. "There *are* no more Healers," the makeshift Master Steward was telling them. "So you've little choice but to tell your fellows that if they're unwell, they ought to stay home and try herbal remedies. Just adjust the roster."

My heart squeezed as the three fell silent, turning to us. The stand-in, whose name I thought might be Romwell or Roswell or Wellross, paled when he saw me.

That didn't usually happen. Not to me. My father, yes.

And with my father in my mind, I asked, "Are we likely to struggle to fill patrols?"

The two guardsmen shared a grim look. Romrosswell bowed to me. "This is a matter for the guard, my lady. Not the likes of you and I."

Ah, a problem not belonging to us, a Master Steward specialty. I noticed the look the steely-haired guardsman gave Thomas over my shoulder. It wasn't a happy look, but it spoke of shared experiences. "How fares the Captain?" I asked, going off-script again in a way I suspect my father would've approved.

The makeshift Master Steward's expression was fixed in lines of calm. "I've named Smythesson as Acting Captain until he recovers."

Or dies. "You did?" I smiled. My hands hung awkwardly beside my body, but I didn't let them lift to cradle myself. "I'm sorry, Master Steward, what was your name?"

The young guard ducked his head to hide a grin. Behind him, the old guard stood, stone-faced.

"I'm Acting Steward Romwell, my lady. Can I arrange a time to discuss this with you?"

"What's 'this?'" I asked. The color in his cheeks rose, and I realized I'd accidentally antagonized him, but I had no regrets. I discarded the line of questioning instantly, though, redirecting to the information I needed. "I understand Smythesson is a loyal La'Angi guardsman. I was hoping to enquire after his qualifications in running such an elaborate organization as the guard."

"Certainly, my lady," Romwell said stiffly. "If you'll step into my office?"

I hesitated, looking between where the assistants had their desks and the Master Steward's rooms.

Cheeks red, he stepped back and indicated the Master Steward's rooms. I'd insulted him a second time, and that one I *did* regret, though probably not as much as I ought.

The office had space for me to sit, a tray of tea that no longer steamed with browning herbs floating in the water, and a decent view of the city.

I paused on the inside of the door, though. The Acting Steward made as if to turn, but the older guardsman stepped forward. "Romwell, this isn't tenable. There are no precedents we can draw on—"

Romwell's hand snapped out, closing around the older guard's gambeson. "Send me Smythesson, then. And if you're so concerned, go and make yourself useful."

Confident I wasn't supposed to see that, I eased out of the doorway. The old guard didn't so much as glance at me. I realized I wasn't breathing as I let myself into the office.

The guard and the Master Steward worked hand-in-glove. They had to. But they were also overseen directly by my father.

"If I need to explain every decision I make to every person in this castle, we'll be in a sorry state by the time the Duke gets back," Acting

Steward Romwell said out in the hallway, and there was no mistaking the threat in his words. "I don't expect he'll have my patience."

There came some murmured conversation. I recognized the tone of platitudes and tried to breathe. My father would be gone for years, but more importantly, he couldn't manage a crisis from afar. These power plays would never have been allowed to draw breath under him.

Romwell was still red-faced when he strode in, papers ruffling in one arm. His hand where he'd grabbed the old guard was muddy.

I'd thought he'd be someone I could put my weight behind. Was I better to stand behind someone who would cause division, or allow the fractures to happen and throw in with someone I liked?

I didn't know enough to choose a good representative for the job of Acting Steward. I knew about supply and demand, I understood distribution and logistics, but I didn't really know what people would *need*.

But I was confident what people didn't need was an ego bigger than this keep.

My carefully scripted options vanished from my mind as I watched him take a seat opposite me. Was it fair to judge his ego so harshly? Would I act any differently in his shoes?

"My lady," he said with a tight, tired smile. "Would you like some tea?"

My stomach curled. "No, thanking you, Master Steward."

He nodded and poured himself a cup. It didn't steam. "You're concerned about the plague," he said, and I nodded. "It's concerning, my lady, so that's the right response. However, I question your judgment in surfacing from your tower so soon."

I'd expected that. "I question Steward Daniel's judgment in leaving."

Romwell's smile was razor thin. "As do many, my lady. There could be extensive unrest, but such things are not uncommon during trying times. Regardless, the safest course for you is the one he explained."

"Not uncommon?" I shook my head. "What time was it not uncommon for all the mages to be dead and gone, the herbs ineffective, and the guard unable to man the walls?" He opened his mouth to object, and I shook my head, hard, because mayhap the guard *could* man them now, but why had those two been so worried if it wasn't on the horizon? "How many of those burning houses were sanctioned by you?" I asked him, and he looked surprised, as if he hadn't thought I'd see the columns of smoke.

He stood, the chair scraping heavily. "And what is it you would have me do that I do not, my lady? I saw the mess you made of those in the hall, what wisdom have you gleaned from your actions?"

The world spun slowly around me. I felt the words crowding in my head. "Turn the tourney grounds into a field hospital," I said, before I could be silenced. "Offer support to transport the sick *out* of the city. Somewhere warm to sleep, food, and company are all things we can offer, and the tourney grounds has space." He was staring at me, but I'd practiced this. "Offer free meals as rewards for those who help bring their sick fellows in. The rich won't want to go to the lower marketplace for treatment, and the poor don't deserve to have the majority of the plague hosted alongside their homes. The tourney grounds are more neutral." He went to argue, but my momentum carried me forward. "If it comes to mass graves, it'll be simpler to manage from the tourney grounds."

He scoffed at me. "The tourney grounds? Free meals?" He shook his head, nose wrinkled as if disgusted by something on his shoe. "We need the harvest so we don't starve this winter. There will be no free meals for anyone except you. Go back to your lessons, my lady. You'll have babes soon enough to fuss over. Enjoy your peace while you can."

The floor opened beneath me. I'd expected refusal, but that hurt. "Your decisions will be documented," I told him, as he put down his armload of papers and gathered up another. "And weighed."

"Yes, my lady," he said tightly. "Good day."

He walked out, leaving me with his untouched tea and the crumpled stack of reports.

I'd be fed, even if no one else would. Why did I hate that so? Yet, if it came to it, yes, I wanted to eat.

"The tourney grounds are a good idea," Thomas murmured. "Get the sick out of the city. Offering free food'll do it, too."

"Of course it would." I glanced up at him. "What's happening with the guard, Thomas?"

He glanced at the door. "I don't know what you mean, my lady."

I stood and shut the damned door. Romwell had basically volunteered his office to me, anyway. "Who is Smythesson, who is standing in opposition, and why is Romwell choosing Smythesson?"

Thomas glanced around, clearly uncomfortable. "My lady…" I waited, watching as he shifted from one foot to another. "Smythesson is no one. He's never done anything. But he's loyal."

That was predictable. "And the opposition?"

His eyes darted again. "My lady, I've never been much for gossip. Truly, I cannot tell you much."

Thomas was hiding something, though. I was sure of it. He knew something. Otherwise, why was he so nervous? "What *can* you tell me?"

He wet his lips, looking at Isolde and then at the tips of my slippers. "I know Kaelson disavowed any position of responsibility after…"

I waited, but the word just faded. "After?"

"Wolfswail."

As would any human with a heart. And the older man, who'd looked at Thomas. "Was that Kaelson there, earlier, speaking to Romwell?" The one with the dirty gambeson who Romwell had been comfortable enough to threaten?

"That's he."

I thought of that ink-stained hand curling in the fabric, and rage-filled, childish screams echoed in my head in warning. "Why did he disavow a position?"

Thomas shook his head.

"War's bitter," Isolde said by way of answer. "The Master Steward named men he can control, not men who will question."

"I can't say, mistress," Thomas answered, head bowed.

It made sense, though.

I wasn't an expert on any of this, and curse Chay's jangling belt, interrupting my thoughts! But if Kaelson had served in a major position during the war, he'd know better than I what to do. And he wouldn't jangle. "If I speak to him, is he likely to be reprimanded?" I asked Thomas.

He hesitated. "Mayhap. If you were known to be seeking him out…"

It'd be seen as going against Romwell's directives.

"Fine." I pushed down the hopeless guilt. "Next stop, then. I've a prisoner to meet." I paused to glance over the papers Romwell had left, but it was all just anticipated harvest numbers. "All in all, that went better than I expected," I said to Isolde. Shock, and then amusement, flared in her gaze. I was treated to a rare toothsome grin, ruthless and full of mirth.

"It's early yet," she said, and the words held both threat and laughter.

CHAPTER THIRTY

ISOLDE

"Different locales will have different healing herbs available. When traveling, enquire at the Wife's shrines. Local women will be able to suggest to you options that grow locally and supplement your existing stores."

~ Growing Greatness: Common Garden Plants in Arcanloc

I stretched my legs to keep pace with her longer gait. The bite of the wind and the hum of my own power took me back to another world, where we'd traveled through trees and clearings, over mountains and rivers, bringing aid to our sisters.

I drew in a deep breath, reveling in the hum of tension and conflict faced head-on. Inside my gloves, my hands flexed. I didn't bear my bow or knives, not today. But I may as well have.

Audrey's hand on the mess room door was big and sure. She opened it with more force than she'd intended, but I doubted anyone else would've picked up the flicker of surprise on her face the moment before it crashed against the wall thunderously. The men within all scrambled to attention as she swept through. Beside her, Mortemon's sunken eyes narrowed.

She didn't pause to acknowledge them as they bowed. I knew it was because she'd struggle to restart once she stopped to consider her actions. I also knew it looked like confidence from the outside. And in a way, it was.

The confidence of hurling yourself into a situation and trusting you'd be able to manage it. That's what she had. The confidence of knowing that there was no better alternative.

The office door of the Captain's rooms was opened. A young, fresh-faced, golden-haired man with a square jaw and dimples stood there, his brows drawn and lips pursed.

"Smythesson," Audrey said, and his eyes widened. She didn't pause in her forward momentum, and he didn't give way. She was as tall as he, and he was unprepared. "Apologies," she said as he staggered, and she let herself in.

He looked at her as if she'd been summoned by forbidden blood magic.

"I require a key to the prisoner in the dungeons," she said, sitting uninvited, with little grace but great aplomb. "I wish to ensure her well-being, as she was a valuable captive of my father's."

"I—my lady." He bowed. "I—of course. If that's your wish, it should do no harm." It was about to do a lot of harm, but he didn't need to know that. "How fare you?" he asked, as he turned to the wall of keys behind him, all carefully labeled.

"Well, thanking you."

I stood behind her chair, Mortemon and Thomas by the door, as Smythesson searched the wall of keys. I knew the moment Audrey had spotted her quarry from the way her breathing leveled out, and her eyes stopped their scanning.

"How many of this key do you have?" she asked, as he kept searching.

"Uh—there ought to be at least three, my lady."

"How many do you have access to?"

"Me?" He paused, as if the concept was entirely foreign. "I—One, my lady."

He had no idea. But Audrey smiled at him. "I'll see I return it, then, every time I borrow it."

"Oh." He turned back to the wall, facing again an area he'd scanned. "Of course. If that's your preference."

It was an excellent excuse to speak to the guard generally, and keep an eye out for Kaelson, which is what I suspected was her plan. There'd be no diffusing suspicion if we vanished the same time the prisoner did, unless we pretended to return to the tower. But I suspected that ship had sailed. The way she'd made people jump to attention today would have consequences.

Eventually, she took pity on him and said, "Is that it, there? Near your left hip? A bit further. There are just so many keys. I'm glad I don't need to keep track of them."

Panic flickered over the man's handsome face. "This room is secure. It's in the center of the barracks."

Which meant it was as secure as the guard wanted it to be. I knew Audrey made that connection, too, when she glanced at me quickly, her smile glued on.

I took a moment to run my eyes over the oft-absent Mortemon, noting the depth of his pallor and the size of his pupils. He was, quite clearly, unwell. It would be a small thing to ask him to stay away whilst he "recovered". The trick would be doing it *before* he infected the rest of us.

He shrugged his cloak to better cover his folded forearms, hunching into the cloth as I watched.

The opportunity to meet Kaelson didn't present itself on the way out. The bleary-eyed guard stood smartly as she left, eyes ahead and shields up.

That was going to make it hard to have conversations.

The trip over the bailey was brief, and the clouds hung heavily in the sky. I folded my cloak tighter against the chill that crept into my bones, missing the warmth of summer—or better, the warmth of my tribal forest, where the summers were long and dry, but the rivers deep and cold.

It felt so far away as we made our way through twisting passageways into the bowels of the castle's dungeons.

Every time we lit a Bloodfire, we knew it could be our last. We celebrated our lives and mourned the dead on the bones of the fallen who'd been fortunate enough to be carried home. I had a feeling when I'd walked away from my tribe that I'd danced at my last Bloodfire. I'd thought I was at peace with that. But I wanted to be back there with a ferocity that took me off guard after all these years. I wanted the sweet bite of mead and the drum that spoke to my soul. I wanted to dance and mourn and celebrate.

Thomas stepped in front of Audrey, shield up and spear left by the door in deference to the close quarters.

Audrey followed him, torch in her hand. The writhing shadows mocked my treasured memories of Bloodfires back home, casting cold, grimy stone into relief and then plunging it into darkness as it flickered.

"Quite a crowd." The would-be assassin was sitting in the far corner, one knee up, head tipped back. "Smells like death up there. Does this mean I won't be left to starve behind bars as you all succumb?"

From where I stood behind Audrey's shoulder I could see the knife Thomas held behind his shield, his grip white-knuckled.

"What's your name?" Audrey asked.

"Ylva. You can call me honey, if you'd prefer."

I sighed. "She doesn't want to fuck you, and if she does, she won't admit it in front of us. But she does want to be your friend. Can we shelve the bad flirting? Just for now?"

The woman stood as I spoke, her eyes on me. "Stay back," she told me, positioned defensively.

I felt mildly insulted. "That was my intention."

"Why?" Audrey asked, at the same time.

"She's got it," Ylva said, the words hard. "Get her out."

A chill went up my spine. Audrey was demanding explanations, but my eyes fell on the dirty silver bands at her wrists.

My mouth dry, I eased out of the small room, past Chay, and to the top of the stairs leading down to the dungeons.

Audrey hadn't shared the information on the plague the Master Steward—Steward Daniel the Deserter, as he ought to be known—had left her before he'd fled. I hadn't asked.

I didn't need to hear the explanation the woman spun, and I doubted Audrey would believe any truth she was told. That prisoner was part of an inconvenient reality that Barloc hadn't managed to weaponize and the majority didn't know of. And it didn't matter most of the time, because they'd been brought to heel so hard so often that when they did snap their chain, they weren't the fearsome force they could be.

But I had no doubt she could smell that plague.

She knew Audrey could take her in single combat. But mayhap she thought it had been luck and had seen her opportunity to attempt to drive me away.

But I couldn't put all my hopes on that.

The future stretched out before me, bleak and brief. Everything I needed to do crowded my head, and my heart sat heavily in my chest.

When Audrey appeared, her skirts were bundled in her hands, and her cheeks were pale. "We need to get you inside."

I shook my head. I could hold the line for her. "Say you're sealing yourself in the tower again," I said, and she looked at me, stricken. "If you'd had it, she would've told us," I explained. "You need to go before you do. I can buy you time."

But she shook her head, her mouth a thin line. "No." And there was a note of finality in her tone, like the cracking of a whip, that reminded me of another time, and another order.

Hope stirred deep inside of me. "Well," I said. "What's your plan?"

CHAPTER THIRTY-ONE
THOMAS

"There is a place for everything." ~ *Barloc's Wisdom, compiled by F. Bergsoniir*

The torches weren't all lit as I walked back to my rooms. Most were, but a few had burned out and waited, yet to be replaced. I didn't stop and feel for warmth on the stubs, but I considered it.

Further evidence of how hard the plague was hitting us wasn't necessary. I could see it out the windows on the castle wall where there ought to have been groups of three patrolling each segment. The group I could see were covering two segments, though.

If I saw nothing except that, I'd still know we were in trouble.

I hadn't seen Isolde since she'd been declared sick by the Worg in the dungeons almost a week ago. And that was as unsettling as the thin patrols.

In the mess, Riyad hailed me. He didn't stand from his spot, his face long and tired. Knowing what he was like, I grabbed some extra bread for him before I went to sit. "They found the source, did you hear?"

I spooned up some thin soup, fighting against my disbelief. "Did they just?" I asked, trying not to sound too doubtful.

"It was a fisherman's family who died first," he said, taking the bread I'd given him and ripping it open. "So they're burning all the fish. And I hear there's to be a new infirmary, set up at the tourney ground. I'd hate to be the bastard out there."

I forced more food into my body. Seven days ago, Steward Daniel had left. Four days ago, Acting Captain Smythesson had been found drunk beneath his desk. Two days ago, he'd become Captain properly at the passing of his predecessor. He hadn't been seen sober since that hurried ceremony, from what I heard. One day ago, Mortemon had gone entirely missing, presumed dead. Today, Acting Steward Romwell had greeted the lady from beneath his thickest winter coat, veins visibly dark beneath his eyes.

"How's it going, being with the lady?" he asked me, grinning, his gap-toothed smile not entirely kind.

I missed my Rose, suddenly. I wanted to bury my face in her hair and fall asleep. I'd wake to that damned cat without complaint and fetch the babe for her for feeding at any hour he demanded.

"Can't complain," I said instead. "Still on the Outer East Wall?"

"Nah." He snorted. "Everywhere nowadays, and not in the fun way."

I was going to run the field hospital at the tourney grounds tomorrow. I'd agreed to it. Helped the lady set it up. She didn't know what it took to run an army camp. I was no expert, but I was the closest she had. Everyone else who had the know-how and was still fit was desperately needed to hold the city together. If it worked, the unrest would ease, and I'd be supported more. If it didn't work...well, then it wouldn't matter.

The lady had asked with tears in her eyes after another trip back from the almost deserted mess hall. She knew the risks I was running. She'd done what she could to reduce them.

I'd sworn I'd never put myself in the position where I'd be in charge of people, but that had been under the Duke. Riyad was yapping away, and I just stared at the bits of cabbage bobbing around in the thin liquid.

The little lady, she wasn't the Duke. Not even close. But he'd be back one day. He'd be taking the reins from her hands.

"…like fish," Riyad said, and grinned. "But there'll be plenty of knappchs to be taken."

Riyad wouldn't know knappchs if an apple came and pissed in his cup. "It's not going to be over soon," I told him, the words razors in my throat. The wind screamed around us, but the lamp didn't flicker.

He pulled back, affronted. "But the fish—"

"If it's the fish, then it'll soon be stopped." By the One, I hoped it was the fish. I could live without them for the rest of my life if needs must.

"But I'm not holding my breath, old friend."

The next day, when I entered the bailey, I found a horse saddled and waiting for me. Ready to go already were a handful of guardsmen who'd offered to come along in exchange for their own families being provided with shelter and care.

To my shock, beside them was the lady herself on her dignified gray mare, and the missing Isolde on a pleasant piebald. Nearby, Chay stood holding their reins and those of his own warhorse.

"I need to travel to the city," she told me, before I could ask. "I may need to go with a reduced escort at times, but today, I thought I could see you off and run my required errands."

If I hadn't known how regularly she flaunted her father's rules, I'd have thought it a sensible way to navigate a difficult situation. But with Mortemon dead, she had limited choices.

I hefted myself into the saddle and barely even noticed the aches in my hips, in one knee where I'd broken my leg decades ago. Chay was already mounted, and as our group moved off, I caught a glimpse of a stableboy, his cap pulled low and a scarf pulled high over his face, watching from the shadows.

The upper level of the city was, if anything, busier than usual. People stood in groups, talking. Whilst expressions here weren't grim, there was a strange intensity. Lady Audrey was hailed by a few friendly faces I didn't recognize, but she didn't stop and none of them tried overly hard to persuade her to. A cart heavy with food trundled past us.

We moved through the streets, and it felt odd. The hawkers were thin on the ground, foot traffic was thick. Twice, I saw groups of guardsmen moving together with carts, and the sight of the bags in the cart made my blood run cold. I called myself a fool. We weren't at war.

Well, we were. But the war was far away, over fields and rivers. And I was safe, me and mine.

Lady Audrey and Isolde steered us through the city toward the docks. I didn't realize their destination before I smelt the brine, though, too intent on the faces watching us from shadowed lanes and windows, from doorways and the side of the road. There wasn't a war here—but it *felt* like there was.

A woman hauling wood stopped to look at us, a cat fled into the shadows at our approach. Children playing in the street went silent and hurried away. There was snow on the wind, and I couldn't shake the thought that we were walking into an ambush.

The tension was heavy, and it had me by the throat.

To my relief, the main road to the docks was blocked. A makeshift barricade of repurposed carts and crates filled the street, with two green guards hastily stowing dice as soon as they saw us approaching.

"No passage, milady," said one of them, with a bow that wobbled as much as his voice did. They were recruiting hard. I'd never seen the boy in my life.

Silence met this news. I glanced, from the corner of my eye, toward the little lady. She was looking past them, lost in thought. "On whose orders?" she eventually asked, bringing her gaze back to the young man who'd spoken.

His skin reddened under her gaze. "Th—The Master Steward, milady. 'Tis—'Tis to contain the plague."

"I see." Her tone said whatever it was that she saw wasn't pleasing. "I spoke to the Master Steward this morning. I am checking on the situation for him. I thought he would have sent word to expect me."

Her lie made my heart ache. There was no chance she'd had time to check in this morning and still been waiting for me. But at least she didn't remind the lad there was no Master Steward in La'Angi, currently, only an unwell Acting Steward.

"My apologies, milady," he said, stepping aside and waving us through, his eyes wide. "I never—I meant no—"

"I respect you doing as you've been ordered," she said crisply, as she led us past the barricade.

I waved on the guards I was taking with me to the hospital. "I'll meet you at the lower market to gather the last of the supplies," I told one who hesitated. "Or at the tourney grounds." Whatever was coming, I couldn't leave the lady to face it alone. Not without feeling the burn of my oath, and not without feeling like a fraud.

We rode on. The streets were empty of people. The buildings stood silent, crowding around us. "We shouldn't be here," Isolde said, as we turned yet another corner to leave the barricade behind us.

I silently agreed with her sentiments. I'd seen emptied parts of the city before, but never for a good reason.

"There are no ships," the little lady said, her eyes fixed on the water behind me.

My gaze moved away from the open shutters on buildings, the doors hanging on their hinges, and went to the bay.

She was right. It was a sight I'd never before seen. Not a single vessel waited in the sheltered bay. Fishing craft lay smashed.

"If you're thinking of investigating that smoke, so help me, Audrey," Isolde said, the words threatening.

I raised my eyes again and found the pillar of smoke Isolde had mentioned. "I need to know," the lady said, her words soft and full of pain. "Isolde—I need to."

"Fine," she snapped, and her eyes cut across me like a lash. "Keep her safe," she ordered, leaping down from her mount with none of the decorum I expected. I looked away as she kicked her skirts up and kilted them to the side, and simultaneously broke into a long-legged, loping run.

"I need to see the markets," Audrey told us, the words wooden. But she made no move to leave.

Chay climbed down, took the reins of Isolde's mount and gave the animal some attention. It seemed not at all bothered, though. Not like us. Chay sent a long, meaningful look my way. I lifted my shield from its spot on my saddle, strapped it to my arm, and turned to face back the way we'd come.

Isolde wasn't gone for long. "Mostly nets, boats, barrels, and fish," she reported to us, taking her reins back and leaping up lithely, flicking her skirts to resettle them. "Some bodies," she added, matter-of-factly. "Not as many as I expected."

The chill in my breast spread to my bones.

"Did the plague kill them?" Audrey asked her, her voice heavy with the question.

Isolde drew a deep breath. "I didn't get close, Audrey." The little lady waited, and Isolde let out the air she'd so carefully drawn in. "Damn it," she muttered. "I saw one—*one*—that was clearly cut down. But most of them were too burnt to tell."

"How many?"

Isolde's patience surprised me when she said softly, "I don't know. The pyre was huge, but as I said, it was mostly nets and wood from what I could see. Lingering there is no wiser than lingering here."

"If it's spread via the fish, we're safe here," the lady said, but she was turning her mount.

"Yes." The word was brief, sharp, as Isolde came toward me to take her place at the front. "If."

Audrey hesitated a moment more, clearly wanting to explore for herself. Behind her, I watched Chay watch her, waiting, his face a study of neutrality. "Which market should we head to, my lady?" I asked Audrey.

She started for a moment, clearly being torn from her thoughts. "The main," she replied grimly.

"Market?" Isolde demanded, turning to look at Audrey incredulously, her cheeks pale where her scarf had slipped.

Audrey lifted a hand toward the barren bay of La'Angi, her expression somber. The wordless explanation made Isolde close her eyes for the briefest of moments. Grief? I doubted it. Anger, more like, that the lady risked herself.

I wanted to ask them how long it would take before I was free to do my duty, but at the end of the day, protecting Audrey *was* my duty. The question clawed at my chest as we made our way through tense streets, as we stopped to let a group of men pulling a cart covered in thick burlap toward the lower levels of the city, their faces shrouded with cloth, expressions bleak. None of us asked what was in that cart.

The market wasn't empty, as I'd half feared; however, the stalls usually full of vegetables were all but bare, offering only the poorest selection of sad-looking wares. The bakery had a sign up saying they were out of stock, and the butcher's hooks were clean. The fletcher and the furrier were still there, but no one stopped at their stalls.

We rode through as we could never have done safely on a normal day. The crowds that usually clustered were replaced by hurried, grim-faced, shocked-looking individuals. None of us spoke as we rode. Audrey led us along a path through the main market into the park.

As we approached the Bonetree, I kept my eyes ahead. There was still a patrol on it, but only one pair. The wind whispered through the hollowed bones craftsmen had turned into chimes and hung high in its branches, making haunting music.

I remembered shimmying up that trunk as a boy, before the punishments had been so severe. I remembered my ma whispering words and tucking little bundles of whatever she could find into the gaps where the roots lifted themselves forcefully from the ground. Back in those days, for a bit of copper, you could play as long as you liked, and no one would remember. Now, the price was silver, and you had to be quick.

Even the lady got suspicious looks from the guardsmen on duty. She stared at the tree, frowning, but didn't stop. The sky threatened us with dark clouds, but we kept the same pace, taking another route back to the castle. We stopped twice for groups of guardsmen—once taking an empty cart toward the lower levels of the city, once for a group with a full cart returning. They saluted the lady smartly as they passed us by. She watched, unblinking. I saw Isolde looking down at her own fist on her saddle horn. The gloves hid her skin, but I knew she must be ill and was no doubt hurting.

"Who's in charge of the guard today, Thomas?" she asked me as that heavy cart was pulled through a lesser gate toward the castle.

I shrugged. "I don't know, my lady." It was the truth.

"Is anyone, really?" she asked me.

All I could do was repeat, "I'm sorry, my lady. I just don't know."

CHAPTER THIRTY-TWO

CHAY

"Growing certain plants together can encourage faster growth, provide ground cover and shade, improve your overall soil nutrition, and also increase both the size of your harvest and the flavor of your crops. These plants will be referred to as 'companion plants' for the remainder of this text."

~ *Growing Greatness: Common Garden Plants in Arcanloc*

As soon as I walked out of the entry chamber and saw her scrambling up from the ground, I knew exactly what I'd interrupted.

Audrey's cheeks were flushed, and her skirts didn't sit smoothly. The pillow she tossed onto the chair, then launched herself onto, I'd not seen since I'd helped move her into the tower.

If she'd been a friend, I'd've apologized and left. But I needed to speak with her, and she wasn't my friend.

So I shut the door behind myself and walked further in, ignoring her quick breaths and the hands that trembled a little as she reached for the sheafs of parchment never far from her elbow.

As I warmed the back of my thighs and my behind, I considered that she and I probably *could've* been friends, under other circumstances.

She let out a frustrated sigh and shifted in the chair. Her cheeks were still flushed.

"Something wrong?" I asked innocently, in case she hadn't learned her lesson. "Anything I can help with?"

The color in her cheeks deepened. Her gaze skittered away, settling on the hilt of my sword. "No. Thanking you."

The breathlessness of those words went to my head. Or mayhap it was the way her lips were slightly parted. Irritated with myself, I considered calling her out.

She had access to five other rooms over two other levels. She could've grinded up against plenty of stuffed objects all over the place because there was only *one* other person up there.

I didn't bother pointing out any of that. If she hadn't figured it out for herself, she was too foolish to use the information anyway. "Apologies for the interruption," I said.

She nodded, as if her skirts weren't all tangled around her calves. I tried not to think of how, if she liked to grind, it would be so wonderfully easy to angle her just so, and I hated that I even had that image in my head. *Butcher's daughter. The cause of the deaths of children. Magically bound to me against my will.*

It worked to cool my blood until she said, "You didn't interrupt anything, sir."

I snorted. "Since I'm so clueless, you ought to probably just tell me straight. Next time, should I offer to angle the pillow differently to help you get off? Off the pillow, of course."

A twist of guilt went through me as the words left my mouth. She *was* a gently raised woman, for all her matter-of-fact presentation. There was so much blood in her cheeks, I wondered if she'd grow dizzy from it.

"I doubt you have the necessary skill set, sir," she said without missing a beat.

Humor twisted through me at her self-conscious attempt to one-up me. "Oh, I didn't realize heirs to a duchy had unusually complex needs. My mistake."

She waved a hand in a dignified dismissal. "Worry not, for I can manage quite satisfactorily by myself, allowing you more time to practice doing your job." I stared at her, torn between wanting to laugh at her and shock that she'd actually engaged in the conversation so wholeheartedly. "Is there a reason you're here, attempting to speak to me?"

There was. I tried to recall it, but her skirts were bunched around her calves and her chest still rose and fell in an exaggerated rhythm. My own breath was quickening in response.

"You said yesterday you wanted to see Ylva in the morning." That was it.

The look she sent me was one of irritation, but she stood, scooped up her pillow, and said, "I'll be down later."

I didn't watch her go. But I did see, from the corner of my eye, the spring in her steps and the curve of her neck.

I let out a long breath, and then another, moving away from the fire as the backs of my thighs grew too warm. They matched the rest of me.

It took her some time before she made it back downstairs.

It would've been faster had she stayed.

SHE'D MOVED Ylva to a suite of rooms that had sun and air, at least. I figured the prisoner would escape at some point, when she got tired of toying with Audrey.

So far, she hadn't, and I wasn't quite sure why that was, but I didn't overly care. I'd probably be blamed for it when it did eventually happen, even after warning Audrey.

I *hadn't* warned the guard. I'd rather Ylva break free and deal with the lecture and another stay in the dungeons. It was all I could do to stop myself from dropping the keys in the heir's lap.

They sat in the sun around a chessboard, and I tried not to fall asleep in a chair. They didn't speak. Audrey had asked basic polite questions for the first few days, but that had given way. They just sat in silence and played chess. Every day. For two weeks.

It occurred to me that Audrey was probably lonely.

It occurred to me that she didn't once attempt to speak to *me.*

So when I heard Ylva say, "You've got quite a problem out there," I paid attention. There was nothing else for me to do, anyway.

"I do."

"You know this plague is magical, right?"

I watched as Audrey's fingers hesitated over her knight. "I don't know much about it."

Ylva's smile kicked up a little. "Shame you're on this side of the battle lines. I'd have a bow in your hands in a moment if we were at home."

There was enough regret in that statement that I went to stand beside Audrey. Ylva could escape whenever she damned well wanted, but she wasn't murdering the person I was bloodsworn to protect on her way out. At least not in my presence. And with Thomas settled in the camp and preparing to face the approaching winter, that meant she wasn't murdering this woman at all.

"At ease," Ylva said, not glancing at me. "She can take me." And this was followed up by a leer that gave me secondhand discomfort for Audrey, who surely knew she was being mocked.

"I understand those thoughts must irritate you," Audrey said, shifting her knight defensively. "But the only place I want to take you, Ylva, is to the orchards with a good horse and some supplies, so you can go and cut throats in peace."

It was Ylva's turn to still, and I watched as the fine silver chains in her ears shivered, giving away her tiny movement. "You know how to woo a Worg, my lady."

"Sit down, Chay," Audrey said, and the utter disinterest in her words made the boy inside me shrink. Rather than follow her command, I wandered to the window, folding my arms over my chest as though I held that boy to my chest. I didn't block the sunlight falling over Audrey, but I did take what I needed, turning my face into the warmth, and I breathed.

I didn't need to exist in the shadows. And no one would make me.

"What's a Worg?"

Ylva looked at her, eyes wide. "Seriously?"

"What I don't know could, and does, fill hundreds of books," Audrey said with a shrug, and her shawl slipped just a little, hugging her strong arm. "Enlighten me, while we're both stuck."

"You aren't stuck," Ylva said with a snort. "You could do *anything.* You've the money and the power."

I remembered someone accusing Kadan of the same. He'd laughed at the lie, but Audrey didn't. "I can do a lot," she said, straight-faced. "I don't know how. What's a Worg?"

Ylva glanced at me, unsettled, but I just met her look blank-faced, so she turned back to Audrey. I didn't know how to take the comment, either. I remembered the day in the orchard. She'd burned, then. I'd seen glimpses of it, but that fire was hidden.

I was glad. It consumed what it touched.

"Why do you put up with it?"

"Put up with what?"

"This." Ylva flicked her fingers in a movement that was both contained and aggressive.

Audrey sat back, her eyes still on the chessboard. I resisted the urge to explain that Ylva meant her situation at large as the prisoner made a swift move that sacrificed one of her pawns and put Audrey's knight in another dire situation. I didn't like the symbolism of that.

"I don't know how to shift the power," Audrey responded. "Not properly. I could drop some matches on the city, but they'd rebuild it on the bones of the innocent. I could throw my father's wealth to the wind, but he'd just seize it at sword point. I could leave, but he'd just adopt."

Ylva picked up her queen and tipped it at a jaunty angle. "Have you considered, and I'm just throwing this out there, mind, but have you considered sticking a knife in his eye?"

I couldn't help but glance toward the door. I'd been in La'Angi too long. It was making me jumpy.

"How'd that work for you?" Audrey asked sweetly.

Ylva dismissed that with a flick of her fingers. "It wasn't me, it was my cousin. If it'd been me, he'd be dead."

Audrey didn't laugh at her bravado. I suspected my gently reared lady didn't see the offer of a shared joke in Ylva's eyes. I smiled to make the prisoner feel better, but she didn't seem to notice.

"And without my father, what changes?" Audrey asked her.

"That depends on what else is in play." Ylva leaned forward. "What else do you have in play, Audrey?"

She looked at her chessboard with a curiously blank expression, and I was back staring at Kadan's broken body, hearing Darrius' efficiently summarized plans. "Nothing," she said softly.

CHAPTER THIRTY-THREE

CHAY

"A smart man might hope for the best, but he'll be prepared for the worst."
~ Barloc's Wisdom, complied by F. Bergsoniir

I half-shoved Audrey's noble self out the door, keeping myself between the poverty-stricken Southerner and the sad-faced duchess-in-waiting.

"Smooth," I said through my teeth, my heart aching for the Wuurgard heir as I dropped the bar over her door. One of these days, I'd forget to lock her in. It might even be an accident.

"It's true," she told me. "If I had any allies or power, I wouldn't be sitting around playing chess."

"Well that's lucky, then, because your strategy is dreadful," I snapped.

She threw up her hands and stormed off toward her rooms. "I want to make things right, but I don't know how!"

The depth of rage in the words sparked answering frustration in me. I'd seen this dance many times before. My mother had thrown her hands in the air, too, after we'd been whipped. "*Why didn't you stay away from him?*" she'd ask us. *"What am I supposed to do now? You know what he's like when he's in a mood."*

"Ah, of course *you* need to have discovered the answers for them to be right," I said to her back. "Far be it that you actually *speak* to the *affected parties*!"

"Oh, yes, they all want to speak to me," she bit out. "I can't even get a look from Kaelson, much less a meeting with him, and he's basically on my payroll now that the Acting Steward is nine-tenths dead and Smythesson isn't far behind. I expect folks in the city who despise my father can't *wait* for an audience with me!"

"Why the fuck would they want an audience with you?" I asked, genuinely confused by this woman's brain.

She spun and leveled a finger at my nose. Her whiskey eyes burned. "Don't make this sound simple, you cur, because we both know I can't toss money and power randomly out the window of a carriage as I go past and expect it'll help."

I flicked her finger out of the way. "Why not?"

"One," she said, getting out a finger, "*power* isn't something that one can throw, much less catch, and two, how do you think the guards would treat the folks who scooped up that wealth?"

I hated that she had a point. "That required you to count on your fingers? You can't keep two arguments straight?"

"I don't keep much straight," she said, giving me a derisive look up and down. "Thanking the Wife."

Laughter wedged in my chest. If she expected me to care that she had a crush on our prisoner, she was sorely mistaken. I'd figured that out from the get-go. But before I could respond, she pressed one hand over my mouth and tangled the other in my sword belt, dragging me back into the shadows. Frozen, I felt the pressure of her fingers over my mouth, the pressure of her hand on my belt at my hip, and her breath at my ear. Heat flooded my body. I held myself still, resisting the urge to turn into that warmth, her attention on the hall leading toward the kitchens.

Two sets of rapidly approaching steps were a welcome distraction from the fact I hadn't been so close to anyone in what was clearly far too long.

"Jillian," a man called. "Stop it. I'll just come by tonight."

A woman, basket in her arms, slowed at the point where the hall we were in joined the one they traveled on, positioned between both passageways.

My heart beat heavily. I knocked Audrey's hand off my face, and she shot me a look that would've made her servants weep. I just ignored her.

The woman was dressed for the kitchens, and from the flush in her cheeks and the tendrils of sweat-dampened hair sticking to her temples, she hadn't been gone long.

"Winn, I haven't anything to spare."

Winn stopped close to her, a middle-aged man with a neat tabard in the colors of the guard. "You always say that. You know if I have to chase you, it gets worse." He held out his hand. "Give it to me."

She took half a step back, clutching the basket to her chest, and the guardsman's hand settled on the wicker, preventing her from taking flight.

Audrey was on the move before I could act, her eyes on the man.

I remembered, fleetingly, fighting beside her before I'd been forced into her service, when it was just she and I against Mikus and his buddy.

"Don't run, Winn," Audrey said, and the guard's eyes widened. He dropped the basket and bowed.

The woman curtsied, the basket bobbing in her hand. "No, my lady," Winn said. "Jillian was just sharing a bite with me. She promised she would, you see."

La'Angi was painfully shorthanded and spilling blood over a few loaves of bread seemed like a bad stampede to get moving, but Audrey was already inserting herself between them. "No, she isn't. She's leaving now." And she gave Jillian a hard look that made the other woman shake her head sharply.

I felt sick, imagining the repercussions.

"It's as he says, my lady," she said, and the words didn't shake at all.

The man opened his mouth, and Audrey lifted a hand, demanding silence. Winn didn't seem to take note, continuing, "My lady, I'm not sure what you think is happening, but as Jillian's told you—"

"No, you don't speak," she said, the words clear as glass and just as sharp. "That's what it means when I hold up a hand like this."

He cleared his throat and stood a little straighter. "Of course, my lady. Only I've got the Watch in a half-hour."

I saw her close her eyes and draw in a breath. "Hey, buddy," I said over her shoulder. His eyes flicked up to me. I jerked my hand across my neck in a *cut it out* motion.

Audrey turned to the woman. "If I let him go, he takes this out on you."

Her mouth opened, then closed.

I held in a breath rather than tell my illustrious liege lady what a fool she was.

"If I send him away, he spreads the poison."

I let the breath out. Well, she was considering her options. I didn't like the one that was left.

"If I execute him publicly for harassment and stealing—"

"I haven't stolen anything!" he objected. "My lady, this is unfair!"

"Oh so you *did* harass someone, *will* take it out on her, and *will* spread the poison, then? Noted."

He made a noise of frustration. "That isn't what I said. I'm a good solider."

"If you were a good solider, you'd be dying at my father's whim," she said, and I liked the way that barb of hers made him flinch. To make sure he knew it, I grinned behind her.

The look he shot me was pure venom, but I was immune. My grin widened.

"If I execute him publicly, it'll force the guard to hide how they're terrorizing civilians," she went on. "Sir Chay, you've got *all* the answers tonight. I only have one option, don't I?"

"You're shorthanded," I reminded her. Winn retreated a step, unconsciously mimicking the way his quarry had stumbled back earlier. I had longer legs.

"You're right," she agreed. "It feels like the price I'm willing to pay."

Mayhap I'd been in La'Angi too long, but I understood my cue. He went to argue, and I reached for my sword.

A split second later, he did, too.

She was in motion already, and his knee was cracking sickeningly. The noise of pain he made between his teeth as he fell caught me off guard, and she followed up the blow to his joint by grabbing him by his precisely shorn hair and driving her knee into his face.

I stepped back, disoriented by the flurry of violence.

She let go of him and turned to Jillian. "Go home," she said, the words a little breathless. "Sleep well. You never saw him, and you never will."

This time, her curtsey shook.

The fool of a guard tried to get to his feet, but he just fell.

I drew a bracing breath. I'd never executed a man. Not in cold blood. Those children I didn't count as executions. They were a mistake. A hideous, life-changing mistake.

I hadn't drawn my sword since that day. I hadn't trained. No one noticed to ask why.

I didn't know why.

It felt heavy in my hands.

"Help me get him into the garden," she said, and there was something far too normal about her voice as she made that demand.

I sheathed my sword again, relieved at the respite. My hands hooked into the depressions beneath his arms. He screamed when she took his legs, and I wished her knee to his face had done more than make him eat a few teeth. A dead weight'd be harder to haul, but if this was a stealth mission, we were failing at it.

The door to the side garden wasn't too far, though, and as soon as we were on the ground, she dropped his legs. He was babbling pleas, and I was feeling sicker.

"Thomas' field hospital might be worth considering," I offered.

"He wouldn't be there long enough," she said with a quick shake of her head. "Men like him have long memories." She cast her eyes around and leveled a finger at the seawall. "There." He was struggling to sit up and she knelt, one hand going around the back of his neck, the other in his collar, fisted hard.

His struggles ended before I could do more than grab one of his hands and stop him from clawing at the collar she used to choke him.

"Obviously," she said, still choking him, "we need to avoid being spotted. If you hear the Watch, we head to the nearest shadows, and *you* stay as still as you can."

The world was upside down. In a hall nearby, someone hurried past holding a torch. They never paused, though, to come our way. He jerked and went still.

Her hand relaxed on his collar, and she straightened, stumbling a little on the hem of her skirt. I went to catch her, but she flinched back. Before I could figure that out, she said, "Get his feet."

"*You* get his feet." His shoulders would be heavier.

She shrugged, quilting up her skirts as I'd seen Isolde do earlier, a few economical movements that didn't stop them from getting muddy but would protect them from more damage than they'd suffered and free her up.

I took him under the shoulders this time. His head lolled. I was right about him being heavier as a deadweight. Her cheeks puffed out as she took him by the ankles, but there were no screams.

I couldn't see where we were going. My prediction was right—he was both heavier and quieter like this—but I hadn't accounted for my own nausea. The last of the sun's light guided her, and I trusted her to know these gardens well enough to steer me.

"Past those lamb tongues," she said. "The silvery-leaved plants. The lamb tongues, there? Go *left*," she said eventually, huffing with impatience. I went left around a bundle of plants that looked light green, not silver, into the soft bed of the garden. "A little more left. That's good."

Part of me wanted to ask if it was right. But I didn't joke with her.

That wasn't what our relationship was like. I certainly didn't joke with her while I carried the body of a man I suspected was still breathing. If he was, he wouldn't be soon.

He hadn't been sick. How many guards did she have who weren't sick?

She put him down in the lee of a large bush and slipped away. If I hadn't been staring at her, there's no way I could've tracked her movements. She didn't vanish the way Isolde could, hiding in plain sight, but she melted into the shadows like a native predator.

Which she was.

I heard booted feet along the walkway above us and stayed where she'd left me, my heart drumming as I waited for the cry of discovery.

The steps had moved past me when she reappeared at my side, though, somehow condensing out of the darkness. Her fingers were stained with ink as they settled over the man's throat, her eyes on the walkway above us, her expression entirely blank.

In the darkness, I couldn't see what she was doing. I didn't know if she was tracking his pulse, limiting the blood reaching his brain, or preparing to strangle him if he made a noise. The rise and fall of his chest was shallow, but still present.

My heart rate didn't settle as those boots moved further away. But at some point, she stood and murmured, "Up the stairs and to the east, just a few steps, there's a lookout spot."

Where we'd hurl him, unconscious and barely breathing, off the wall? Or would we murder him first? I took his shoulders again, the dead weight dragging, and again walked backward through the garden.

The stones were damp and slippery, but the sea wall wasn't high. That it existed at all spoke more to vanity than necessity. I couldn't imagine anyone attempting to navigate the aggressive swell and rocky outcrops to scale the cliffs to take the keep, wall or no. The course to the La'Angi bay was signposted by magework; it was so hazardous that the route safe for ships was carved into the stone in the seabed by old magics long forgotten—deep enough to let them pass safely, but only if they were cautious. Even Luca's shortsighted plans would never include incursion by sea.

The guardsman's head bobbed up and down, and the pressure on the bones in his neck made my stomach writhe. There was something honest about a sword to the gut.

I remembered the dark morning I'd been sworn into this woman's service, and how one of the big guards had turned on Mikus, mace in hand. But Audrey had stuck her dagger in Wade's eye. Was that because any other method would put her at risk, or because she wasn't the monster her father was?

The stones on the wall were even and well-worn, and the crash and tumble of waves below grew louder. Wind whipped my cloak around my legs, but the stones came up to my chest, and I had nothing to fear from an accidental trip save injuring my ankle and dropping the man who may as well be dead, anyway.

I knew sticking a knife in this man's eye would've left a trail of blood so wide we'd've been bound to be discovered. I could respect the decision Audrey had made to try to look after the woman when there had been no good options. But as we stopped in the viewing area, with the sea dark below us, and the sky blanketed with clouds, I just felt cold. Sick and cold.

To the best of my knowledge, Kadan had never once ordered anyone killed.

"Set him down on the bench," she said.

I did, remembering the way she'd held him even after he was limp, and had given me instructions whilst choking the life from him.

The same woman who'd staggered and frozen at the sight of angry children.

I stepped back as she positioned herself near his hip, glancing along the wall from the little sheltered pocket. There was no one in sight, but there wouldn't be. We were inset in the wall, a step down, and here it only came up to my hip. The early fog was a blessing for whatever she planned, but even with numbers as reduced as they were in the guard, I wanted to get out of here.

One of her hands took him by the belt. The other fisted firmly in his collar. Before I realized what she was doing, she lifted and swung, letting out a grunt of exertion as she threw the entire man, a *dead weight,* off the sea wall.

I didn't know if I even heard the splash he made as he hit the water, or if it was just a wave against rocks.

My belly churned as she untied her skirts and settled them once more around her boots with a few practiced flicks.

Had his death bled off any of the rage she carried? A moment later, the memory of when I'd fought my first skirmish against the Steppe nomads, and my first kill, flooded my mind.

It was for a purpose, but not rage.

"Isolde'll be proud," I said as she turned to go back to the wall.

"Isolde would've done it faster and neater," she said dismissively. "I'd have a dozen things to improve on for next time." That wasn't accompanied by a look toward me for feedback. She led us back along the parapet, her eyes clear and steps sure. I followed her to the garden, but she paused to visit the plants she'd called lamb tongues, straightening bent stems and obscuring our prints with sprinkles of damp soil and fistfuls of scattered leaves.

Unconscious, full-grown men weren't light. She'd lifted him with a strong stance, her core braced, and her knees bent. But still, she'd feel that when the rush of violence wore off. I followed after her down the path, sticking to the shadows, deep enough in the gardens I wasn't too worried anymore.

She'd taken me to the ground and kept me there with ease, that day in the orchard. I'd known she was strong. But I'd seen her shrink and hesitate more often than I'd seen her roar.

I didn't know how to comment on that, though. I didn't know how to check in with her. I doubted she murdered men as part of her daily training exercises. Isolde would've bragged about it by now.

"Are you okay?"

She glanced at me, then unsettled a patch of stones with the toe of her boot and scooped them up to toss them over the path where a deep boot print had been left, presumably by me. "Well. Thanking you for checking. You?"

Was I fine? I had no idea what I was. "That was not how I expected the evening to go." One minute, she was missing opportunities to flirt with the heir. The next, she was breaking knees and tossing men to the sea.

"Apologies," she said. "I don't have the reach or time for the long-term solution of attempting to show someone like that the error of their ways." She glanced up at the sky as if concerned about the hour but didn't comment on it, opening the door to the keep and holding it for me.

There was no sign of what had passed in the corridor except a few splatters of blood that blended with flakes of mud from someone's boots. I glanced down at myself and realized with a start that somehow, I had a crimson stain on the hem of my cloak, a long stream of it, like from a slow nosebleed or a nicked finger. I twitched the cloth closer and ran my eyes more carefully over her as we passed through torchlit parts of the keep.

There was no blood on her. Not even her sleeves or the hands she'd fisted in his shirt.

Mayhap that was a family trait.

She finally looked toward me. "I'm not injured," she said, and I realized she'd caught me staring and assumed I was concerned.

Considering the reasons I *could* have been staring at her, that was probably about the best. "Of course," I agreed, turning my eyes forward. But for once the silence between us wasn't comfortable. "Why are you still here?" I asked.

As soon as the words were out, I wanted to snatch them back. In my mind's eye, my mother's hands made aggressive downward motions behind her skirt, trying to shush me. The boy in my chest recoiled.

"When I could just kill people between me and the horizon?" she asked flippantly. "Oh, I don't know. This place has a nice view."

Something about that, the irreverence or the way she delivered it with a straight face, reminded me, achingly, of Kadan. Except I'd never bought his bullshit. And I wasn't buying hers, either.

She'd specifically asked me to set the guard down. I went over it in my mind, the way we'd carried him up there, the way she'd positioned herself so carefully. She couldn't have tossed him over the regular height part of the wall. *I* could've, and together, it would've been simple. Instead, we'd carried him farther so she could do it alone.

Ego? Rage? Distrust?

We were at the door to her tower. I lifted the key, but held it in the lock and turned to her. "Why was it important you do it yourself?" I asked her.

She met my eyes. Something about it felt forced. I couldn't remember the last time she'd met my eyes. "I'm done asking anything of you." It knocked the wind out of me, but she was frowning, shaking her head. "That came out more forcefully than I intended. I'm sorry, Chay. I simply meant to uphold my promise." She looked down at the door. "I didn't mean it to sound unkind. It isn't, really. I said I won't expect you to kill for me. I don't. I apologize you were so complicit tonight. I acknowledge the weight of your oath must be significant."

The lock clicked open, and I shoved the door, my tongue thick in my mouth. I'd known exactly what she meant because she'd said it plainly. I hadn't needed the over-explanation. It wasn't ego, or rage, or even distrust.

She was just doing what she said she'd do. Nothing more, nothing less.

And I had no idea how the hell to feel about it.

CHAPTER THIRTY-FOUR
ISOLDE

"Action is easy." ~ Matri'sion proverb

I knew Audrey wouldn't open the door between us. I'd told her not to, and she understood and respected that I refused to be the one to make her sick. That was as complicated as it needed to be for her.

Knowing it was safe to do so, I fanned my hand over the wood separating us, listening to the rise and fall of her voice as she told me what she'd done.

I should've been there to hold that space for her. I should've held her when the battle energy ebbed, and the shakes took over. I heard the tears in her voice and swallowed my own, taken off guard by the show of emotion. Even locked safely away from her view, it still didn't serve us.

"…but Ylva actually talked to me today, so that's something. Do you know what a Worg is?"

Ylva *had* talked. "It's a curse," I told her, because I'd never lied to

Audrey before, and I wasn't starting now, regardless of how much I wanted to hide that truth. "And she's a victim of it. Keep silver against her flesh, and she won't need to deal with it." Before she could launch more questions at me, I refocused on the key issue. "The body might be on the rocks below."

"I know," she said through the wood. "Well, actually, I guessed that. I don't really know. But we're so shorthanded, and those areas are patrolled only intermittently. I've got a meeting tomorrow with the Acting Steward, and if he mentions he's shorthanded, I'm going to recommend that he pull people away from that area, among others."

I stared at my nails, hating the sight of that gray. I shoved down the hopelessness that tried to grab me by the throat. She was doing well without me, and that was all I ever wanted for her. "Good. Make sure you bury it amongst other suggestions. Not at the very start or the end, because people remember the first and last things the best, but mayhap second or third." I'd told her this a million times, and I hated that I knew that, but I couldn't halt myself, all the same. "Not the middle. Few remember the middle." I didn't wait for a response. I didn't need one. *Get it together, archer.* "Do you know the woman's name?"

"No," Audrey said. "Or I'd seek her out."

"Better to give that job to—" *me.* I cut that off. I could still walk, but I needed to save that ability. Weakening myself now would be an error. "—someone else, or let it sit for now. You don't want her thinking about you more than she already will be if that death is uncovered." Audrey wouldn't hang for murder, but there would be assumptions made as to what the guardsman had wanted from her and the woman, both.

After all, we were only good for one thing.

"I've got plenty of other problems," she told me on a sigh that I could hear clearly through the door. "I still don't know what to do with the guards who are hoarding food and wealth."

We'd spent hours going over this together. There was no good answer, only varying levels of risk. I didn't ask if they'd progressed the cure at all. She'd tell me the moment she had even the whisper of an update on that front.

My tribe will welcome you. I wanted to tell her. *You could find this woman and escort her yourself. You know the way.* The image of her riding into the sunset flashed into my mind. It was the first time I'd imagined her doing it alone, and I hadn't been terrified of the thought—it brought me a measure of calm. I withdrew my hand from the wood, using it instead to anchor the blanket closer to my shoulders.

Whatever happened, she'd be okay.

I closed my eyes to blot out the door keeping me from her, but her expression was burned on the inside of my lids. The way her head had snapped up as a child, like a rabbit hearing a hunter. *Go,* she'd told me.

But what if we hadn't?

"You need to take control," I told her, allowing no trace of doubt or worry into my voice.

"What would make me able to run it any better than the Acting Steward and the Captain?" she asked me. Her brows would be all bunched up and there would tears in her eyes as they stayed fixed somewhere to my right.

I hadn't hugged her enough. I needed to remedy that when I was able. "You listen," I told her. "You learn. You acknowledge you don't know shit." From what I'd seen, the best all started like that. "You're willing to put in the time, and you put people first." She was quiet, and that worried me. It was rare I couldn't predict her reactions, but I wished I could assess which of my assurances had the most impact.

I missed her.

"You aren't trying to accumulate more wealth or power," I added. I couldn't make out the exact words, but whatever she murmured sounded like a disagreement. "Wealth, then, and the power is purely what you need to seize to be safe. Isn't it?" She was silent, and I rocked on my haunches, frustration clawing at me. "If you keep giving these men your power, they'll keep taking it."

"I know," she said clearly. "I know they will. And they're taking it from others."

And she was positioned with enough of a leg-up that she could have half a chance at disrupting the locways. "This isn't a pitched battle on an equal field," I reminded her, keeping the frustration from my voice. "Your guilt is irrelevant unless you can weaponize it against the powerful. The situation is what it is." And she wasn't going to stop the prophecy if she felt *bad* about it. "If guard numbers are as low as you say, and the ranks are so badly fractured, then a few public killings as you take control and seize the reins is a kindness. Short-term cost, long-term profit." She was quiet again, and this time, I wasn't worried about it. I probably shouldn't have mentioned how she'd need to roll some heads to be taken seriously. Not after what she'd done today. "You've got people to ask for advice, don't you?"

"Kaelson," she said, and the word was thick. "He seems like he knows the score, if I can ever get hold of him. And Bernadette. Graff, mayhap."

My heart ached. How many leaders listed a cook and an errand boy as their advisors? *Not enough.* Bernadette had her own agenda, which could be both a boon and a barrier, but Graff was a good choice. His mouth stayed closed, and he heard and saw a *lot.* "So, start there."

"But I can't," she objected. "I can't staff the city. If I seize control of the guard and there's in-fighting, we'll lose more people. We'd become vulnerable. If I pull us back a level in the city so we're only defending the inner walls, we could have bandit camps in the lower levels. Flushing them out later will be harder than keeping them out now. We'll be pinned down with limited supplies and no hope of lifting that until ships arrive, and I've no clue when that may happen."

"But you can't keep them out *now,"* I pointed out, like I had yesterday. "You can't feed people *now.* These problems all already exist. We've been over this."

She gave me all the reasons, all the risks, all the things she was afraid of. My body ached, and I listened to it, held it all for her. It was all I could do from here.

I needed to draw a new bath. The warm water renewed me, and it was one of the few benefits of being locked in here endlessly. That, and the sewing I'd been able to progress.

When there was a break in the flow of negativity, I asked, "When did you last go for a ride?"

She was quiet for a moment, and I could imagine her gaping at me. "A *ride?*"

"Yes, a ride. Just for the joy of it and to keep your eye in and your bow limber." And to remind her that she could exist outside of these stone walls.

"I don't know," she said impatiently. "I don't have time for that, Isolde. People are *dying.*"

"They're dying while you worry, too. Your guilt is irrelevant. Get out. Clear your head."

"Thomas is at the field hospital. I can't go out without him."

Curse the Duke for that. "Audrey, I think people are more worried about whether they'll live through the winter than whether you've got one knight behind you, or two." If they weren't, they should be. "You're moving around the castle already with just Chay. It's no different."

She was silent again, and I knew she was running through all the arguments in her head, weighing them all up. "Mayhap," she said eventually. "Can I get you anything?"

"No." I had everything I wanted, and it left me feeling strangely tired. "Go do your nighttime drills, and then rest. Tomorrow, I want you to ride."

She mumbled something that wasn't agreement. I listened to the sounds of her exercising, but didn't move myself to do the same. I'd taken to doing just small spurts of activity. My body didn't manage more, and there was no point pushing through.

Aching and hollow, I sat against the door, listening to the sound of her readying herself for bed. I could remember every step of our routine so clearly, I could just about feel her hair in my hands as I brushed it out.

Go, my heart said. But what I truly wanted of her was not flight, but fight.

CHAPTER THIRTY-FIVE
THOMAS

"Treat diseased plants immediately, lest the sickness spread."
~ Growing Greatness: Common Garden Plants in Arcanloc

When I'd been sent, I expected a few poor, desperate people, and I got them. We dug the latrines and set up tents and cookfires. It looked as neat as any La'Angi army hospital ever did, and I took pride in that.

What I didn't expect—and I should've—was that they came in family groups. Sometimes, it was a mother with sick children, sometimes children with sick parents—none of the groups that arrived were *all* unwell. And it made sense, didn't it? Not only was I running a field hospital with a handful of good men, but I was also organizing a group of volunteers.

There was little to do for the sick, but they wanted little, anyway. Somewhere warm and safe was what I could give them, and most of their families were happy to either sit with them or make themselves useful around the camp. There were no Magework Healers to be found, but after seeing one dying of the plague, I wouldn't have had one anyway, not to work. Instead, herbalists had made poppets, tinctures, potions, and oils. What good they did, I didn't know—they were gratefully taken, and that was valuable, too.

They came looking for hope. What I could give them was order.

The lady arrived—to my horror—on foot and leading her horse, when we'd been there almost two weeks. In her saddle sat a wizened old woman, and by her side was a tight-lipped Chay. She brought more tents, more blankets, more flour, and salted meat. I made time to talk to her, but she was helping cut vegetables beside a cookpot, speaking to two older women.

"I wouldn't have said so myself, my lady," one of them demurred. "But if others do, then I can't speak against it, either."

I hung back, but the oldest woman looked sharply up at me all the same. "There's just a few who're the problem," she said very deliberately. "I don't envy you trying to manage them, milady."

"Oh, I'm just helping out where I can," the little lady said, her smile sunny. "I'm more use here, cutting potatoes, than I was in a castle, worrying."

I watched from behind her as she peeled them deftly. Rose lost less of the vegetables, but it would be a near thing.

Who'd taught my lady how to peel a potato?

For some reason, seeing her smile and chat made me feel better about the day. I spotted a lad who'd taken on runner duties coming for me from between the tents, and there was some hope in my heart. It felt good. "Sir, we've nowhere the new group can fit together. Should we set up another pocket of camp?"

I resisted the urge to smile at the term, and that surprised me. "How short are we, and can we rearrange any of our families?"

He shook his head. "Not unless someone dies, sir." Then he looked up at me, horrified. "Or leaves."

The joy I'd felt was gone again. "Then yes, we'll set up some more tents if we've got them. We want to keep families together."

He nodded and ran off. I turned back and saw the women around lady Audrey in deep conversation. She kept her eyes down, peeling her vegetables. But that girl knew what was going on.

Steps beside me made me glance over as Chay stopped at my side, shield tossed over his shoulder and hand on his belt like a cocky sellsword. My young counterpart had a good heart, but little sense.

"I checked, and there's no letter from your family," he told me, pitching his voice to carry only to my ears. "Bad news travels fast, though."

I hadn't asked it of him, and I was caught between gratitude for his thoughtfulness and worry for my family.

"Thanking you," I said, because I didn't know what else to say.

He shrugged, glancing around quickly. "Situation with the guard isn't good," he said even quieter, his eyes moving slowly over the gathered people. "I don't know any locals, and Isolde isn't able to go out."

Worry flared. "Is she so unwell?"

"I'm not sure. I haven't seen her in weeks. I haven't asked Audrey, but…"

"The lady would tell you if it was important," I said, emphasizing her title.

Chay didn't seem to notice my pointed correction. "Perhaps. I think we're in a bad spot." He looked at me levelly. "I suggested to Audrey we should all visit your family."

Gratitude and fear, again. I didn't look around, trusting he wouldn't be speaking so if anyone were in earshot, but I still leaned in a little to say, "What'll people say if they hear you calling her by name, boy?"

One of his brows rose. We both fell silent as an older woman passed us by, an apologetic smile on her lips and herbs in the basket in her hands. We watched her go together, and Chay said, "I think we've bigger issues than Audrey's reputation, Thomas. It isn't like I'm moaning it at night, after all."

I looked at him hard, not convinced by the casual way he looped his thumb into his belt. For those thoughts to even be in his head meant we were in more trouble than I'd realized. "I take the Duke just as seriously as I take this plague," I told him, putting as much force into the whispered words as I could. "I'd recommend you do the same, lad." At the flicker of irritation on his face, I added, "If not for yourself, then for her."

His expression smoothed at that reminder, and rather than settle my fears, his reaction only solidified them. Whatever had been running through that boy's head, I was confident it'd get both of us killed.

Before I could even consider letting him have the sharp side of my tongue, he said, "The point is, the situation at the castle is grim. She's vulnerable, and there's an easy solution."

I bit off my frustration with the boy. His idea of *easy* didn't match mine, but mayhap the simple life had spoiled me. "When do we leave, then?"

His eyes cut over to where she was now stirring the pot. The older woman was sitting, cup in one hand and swinging the other wildly. The younger was nodding along, scrubbing more vegetables in filthy water. I was eons away from that group of women, but the little lady had slipped right on in. I felt even further from the knight at my side, wearing the same tabard as I, sworn to the same cause. He didn't even *try* to disguise his interest as he stared at her. I opened my mouth to tell him that look would get him flogged, and then I saw his eyes dip. The little lady had gathered her skirts and was taking a seat, ready to peel more vegetables.

Fury pulsed through me as I followed his gaze to the curve of her calves above her low riding boots. She shifted a moment later, skirts resettling, and his eyes bounced back to me, but it was too late.

In my mind, I could see myself plowing my fist into his mouth. I could feel the burn of my own bones splintering as I used them to crack his.

In reality, I lifted that hand and put it on his shoulder, leaning in. It didn't matter who saw, now. "You're not local," I murmured in his ear, forcing the words out past my teeth. "You don't know your manners, and it's showing. Don't let it show again."

His mouth thinned, a silent objection, and my hand tightened on that big shoulder of his.

"You were a big fish in a small pond," I said, reaching for my patience. "Here, boy? The pond is bigger, and you're at the bottom of the food chain. Keep your eyes off her."

"The One, the Wife, and the Son," he muttered furiously, brushing me off, and I let him. "You're so bogged down in your own fear you can't see what's coming." He stayed in close, his voice low and furious. "The Duke is gone. Your buddies are 'taxing' everyone, choosing the shifts they attend, and killing those who disagree. I don't have to like her to know I've sworn to keep her alive, and this is *not* how we do that."

I felt sick. "Use the courtesy your mama taught you, then, when you address her, and we can deal with the next issue."

He laughed, a low and bitter noise, then stepped back. "I am. I'm using exactly what she taught me. Forget it, Tom." He turned and stalked off in the direction of his horse. People scurried out of his way.

I wondered if he knew people had fled from Mikus the same way.

When I glanced over, Audrey met my gaze fleetingly, her expression somber. My heart dropped further.

She'd seen the exchange.

Scrubbing a hand over my military-smooth chin, I wished I, too, had somewhere to retreat to. But Audrey didn't question me when she extracted herself. Not about that.

"There are a few houses that have been turned into storage for bodies," she said, brushing a stray hair from her eyes and leaving a smear of dirt on her cheek as we wandered back toward the horses. "While they dig graves."

I'd seen it on the way out of the city. They had tried to put the graves a sensitive distance from the city wall, but they needed road access for the dead carts, and burial duty was unpopular. No one wanted to go further than was needed, and no one had time to, either.

"Logistically, the winter will cause issues," she went on. "Do you think it's fair of me to request additional graves dug now, before the ground freezes? I don't want to be the voice of hopelessness, but if winter comes and bodies are left lying about..."

"Fire cleanses," I reminded her softly.

"Fire also spreads, and we've limited people to control it." She paused on the edge of the area her horse had been tethered. Chay was with his own big, grumpy beast and hadn't glanced over. They deserved each other. "I agree it would be a good option, but a pyre for so many would require space and management I don't have, not to mention transporting all those resources."

My head ached, and the wind whistled around us. Her shoulders were too broad for a noblewoman, but not broad enough to carry this unaided. "I'm not familiar with burial in situations like this," I admitted, the words coming from far away. "But I know the corpses can enrich the soil for future generations if we treat it right." Or we could add some salt and poison it. Let them plow fields to find skulls of their kin. I heard the creak of the cart and the smell of blood and snow.

"I don't know how long this plague might exist inside a deceased body, if it does at all." She blew out a breath. "Still, it's relevant. Hopefully, we'll be rebuilding one of these days. We'll need all the help we can get."

"As you say, my lady."

She looked up at me, her eyes old in her face. "How are you, Thomas?"

I watched from far away, resisting the urge to lick my thumb and clean the smudge of dirt off her cheek. "I'm well, my lady. Don't you worry about me. It sounds like you've enough to concern yourself with."

"Oh, really?" she asked, brightly. "I hadn't noticed anything amiss!"

I didn't realize it was an attempt to joke until I saw a smile tugging at her mouth, and then I didn't quite know how to respond. "Yes, my lady," I agreed, stepping back. "Safe travels."

They rode out on opposite sides of the trail, and I was glad to see that gaping space between them, though it highlighted the lack of handmaid *and* second guard. Unease tugged at me, so I turned away, hoping that it was never even mentioned, so full were people's minds.

The rain came that night. Trenches dug by inexpert hands around tents were deepened, fires were fed, and soup was held close. I slept with aching bones and a heavy heart in the tent kept for the guards, but was shaken awake in the early hours of the morning to find we'd suffered our first loss.

Digging graves was no small feat. You had to dig them deep enough that they didn't get dug up again. It was hard, soul-crushing work. And with the rain and the cold, it was also dangerous work. I had volunteers. We all knew it had to happen. The dead couldn't just sit. But where to bury them? Not close to the tourney ground—we didn't need their bodies under us during the festivities next year, should any of us survive. We certainly didn't want to risk them decaying and adding to the sickness we swam in here.

In the end, we buried our dead in the orchard. Graves were marked with handfuls of dandelions and other posies gathered by children or prettily arranged leaves. I listened to speeches in sunshine, in wind, and with rain dripping off my nose. Sometimes, when there was no one else, I did my best to say a few words. And as my skill increased, I wondered how many more times I'd have the time to stand beside a grave. How many more people would be buried by themselves, with dignity.

CHAPTER THIRTY-SIX

CHAY

"Rather than try to train a defensive horse, you should first gain its trust by existing alongside it without placing demands."

~ How to Tame Your Brumby: A Collection of Raider's Ban Wisdom

I let myself into the tower for what felt like the millionth time today, settling yet another basket of coal beside the dense logs deigned fit for the lady to burn. We kept the tower warm, to help Isolde, who Audrey reported was still doing well. I hadn't seen her. I also hadn't seen Audrey since yesterday morning, when she'd tried to use the Acting Steward's influence to gather the merchants, and none had turned up.

I stoked the fire, then glanced up the stairs to her room. I hadn't been up there since Isolde asked me to train Audrey in the sword, and she'd burst into tears. I struggled to match that woman against the one who'd broken a guardsman's knee, then choked him until he was unconscious. And I struggled to match both of those people against the woman who'd lit up with joy as her horse charged toward the horizon when she'd dragged me out for a ride the other day.

The tower was silent.

I didn't mind her quiet. It was broken by little sounds of her fidgeting, the rhythmic scratch of her quill as she traced strange patterns on scrap parchment, or the turn of pages. I'd had a lot of time to observe her.

I didn't think she'd been noticing me much.

It had been a very long time since I'd walked halls like these, feeling distrustful glances and speculative looks being thrown my way. I'd gotten out of there, and I was getting out of here, too.

But I didn't dislike the idea of getting out *with* someone this time.

Steeling myself, I went up the stairs with a quick, "Coming up," in case she had her cushion out again. The thought made my steps lighter.

She was curled up in a pillow fortress in the center of her bed. It was late morning, and from someone I was reasonably confident rose with the sun, this was unusual behavior.

"Is there a problem?" she asked me.

There was no *give* in the woman. But that wasn't right, either. I'd seen her be thoughtful. The way she had chosen a specific room for Ylva because of the sunshine, the time we'd stopped by and she'd shared her skeins of thread with one of the cooks, who was low on greens. She didn't say nice things, but she did them.

"Sir?" Her formality was made even more devastating by the messy tumble of her hair and the blankets draped over her shoulders. In her hands, parchment rustled. Would she *always* "sir" me? I recalled her saying my name, but it felt like it was so long ago I couldn't bring up the precise memory any longer.

"Are we in hiding?" I asked, maintaining my focus. "Because, if we are, I ought to lay in more coal."

"What should you be hiding from?" Isolde asked from the other side of the door.

Beside that door was a chair still draped with the blanket Audrey must've wrapped herself in when she sat there to speak to Isolde. It was a familiar one, a dark green I'd seen her wear like a shawl a few times. A candle had burned out beside it, leaving behind a puddle of wax in the saucer.

Something about that made my heart ache.

What should we be hiding from? *Everything.* I looked into her whiskey eyes, and she looked straight through me, then dropped her gaze back to the words she'd been studying.

"Nothing's changed," Audrey told her, turning a page.

Fury gnawed at me. I was tied to this woman. "Should I exercise your horse?" I offered, because that at least would get me out of here, and her mare hadn't been as middling as the chestnut she'd ridden through the orchard when we'd met.

"No." She set her book aside heavily and flung an arm back with more drama than was necessary, sending a few pillows tumbling and breaking the surface of her bed. "I'm coming."

"You don't need to." But I glanced at the cover of the tome as she shook herself free from her layers. *The East Arcanloc Trade Company: A History.*

"If I don't need to, why are you here?" I had no answer for that except that I was tired of sitting in a silent room alone. She looked at me, blanket held tight around her shoulders, waiting.

"You're the one who's been agitating for action," I reminded her.

She barely blinked. "So I *do* need to."

"No, you don't." Her toes were bare. I could see the way her feet were positioned mostly by the way the blanket draped, but a few digits peeked out. There was something strange about that combative stance and those naked toes. "But I've been waiting for you, assuming today, like any other day, you'd appear and announce what it is we're doing, and I'd be expected to trot after you like a good boy."

"Did you hear that, Isolde?" she asked, laughter in her voice as she turned away from me. "He's a good boy."

"I don't recall seeing such a thing, but I've obviously missed a lot," Isolde said, the honey dripping off her words.

In front of me, Audrey tossed the blanket to the side. Her nightgown wasn't like the ones back in 'Ban, shorn off at the knees. I'm sure Thomas would be scandalized that I knew the regional differences between women's nightclothes.

I bet he wouldn't like to know that the extra length didn't hide the curve of her ass beneath the cloth as she leaned forward. She didn't pop her hips to accentuate the movement, rummaging through ribbons, jewelry, pins, and pots. Embers blew to life low in my belly. The fabric stretched over her back. She had strong shoulders with defined musculature that I wanted to explore. Impatient fingers unraveled the tie in her hair, and I was jolted back in time to the tourney I never should've fought in.

She'd helped me accomplish a dream without being gutted. I don't know that I'd ever shown her gratitude for that.

As they had then, her fingers tangled up in the auburn strands. I watched as she tore the tie free and broken wisps of hair fell to the floor. She muttered in annoyance, shaking it free. I fought not to grab her hands and force them to still.

I fought not to bury my face in her hair and pull that ass against me.

"If you're trying to convince me you're a lost pup," she said, and I was torn from my thoughts, "you've failed." She glanced over her shoulder, but I was already on the move, my feet like slabs of meat at the end of wooden stilts as I tried to navigate back down the stairs. There was something, though, some flicker on her face as I left. *Guilt.*

I got to the common room and braced myself against the fire, which may as well have been my post for the hours I'd spent there. This time, I didn't need its warmth.

Don't go there. She's the Duke's daughter. *You killed* children *for her.*

That could be true, *and* she could have an amazing ass. The quality of her curves would never cancel out her personality.

Anyway, it was probably a breach of my oath to fuck her, because there's no way word wouldn't get out, and it wouldn't do harm.

Her hands hadn't been impatient when she'd caught me up in her limbs in the orchard. They weren't impatient on her horse's reins, or when they lingered over the corner of whatever she was studying. Why were they so impatient in her own hair?

As she appeared, pinning her cloak at her throat, I resisted the urge to offer to assist her with it.

"We'll go to the kitchens first and take Ylva a hot meal, then see if the Captain has returned." The Captain was either dead somewhere, finding the bottom of his tankard, or sleeping off attempts to accomplish those things. She opened the door and held it for me to pass. "If I can't find him, I'm going to start talking to anyone who's there to figure out who's drawing up the roster. I need to make sure Thomas is given rest time. We'll probably be headed there tomorrow, but I don't know right now." The thought of visiting the field hospital wasn't the worst. I closed up the tower and walked beside her. "I've got three primary issues right now. Military, medical, and economic. I'm putting them in that order of priority because that's the order they'll kill us."

That was a lot of information. She must've been feeling bad. "Where does Ylva fit?"

"Pleasure," she said, without a hint of shame or any further explanation.

I didn't see it, myself. Ylva was too sharp, too sly, too unbending. And I suspected she wouldn't bat a lash while she cut our throats.

"She's using you," I pointed out.

"I imagine we're using each other," Audrey agreed. "Isn't that how people work?"

The thought was disturbing. "Not good ones."

She tossed me a pitying glance. "If everyone is happy with the trade, then you're still using each other."

"Is that what you're learning from the history of the East Arcanloc Trade Company?"

"You can laugh, but a lot of strategies used in trade seem like they're useful in life." She shrugged her cloak a bit higher, then picked absently at a nail. "Similar tactics are used in relationships as they are in large organizations. But no, I didn't learn that so recently. Do you want to know about the EACo, as it's become known?"

She looked at me as if she genuinely thought I might say yes.

"No."

I expected a flicker of disappointment or disapproval. Instead, I saw nothing but acceptance, as if it wasn't just the anticipated answer but the *correct* one.

She swept into the kitchens ahead of me, and I was left staring after her, feeling like we were both failing a trial.

CHAPTER THIRTY-SEVEN
AUDREY

"As the moon vanished, Hruudwulf looked across the fallen stones and bloody ground. It wasn't until he saw the tears on Gaelena's cheeks that he realized his belly was now full." ~ *Southern lore*

I watched the young woman's hands working the dough before her, hypnotized by the graceful movements. "…in the riot last night," she was saying, cheeks bright, words breathless. "Richard says his cousin's neighbor's family hasn't been able to get aught to eat for almost a week. Everything's gone."

The three guards in the corner stood as they saw us, scraping their chairs back. Dice disappeared into pouches. I stopped beside the cook, ignoring the bows they sent my way, and deliberately turned my back on them.

My heart drummed as I looked up and met her eyes. I didn't know where to put my hands. I hated that I had to worry about that while trying to figure out what the crinkles between her brows meant and that pinched twist to her mouth. Annoyed? Worried? "Why are they here?" I asked her quietly.

"My lady!" she bobbed a curtsey but didn't stop stirring. "Why, I've just sent you up a good bit of soup."

She didn't want to talk. That was the only answer. "I'm here for the prisoner," I said, playing along. "Could I have another bowl, mayhap?"

There was quiet around us. The cook smiled. "Of course you may." The guards watched her measure it out. "Would she like some bread, do you think?"

There was a combative set to the woman's shoulders. "This will do," I replied, wanting to get out of there. "Thanking you, Bernadette." I leaned in close to take it. "Cough if you're in danger," I murmured.

She smiled, but there was determination in the line of her mouth, not joy. "You stay well, lady Audrey. Come back down once you're done with her. We'll have some pie, then."

I noted that and nodded, doubting the invitation had anything to do with pie. But she didn't cough. "I'm hoping to speak to the Captain. Do you think it's particularly good pie?"

She considered it. "Tomorrow it'll be cobbler. If you're happy to wait, we'll always have something for you."

I walked out, wishing Isolde was with me to confirm she really *had* been trying to give me some sort of message. Could she just be trying to feed me pie? It wouldn't be the first time, but there was something off in the way she'd spoken, and in her body language.

Finding the Captain, or an alternative, was definitely becoming urgent.

In the corridor outside of Ylva's room, I stepped over some refuse and then stopped, looking down in horror at the body lying in the lee of the door. She'd died with one leg outstretched, her hands tangled deep in her shawl.

"They'll get her in the evening run," Chay said, urging me on.

"The evening run?" I repeated, struggling with the concept. "They…gather bodies? Multiple times a day?"

"They're supposed to." He drew out the keys. "They're shorthanded, though."

I was still trying to fit that knowledge into my understanding of the world when Chay opened the door to Ylva's room. He was pulled forward violently with a crash and jangle of equipment. Instinct, or muscle memory, or some part of my brain that worked without my knowledge took over, and I dropped my weight in time to go down in a tangle of limbs with Ylva, rather than let her throw me behind her as she escaped.

She swore and writhed. My heart roared. I ignored her blow to my ribs and tossed her onto her back. Fabric tore, giving way like butter beneath me as I held her down. From the corner of my eye, I saw Chay climbing to his feet, unhurried, as he watched us. She kept fighting, and I adjusted my grip.

She'd scratched my neck, somehow, and my thigh ached where she'd tried to take out my knees.

"Fuck," she said, thrashing furiously. "*Fuck you,* bitch!"

My belly twisted, but my hands didn't soften.

I wanted Isolde.

She collapsed beneath me, but her eyes went to the window. Tears sheened in them.

There was no question that she wasn't defeated, just delayed. I knew that feeling well. And still I didn't soften my hands on her.

The way I'd pinned one of her arms exposed the pale scars where I'd shattered her forearm. My father must've paid for a mage to heal her. It was the only explanation. And above them were other scars—deep, ugly, purple marks. I hadn't seen them that night. They looked about as healed as the marks her bones had left from driving through her flesh, back in the autumn.

As she panted beneath me, my mind went to the guards in the kitchen, in the corridors, beside covered carts, and standing in front of silent buildings.

Everywhere except at their posts.

"You need to get out of here," I said quietly. "You won't be safe for much longer."

She looked at me with such disgust I suspected she considered spitting on me a waste of energy.

The ground threatened to swallow me whole, but I didn't loosen my hands.

She'd never been safe. Not here. And she never would be. Even my limited protection was running up hard against its limitations. My head ached.

I needed to deal with the Captain.

The woman who basically kept the whole keep running was being bailed up in her own kitchen.

I didn't have time for this.

"I'm going to let you up," I told her. "I want to make a plan with you. If you don't want that, I'm going to pretend you just bested us, and hope your road was paved by the Son."

"Keep your Son," she said through her teeth. "I've got Khazari's kin in the wind."

The name meant nothing to me, and I saw no response on Chay's face, either, but she said it the same way someone would say *the One.* My heart still drumming, I eased myself away.

She made no sudden movements, just rubbed her limbs.

"If you attack her, I'm oathbound to kill you," Chay offered.

"I just did."

His brows rose, but before he could respond I flicked my fingers at him to stop him from getting in the way, gaining my feet. A few layers of underskirt were ruined, but I could repair them later. For now, I scooped the mess up and closed the door. I needed a way forward. That was all. I just needed this sorted so I could deal with the guard, somehow.

"Get me a horse," Ylva demanded, the words icy. "Or you'll regret it."

"That's not really how bargaining works." The soup was all over the room. I avoided it. I tried to gather my thoughts, but they were buzzing in my head. I didn't know *how* to deal with the guard. My leg ached, and I felt very small. "What's the next step?"

She looked at me like I'd grown two heads. "I'm not bargaining." Then she glanced at Chay. "What do you mean, the next step?"

Frustration twisted inside of me. "You want to go? Fine. I've got bigger issues." I was going to miss her, but that didn't matter. What mattered was the knife's edge this city was poised on. "I just need to figure out how I can get you out without disrupting—" I waved a hand at the castle, trying to find a word for the hideous maelstrom we were in, and failing.

Ylva's eyes narrowed. "Are you okay?" she asked me, but there was no kindness in the words. Only mockery.

I felt sick. If she walked out, she'd probably be stopped. They'd underestimate her and end up dead.

Or she'd double back, and *I'd* end up dead.

She could come back even if I escorted her out. But if she was properly clear of the city, with a decent chance of getting away, I suspected she'd cut her losses and flee. She was a sensible woman. And then we'd come back home, and I'd figure out the next thing.

Beneath me, the rug on the floor was faded and thin. I wished I could've looked to Isolde, assessed her thoughts on the matter. She would've stepped in if I was putting my head on the chopping block.

Chay would, I suspected, when crunch time came, but I didn't know if he'd see the issue before it arose.

"We're going riding," I said, then drew in a deep, bracing breath. She might pass as Isolde if I borrowed my friend's riding habit and horse. Their builds were nothing alike, but with a cloak drawn high and a kerchief over her face… "You're going to die of the plague," I told Ylva. "And Isolde is going riding with us, Chay."

He shrugged, straightening.

Ylva didn't move. "You can't be serious."

"I can be," I disagreed. "When I need to."

She looked like she wanted to hit me again. "You're scared."

It wasn't a question, so I didn't bother to agree. "Wait here. I'll return with Isolde's clothes momentarily." The other problems I couldn't deal with just grew larger, but this one, this small thing, fell into place neatly and brought me a measure of peace. "I'm sorry I didn't think of this earlier," I admitted, struggling against the humiliation of my error.

"I'm sorry you didn't, too," she said, but there was less sting in the words. "Bring me with you." I opened my mouth to object, and she silenced me with an angry hand gesture. "Trust me, *fina.* You don't want that storm blowing in, and I don't want to sit in this cesspit of death another moment."

I glanced out the window, surprised to see the sullen clouds from yesterday had become a dark, threatening mass on the horizon.

And the wind was blowing from the south. The wind *never* blew from the south.

"You'll explain on the road?" I asked her, unease prickling the back of my neck. She hesitated, and I pressed, "If I let you out now, you'll tell me what's happening?"

She was silent for another moment, then nodded her head in resignation. "Fine. Sure. Rivers and snow, this is not how I expected any of this to happen."

Finally, we'd found something we agreed on aside from wanting my father dead.

CHAPTER THIRTY-EIGHT
CHAY

"If the end isn't happy, it isn't the end." ~ Raider's Ban proverb

"Tell Isolde," Audrey said, glancing toward the stairs to her rooms as Ylva began nosing around the tower. "I'll wait here with Ylva."

It was clear I wasn't fit for guard duty in her opinion, and for some reason that rankled. I'd been dismissed from her company though, so she wouldn't even see it if I glared at her.

There hadn't been too many reasons for me to climb those stairs before. The turns weren't too tight, but I had to put my hand on my scabbard all the same to stop it from knocking against the stone.

Her nightgown had been tossed over the back of the chair before her dresser, and an Audrey-shaped divot was in the middle of her bed. She'd fit in there so neatly. Her skin would be so warm, her smile sleepy.

"Isolde," I said, with more annoyance than the woman had earned. "We're disguising Ylva as you and releasing her in the orchard. I need a cloak or something." There was no way Ylva would pass as Isolde. They were both humans and both sharp-tongued. Their similarities ended there.

"What?" she demanded through the door. "Where's Audrey?"

"Down below with Ylva."

My eyes wanted to wander over the room. I forced them to stay locked on the door as I waited for her response.

The time crawled by, and it didn't matter that I wasn't looking at the bed because it was right behind me. I tried to remember the smell of her from the orchard, but it was the feel of her atop me that filled my mind, not the woman's scent. It'd be all over those pillows, though. Not that I was planning on sniffing her pillows, especially knowing how intimate she was with at least one of them.

But the thought teased me, still.

The door in front of me opened, and I stepped back instinctively. Isolde, pale but otherwise fine, strode past me, basket on one arm. "There's a stack of spare guard uniforms in the spare wing of your barracks," she said, directing the words down the stairs. "Get into a tabard in the La'Angi colors, Ylva."

How she expected Ylva to hear that from downstairs I had no idea, but I followed along behind Isolde and, as we emerged into the common room, I saw Ylva's cloak vanishing around a corner.

Apparently, she *had* heard.

Audrey was staring wide-eyed at her mentor. "Don't complain," Isolde said, irritated. "I'm fine, and I needed to stretch my legs anyway. Why now?"

Audrey shook her head. "She tried to escape. It made me realize she really ought to. There were guards in the kitchen."

So, she *had* identified them. The unkind part of me wondered why she hadn't killed them, like the other guard who'd been clearly abusing his power, much as these men had. It wasn't an entirely fair comparison, and the righteous indignation I reached for didn't sit well in my belly. I wandered over to my station before the fire, annoyed that I hadn't been able to read her. The woman was just so changeable. I missed Kadan.

Sunny one day, cheery the next. You always got what you expected from him.

This woman was murdering children one day and tossing men over the seawall just to save my feelings the next.

And then ordering me about.

Heart sufficiently hardened, I turned my attention back to where they stood near the window, speaking quietly. Isolde mostly listened, nodding every now and then, her eyes on the horizon.

Ylva let herself back in quietly. Her hair was tied back at the base of her head and tucked into the collar. The broad uniform made her look smaller than she was, but it hid the few curves she had. "The hair's a problem," I said. "They don't let anyone don the uniform if your hair isn't done just so."

She looked at mine with distaste. "Well, I'm wearing their uniform whether they approve of my hair or not." She plucked at the fabric. "It's vile."

"Agreed." I went to my small bundle of items and drew out a scarf, passing it over. "A lot of people are covered at the moment."

She wrapped it over her head with quick, impatient movements. Before I could get Audrey and Isolde's attention, they turned toward us. "Let's get it done, then," Isolde said.

"You're more concerned about Ylva than infecting Audrey?" I asked, because this wasn't making sense. If Ylva was truly such a great threat, why had she allowed for visitation in the keep?

"We'll be in the open air," Isolde said briskly. "And it isn't Ylva I'm concerned about."

I glanced out the window at the threatening clouds, ignoring the smug look Ylva directed my way as she fell into step beside me.

From the corner of my eye, I kept track of Ylva's body language. Everyone else seemed to know something I didn't, and it all seemed to center around her. She didn't lean away from Isolde any more than she had from Audrey, and didn't seem in the least anxious. If anything, I would've called her cocky. I didn't know if the swagger was natural or part of her disguise, along with the uniform she'd donned.

We barely encountered anyone, though. We'd seen no one at all on the way to Audrey's tower. The chances of us getting away with it grew with every step. I knew I ought to care because it would put Audrey in danger later, but it was hard to get excited about executing an escape for someone else while we remained trapped.

In the stables, Isolde pointed to a deep-chested gray mare confidently. "Take that one," she told Ylva. "She'll carry you far, and she's compliant."

Ylva's grin went unseen behind the carefully draped scarf, but her eyes crinkled with mirth. I turned away rather than pick up that joke, heading to where Bliksem was housed near Audrey's mare. There was no sign of a stableboy, and I tried not to worry about that stroke of luck. *Some* good fortune was welcome, but too much felt suspicious.

I pretended not to notice the bundle of rags in the corner of the stables and the rats scurrying away.

Mayhap there wasn't too much good fortune, after all.

Isolde led her horse to the mounting block, and I watched as she climbed into her saddle, unsure if the weakness was real or for show. One quick, razor-sharp look from her ended my doubts. Realizing I was supposed to be the lady's guard, I moved to boost Audrey into her saddle, but she was already taking her turn at the mounting block. I returned to Bliksem as Ylva climbed into the saddle as if she hadn't spent weeks in captivity, settling in comfortably. She'd been given a La'Angi issue sword and plain shield, which she wore slung over her back.

No one had said anything to me. Was I so superfluous?

The scene in the city remained unchanged, except now clots of people cast glances to the storm on the horizon. Audrey set a pace that bordered on impolite as we hastened out of the city, but the roads were almost empty, and the pressure of the quiet was immense. She never once paused to look back at Ylva or check on her. Isolde wasn't the only one who played a close game. I'd lived alongside this woman for more than a moon now, and I still didn't know her. It made me feel oddly hollow.

Audrey didn't slow until the apple trees sheltered us from the view of the gates. Then she turned to Ylva and said, "Where are we headed?"

She pointed. "To the *ceiyemmyah pbettra.*" And it was said as if Audrey should've known that, and also know what the words meant.

I watched as my liege lady glanced at her mentor, a quick, searching look that went unanswered. "Where?" Isolde asked.

"The *ceiyemmyah pbettra*," Ylva repeated, frustrated. "Surely you must know them?"

"Possibly," Audrey agreed. "Under our own name."

"The stones?" Ylva offered. "Big. Old magic. Pre-dates your shitty, drafty pile of pre-rubble, there."

I enjoyed the term *pre-rubble* while I saw Audrey glance toward Isolde again. This time, Isolde met her glance.

"Should I stop to change to a proper saddle?" Audrey asked. "Or is it a short ride?"

"It's not close, but we'll make it before nightfall."

Another quick look between the women, and I resented being left out entirely. At least when Thomas was here, he'd look at me. I felt invisible.

"We need to be back by nightfall," Audrey explained. "Or they'll send a search party for me."

"Then go," Ylva said with a shrug. "I don't need to be accompanied."

At least I knew enough of Audrey's character to predict her terminal curiosity. She shook her head, and they set out in the approximate direction of Ylva's pointing. "We'll stop and change saddles," Isolde said.

That they kept proper saddles stashed somewhere didn't surprise me. Audrey had been using one, albeit only barely, when we'd first met. But I'd never seen such a swap happen, and mayhap the Duke's daughter wasn't the only one who was curious.

At one stage, Ylva pointed and said, "We're off-course."

Isolde glanced over her shoulder. "You'll benefit from hitting our cache. We aren't far and, we'll travel faster with proper equipment."

Of course she had a cache. I'd be surprised if she only had one.

Apparently mollified, or perhaps also curious, Ylva and I followed along until they came to a long-abandoned little home that looked to only provide shelter to animals now. Both women dismounted, and their horses—clearly feeling at home—went to work cropping the grass that had grown undisturbed in the small clearing.

I saw Audrey murmuring something quietly to Isolde, who sent a quick glance toward Ylva. "She knows where it is already," she told Audrey with a dismissive flick of her fingers. "There's no point worrying about that now."

"I've a nose for secrets," Ylva agreed, dismounting.

"If you don't have a tongue for them, we've no issue," Isolde told her.

Ylva grinned, the scarf down off her face. "No, Sister. I wouldn't waste my talents on talking." Impervious to Ylva's charms, Isolde rolled back what looked like grass but had a pattern-like fabric beneath it, revealing a sturdy wooden door to a cellar. "Odd to see a wolf run so far north," Ylva mused, hands on hips. "Have you a longbow, Sister?"

"Recurved only, and none to spare. But I've knives. Ylva and Chay, remove your insignia."

I did as I was told, then held the reins of Ylva's horse while the three of them vanished into the hole. They were only gone a few moments before reappearing with saddles. Isolde set to work swapping them over, and Audrey vanished again.

Horse care was something I *could* do. Wary of Audrey's mare, who I'd seen nip at a stableboy who'd been too hasty with her, I helped Isolde ready the animals. Audrey reappeared, and I had to force myself not to visibly react to the change in her.

The riding habit was replaced by sturdy winter men's clothing. A wide belt rode on her hips, a quiver on her left, and a wicked knife at her right. The curves of her legs were obvious in the boots and figure-hugging pants.

She hadn't worn the quiver when we'd run into each other.

Isolde saw it and gave a nod of approval. They swapped roles almost seamlessly. I didn't offer Audrey a boost into the saddle, and she clearly didn't need one. The strung bow she hooked onto her saddle as if she'd done it a hundred times before was at my eye height.

I'd seen the like before in the hands of the Steppe warriors. Bone and wood, beautifully carved, passed down through generations. That bow would have tales to tell.

"Thanking you," Audrey said to me. "It's much faster with an extra set of hands."

Surprised to be acknowledged, I said nothing.

"Are you sure you're happy to part with this?" Ylva asked Audrey from her own saddle, turning a knife over in her hands.

"Mayhap it'll find its way between my father's ribs," she said, with the same semi-bored speculation I'd heard in her voice as she'd once said to Isolde, "*I wonder if cook's making upside-down apple cakes one day soon.*"

Isolde returned dressed similarly to Audrey, then stopped to tie a bedroll on the horse behind Ylva and pass her a small but heavy bag that chimed with coin.

Ylva didn't look so cocky now. She cleared her throat. "We need to move."

"We will." Isolde closed it up and spent a little time with her hands in the grass where it had been rolled up, fluffing up flattened stalks. She didn't eradicate all signs of her hidden cellar, but there was nothing to set it apart, at least to my eye, once she was done.

Now, Ylva led the way. I followed along behind, ordered to participate by a man none of us respected. I could think of many situations where I would've gladly ridden along as a shield on such a rescue operation.

"Who's Khazari?" Audrey asked, when we were forced to a walk due to the undergrowth.

"He breathed and made the wind," Ylva told her, without looking away. "He angered and made lightning, then cried and made rain." I wondered if Ylva knew how firmly the La'Angi locals held their beliefs of the One, but I put most of my attention to the rapidly approaching incline, assessing the best path for Bliksem. "His children are those who dedicate themselves to the air and sky. And they're waiting for me."

"Wait. Khazari is your name for the One?" Audrey asked. "There's a priest here?"

Ylva snorted, leading us straight toward the hill, straight into the wind that whistled through the trees and made leaves stir wetly against branches. "Khazari is not the One. There is no One. There are only many. Arrogant northerners."

Before Audrey could respond, a bird sang nearby, and then silence descended. Grateful for the quiet, I watched the way Audrey held her seat in the saddle, critically. If she broke her neck riding, I suspected my oath would consume me. I did, after all, know she needed practice.

She wouldn't enjoy being pulled up and told to walk her horse, but the hill was such that it was probably the safest option.

She was fine, though, letting her mare pick her own way and moving well with the horse. I followed closely but noticed, once we'd reached a more level part of the trail, that Isolde seemed unconcerned.

I'd never thought to ask what had gone wrong with Audrey's horse on that day, whether it was simply because it was an unfamiliar animal or whether something had happened. That oversight made me wonder how many other things I hadn't thought to ask.

I could just about hear Kadan telling me, "You don't know what you don't know, brother. That's why you make friends with folks who do." My heart ached.

Neither he nor I would ever be the same people we had been before we'd come to La'Angi.

Leaning low over Bliksem's neck to avoid a branch, I caught a glimpse of the storm clouds up ahead.

There were a lot more types of magic than those used in our own fair country by our lily-livered excuse for a king. But Audrey might not know that because she didn't know what she didn't know, either. And if we were riding up to someone proficient in magics we couldn't understand, how could we hope to defend against it?

"What're the odds this is a trap?" I asked Isolde, keeping my tone unconcerned.

"High," she told me without looking. "If they turn on us, I'll put an arrow in Ylva's throat. It's her they want enough to risk coming so close. You get Audrey home. Don't wait for me."

Despite her bravado, I realized she sat low in her saddle, her cloak pulled tight. From my position to the side of her, and with the poor light, I could see how pale she was.

Ylva sent Isolde a long look that left me with no doubt that she'd heard every word. Isolde clearly had known that would happen. If there was a hidden meaning I was supposed to take from that plan, some sort of secret alternative option, I wasn't finding it. The best I could do was follow Ylva and Audrey's path.

There was smoke coming from off to the west when we next slowed enough to speak, but the silence was broken only by the splashing of our horses crossing a creek. With another slow incline before us and the sun sitting low, we focused on the path ahead of us.

If Audrey was wearying, I couldn't tell from her seat or her focus. Isolde, on the other hand, sank lower again in the saddle. Audrey was in front of her and hadn't noticed. In the gathering gloom, I was watching for a spot of relatively clear riding so I could draw Audrey's attention. Before one came, though, another burbling bird call met my ears. This time, I saw Isolde lift her fingers to her lips to make the sound.

It was a disorienting reminder I was riding alongside a Matri'sion. But it was more than that for Audrey, who had an arrow notched and crowded her horse closer to Ylva.

Ylva just laughed. "You're sharp," she threw casually over her shoulder toward Isolde.

And then chaos erupted.

CHAPTER THIRTY-NINE
ISOLDE

"It was that night that Hruudwulf's sorrow was heard. From that day forth, that place was known as Wolfswail. None can walk there without sensing the grief of his betrayal soaked into the stones." ~ Southern lore

I didn't bother trying to give Chay directions and didn't dare distract Audrey. My horse had lost its head in the blast of wind that had forced my eyes closed, and I steered it best I could, loosing an arrow based on my memory of Ylva's position.

Branches were groaning and cracking under the force of the wind. I could hear hooves and cleared my vision enough to see Ylva clutching at the arrow in her chest. My horse wanted me to flee in the direction Audrey had gone, and that sounded perfect to me.

My heart beat heavily. I felt slow, but I'd been fast enough to cost them their princess, at least.

Leaning low, I hugged the side of the horse and let it have its head, keeping track of Audrey and Chay from the sound of the crashing underbrush and their horses' heaving breaths and terrified whinnies.

Breathe, I willed of Audrey. *Breathe. Guide her.* I felt an arrow pass me by, and fury pulsed through me. Regardless of what I'd said to Chay, I *hadn't* thought it would really be a trap. I would never have allowed Audrey to take such a risk. I didn't expect Ylva to be our ally, but if she was a neutral party, that was better than an enemy. And Audrey was going to need allies.

My legs straining, I pulled myself up and tried to see ahead. They were silent to our ears.

Magic users didn't use bows.

The Worgs had come to fetch Ylva.

Ahead, I caught glimpses of a clearing through the trees, of Audrey fighting for control of Storm, and of a posturing Raider's Ban warhorse in his element.

Well, he wasn't the only one.

Against other foes, I'd've sent my horse on its way and laid in wait, but I wasn't fooling these people's superior senses. Instead, I reined in my girl, slowing her as she broke into the clearing.

"How many?" Audrey was shouting.

I had no idea. I'd caught a slight movement from the corner of my eye. That, and the tightness of my gut, had told me all I'd needed.

"They're Worgs," I said to the pair. "They'll hear you coming, they'll smell you. Use a stream to muddy your scent."

Chay pointed his sword at the sky. "Magician," he said grimly.

My bow followed my eyes, but my arms felt heavy, and even with the battle energy forcing my heart to beat harder, I still felt too damned *slow.*

The sorcerer was a dark blot against the clouds. He dipped from my view, vanishing into the trees like a leaf fluttering from the sky. I struggled to make sense of that when I saw Chay moving, shield on his arm, and his horse high-stepping arrogantly.

Arrows bloomed in his shield, two of them. I blasted a whistled warning. Audrey twisted, dropping down beside her horse as we'd practiced. But she kept falling, graceless, tangled.

My heart twisted, too. Just as graceless. Just as tangled.

I was in my forest, and it was early morning. *Giselle lay before me, her body still warm, her eyes glassy. I reached out, dirt on my hand, and closed her eyes. But they didn't close the way they did when the Commander did it. Her lashes prickled. I tried to get purchase on the skin of her lids and ran the pad of my finger over the moist softness of her eyeball. My stomach rebelled. I tried again, dropping my bow so I could hold her head still.*

The wind gusted around us. Chay's sword came down against Storm's side, and the horse danced around Audrey, lashing out at him. She rolled free, staggering toward the closest source of cover, a big, moss-covered rock. Her saddle slipped drunkenly where Chay had cut it loose.

I drew in a breath and cast my eyes around for targets, sitting high to make myself vulnerable. "And I heard Worgs shot like 'sion riders," I said derisively. "That's five shots I've counted you've missed. How many more arrows did you loose?"

To prove my point, a shaft skimmed past Audrey, and she fell back against the stone. She'd saved herself, barely, falling backward hard. Her hands dropped to her sides, and she made a noise of pain that I heard against all reason, over the horses and the wind, over my own drumming heart and the roaring in my ears.

There was no target in the trees, though. There was nothing except the blur of more shafts. Not even coming at me. And they were so far from me.

Chay whirled hard. I heard the arrow sink deep into the wood of his shield. But beyond him, another flew toward where Audrey was prone against the stone.

It struck the air before her like it was made of wood, too. The shaft stood, bristling, like those Chay's shield boasted. Almost immediately, another split it.

I didn't know what magic that was, and I didn't care. I steered hard to Audrey and kicked one foot free, readying myself to help her mount up and flee.

"Truce!" a voice shouted. "Unless Ylva dies."

There was no way she wasn't dying, and now wasn't the time to wonder. "Get up," I told Audrey, landing beside her. One of my knees gave out, and agony screamed up my legs. I kept my face blank. She didn't notice, her eyes on the arrows ahead of us. Blood streaked down the outside of one arm, nonfatal. As she stood, the arrows tumbled from the sky like they'd been dropped by whatever magical force had stopped them mid-air. I boosted Audrey into my saddle.

Over my horse's rump, I saw a man striding into the clearing, longbow at his side and quiver over his shoulder. The fur-lined cloak he wore strapped over his chest, and his long hair pulled back in a club both marked him as Southern.

"The earthworker says we shouldn't kill you," he called. "Let it be known that is the *only* reason you are still standing."

Chay snorted, and so did his horse.

"You're coming with me and will be thanking her," the Southerner called.

I shared a quick look with Audrey. "You actually shot her?" she demanded, taking my reins.

I didn't bother to point out the Worg had led us into an ambush. My quiver was on that saddle, and I only had the fistful of arrows I held and my knives. None of them were useful against invisible targets.

My bones ached. But over the Southerner's head, I saw a dark form move in the trees. Judging from the number of arrows loosed, I suspected there were mayhap two more after this crusty cocktugger, at most.

I didn't hate those odds, if I had eyes on two of them.

Deliberately, I looked up and caught Chay's gaze, drawing in a deep breath. I didn't question the flicker of compassion that was swiftly disguised, simply noted the way he sheathed his sword to take up his reins.

Go. I whistled and swung my bow up at the same time, letting fly at the figure lurking within the shadows and then charging toward the man in the clearing.

He spun. Horses screamed in fury, and hooves churned the ground. I dodged the arrow stabbed toward me and kicked out. A shaft whistled past me from the shadowed area where someone had lurked, and I knew that while I'd missed my secondary target, I'd accomplished my main one.

Safe travels, I thought to Audrey, sending another arrow into the darkness.

A foot in my abdomen drove me back, and a little further from the crusty cocktugger, I saw another emerging from the shadows.

"Enough!" the man roared, his face twisted in fury but his hawk-like features were still strikingly familiar. If he wasn't Ylva's blood, I'd cut Audrey's throat myself. "Cut her string!"

I dropped my arm so the man before me missed my bow, and I ducked to the side. But my legs weren't as sure as they should have been, and the ground gave way a little.

There was really no other way it was going to end than this brute pointing his drawn bow at my chest. "Do we take this one?" the man in front of me asked.

I could just about *see* Ylva's kin considering whether it was worth it to rough me up. "The Butcher's Brat won't come back for her." Fury pounded at my temples, and he smiled. "Will she?"

"You'd better hope not," I said quietly. "She was gentle with your sister. She wouldn't bother with you."

"*Gentle?*" He raised a finger. "Walk, bitch."

I considered fighting against it, but by now, the two other men would have a solid line on me. I had two arrows left.

If it came to it, I'd kill Ylva's poor-tempered kin and let her live.

So I walked, biding my time, ignoring the exhaustion and the agony that had settled deep in my limbs. None of them got within range of my fists. The third man stayed mostly out of sight. And while I could hear the occasional noise that could be from Audrey and Chay in the distance, I wasn't certain of it, though the men around me would be. They'd know their location, but more, they'd know whether their hearts beat too fast under duress, or whether their horses stumbled. They'd know if they were angled into the wind and whether they'd be home, safe, by nightfall.

It was beyond me to not resent them for the knowledge of my charge that I so desperately wanted. I remembered the blood on Audrey's arm, the fistful of arrows she'd held. She'd done fine. Not well, perhaps, but fine. And Chay had been the boon I hadn't expected. Apparently, he *could* use a shield when he was on a horse, at least.

Ylva was lying on her back where she'd fallen. The arrow shaft lay beside her. Her skin was pale, and the woman bent over her didn't look up from her hands, folded over the wound, and slick with her blood. She had the strange stillness of a magic user at work.

I had no guilt whatsoever. But the sight of this mage made me uneasy. I didn't know enough about Southern magic to know if she ought to be my primary target. She hadn't been the greatest threat earlier, and potentially had even halted those arrows to protect Audrey. But was that just because her primary focus was saving Ylva?

"Don't even think about it," murmured Ylva's relative behind me. "Her life is worth a thousand of yours."

I assumed he meant the mage. I studied the woman's bare, dimpled knee, soft forearms, and long brown hair that seemed to ripple in wind I couldn't feel. Whatever storm had been blowing in seemed to have calmed.

"If we came this far, and she dies…"

I cast an unimpressed look at Ylva's bearded double. "You'll kill me?" I held up my hand. The movement made the splinters of agony in my bones scream. "See those black nails? I've got the plague. So does more than half of that city you were planning on slipping into. Those two who you couldn't kill despite your best efforts?" I folded my cloak tighter around myself and leaned back against a tree. "Pretty much doomed. You'd be wasting your time going after them."

"You just sacrificed yourself for fun?" Ylva's kin asked me, his mouth kicked up in amusement. "I appreciate your service, Sister."

"I want to see if she pulls through," I said, jerking my chin at Ylva, and it wasn't entirely a lie. If Ylva had called them off, was it because she didn't intend for it to be an ambush, but wheels had already been turning? Or did she just think better of them all dying on our arrows? "When I shoot a man, he stays shot. Lucky Ylva's a woman, isn't it?"

"Your bravado would be more convincing if I couldn't hear your heart laboring like a fish trying to breathe air," her kin drawled, then picked at one of his teeth.

If only *he'd* been the one the Duke had captured, I'd happily have let him rot in the dungeons. He was top priority to turn into a pincushion. The mage could live if he needed both my remaining arrows, and so could Ylva.

"Why'd you come after her?" I asked him, realizing they were risking much, sending a mage *and* another member of the royal family for a princess never destined to be heir.

"There's too many women for me to keep satisfied," he told me, his eyes on the mage. "I need someone to tag in, and I've heard she eats cunt almost as well as I fill it."

"That's not what I heard," murmured the other man, and the quick, annoyed glance shot his way by Ylva's brother made both the other man and I grin.

I was wrong. He wasn't the crusty cocktugger. Ylva's kin was. "What's your name, hero?" I asked him, keeping it friendly.

Dark eyes above Ylva's hawk-like nose flicked back up to me. "Wuden," he told me after a moment.

I considered it. "No, I haven't heard of your prowess."

In the darkness, I saw the man opposite me hide another grin. "You wouldn't," Wuden said icily. "I don't stick my dick in northern bitches."

Without hesitation I responded with, "Speaking on behalf of northern bitches, we're grateful."

The mage before us stirred, then fell gracelessly back onto her bare backside with a heavy thump. A pretty, heart-shaped face was turned toward us, and the look she sent me was full of disgust. "She'll live. What's this one doing here?"

"She's a guarantor," Wuden said, shooting me a smile.

"She's a hazard," the mage shot back. "And she's infectious. Get rid of her before Ylva gets sick, or I'll heed the wind's call."

"Reckon she'll make it through the night?" Wuden asked the man beside him.

"I've got two arrows," I told him, making my eyes big and round. "It'd be a shame to die with them unspent."

His attention narrowed on me again. "Go. You might just get lucky and need those to bring down game. It's a long walk back, and your time is short."

He wasn't wrong, and we all knew it. "Tell her I'm sorry," I told the mage. "I thought she'd led us into a trap."

"She knew," the woman said with a nod. "Gaelena ease your path, Sister."

I touched the back of my knuckle to the circlet I hadn't worn in more than a decade, suddenly feeling naked without it. "Walk tall," I told her.

"Die standing," the woman returned, as few knew to. "I'm sorry, but I've no magic to spare for you."

I waved her kind words off rather than think on what they might mean, drew my hood closer, and headed into the darkness. It, at least, I could face.

CHAPTER FORTY
THOMAS

"We are stronger than we think, and also more fragile. Listen to your body, because nowhere else can you find an accurate assessment of your limits."
~ Matri'sion lesson

The boy shifted from foot to foot as I pulled on my boots, my bones protesting the movements. "...and I think she's *bleeding,*" he told me, yet again. "And she's dressed like *us.*"

My heart sank.

I arrived to find Audrey had already been moved into a tent. I heard rustling from within and the occasional low murmur from an older woman.

Chay lifted a hand. He wasn't wearing a tabard, and his shield, at his feet, was studded with arrows.

"How's the road back to the city?" he asked me. "Passable at night?"

I assumed he meant on horseback. "I don't have enough riders. What happened?"

"Brigands," he replied. "We were trying to be less conspicuous."

That was the story behind his lack of tabard? I saw the wide-eyed youngster lingering by the fire and didn't question him further. "Isolde's still out there. She's sick."

My heart ached for the lady. "Is she…" I cast my eyes toward the tent again.

"She bought us time to flee," Chay said, his voice neutral. "Audrey wants to return immediately. Isolde will be on foot."

My bones could attest to the dip in temperature but not to whether they'd find a live woman or a corpse. "You're thinking to return to the city, get aid, and take them back to the site?"

He nodded. "Bliksem is fine for the journey, and I know where to go. Isolde's horse will make it to the city, but much further and she'll be harming her. But there are other horses."

The lady had been on Isolde's horse? Before I could get the details, she emerged from the tent, her expression eerily reminiscent of the Duke when he was a hair's breadth from a full-blown rage. A bandage was neatly tied around her upper arm, and her skirts were a few fingers too short for the length of her legs.

I caught the look the cook sent me as she, too, emerged. Whatever had happened, we didn't need rumors exaggerating the cost to the lady. If it was known she'd worn a different skirt home…

"Thanking you for waking me, lad," I told the boy. "Could you get my horse ready, please?"

"I'll get you some torches," the cook said primly, and made herself scarce.

"Thomas, you don't need to do this," Audrey said, shaking her head. "We'll be safe on the road back."

"They'll do without me for half a day," I told her. And the thought of seeing Sandra made me glad. I didn't like to think of her huddled in a dark corner, waiting for the terror to subside before it was safe to emerge.

By the time tomorrow night rolled around, I was going to be an exhausted shell of a man, but that wouldn't change me overmuch.

It took me only a few moments to tap a few people on the shoulder so they'd run it without me whilst I was gone. By the time we got to the horses, they'd been fed, watered, and were ready for the short trip to the city.

I suspected Chay left the arrows in his shield as some sort of proof of their trials. It worked, too. No one looked too closely at Audrey's skirt with the bandage on her arm and the arrows in his shield.

Audrey's saddle had been switched to a man's, but I didn't comment. There must've been reason for her own to have been replaced.

"How are…people?" Audrey asked as we set off. "Everything."

"Well," I told her, because she wasn't going to hear much information, and I didn't want to share delicate details within earshot of half the camp.

She nodded, her eyes locked on the road before us. I let the two of them ride abreast and followed along behind, making the most of the light of their torches for my nervous horse.

The road between the city and the tourney grounds had been immaculate before the tourney and maintained during the festivities, but that was weeks ago now. Rain and use had seen holes develop in the road. Stones jutted up, and puddles had softened patches to mud. It wasn't a ride through the orchard, but it wasn't a well-lit, cobblestone street, either. The two of them obviously weren't worried about the risks each of those holes provided, but I wasn't the world's greatest horseman, and I had no shame in that. My two feet had carried me further than those two had ridden, of that I had no doubt.

I was relieved when the city walls came into view. The roads were silent, and the gates were down, but they'd open for her. They *should* have search parties out, too.

But when we made it to the heavy wood and steel gate, no one responded to my shout of "Hoy, friends!" or "Raise the gate!" and I wasn't announcing the lady's presence at the top of my lungs, just to have any listening ears squirrel away that information.

The three of us stood there in the quiet of the night.

"I didn't see anyone along the wall," Audrey said softly. "Did either of you?"

"No," Chay said.

I'd been watching the road. "They've probably got search parties out."

"They've probably not set the Watch properly," Audrey said, her tone icy. "It's too cold for her to be out overnight. If she was healthy, and they hadn't had a mage—"

"Raise the gate!" Chay bellowed, and the lady winced.

"They had a mage?" I asked hesitantly. "Are you sure, my lady?" Mages weren't found in brigand groups.

"Not like I've seen them," she told me grimly. "I didn't get a good look at them, but they blasted us with air and looked to be gliding."

A chill went through me. I held my torch up, studying the arrows on Chay's shield again. The wind around me screamed, and it smelled like snow. My heart worked like a smith's hammer against my chest. "We need to get in." There was no way to get her in those walls, though. They were impenetrable. But we had to find some way.

"Do you know that sort of mage?" Audrey asked me.

I focused on keeping my tone even. "Mayhap, my lady. We should ride to another gate."

Chay lifted his torch to the side. The land was clear, the grass trampled from the tent city that had sprung up during the tourney. Now, it was a field of muddy pits and furrows.

"Sorry," he said, sounding anything but. "I'm not taking Bliksem through that in this light."

But urgency was clawing at me. "We can walk them." We wouldn't be expected to move alongside the walls, would we? And we might stumble across someone on duty who could raise the gates, too.

"Someone is just as likely going to patrol past," Chay disagreed.

Terror drummed. "We need to get inside the walls."

"He's right," Audrey said in a monotone. "The longer we're out here, the longer Isolde is out *there.* Do we wait, or do we go get her ourselves?"

The thought of heading *toward* that mage…

"She bought you time so you could flee," Chay said bluntly. "That was her wish. She gave us instructions on how to do it."

"So *you* go back!" she told him furiously. "I'm safe, now!"

He was so unmoved that I suspected it wasn't the first time he'd heard that demand since they'd fled.

My skin crawled. "I'll go," I told her, ashamed to hear my own voice crack. I cleared it, hoping she just thought I was sick. "I'll go at sunup, with others. We'll find her." We'd need the dogs. I didn't tell the lady that, though. "I'm sorry, my lady."

When she turned to me, there were tears on her cheeks, but her expression was fixed in a compassionate smile. There was something deeply unsettling about that. "I understand," she said, but I didn't know what she understood, or why she looked like an effigy of a demon attempting to disguise itself as the Wife.

She climbed nimbly from her saddle, not slowed by the injury to her arm. I followed her lead, my knees clicking and grinding, bracing myself to walk. The big knight and his proud pony could sit here and be too fancy for the fields. The lady and I knew how to make things happen.

She was pulling a length of rope from the saddlebags, though, sniffling quietly, dashing tears away. "How many knives do we have?" she asked in that monotone voice.

Puzzled, I watched as Chay shook his head. But she wasn't looking at us. Two big, wicked-looking hunting knives appeared from those saddlebags. "Whose bags are those?" I asked them. Chay looked at me for a moment, his expression unreadable, then shrugged.

"Mine until Isolde gets back," Audrey said, working with the rope.

"If you're trying to make a grappling hook, no you aren't," Chay told her. "That'll never hold you."

"I'm used to that," she told him with another unladylike sniff, then she tested the strength of her knot with a hard tug.

My heart ached for the child. "I know you're scared," I told her, like I would've if she were one of my girls. "But look on the bright side.

We're here and healthy. As soon as someone comes by, we'll rouse a search party."

She didn't respond but set to work on the second knife, knotting it a little further along from the first.

Chay blew out a long breath. "Pretty sure this place's whole claim to fame, aside from your father, is that it's impossible to get into," he said, frustration in the words. "This is ridiculous, Audrey, even you know that."

She tugged on this knot, too. "Going to tell me I can't do it?" she asked, monotone again.

"Far be it from me to speak facts. That rope won't even reach the top."

She didn't respond, just paced a short distance away, and started to swing it as if it *was* a grappling hook.

"Does she know you were set on by Southerners?" I asked Chay quietly as she let it fly, and it fell short, hitting the stone with a loud clatter and falling to the ground.

"Yes."

She'd know, then, that they wouldn't be inclined toward mercy. My heart sat heavily as she set her feet, eyed the top of the wall, and started spinning her makeshift hook again. "That maid's the only one the Duke let her be close to," I told him, hoping his frustration might mellow some if he could understand. "I bet she's been a right pain in the backside, but..."

Chay sighed and climbed down to stand beside me, shoulder to shoulder. "We can't let her go back out."

"The risk is too high," I agreed softly. The rope clattered again. She jogged over to it, yanking it fiercely. "You were smart to remind her of Isolde's wishes."

But he wasn't mollified by my soft words. "She doesn't need to be there when they find Isolde's body."

I was relieved to hear he was thinking along the same lines as me. Grim reality was better than dangerous optimism. "It might be hard to convince her to stay. I could ask her to help at the hospital. It'll keep her busy."

"And get her sick. No. We need to think up something closer to home to keep her busy."

I dug out my hip flask, offering it to him. The light from the torch in his hand flickered over the metal surface, showing the rose my wife had paid dearly to have engraved on the surface. Chay shook his head, so I unscrewed it. The cider was body temperature and tasted like coppers, like it always did from this flask. I loved it all the same.

"Mayhap Sandra," I suggested, keeping the words soft. "I could tell the lady she needs company. Do you think that would entice her?"

"I've no idea what entices that woman," he said, in such a way that I looked at him hard. The planes of his face were harsh in the bright light, the growth on his jaw light and shadows under his eyes dark. "No," he breathed. I followed his gaze as he said, louder, "Wild horses, woman, what are you *doing?*"

She was off the ground already, feet scrabbling for footholds, hands locked around knife-hilts. The blades were buried deep in the cracks of the wall.

There was no way she'd make it to the top. "Get down!" I ordered, not realizing I spoke to her like one of my own until the words were out of my mouth. Chay was already at the wall, hovering beneath her, I a few steps behind. My heart was in my throat. I could see the pale flecks of stone where she'd cut herself a foothold at my eye height. "My lady, that is *not safe.*"

She didn't say anything. The rope dangled above her, hooked as it would've had it been a proper grappling hook, at least from the look of it, and my heart sat in my chest like a lump of ice as I watched her pull a knife from the stone.

One of her feet slipped, and she leaned in close to the wall, her breathing deep and quick, her eyes turned upward.

Neither Chay nor I said anything as she found purchase with her unsteady foot higher and drove the knife in again, using it like a climbing spike.

I closed my eyes.

Southern mages, dead handmaids, plague, and a guard who couldn't or wouldn't maintain the peace.

We needed to leave this city. Even the appearance of safety was gone, now.

The whisper of rubble falling made me look again. She was higher than she'd been a moment ago, but not even halfway to the bottom of the rope.

I tossed my shield away and braced myself to catch her. Beside me, Chay did the same.

From the corner of my eye, I saw movement along the wall, and hope surged through me. "There's someone to open the gate!" I called, my heart in my throat. "My lady!"

"Who goes?" someone shouted.

"Raise the gate!" I called back, feeling sick, unable to take my eyes off her as she reversed her progress, finding the holes she'd used already, the same footholds.

The lone figure broke into a jog just as the little lady slipped.

Time stopped, just as it had when Beatie had tumbled off the edge of the drain and into the water below last winter. And just like then, I stayed back, trusting others to fulfill their role. I was in the wrong position, and I couldn't remedy that. If I'd moved, I would've knocked into Chay, who was in the perfect position.

She caught herself, though, with a noise of pain through gritted teeth, then skidded down the wall. I remembered the local butcher's boy holding my little girl up, covered in algae and ready to cry from the terror of it.

Just like Beatie, when Audrey finally hit the ground, she was shaking and breathing heavily.

"Show yourselves," the man above the gate called.

He was on the other side, away from the little lady's makeshift grapple. Hoping we wouldn't need to explain that, I grabbed Chay's torch and strode over to the horses, holding the light to my tabard. "You're looking for us," I called up.

A moment later, I heard the wheel turning.

I glanced over in time to see the lady knock away the hand Chay offered to help her up, standing on legs that visibly shook. She went to her horse and took hold of the saddle horn, then let it go and took the reins, still gulping in air and expelling it in what could've been pain or distress.

"We're going to get her," I promised Audrey, feeling the cold biting at my fingers. The ground was soft beneath my boots, though, not frozen. I'd heard tales of it opening and swallowing men whole. "It's going to be okay."

Still making those strained noises, she nodded and led us into the city, her hands white-knuckled on her handmaid's reins.

CHAPTER FORTY-ONE
AUDREY

"The One does not remove the pain we feel, but he gets us through it."
~ *The Book of Bread and Salt*

The first thing I heard was the crackle of fire. My whole body hurt, and I felt tender to my bones.

Vaguely, I recalled the empty barracks, the unanswered call for help, and the rage that dragged me away from anything resembling sense. I remembered yanking open doors. I didn't remember screaming, but my throat ached. Had there been people? I recalled finding the Captain, the way his cock had gleamed in the torchlight, and how he'd clutched his pants trying to hide it, but I had no idea who'd held the torch or dealt with the man.

But I knew he'd refused to help.

And I knew Thomas had hugged me.

I pulled the blankets up higher and wanted to weep, but I just felt hollow. I'd made a fool of myself. I didn't need to recall every moment to know that whatever had happened, it'd been public.

Killing the Captain would certainly solve issues around how to deal with that going forward. Not that he'd want to talk, I suspect. Not considering who had been in his bed. You didn't just bone the wife of one of the most influential merchants in La'Angi and get away with it. Especially with your *boots* on. Who left their boots on?

Disgusted with my own brain, I threw back the blankets. The fire was full of bright coals, and a little note was folded in front of a jug of cordial. Some hard bread and cheese sat beside it.

I went for the note and poured myself a drink, ignoring the discomfort in my body and mind. In plain, somewhat blocky script, it read:

Audrey,

Thomas and I have gone to get Isolde. We've a group of volunteers. Situation in keep is bad. Stay in until we return. Eat and drink, even if you don't want to. You need it.

Kaelson is taking over running the hospital for a few days to give us time.

C.

My head spun. I turned the page over, but that was the entirety of the message. I tossed it into the fire and looked at my fingertips, pleased to see that while they were scratched, they weren't a shredded mess the way they'd been the first few times we'd practiced scaling the wall deep in the garden.

I'd been taught to always have an escape plan ready. But escape didn't always mean getting away, and I hadn't understood that at the time. Sometimes, escape meant finding a different way forward.

I would've gotten over that wall if that guard hadn't come along. I could've done it.

I'd lost myself afterward, but in the moment? She would've been proud of me.

The cordial sat heavily in my stomach. I stood, but it was no better. I drew a bath and took my time about it.

That mage who'd come for Ylva had manipulated wind and storm alike, but that wasn't magic I knew about. Magic-manipulated machines. They worked to make processes simpler or more efficient. Old magic might've interacted with the world, but no one knew how to use that anymore, and the cost was paid in blood. Had the mage been using blood magic?

My intuition said *no*, but I couldn't put my finger on why. I let the thought rumble around in my head as I filled my bath. I wondered what it would cost to fuel that sort of spell. If one paid in blood, how much blood was required, and did it need to be fresh? What if it spilled and soaked into the ground? Would corpses work?

Had Ylva planned to kill us all along?

I'd assumed they'd clearly see she was free, even *armed*, and riding willingly alongside us. I didn't think that was such an unfair assumption. Still, she'd had no way of organizing it in advance. More than likely, she was as much a victim of circumstance as we were.

I hid my boots, belt, and knives, though I hadn't seen the servants in days. I burned the skirt that wasn't mine. Avoiding questions was easier than answering them, and I had no words to spare for casual conversation. Those questions weren't a threat now, but would be soon.

When Isolde got back, she was going to be exhausted. I scrubbed dirt out from under my nails, ignoring the pain of the movements, and started compiling a list of what I needed to have ready for her to make her recovery easier. I paused, the world doing a sharp half-turn around me.

My nails weren't black. Slightly blue, of course. It was cold, and I'd drawn the bath at a snail's pace. Blue was normal. The One knew my body wouldn't be acting properly after the short-changed sleep and copious stress of the last few days.

Distracted, I tried to recall where my mental list had gotten to, and couldn't. Instead, I focused on getting my hair clean and tangle-free before Isolde returned. No matter how sick she was, if she saw something that needed doing, she'd do it. I didn't want that for her. So I rinsed, lathered, and combed.

Storm was gone. She'd been my girl for almost a decade now. She was my *friend.*

Breathing deeply, I refocused on what I had to get done. I was mostly dressed when I saw the pile of cushions and blankets on my bed and started tidying them. Isolde might not be comfortable with taking my bed unless I made up a good reason. It did have better warmth, with the main fireplace being in the room itself, but I doubted that alone would convince her. I gathered up an armload of covers and carried them downstairs, making a nest for myself on the divan before the fire. Chay had refilled the fuel supply, so I took some upstairs, then more. She'd need to keep it burning high. I started to light it myself, then realized I hadn't finished getting dressed.

By the time I heard a commotion in the bailey, I'd finalized more tiny tasks than I'd started, but they all fell out of my head as I moved over to the big window.

Chay's horse was obvious from this angle, but it wasn't him in the saddle. My heart lurched to see how Isolde slumped low, barely staying in her seat. She didn't climb down herself.

I ran to the fire and threw on more logs. I should've gone to get herbs or posies. See if there was another mage about.

Rushing downstairs would only slow them down. Instead, I ran back up and continued throwing my ribbons in their box, then spotted the nub of a candle and tossed it into the fireplace. If I went down, she'd feel obligated to greet me. We'd have to pause to talk. She needed warmth. I needed to stay up here until she got up here, and *then* I'd see her. I'd done most of the waiting. It wouldn't be much longer. I might have time to get her soup, though, and mayhap soup would help her? She wouldn't have eaten, although Chay might've taken the rest of the bread he'd left me with himself.

I blew out a hard breath and scrubbed my hands over my face. *Stop it. Just stop it.*

"I'm stopping," I told myself, firmly. "We're okay. It's going to be okay, eventually." It was too hot, so I went back downstairs and spotted a quill that needed to be returned to its stand, and a chair that was off-center.

When the door finally opened, Isolde stepped through. The relief was so overwhelming that I was frozen to the spot, watching her drag herself forward. Chay and Thomas stopped what felt like a respectful distance back.

I thought about moving forward to help. And I thought about the energy that refusal would take from her. I followed a half-step behind instead, taking in the tiny rips in her skirt, the fine twigs and leaves caught in her hair, the mud caked on her boots and lining the bottom of her skirts. There wasn't a drop of blood on her. She was bent almost double and labored up the stairs without pausing, as if fearing that she may not be able to start again if she stopped.

"Take my bed," I told her when we reached the top. "I've moved my things down. You'll be warmer."

It was proof of how ill she truly was that she did exactly that, collapsing at the foot of it like an exhausted hound.

I drew blankets over her. "Leave me," she said, though the words were sturdy as wet parchment. "Sick."

"I know you're sick." I added another blanket and put a pillow near her head, but didn't want to disturb her.

Her cloak was damp around her pale face. The veins beneath her skin looked like cracks in fine ceramics. I put yet more fuel on the fire.

"Go," she said, or I thought she said.

I went.

Downstairs, Thomas and Chay broke off their quiet conversation. Thomas bowed to me. "I think I can get Kaelson to step in and support the Captain," he said without ado. "If it's your wish, my lady."

I remembered little from last night, bar the Captain's disinterest in helping and the crushing waves of fury. "How would he feel about *being* Captain?" I asked.

Thomas clasped his hands before him. "My lady, I understand your disappointment, but the Acting Steward appointed the Captain."

"Actually, the Master Steward appointed the Captain," I disagreed. "The Acting Steward can't appoint a Son-struck thing."

"Neither can you," Chay said, then shifted, making his belt jangle and setting my teeth on edge.

In my mind's eye, I could see myself striding down the halls, the swirl of the skirts around my feet, the drag of my cloak in my wake. I could feel the weight of the knife in my hand. I could see the Captain's eyes wide with shock. I'd sidestep the spray of blood from his throat. Kick his body over, too, because he could at least fall on cue. He did *nothing else* right.

"Check with Kaelson," I told Thomas.

He bowed again, and left.

"That man barely slept last night and hasn't stopped since," Chay said quietly. "Be careful how often you use spurs."

Disoriented, I shook my head. I hadn't meant today. A quick glance at the window indicated there was enough daylight to return to the field hospital, barely. But by the time I'd processed that, Thomas was already gone. I could've run after him, but what would it change? Would he opt to stay and rest?

The reality was I needed Kaelson here, making it work. La'Angi was vulnerable to external and internal forces, and damned if I was letting it get to trial by combat just to survive a day in this city.

Not that it'd ever been much different, I supposed. And mayhap removing the veneer was good. Mayhap it helped us all see.

"What happened?" I asked Chay.

"I gather she sheltered overnight with a beekeeper, then made it to your stockpile."

The cache. It was known to Ylva, now. Isolde wouldn't want to replace what we'd lost from it, but find another somewhere nearby. She liked to keep one along every route out of the city. "She escaped unscathed?"

"Apparently. She didn't say much. The weather did her no favors, but that beekeeper probably saved her life."

"The Southerners?"

"No sign of them, but we didn't go even half the distance to where they attacked us." He poured himself a cordial. "I can't believe she got away and made it so far on foot, sick as she is."

If he still needed convincing, then I didn't know how to help him. "I know I lost my head last night," I said, just to have it done. "I'm sorry." I wanted to offer some sort of assurance on how I'd deal with it next time and what I could do to avoid it, but I didn't know what tomorrow held, and any assurances would be a lie. It *would* happen again if we all lived. It was just where and when I couldn't be sure of. And I didn't have the energy to explain any of that to this man, who rightfully resented me.

I was sorry he'd come after me all that time ago. I was sorry he'd sworn that oath. I was sorry I hadn't let him take his chances with Mikus in that tourney and limp home to lick his wounds. I was sorry I'd gone riding that day and fallen into his eyes.

"I'm sorry," I repeated, letting go of old regrets and turning toward new ones as I went up the stairs to Isolde.

CHAPTER FORTY-TWO

CHAY

"An army in step is an army unstoppable."
~ Barloc's Wisdom, compiled by F. Bergsoniir

I lengthened my stride to get ahead of the man I'd found healthy enough to help carry wood, juggling my armload and the keys too. "We're lucky to have the lady," he told me, eyeing the big, imposing door to the tower with its beaten metal scrollwork that doubled as iron reinforcements.

If he thought the outside was ugly, he should see the inside. There it didn't pretend to be anything except what it was—a jail. And I it's keeper.

I said nothing. Were we lucky to have her?

She was behind her desk when we came in, rolling the merchant coins I'd seen her playing with between her fingers. We were greeted with a smile, but it was an absent one, her quill scratching swiftly across parchment at irregular intervals as she poured over what seemed to be three tomes at once.

"Sorry to interrupt your studies, milady," the servant said tentatively. "If you're agreeable, I'll bring up another load."

She tore her eyes away from the tome, her smile wide and warm. "Studies? I suppose it is. Trying to take on the job of a Master Steward without all the information makes it feel more like a puzzle, though. I'd appreciate the extra wood, thanking you, sir." He bowed low to her. I went to leave with him, and she stood. "A moment, sir Chay?" she asked, and there was no way I could avoid those soul-warming eyes.

I thought I saw approval in the man's gaze as I bowed to her, too. Thomas' warning about modesty and reputation rang in my ears as the servant let himself out, his steps loud in the quiet of the tower. Hers were barely a whisper of fabric swaying around her legs as she came over to fold herself in the chair by the fire absentmindedly. The pile of blankets she'd slept in last night still bore her imprint.

My mind went to the reason she was sleeping here, and I kept my fleeting misgivings to myself. A shattered reputation killed slower than the plague.

"Have you an errand for me, then?" I asked as her gaze settled on the coals.

She took a deep, bracing breath. The glow of the fire was reflected in her eyes, in the orange in her hair. "Kaelson visited while you were gone."

Our pause after that statement was filled by the crackle of the fire kept stoked high. Isolde hadn't recovered properly. I hadn't seen her, anyway. And Audrey said little. But the heat, apparently, helped.

Thomas had come and gone twice since we'd last seen Ylva with an arrow in her chest. Kaelson had been unofficially pulling strings in the background. There were people on the walls, now, consistently. There were organized duties.

But there was pushback, too, from a small faction who wanted what they wanted. If things continued as they were, we'd all have much bigger problems than who'd ransacked which house on Big Wig Hill.

"I might be executing the Captain, come morning. If he continues to interfere with Kaelson trying to do his job for him."

She said it without inflection. And I didn't even wonder if that was the royal "I."

"What do you need from me?" I asked, and it might've been the first time I'd aired that question.

"Nothing," she said, the word a tired statement of fact. "I thought I ought to warn you what tomorrow might hold, since this time I can."

It took me a moment to untangle the meaning of her words. Usually, she couldn't warn me, but this time she could. It was a courtesy message, no more or less.

"Have you considered how it'll look if you execute him yourself?" I asked.

"No," she told me, her eyes going wide and innocent as she tugged her shawl tight around wide shoulders. "'Twas just a spur-of-the-moment decision. Why, do you think it might have consequences?"

She couldn't do that, be thoughtful one moment and a raging harpy the next. "Pardon me, my lady, merely attempting to do my job and keep you whole."

At least she didn't tell me I wasn't needed. Not aloud.

I took my useless rage and went back out to do a poor job of splitting wood. Along the path, I saw no one. I knew there were pockets of people secreted away, with stashes of supplies and makeshift cures that eased their hearts more than their symptoms. Sometimes, it felt like the keep was awash with people, like they all were drawn to one another and came out just to remember the world *was* unchanged.

And sometimes, I felt like I could be the last living soul in the whole city.

The job was physical enough that it bled off some of my frustration and was monotonous enough to be soothing. The sawn-up pieces of wood that had been piled in the shelter nearby were dwindling faster than the population might suggest. I wasn't surprised. I'd seen, over a pale woman's shoulder as she came out of a suite of rooms in the lower levels, a chair burning in a fireplace. There was probably good coin in selling wood to the desperate.

With that in mind, I loaded our stockpiles higher throughout the day.

The cook Audrey liked wasn't there when I went to the kitchens to find food for us, but I was assured she was just taking her day off. "She'll be back tomorrow," said her replacement, a sunny-looking older woman with flour on her forehead.

I nodded, noticing a lack of guards today, but was unsure if that was good or not. The platter of food filled both my hands, and I didn't complain about that because I knew, one day soon, there wasn't going to be food.

"I can't go," Audrey had told Thomas and I when we'd urged her to flee. "People need us."

People needed a miracle, not us. But at least she came out and said it. She wanted to save the world, one piece of parchment at a time.

The bitterness carried along with me as I let myself in and set the food down on the low table before the fire. I had to move some of her piles to do it, which always made her huff impatiently, but she wouldn't need to huff if she was less disorganized.

My eye fell on a letter that looked less formal than others. I hadn't meant to pry. It was addressed to a Yasmine, and seemed to be continuing a conversation about casualties, remedies, and their worries.

I helped myself to the stew while it was warm, assuming she was just up caring for Isolde. I didn't know what caring for Isolde involved, because I'd been told not to worry about it. I didn't know how aware Isolde was, either. I was confident she wouldn't want Audrey near her.

My bowl was only partway done when Audrey came down the stairs, handkerchief pressed to her face like it might hold in the tears streaming down her cheeks.

The air sat in my lungs like it had become rocks. "What happened?"

She shook her head, unsuccessfully trying to muffle the sobs.

Isolde was dead. It was the only explanation.

I set down my food, suddenly wondering how I was going to dispose of that particular body in a way that didn't traumatize this poor woman.

"Audrey," I began, and then wanted to wince at the impatience in my voice.

"I know—" she sucked in a breath. "I know you've lost everything. I know you probably don't care. But she's my only friend, and she's very sick, and I'm scared, and I'm going to cry but I *can't* do it up there and disturb her, so just—" she sucked in a breath and, on a sob that twisted the knife in my heart, said, "Just leave me alone, please."

Not dead, then. The air filled my lungs again as she collapsed, picking up the pillow she'd slept on and burying her face in it.

Not dead, yet.

For a moment, I watched Audrey sobbing into the pillow, muffling the noise as best she could, her fingers turned to claws in the fabric, and her body shaking with the force of her grief. And I wanted to cry, too. I wanted to smooth my hand over her back and let her tears soak my shirt, and we could both cry for how fucked our lives had become.

Swallowing my tears, I turned away and gave her space to grieve.

CHAPTER FORTY-THREE

ISOLDE

"Before you can administer the antidote, you must know what the poison is."
~ Matri'sion proverb

Everything hurt. But nothing hurt worse than the cold. I'd almost wished I'd gone out, there and then, in a whirlwind of violence. It was how I imagined I'd go. I'd never expected I'd die in my charge's bed, counting the minutes left to me.

For the occasion, I'd forced myself to bathe. The heat and fresh water, or the herbs, or the simple act of caring for myself always made the pain a little more bearable. I didn't know why. I'd spent hours silently speculating, but expected to go to my grave ignorant.

That, at least, was exactly what I'd predicted for my life.

I dressed in fresh, warm clothing, layering the cloth carefully to preserve my warmth, then took the comb with me downstairs to the window.

I felt the sunlight as if I were at the bottom of a deep lake. As though it couldn't really reach me. Still, I turned my face toward it and slowly worked the tangles from my hair to have something to do while I waited.

A crowd gathered in the main bailey. Folks stood in groups, shoulder to shoulder, their eyes on the barracks.

The door opened. Kaelson walked out first, then Chay, then the Captain, and finally Audrey. The Captain's hands were tied behind him, and his feet were hobbled like a horse. It was a nice touch. I expected it was hers. Chasing down her quarry would distract from the purpose of today's little showing.

I couldn't hear what Audrey said as she addressed the people gathered. But I'd heard her rehearsing it a million times, in a million ways, heard her running through every possible scenario as she'd paced in front of the fire. I'd been at a low point, then. I hadn't been able to tell her it was grand, that she was doing the right thing. That a Captain who allowed vulnerable people to be robbed shouldn't remain Captain.

Of course, all Captains before had done that, too. This one just had the poor luck of being more obvious than usual, and Audrey being the one in charge, not her father.

The comb hung heavily in my hand as I watched the crowd react. Nods, hands pressed to mouths, tears, shaking fists. She had them on side. *Anyone* who addressed them right now, with a fleck of awareness, would have them on side. They were desperate for hope.

Above them all, a trio of birds glided on the wind. If only Thomas were there, I'd've found the strength to show him.

There was no Butcher to feed them today. Just one woman as lone executioner.

She knew she'd have to follow this up with real change. Killing a man was easy. Upending the whole city's belief in the locways? Less so.

They watched as Chay brought over the chopping block. I wondered, absently, why she hadn't had the Captain hung.

She didn't use an axe, though. I saw the ripple of shock as she took a knife from Chay. Leaning against the bar on the window, I smiled, but on the inside. Where it took less energy. She cut his throat neatly and avoided the spray. *Well struck*, I thought, the world swimming around me, the agony in my bones exhausting.

She was going to be okay.

The way she cleaned her knife quickly on his cloak was probably not the most sensitive choice she could've made, but it was sensible, and it was how she'd been taught. We aimed for efficiency, not sensitivity. Mayhap I'd been remiss, but I hadn't thought to discuss how an execution should be run. That, surely, should've been her etiquette teacher's job.

Amused, I turned and braced myself for the journey back up the stairs. But my eyes fell on the parchment on her desk, anchored flat by that horrible chain of merchant's coins Luca had given her when she'd been a child. *Howe the Gyuildstonnes Helde Back the Giantte Wahv of Tommorroww at Mysctheras.*

The world spun around me. I didn't know about giant waves. She'd had some strange interests in her time, though, and it didn't surprise me that she either did know of such things or was about to. With the amusement burning like a coal in my chest, I went to move on and then saw the sketch beneath that page, done on the same painfully yellowed leathers.

It was La'Angi, but there were no apple trees around it and gently rolling hills on either side where only cliffs were now. A giant wave was pictured hitting an invisible bubble around the city.

Unsettled, I reminded myself she was doing real, concrete things now. That was what I'd wanted for her. I'd told her there was no such thing as a bloodless revolt. She knew the currency most valued in La'Angi was freshly severed heads.

It was a matter of supply and demand. She understood those.

CHAPTER FORTY-FOUR

CHAY

"As the twig bent, the tree grew." ~ Southern saying

"Have you a moment?" Audrey asked Kaelson, though she'd been called to his office.

"Of course, my lady." He waved her in, and I followed after her, closing the door gently. "I've been meaning to put together a report for you."

She waved it off. "Report when you need me or want to celebrate. Daily running I don't need to hear about, unless it pleases you to share it." Kaelson's face didn't falter from its polite lines as she spoke. "I won't waste your time. We've had thieves taking too heavily from the larder. I'm opening up the mess hall to anyone who'd like to access it, but I want to secure the kitchens, and we need to reclaim some of the hoarded food."

Kaelson nodded, regret in his face. "I like that move, my lady. It ought to help some. Better if we could deliver food to those who need it.

We had the men to do that a moon ago. I don't know if we've even got enough to put a decent guard on the larder, though."

It wasn't what Audrey wanted to hear, but to her credit, she heard it nonetheless. "Can I recruit people from the public?" she asked. "Have someone with integrity tracking it?"

He shrugged. "It's the same issue, my lady."

She looked down at her hands, and I stood, as useful as ever, holding a shield in the doorway. Everything was unraveling, and here she was, trying to hold onto only the best parts of a pattern she hadn't chosen herself. I wasn't a monster. I respected that.

"Can you see any way forward?" she asked him.

He shook his head slowly. "Declare the kitchens open. Ask for donations of supplies to be shared or offer to trade uncooked for cooked. Lock what we have securely. It's the best we can do."

"Then that's what we'll do," she said. "Do you think, if I loaded up some wagons and sent them around with bread, that they'd be safe?"

Kaelson hesitated. "Today? Probably. But next week?"

Beneath the desk, where he wouldn't see, she was strangling her hands together. Her voice was perfectly even as she asked, "What if I paid volunteers to transport people? Instead of taking the food to people, I could bring people to the food. The castle needs staff, so I'd have work for folks."

"Bernadette told me she's shorthanded," Kaelson agreed. "Run it past her, but I'm in favor."

"If we need to fall back into the castle, it'll simplify things," she noted.

His expression was as neutral as hers. "It will, my lady. And...I had considered that may need to happen before the spring, unless a regiment returns early."

"Have you requested that?"

"I have."

She nodded. "Thanking you. It'll add weight to my own request for immediate aid."

His brows furrowed. "When did you write the Duke, if I may ask, my lady? You hadn't mentioned it."

No, she hadn't. I watched her quick shrug. "After Steward Daniel left. Respecting his intelligence, I thought it wise to take his concerns to heart. Since then, I've contacted all my father's liegemen. Every response I've received states the plague is everywhere."

I thought of Ylva and the Southerners, the lost opportunity to question them. But Kaelson just nodded with a gusty sigh. "That matches what I'm hearing. It's good to know help is on the way, though."

At no point had Audrey said that, but it was stated so firmly that she didn't question it, though I saw the sharp look she shot him. "Indeed," she agreed, a little awkwardly. "Thanking you for your time, Captain, and your service."

"Don't," he said brusquely. "But do be safe, milady."

She accepted that with an awkward half-nod, then stopped partway out the door to curtsey. His door closed behind her, and she shook her head aggressively, muttering something under her breath. But the moment she saw me looking, her expression smoothed. "Not all bad news, I suppose," she said brightly. "A path forward is a path forward."

You could go forward through hellfire, too, but I didn't tell her that. In the bailey and out of earshot of anyone, I asked quietly, "Are you well?"

"I am, thanking you for asking. And yourself?"

The polished, practiced sentence was jarring. The last time she'd spoken to me like a real human being, she'd been begging me to leave her alone.

I almost preferred it to this shiny layer of bullshit.

She used a less formal version of it in her interactions with the cook who'd taken over responsibility for the staffing, and a more formal version of it with Kaelson. But I knew what she looked like without those layers of expectations.

And I knew what she looked like when those practiced layers of politeness shattered, too.

As she spoke with Bernadette about the suggestions she and Kaelson had, I wandered through the quiet places in the kitchens that probably weren't usually quiet, preferring to find patterns in the mayhem that was the heart of the castle rather than dwell on the night she'd screamed, smashed furniture, and tried to crush her skull with her own hands.

She loved Isolde. I could respect that. And everyone had their breaking point. Now I knew where hers was.

It wasn't just the old magic tangling us all up that made me want to help her stop *before* she hit that point again. But, aside from a miracle to save Isolde's life, I didn't know how to do that.

From the open window that carried in the sea air, I could see Audrey's tower and the smoke coming from the chimney. I thought of the woman up in that tower who, by all accounts, probably should've been long dead.

We started the slow walk back up to her tower, mission accomplished, and plan in place. Only then did her shoulders slump. She pulled her cloak tight about herself.

She was pale.

My heart sank.

It was strange, being in the middle of a crisis but having nothing to do and nowhere to go. I opened the door and held it as Audrey entered the warmth of the tower. She folded herself down amid her blankets, fluffing them around herself, her nose buried in old scrolls. She'd taken her gloves off to handle the reading materials, and I caught glimpses of dark nail beds.

She'd worn gloves a lot recently. Scarves, too, and fur-lined cloaks and caps. It was winter. I hadn't thought anything of it, being the amazing guard I was.

If she died from the plague…if I did everything I could to defend her…I was a free man.

The realization felt hollow.

I looked at my whittling, uninterested. I wandered to the window, but the scene was dull. Heavy clouds filtered sunlight. Shades of gray as far as the eye could see. The words sat, unsaid, on my tongue. *Why didn't you tell me?*

Because I'd given her no reason to tell me anything. Because I had no reason to listen. Both of those things were equally true, and yet they didn't quite feel right. And I had no clue how to remedy it.

"Would you leave me?" I forced myself to look at her as she glanced up from her scrolls, her brows knitted. "If you left tomorrow, if Isolde was well and there was no plague, would you leave me?"

Her frown grew deeper. "I don't know. You couldn't come into the Matri'sion forest with us. I don't know if your oath would let me go without you. If I escaped from you against your will, you'd be safe."

A knot in my belly unraveled, and those warm whiskey eyes fixed on my collar. She'd abandon me tactically. For my own good.

"Should you ask me how I feel about it?" I prompted.

She blinked at me, those eyes flitting further up to settle in the vicinity of my nose. "Chay, I don't mean to disregard your feelings, but you're bloodsworn. Even in this scenario, you *cannot* give me unbiased information."

"I can tell you you're being a shortsighted shit without melting like a cheap candle," I said, irritated.

"My eyesight is fine according to the last mage I consulted," she said, turning back to her pages. "Mayhap we'll get your tongue checked out, though."

Before I could describe all the ways I could prove my tongue worked just fine, a knock sounded from the outer door. I moved to open it and noticed how swiftly Audrey stowed whatever she'd been reading.

Kaelson looked at me grimly as I opened it. "Just me again," he said gruffly. "How're you holding up, lad?"

It was possibly the first time anyone in this icebox had asked me that and meant it. "Loving your city, Captain," I told him.

Amusement lit his face up. "You and I both. I'm Kael to my friends." I must've missed when we became friends, and mayhap that showed on my face because he said, "If you aren't threatening to stick a spear in my gut or a knife in my back, we're friends." He clapped me on the shoulder and walked in as he said, "Sorry to disturb you so soon, my lady. I've a situation I need to raise with you."

"What happened?" she asked, pouring him a cordial.

He waved it away. "Nothing yet." He offered her a crisp, well-oiled bow. "I've news that there's a group of folks—desperate, hungry folks—who're poised to hit the field hospital supplies as they leave the city. They're in the lower level, milady, where Victor's Road crosses with Red Row."

"How many?" she asked, her eyes slightly narrowed, her shoulders straight.

This layer of bullshit looked a little like her father. The way she seemed taller, the way she took up more space. I was sure I'd seen him do the same. But I didn't believe she was deliberately mimicking him. Part of me wanted to.

It was safer, thinking of her as the Butcher's daughter.

More likely, it was testament to the self-belief Isolde had unlocked within her. I looked down at the ground. There wasn't anything I could do about the past, and the future looked grim, too.

"The exact numbers I don't know that I can trust," Kaelson was saying. "Begging my lady's pardon, but the young chap who told me was scared and didn't see a lot. He guessed at a dozen. But I wouldn't put money on it, myself."

"A dozen?" she raised her brows. "Surely we can hold off a dozen? Untrained, poorly armed, yes?"

"Usually, yes, my lady," he agreed, bowing his head. "But today?"

The bleak picture painted sat unchallenged for a time. Audrey paced over to her desk, picking up her favorite quill but not drawing with it, just running it idly between her fingers. "Even if we called Thomas back right now, he couldn't be here before tomorrow at the earliest," she said quietly. "If we change the route, they may well just ambush us where we don't have advance warning. I assume the caravan is guarded well enough to dissuade a small handful, just not an organized group?"

"You assume correctly, my lady."

She nodded and looked up, squarely at me. It was like a punch in the gut.

She wasn't asking me to take a life. But she was asking me to save them.

I didn't curse, but only because Kaelson was now my friend, and I didn't want to lose him so easily. "My place is defending you, my lady."

"So we both ride."

She was sick. She didn't need to be out in the cold. Even if she could handle herself—which I suspected she could, if she kept her cool—she couldn't hold back the plague. Isolde was proof of that. "The risk to you is too great," I said flatly.

"My lady," Kaelson said with another bow. "It's a kind thought, but your presence will only complicate the situation further."

"My presence means you have the best swordsman to be tested in our kingdom," she said, the words brisk. "*And* his warhorse." The praise felt like false accolades. I could feel the pressure of her favor being tied around my arm, the tickle of her hair against my lips.

Simpler times.

"Pull all the guards from the castle," she told Kaelson with a sharp nod. "All of them. Forget the walls. Get the supplies out. Once the matter is done, send the extra men home again. We need to deal with these threats right now, or they'll nip at our heels and cost us more in the long run. I want to know where they're from. Their people need our support."

Uneasy, but seeing the cold sense of it, I looked to Kaelson, who'd never hesitated to tell her when she was wrong in the past. No one would expect the castle to go unguarded—but if they heard of it happening… "If we did that," Kaelson said, pausing a moment to clasp his hands and rocking slightly on his heels before he added, "It's a trick you cannot repeat, my lady—the next time, it could be a trap."

"I understand."

He nodded, his face a neutral mask. "I won't pull every man. Two on the gates, to keep up appearances."

"How many would we have?" she asked, her eyes narrowed.

"If I pulled those from the castle, less the two from the gate…we'd have eleven extra men."

"Fourteen over a possible dozen." Was she imagining herself with a bow in her hand, rescuing us all? I didn't dislike the image myself, but the cost would be immense, even if she *wasn't* sick. Knowing you drew the sharp bit of a knife over someone's throat was one thing. Making accurate shots from horseback was an entirely different matter. She hadn't taken shots when we'd been riding, the other day. But she'd been looking for them. "The greater our numbers, the safer. Yes?"

"Yes, my lady," Kaelson said warily. "Depending, of course, on different factors."

"In this situation?" she asked, pinning him with her gaze.

He hesitated. "There might be four of them, milady. There might be thirty. They might have staffs and leathers, or full plate mail. The boy overheard a meeting with voices. That's all I know."

She drew in a breath. "Then we'll go, too, as well as the castle guards. Just until the rabble are diffused."

"Do not make me beg you to stay, my lady," Kaelson said in such a matter-of-fact way it made me look at him twice. "My old knees would weep for days at the task."

She, too, looked taken aback. "Kaelson, I…"

"You're all that's holding this city together," he said as if he were commenting on the weather. "You fall, and I've got chaos. So you stay safe and warm here, and let those of us who're paid to risk our necks do our job."

She blinked at him, still disoriented. "I…"

"You're doing it all with more grace than I could've ever dreamed," he said, the words still ruthlessly neutral. "And if I may, my lady, you're clearly your mother's daughter while learning many important lessons from your father, and that's good. You'll need both. But right now, we need you alive."

She wrapped her hands together tightly. My chest ached. I looked away, better to give her privacy to sort out those feelings. "I'll stay here and lock the tower," she promised, her words equally as neutral. "Chay—sir Chay—would you go, anyway?"

I felt Kaelson's gaze on me like a cloud in the sky—but Audrey's eyes were burning holes in my soul. I took a deep breath. It was the first thing she'd asked of me that showed any real trust. Ever.

A small part of me pointed out that she was being kind to me now she wanted me to do something for her. But it wasn't the *fair* part of me who remembered the apologies, the steps she'd taken and never asked for assistance with, the way she shouldered it all herself.

I'd had to offer to arrest the Captain for her. She'd been ready to do it herself.

"Do you need me?" I asked Kaelson, studying his careworn face and clever eyes.

He didn't hesitate. "I believe we might. I also believe we'll lose some. If you're one that we lose, that's a steeper cost than some of the lads, the Wife take me for saying it."

That decided it. "The lady said we can't lose any." I bowed to Audrey, and she looked somewhat taken aback. "I'd best go and see her wishes done."

"They're leaving in a half-hour," Kaelson told me. "My lady." He bowed low, then walked out, leaving a heavy quiet in his wake.

"I'm sorry if I ask too much of you," she said to her hands. "I should have asked you in private if you were comfortable. Next time—"

"Just say 'thanking you,' Audrey," I said, irritated. Did she think I was so precious I wouldn't help defend supplies for the sick? "I would've said if I wasn't comfortable. I can do that, you know."

She folded herself back into the blankets. "Well…I'm grateful. Mayhap more for that than your assistance. I need to know what I can ask of you. I'm no good at guessing."

I wanted to shake her. "There you go, we're in perfect harmony."

"A thing of beauty," she agreed dryly. "We never miss a step."

"Don't go making promises I can't keep," I told her, amused despite myself. "Chances are they've already laid their ambush. I hope there are no archers. I've had enough of them."

She didn't laugh, which I should've expected. Isolde had nearly died that night.

She held the scrolls again but hadn't unrolled them. She just sat there, looking worried and distracted. But she didn't feel quite as far away as she had earlier. Or perhaps I just felt less powerless.

One of her blankets had slipped. I fought the urge to go right it.

She was trying to look after me, perhaps as awkwardly as Luca had attempted to look after her. And no less infuriatingly.

I tried to remember the last time I'd been coddled, and couldn't. Perhaps that was why the concept wasn't so repulsive when it came from her.

"Bar the door," I told her. "I know you can look after yourself, but these are strange times."

"I will," she said, pulling the blankets higher. "Be safe, Chay."

"Haven't got myself killed yet," I reminded her, then added, perhaps brashly, "I'll be back before dark."

As reward for my boldness, she sent me a smile. "You will."

CHAPTER FORTY-FIVE

CHAY

"Don't curse the darkness if you can light a candle instead."
~ Raider's Ban proverb

I left my cloak. The oiled one would protect against some of the rain but would interfere with movement, and I couldn't afford that. I donned chainmail with my tabard over it. In the stables, Audrey's horse stomped her foot as I passed her stall.

"Easy, girl," I murmured, sparing a moment to pause at her stall door. Checking on the horses had become part of my routine, but she hadn't forgiven me for cutting Audrey loose when she would've been dragged.

I didn't mind the grudge. I was just glad she'd made it back somehow. "You rest up," I told her, and her ears flicked back as if she didn't like taking advice from me. *You get that from your rider.* As much as the thought made me smile, it wasn't true. Audrey listened to me. But she didn't trust me.

Bliksem was already saddled and waiting, his breath steaming in the slow, dreary drizzle that had settled over the city. I remembered how she'd wept for those children.

I remembered how I'd blamed her.

Wrong?

No.

Kind?

...No.

I scrubbed my hand over my face and tried to focus on the group of us, assembling quietly and without fanfare in the bailey. Everyone knew what was happening and why. A few bits of information were murmured. How the swordsmen would ring around the cart, how they'd move depending on what angle we were rushed from, where they'd fall back to if it was needed. I was greeted with raised hands and nods.

All I had to do was stick my neck out to save theirs when they had no other options, and they'd treat me like an equal.

We moved out, a loose ring around the three supply carts. We weren't transporting anyone who was unwell, turning back those who came into the streets, for now. Audrey would've hated that. And she'd hate it later when I told her of it.

For today, we just had to keep the tourney grounds supplied, so there wasn't an immediate issue. Then they had to figure out how and where to relocate it so we didn't need to pull this stunt again.

The heavy clouds darkened the streets, so it felt more like dusk than midday as we rumbled along, a big, noisy, slow-moving target. Bliksem pranced a little, sensing the unease as we rolled closer to the ambush location. I didn't even know what the street names were, but I didn't need to, so openly did they all show their tension.

Due to the quality of my armor and the distance Bliksem would defend, I was taking the lead. The true leader was halfway down the wagon's length.

They were happy enough with me being bait, and I was happy enough not to rely on any of them at my back.

I was thinking like a local now.

It said something about how grim our straits were that I found humor in the thought. As soon as I saw movement on the road ahead of me, I hefted my shield and called, "Come on out, we've got you surrounded." The amusement that still laced my words was an unintended but nice touch, and I was pleased with it.

An arrow whistled past my head, and my mouth went dry. My shield snapped up. I heard shouts from behind. Shock, anger, and pain. *Archers.*

Time slowed. I saw the situation in an instant. The group of us surrounding the cart in the center of the crossroads. Exposed. Able to defend from an attack from the ground by using the cart as a bulwark. Almost helpless against archers because I was surrounded by peerless swordsmen and exemplary pikemen. There wasn't a loaded crossbow in sight.

"Do you?" the man on the road called. "Do you really, Butcher's dog?"

I barely heard him. We had to flee or flush them out of the surrounding houses. Flushing them out was too risky. We'd be pinned down and picked off. We'd charge into houses without knowing where they were. We'd be separated, easy prey.

An arrow sped past, and Bliksem stomped furiously. Movement caught my eye. The man who'd stood in the road ahead of me clawed his throat, staring at me in shock. An arrow was in his throat. He held it, his eyes huge, as one knee went out, pitching him forward at an odd angle.

My heart did a slow roll. *It couldn't be.* None of us had bows. Had they accidentally shot their friend?

With my eyes, I traced the approximate path of the last arrow to fly past me to its starting point. A man hung partially out of a window; the top half of his body crumpled over like a long stalk of grass in the summer. He swayed, twitching. Behind me, from the guard, there was a heavy moment of silence.

Audrey?

Surely, it couldn't be. But if it was—and without Isolde to watch her back…

"I did say you're surrounded," I called into the rain, flicking my shield back over my shoulder to better drive home my bluff. If Audrey was out there, in those houses with these folks, infected with the One only knew what this plague was…

I had bigger problems than a stray, inexpertly carved arrow.

"If I have your attention," I called into the shadow-filled crannies, hoping my voice would carry behind the twitching curtains in unshuttered windows, "I've a message from lady Audrey." I hope she didn't mind me putting words in her mouth. "She'd like to know who needs aid. Because these supplies are for sick folks. She's looking after us all. But I've got orders to protect this here caravan. So, your choice. Ask and receive, or fight and die."

An arrow whistled through the air and clattered harmlessly on the stone at my feet. "Death to the Butcher's Brat!" someone shouted from the shadows.

Three guardsmen, their shields locked together, closed in on that nook. A skinny man was pulled out, dripping, his homemade bow broken in his hand, his lip bleeding. He was tossed at my feet. Bliksem stomped his disapproval twice as my heart drummed in my head. *The Butcher's Brat.* It had a ring to it. I thought of her, out there in the rain, freezing, getting sicker by the minute for these people. She'd *better* be in her tower beneath disorganized piles of parchment.

With violence in my heart, I dismounted and leaned over the asshole who'd called her brat. His eyes were round with terror, but his lips were sealed tight.

He wasn't going to say it again. But he wasn't going to apologize, either.

"You can try to kill her," I whispered under the rain. "And when you do, you'd better hope she gets you before I do." I straightened, nodding to the closest guard. "I'll take your spokesman to the lady, then," I called to the listeners hidden behind the rain and gloom. It took me only moments to have him tied to the back of my saddle, far enough that Bliksem wouldn't accidentally crush his skull with a kick.

"Let's get going, then," Paedar said, his words carrying only as far as the closest guardsman, who passed it along quietly. Another guardsman peeled off and paced along behind our captive, spear in one hand and shield on his arm. It was slow going, and as the violence drained from me, I became aware of how cold I was, how I was covered in filth from the road, and how heavy my sodden gambeson was beneath my armor.

If we were lucky, Audrey hadn't made those shots. Some random person who'd opted to help us out just happened to be in the right place at the right time, and knew how to work a bow.

I had no evidence of her presence. None at all. I'd never seen her loose a single arrow. I'd never seen her leave the tower. While she could've quite easily kept pace on foot, why would she?

In my mind, I heard that grunt of effort as she hoisted the guard and tossed him, all by herself, over the sea wall. Because she'd sat beside her fire with eyes that burned like liquor and promised she'd never ask me to take a life.

If she hadn't worn an oiled cloak, I was going to have to respond somehow. Surely, the woman wasn't so stupid.

Inappropriate reactions ran through my head. Shouting, shaming, locking doors, hogtying.

The only thing I could come up with that I could *actually* do that might have an impact was to rat her out to Isolde, who would absolutely dress her down for taking unnecessary risks.

The thought brought me some pleasure. However sick Isolde was, if she wasn't dead, her tongue would be sharpened and ready to use.

She knew I couldn't go to the Matri'sion lands. She didn't want my oath to kill me.

Why did the thought make me want to grab her, shake her, and then crush her to me until her bones creaked?

When we finally got back to the castle, I left the guardsman with the captured bandit, but not before tying up the newly made criminal. No point asking for trouble, after all, not after Audrey had gone to such lengths to keep us all safe. "I'll be back," I told them both.

I went, alone, to her rooms, expecting to find her there ahead of me. I stopped to strip off my chain mail and hang it to dry, knowing it would need love later, so it didn't seize up. The gambeson, too, I put aside.

I knocked on the door to her rooms once I'd removed the worst of the wet clothing, but I got no response. I let myself in, annoyance and embarrassment making my steps heavy. "So, you didn't bar the door," I said to the silent tower, waiting for her to appear on the staircase, straightening her clothes or carrying fresh sheafs of parchment.

She didn't.

Dread gnawed at my belly. *She's in the kitchens. She's bathing.* "Audrey?" I called loudly. "I'm coming up."

There was no response. When I eased into the room, it was warm. Isolde was sleeping, curled up like a wounded creature on the edge of the bed closest to the fire. Quietly, I stoked the fire and checked all the rooms and the upper level, my heart drumming in my chest.

I found the overdress and skirts she'd worn that day. And with that vanished my last hope of it being a misunderstanding.

CHAPTER FORTY-SIX

CHAY

"When entertaining a guest, do not make hasty decisions, for your husband, father, or brothers will have information you will not, and they have not the time to share it. One must look to the head of one's table for guidance."
~ Etiquette in Arcanloc

The shadows got long. Or my eyes made them warp. I ran through scenarios in my head helplessly as I paced, things that could've gone wrong. She'd been caught. Her throat was cut. She'd fallen and hurt herself. She'd been caught and was trying to escape. She was too sick and weak to make it home and was dying in the shadows of a seedy inn.

How long could I keep the prisoner waiting? In the end, I stood grimly and left her tower to return to them. Too long would only make them suspicious. I'd get them gone and then check one last time before trying to retrace her steps.

Having a plan made me feel better. I strode swiftly through corridors and found the guard where I'd left him and our prisoner as sullen as I'd seen him last. Had it been hours? Minutes? I couldn't be sure. "The lady is busy," I told them both. "She'll see you on the morrow, sir."

"Dungeons?" the guardsman asked me, hefting himself up.

I hesitated. I doubted Audrey would throw him in the dungeons. "She didn't say," I admitted, because it felt unfair to do otherwise. I could put him in Ylva's room, but I hadn't heard whether anyone had even noticed she was gone yet. "But, given the situation, it feels like the best choice for today. Make sure he's got a blanket and warm food, though," I reminded the guard, just in case.

He nodded and brought the man to his feet. The bandit shot me an angry look but didn't fight against it.

The ground flew beneath my feet on the way back to her tower. It definitely *looked* darker, but no one was calling the hour, of course. They were all transporting food and supplies to the hospital we now needed to collapse and relocate.

How close was it really to nightfall? With the thick cloud cover, the light was deceptive, and the hours seemed to take on a life of their own. I opened the door to Audrey's rooms and had to stop myself from running through the whole place again. The only wet footprints were my own.

That decided it. I went back to the hearth and banked it high. When I got her back—and I would—she'd need the heat.

Damn it. We hadn't needed her interference! I flew from the hearth to the side room, opened my bag, and stripped off my wet shirt, tossing it aside. I'd need an oiled cloak—not for myself, but for her. I refused to even look at the modest first-aid kit I carried with me. If she needed it desperately, then it wouldn't be enough anyway.

At least it would be easy to sneak out of the keep, I thought grimly, ignoring my tabard as I tightened my belt over a fresh shirt. No one was watching us, anyway.

CHAPTER FORTY-SEVEN

CHAY

"A slow and relaxed breath will help your horse be calm."
~ How to Tame Your Brumby: A Collection of Raider's Ban Wisdom.

Frustration gnawed at me as my mind skipped ahead over the numerous paths she could take just to the tower, much less through the city. The chances of missing her were high. I didn't care. If I could find my oiled cloak, I was out. But it was still eluding my searching hands when I heard the door shut gently.

My heart leaped into my throat as I looked toward the noise in time to see a hunched, cloaked figure pass by, a basket in their hand.

The disguise didn't fool me. Not when those footfalls made no noise. The worry receded, and fury rushed into the void it left behind, filling my chest. I breathed deeply, drew it down into my toes, grabbed my discarded first-aid kit, and went out to drop the bar over the door behind her.

She pulled off a dark, sodden cap as I walked in, glancing up at me. Exhaustion made her look old. Her eyes were almost entirely black.

"Don't tell me you didn't need me," she said, the words reedy. "There were at least two dozen, and they were mostly archers. You would've all been dead, and then I'd be dead, too."

I tossed the kit onto the divan. Her lips were blue. Blue was better than black, though. She made an attempt to strip the gloves from her hands, fumbling with the leather.

Drawing on patience I didn't know I had, I offered my palm, wishing I could just snatch her damned hands and do it for her, but forcing myself to ask first and wait for her to put her hand in mine.

She didn't move.

I stuffed down the hurt and remembered her heartbreak. I'd had my own. Neither of us had dealt with it. Wariness wasn't unreasonable from her, and patience wasn't too much to ask of me.

So I kept my hand steady. She didn't need to know my pulse was racing. "There isn't a single archer in the La'Angi guard," I told her, still waiting for her hands. "You need to fix that."

"Before my father and Raider's Ban had a falling out, we traded," she said, looking disoriented. "'Ban withdrew their support decades ago. We never filled the void."

"Sounds like bad leadership."

"Sounds like ego and oversight," she said. "Specifically. Sorry. Was that—did that come across as disagreement?"

She was okay. Rattled and sicker than I thought, but okay. That was enough. And she was talking to me, too.

I was about to close my hand when I saw her eyes flicker down to it. Time stretched out, and I remembered tearing through the tower, searching for her. After the wait this afternoon for her to return, I could linger here all day.

I didn't need to, though. She set her icy claw-like hand in my palm awkwardly.

My mouth went dry.

Her gloves were sodden and the leather didn't want to move, but I eventually peeled one back to show skin as translucent as moonlight, woven with black veins. "I was as fast as I could be getting back," she told me, as if still braced for a reprimand. "And I'm cold."

I remembered the arrow that had only narrowly missed me. That one archer could've done some damage to us, clustered like we were. If there really had been two dozen bowmen, we were all very lucky my bluff and the genuine threat of her archery had been enough.

"I'll admit I'd have been less concerned if you hadn't been alone," I said, and was proud of how the anger in my gut was nowhere near my voice as I pried the second glove off her ice-cold hand. "I'll get you fresh clothes. Stay in front of the fire."

I received no objections, which turned some of the anger back into worry. I went upstairs and rummaged through neatly hung dresses of all persuasions. I missed Kadan's room, which smelled of sea and horse and was filled with laughter and sand. I found shirts in a bureau and some plain skirts. I don't know where she hid her men's garb—that would've been better, surely, for warmth? The skirts I'd grabbed didn't match. I didn't care. She could wear dry clothes and not die.

By the time I returned, all she'd done was unhook her cloak. I tossed aside what I'd brought. "I'm going to help get you undressed," I told her, tossing her wet cloak further away. "You're too cold. It's dangerous."

I half expected that she'd protest, or rally to do it herself. "Th—thanking you," she said, shuddering.

Her button-down vest disliked me. It was an excellent disguise, and if I admired that, I had less time to worry. Brown, nondescript, the cut hid her curves and was normal enough that it wouldn't attract any interest. The buttons were swollen with the water, but they gave way eventually.

"What held you up?" I asked, pulling her equally plain shirt over her head. The laces tangled on her chin, but she twisted to help me free them. An expanse of pale skin underlaid with dark veins was revealed to me, and a leather garment I'd only seen women from the Steppe tribes wear, laced together hard over her belly and breasts. I turned away to get the dry shirt.

What a horrible time to realize my lady was every bit a Matri'sion.

And of course there was no seemly way to comment on that, was there? She took the shirt from me, her hands clumsy as she pulled it down.

"Can you do the laces?" she asked. I reached toward the shirt, but she waved a hand at her breeches.

I did as she asked, keeping my movements impersonal. She struggled out of them herself, and I turned my back to give her what privacy I could, passing her the skirts without looking. But it was impossible not to imagine helping her. Sliding my hands beneath that wet fabric and letting it fall away. Her flesh would warm quickly against mine.

"Were you a squire?" she asked. Though her voice was still reedy, I drew comfort from the unnecessary question. If she was able to make small talk, she was feeling a little better, surely.

"I was. Why do you ask?"

"The way you helped me change. I felt like I was having my armor removed."

Relief trickled through me, and a little pride, too, because she sounded pleased. "Is that not what I was doing?"

Instead of answering my question, she asked, "Who did you squire?"

She definitely sounded better. "Lord Henry of Ville-under-Sytha. He did a lot of work defending against the Red Hand. A group of nomads who plague Darrius' herds in the west," I clarified. "He was a good man."

"Was?" she asked.

"Poison arrow took him not long after I was knighted," I explained, the grief an old, dull wound. "I understand his children aren't following in his footsteps. He'd be grateful they don't need to."

She made a quiet noise that I couldn't decipher. "These are formal underskirts," she said, a thread of amusement in her voice.

I shrugged. "They're dry."

"They are," she agreed, through chattering teeth. "Thanking you for that. I'm done, Chay." I turned around again as she folded herself down by the fire. I took a blanket and wrapped it over her shoulders, tugging the fabric snugly. If I lingered longer than I should've, she didn't seem distressed. "The warmth makes the hurt less," she admitted, swallowing heavily. "I was pinned down between two other archers. I didn't see them when I got into position. It was lucky they didn't see me when I did." She stopped talking for a while, shuddering with cold. "And then they weren't game to move for a long time. They were sure there was a trap, I think. They didn't go until after the extra guardsmen circled back."

I sat down nearby. Was it appropriate for me to offer to hold her to warm her? Was she looking less transparent, now? I didn't know how vulnerable she felt, or whether asking would make her clam up the way she'd done that day Isolde had tried to get me to teach her the sword.

If I asked, I'd be crossing a line. I knew I would. And not asking would be worse. But I couldn't do nothing.

I slipped the pins that held my cloak at my throat from the fabric. I wrapped it around her shoulders, folding the fabric over her legs and lifting the hood over her head. So close, I should've felt her warmth. She still smelled like rain, and, beneath that, something soft and floral.

The look she sent me was unreadable. But it wasn't one of trust or gratitude. I let go of the edges of the fabric, forcing myself back.

"Next time," I said, acknowledging the anger in my belly, circulating in my blood, "just tell me. If what I say is impossible, say so. I could've worked with you. I could've at least known where to go to look for you if you were wounded." I couldn't demand to hold her, but I *could* firmly request to know where she went and that she didn't lie to me about taking risks. It was important. For my oath.

She sent me a look from under her lashes. In those eerily black eyes, there was a splash of whiskey again, and I felt a knot of worry ease. "You wouldn't have locked me in or begged me to stay?"

Yes, she was definitely looking better. I stood, fetching the meals we hadn't eaten earlier. I tried not to be insulted at the question. It wasn't easy.

"Audrey," I said, doing my best to be reasonable, "I believe that you didn't mean for that to be cruel, so I'll answer honestly. I'm not in the habit of forcing people to do things they don't want to do, even when they're the right thing." Her eyes flickered up, her expression going blank. I'd already realized my choice of words wasn't ideal and clarified. "That isn't an attack on *you* or the oath I was forced to swear. It's just an explanation of my own personal code. I don't like to tell people what is and isn't right. Because I know the right thing can change. Like today. The right thing was for you to save our hides. I didn't know that. Neither did you. I don't like that you gambled with your life, but I did the same." I set the food down in front of her. None of it would be warm. "Next time you assume I'm the same as the Butcher," I told her, without looking, "I'm going to be upset."

She was silent for so long I thought she'd fallen asleep or been direly insulted. I pretended not to worry, busying myself ripping off some bread, and starting the long process of chewing it, though I felt nauseous and exhausted all at once.

"Well, I can't promise anything," she said eventually. "Since you're the first man to even think twice about imposing his views on me."

When she put it like that, I did feel like a heel. I thought of Luca, sitting in a heavy, plain chair in front of a big hearth and telling us earnestly about how he wanted to protect her. My belly ached. "Darrius thought twice," I pointed out, nudging a log further into the coals. "We wanted to talk to you and Isolde that day in the orchard. But you didn't want to talk, so we didn't."

She picked up a piece of cheese with clumsy fingers. "I wish we'd spoken to him now," she admitted quietly.

I knew what it was like to wonder about a life you couldn't have. "Kadan would've made a horrible big brother," I told her without thinking. "If Darrius had been your father."

She let out a surprised laugh. "I—well, I suppose it's lucky he isn't, then."

I wondered if I could keep that levity going. "And the way you gazed at Kadan during the tourney would've been even more improper," I added idly, popping some cheese into my mouth.

She spluttered, and I had to fight not to grin. "I did not!"

I shrugged easily and leaned back on one arm. Kadan would've loved this. My heart ached. "Sure. It was his horse, then?"

"I do happen to like horses," she said airily.

"Not blondes?" I prodded, shooting her a sideways look, unable to hide the smile any longer at her expression.

"I am *not* lusting after your friend."

It was on the tip of my tongue to ask who she was lusting after, but I didn't. There was no good that would come of that answer. "I know," I admitted. "And even if you were, I'd think no less of you. I just wanted to stir you a bit."

She eyed me suspiciously, but apparently, whatever she saw mollified her. "Well, then." She yawned, laying her plait along her knee nearest the fire. "Stirring accomplished, sir," she said around a yawn. "I'm sorry. I don't think I'll be very good company this evening."

I didn't tell her she was never good company because that wouldn't have been true. Instead, I said, "I like your quiet."

Her mouth twisted in a bitter smile for just a moment. "Noted."

"No." I wasn't letting it go. Not anymore. "Not like that. I mean, it's nice. It's just…nice." She was going to make me find words that I didn't have, but that tiny, bitter smile made my heart hurt. "I like your words. But I like the quiet as you're doing things, too."

"You're making this awkward, you know? You just undressed me. You saw my breasts. Now it's weird."

"*Wild horses*," I said around a laugh. "Look, *my lady*, no breasts were seen by me tonight." If I'd been a better man, I wouldn't regret that. "I saw a mastodesmos, as is worn by any Steppe warrior who doesn't like to jiggle about. Seems like a sensible option to me." Thanking the Old Gods that Kadan wasn't present to tell her sensible women were my weakness. "I'm being nice because I happen to not hate you. We both need to get used to that."

She opened her eyes and looked up at me in silence as if sifting through the bounty of excuses and context I'd offered her, trying to make sense of all of it.

"Okay," she said warily. "Can I sleep now?"

I didn't want to move away. The thought made panic flutter in my chest. "Am I stopping you?"

"You do keep talking," she acknowledged and yawned again. "I'm sorry. I want to. But."

But she'd been out all afternoon traveling the city on foot, single-handedly ending ambushes before they really began, saving lives and having her body ravaged by the plague. She was sick and exhausted. She was vulnerable. I shouldn't push her.

I'd never been accused of talking too much in my life.

"Can I sit with you?" She looked at me blankly. "You'll take hours to warm up." Every moment her face remained expressionless felt like a stone slab being added onto my chest. I struggled to breathe. "You don't have to move." I couldn't hold reassurances in. "I won't take your blankets or mess up your pile." I bit my tongue around promises I couldn't keep.

She blinked at me, her expression still blank. I struggled to breathe.

"You won't fit," she finally said around another, even longer yawn. So help me, I felt the blood pooling in my belly and the rush of anticipation. "You probably could," she admitted, and it wasn't anxiety that kept me from breathing now. "I suppose we're pretty resourceful." I locked my teeth around a response and, oblivious, she burrowed in deeper. There was no expectation or artifice in her manner. Her eyes drifted closed, and I felt the drumming of desire in my veins. "You can sit with me," she said, the words so soft they were almost lost to the night. "But you don't need to. I'm fine."

I dragged the chair the short distance separating us, and settled in.

CHAPTER FORTY-EIGHT

AUDREY

"Old friends can be lovely, but question—what is it they want from you, and why are they here? Remember: our duty is first to The One."

~ Etiquette in Arcanloc

Chay was sleeping sprawled all over my reading chair, limbs akimbo and lips slightly open, when I woke. It didn't *look* comfortable, but he was out cold, so it couldn't have been too bad.

My body ached. The gloves I'd been living in ought to have been dry by now, but I left them and just tucked the blanket around myself, going up to bank Isolde's fire and pass her some warm water.

She sat up, shuddering with the cold. She hadn't made it further than the chamber pot in days. "Go," she told me, shooing me with a weak flick of her hand.

I went, once I was certain she was as okay as I could make her. I didn't tell her about yesterday afternoon or how I'd stood in the rain for hours, watching the sliver of a shadow over the road that I suspected, but wasn't certain, was an enemy archer. I didn't tell her about how my veins had looked black, and my bones had hurt so much I couldn't make a fist.

I missed being able to tell her everything.

Tears jammed up in my throat, and I dressed with extra care. There was going to be a lot to do today. We had to relocate an entire hospital, and Chay had taken a prisoner. He wouldn't have killed the man.

He was still sleeping when I returned. Resisting the urge to give his foot a nudge, I curled up in my mountain of warm blankets and rested my aching body, trying to gather up my strength rather than sit and worry. When that failed, I practiced my breathing.

When he finally stirred, I heard the change in his breathing and the sigh of fabric moving against fabric. I opened my eyes to find he was staring straight at me, a crease on his cheek from the arm of the chair and his dark blue eyes shiny from sleep.

"Morning," he said, blinking a few times. "You're looking better."

I'd probably looked poorly when I'd dragged myself in yesterday. I'd sure felt it and hadn't had the energy to disguise it. I wondered if I was allowed to point out that he ought to shave and organize a haircut. Plague or no plague, guard expectations remained.

He sat up and vanished for a while. My eyes fell on my gloves, stiffened now, beside the fire. Then, beyond them, my boots. Not my *lady* boots, but my sensible boots that had returned with me from the wild flight from Ylva's people.

I went and found the beeswax polish and brush and set to work. I'd need these boots again, possibly even today. The less water they'd take on, the better they'd serve me.

The rhythm of the task was soothing. I remembered sitting beside Isolde working wax into leather in silence, a chair under the door. She'd let me lean my shoulder into hers. A few times, when her smiles were soft and free, and her eyes were bright, she'd even pressed a kiss to the top of my head.

Something had to give. How many others were like Isolde, curled up and unable to help themselves, but not yet gone? The soft brush rubbed circles into the leather, and the pieces of the puzzle rumbled around in my head. I felt like they were all there, but I couldn't put them together. And I didn't have anyone I could ask.

Ylva had cited pre-Barloc information. That was treason.

What I'd give to go back to her now, with what I knew, and ask her some equally treasonous questions.

My mind went to those yellowed scrolls I'd retrieved quietly in the aftermath of Isolde's decline, which were also most definitely treasonous to have accessed.

Our library was deep and old. I'd always known it had been cared for throughout the ages by crafty scholars and gutted by warriors expecting no resistance.

But *knowing* and *actively exploring* were separate things. *Discussing* the forbidden was another tier again.

Acting on it, even if I could figure it out? I'd wish I was dead if word got back to the powers that be.

But Isolde was dying.

I reached for Chay's boots. They were the ones he'd worn here, in the cut of Raider's Ban, lower at the back and front, with a soft, rounded toe and an indent for stirrups in the arch. His had decorations stitched across the top, black designs that might've been waves or perhaps horses' manes. Brush already in hand, I avoided the threadwork, focusing on the points of wear, and wondered if the Matri'sion footwear would be different again.

When Chay returned, the crease was gone from his face, his hair was neat, and he was holding a platter of food. His sword belt chimed gently as he made his way in.

I swapped him his primary pair of boots for some food, and he took them with a surprised, "You polished my boots?"

Breakfast was porridge made with more water than milk and a little honey. My stomach rolled, but I took the spoon. "Mine needed to be done, and yours were there." I cringed at the thick sludge hitting my tongue. At least it wasn't cold.

"Thanking you," he said firmly, and almost like a reprimand. "That was kind."

I swallowed down the mess of it. He was still standing, holding the boots. I was tucked up inside my blankets again. He didn't have the expression of someone who'd been on the receiving end of an act of kindness. "My apologies?" I offered, unsure, hoping he wouldn't go back to being as cold and distant as he'd been previously. He'd been grumpier than usual, but at least he'd *talked* over the last few days. "Was it the wrong thing to do? I should have checked." I should have, but I hadn't thought to. They were just boots. But they were *his* boots.

He didn't have much that was just his, I supposed.

"I'm grateful," he said firmly. "Even if it's just a small thing for you, it means I can wear comfortable footwear today. It shows me you were thinking of me."

Heat flooded through my bloodstream. I'd tried very hard *not* to do that. He'd made it clear he didn't want it. And he didn't look happy now. His dark brows weren't bunched up, but his eyes were slightly narrowed, and he shoved food in his mouth like he was forcing himself to eat.

It *was* horrible food.

I needed to figure this out. We needed to be able to work together. "Should I not do it in the future without asking first?" That would be inconvenient in instances like this morning, when it was easy to go from mine to his, just like when I did Isolde's. But I could manage. A bit of forethought went a long way.

"Help yourself to my things any time you feel like doing some polishing," he said.

There was something off about the way he said it. "I'm not feeling very well," I admitted, hoping honesty would carry me through. "I'm going to take that at face value, so if you're mocking me, best to tell me now."

He reached over, closing the distance between us with ease I didn't expect, and nudged my bowl closer with a single fingertip. "I've never been so serious in my life, Embers. You ought to eat."

I looked into the gray, stomach-turning mass. Had it been a spiced pear tart, I still would've struggled right then.

But he was right, even if it was all an elaborate ruse at my expense. So I ate.

We took extra food with us to the dungeons to visit the prisoner. "We don't want the Butcher's *help*," the man spat at me. "His *help* is the reason we're already in chains!"

He didn't want my empathy, either, so I kept it to myself. On the way out of the dungeons, I turned the situation over in my mind. I didn't want to keep him, but nor could I afford to feed him forever. If I released him, he'd just organize his group of hunters again, and we'd become quarry. I could put him to work loading the dead carts, mayhap, but ensuring he remained present would take manpower. Was it worth the investment, for one prisoner?

Kaelson was found in the barracks, within reach of the Captain's desk he fit so well behind. He hailed us. "I was on my way to Bernadette," he said. "We may as well all go. I've dispatched extra volunteers with wagons to start relocating Thomas to the market square, my lady. I suspect we'll need to leave a small contingent out there, though, as local villages are stopping by there first."

"Can we staff it?" I asked him.

"A few volunteers. Mayhap a guard or two."

"And the market?"

"Yes. The hospital itself hasn't been the target of anything much except a lot of unwell folks, and I do suspect that'll continue. No one wants to get too close to plague carriers."

I thought of my own resignation to it. If only Isolde wasn't so worried, I could just enjoy her company now. "What about those already sick?"

"Possible that it wouldn't keep someone already unwell away. But not something we've experienced yet. There are easier targets. I think that's important to remember. We don't need to make it properly secure, just secure *enough*."

It was a strange thought and one I never would've come up with. "I'm very glad you're here, Kaelson."

He sent me a surprised look as we turned into a side corridor that would take us to the kitchens. "I'm not too unhappy with it, myself. Wish the situation was better, I must say, but given everything…"

My eyes caught on a shadow up ahead. Kaelson cleared his throat and stepped forward, blocking my view. To my left, Chay said, "Do you get whales in this bay, Audrey?"

I glanced over, distracted. "Absolutely not. Our beach is too shallow." From here, I could see the ocean off in the distance, over the sea wall. "Do you? At Raider's Ban?"

"Sometimes," he said. "There are a few viewing points along the peninsula, further around from 'Ban. It's nomad country, and there's no access to the ocean there by foot."

Kaelson was moving out of time with us, positioning himself between me and that shadow. I halted abruptly, and Chay cut off his story just as quickly.

A skinny child was huddled in a corner, more shadow than human. Their eyes were black pits, and their head had slumped on their knees. Beside them, a kerchief, like one used to carry baked goods, was open. A few crumbs remained close to the dead child's open, bone-white fingers. There was a hole in their shirt that could only have been made by a rodent.

Isolde curled up like that, in a tight little ball. The thought of rats gnawing into her flesh to get her sweetmeats made my head spin.

Kaelson's hand on my shoulder jolted me, and I was pulled along. "I'm sorry, my lady," he said quietly. "We've people who sweep the keep. They must've missed this one in the morning go-round. They'll be at rest tonight."

I floated, and Kaelson towed me along.

From far away, I wished I'd listened to Chay's stories about whales.

"Oh, here's trouble," Bernadette sighed when she saw us as if nothing was wrong. "You smelled the buns, Kael."

"Half the city smelled the buns, Ettie." I watched as they shared a look that was friendly. Perhaps even on the *very* friendly side of the scale. And I felt hollow. "I found the lady on the way to chat with you. We need to figure out logistics for a hospital in the market square."

Someone had found that corpse, taken the food the child was carrying, and left the body.

Was there another child out there now, starving? Not dying of plague, but hunger?

Bernadette punched the dough in front of her absently. "So your runner said. I've ideas. You're going to love 'em," she told me. "Grab a bun, both of you, and sit down. This might take a little while, because there's a few moving parts, but it might help us recover some of the harvest if we do it right, or at least get the corpses out of the city so the rats don't get too much fatter."

Eating a bun with that image in my head wasn't going to be possible. I held the warm, yeasty treat, shoved down my grief, and listened as she explained the three arms of the organization she wanted to put in place. Food, shelter, and work. Not work *for* the food and shelter, but as an option for those who wanted to, and could help.

And I wanted to weep as I listened. Because these people, they were the ones who knew what was really happening. I was here only for encouragement and to give a semi-official seal of approval.

"I've a prisoner," I told her, hoping she might work her magic on this problem, too. "His people are starving but won't accept support. Mayhap this is a way forward for them? If it's more removed from the keep, and therefore my father's shadow."

They both went silent for a moment, shared a quick look, and then Kaelson said, "I'd be cautious with prisoners, my lady. They're often a lot more trouble than they're worth. I don't wish folks ill, but that particular chap was willing to take bread from a hospital."

And that was that.

While it answered a lot of questions I hadn't even thought to ask yet, they hadn't been able to guide me on the issue of the prisoner.

"How are you faring?" Chay asked me, as we headed back to my rooms.

Restless. "Fine, thanking you, and yourself?"

He sent me a long, level look that made guilt swirl in my belly. "How are you, really?" he asked me pointedly.

I blew out a breath. "You're not supposed to be annoyed. No one wants a *real* answer when they ask that."

"I do."

I rolled my eyes. "You're the *one* person. I didn't know this. I guess you're allowed to be annoyed, but it still doesn't make sense."

"Lots of things don't," he said, and he sounded amused. "I'm thinking of going to give Bliksem a brush. Storm could use some love if you've the energy for it. The kitchens were warm, so I figured you might—"

"Storm's gone, Chay." I'd done my best to avoid thinking about it, and had mostly succeeded. It seemed foolish to mourn my horse when my best friend was dying.

He shook his head. "She made it back herself."

I staggered to a stop, the world spinning. She *wasn't* gone? "Why—how—"

"She's flighty," he warned. "And not in great condition. But she'll be okay, given a good long rest, a nice warm stall, and some love."

The thought of her big brown eyes and happy greetings made me want to cry. She'd been here for *weeks,* and I hadn't known?

I'd been such a coward. I hadn't even checked.

The path to the stables seemed like it went on forever. The thought of grabbing up my skirts and running didn't even occur to me until I finally made it there, so deeply was decorum drummed into me. But my heart beat furiously against my ribs, and I struggled to draw breath until I was in the dark, dusty stables and saw my girl, right where she should've been.

The joy I felt was so pure it hurt. She lifted her head and came over to the edge of the stall, meeting me at the gate and forcing me to watch my feet in the exuberance of her greeting. I buried my face in her neck and felt the warmth of her, the solid strength, and I cried.

She let me hold her, her head over my shoulder, as my heart broke and mended and broke again.

I hadn't really lost much. Not compared to some. But it was coming. I could *see* it coming. I was watching, day by day, as my best friend slipped away. And while I tried my best to ignore that, it seemed, in that stall, with my horse back in my care, to be a burden I could put down, rather than ignore.

I heard a bucket being set down nearby, the slosh of water. "I'm going to give Bliksem some attention," I heard Chay say. "I think this is Storm's grooming equipment. It looks fit for such a wonderful girl, anyway."

I finally went into her stall to find he'd brought what I'd need to get her cleaned up. "Thanking you," I said, but I didn't know if he could hear me, and I couldn't point the words his way. It would mean turning away from Storm, and that seemed insurmountable.

Brushing her was a slow process because she wanted her head to be on my shoulder or her nose to be up in my face. I'd made good progress when I heard Chay chuckling from the stall door. I glanced over her back and saw him offering her a carrot. "Come on, there," he said, his voice low and soft. "You let her get those itchy hairs out. You don't need them all, now, do you?"

She inhaled the carrot and turned back to me, brushing the leafy top over my head in her haste to check on me.

"Want a second pair of hands?" he asked, amused affection in his words.

Mayhap I was too tender, but it was hard not to enjoy hearing that tone, even when it wasn't directed at me. "She's anxious, but if she'll have you, you're welcome."

"Storm and I are friends, aren't we, girl?"

One of her ears went back as he opened the gate, and she put herself between him and me.

"See, best buddies," he said. "Give me the comb. I've seen what you're like with them. I'll sort out her mane."

It sounded like a jab, but it was said with a sort of amused resignation. I didn't know what he meant, except that he was helping, so I handed over the comb and ignored the rest, turning my focus back to her withers.

"How come you weren't riding her the day we met?" he asked me.

In the quiet, calm oasis that was the stables, it was easy to believe the rest of the world didn't exist, that all the worries and fears couldn't reach us here. And still, speaking freely about what Isolde and I did was an anathema. Explaining how she'd hurt her foot kicking a stablehand and how the boy had hit her, and the whole saga, just seemed like too much. I just shook my head. Conversation wasn't what I wanted.

The sound of Storm's breathing slowed, and she relaxed into the attention, letting us care for her. I knew she would've returned home driven by instinct and made it all the way through sheer luck, but I didn't care. It felt personal to me. Like she'd come home to see *me.*

I was grasping at straws, but they were all I had, and this particular straw was worth holding.

CHAPTER FORTY-NINE

CHAY

"Many productive plants need some shelter. Even sun-loving plants, such as the tomato, benefits from shade when the sun is at its peak. Remain aware of your context and modify your garden to ensure all plants get what they need."

~ Growing Greatness: Common Garden Plants in Arcanloc

I must've fallen asleep on one of the chairs by her fire again, listening to the crackle of the flames as she poured over old texts. When I woke, her candle had burned low, and she'd sunk down in the blankets so only her nose and the top of the scroll in her hands poked out. As I watched, she rolled up one end and unrolled the next. Those whiskey eyes skimmed over whatever secrets were encoded there.

She'd be warm under those blankets. Warm and pliant. Parts of her would be soft, other parts, firm. I could almost feel the way she'd fill my hands.

As I watched, a frown creased her brow, and whatever it was caused her to transition from fascinated to disapproving to highly irritated.

"What's wrong?"

She jumped, pulling the scroll under the blankets like a rabbit ducking into its warren. "What? Nothing."

I straightened, stretching the kinks out of my back. I'd blame the woodcutting before I'd blame the chair. For a non-bed surface, it'd treated me pretty well. "Looked like something was wrong," I said around a yawn. "What're you reading, anyway? It must be past midnight."

"I'm sorry I kept you up."

"You didn't," I disagreed, interested in how she was dodging the question. "Is this you trying to be polite?"

"I'm not following, sir."

"Sir?" I asked lazily. "That's awful formal, considering how recently I untied your pants." I probably shouldn't have said that out loud, but I didn't mind the way her eyes glittered dangerously at me in response.

"I was deeply unwell," she said primly. "And I appreciate your assistance under those highly *unusual* circumstances. Even though you were bloodsworn."

"I wasn't oathbound to undress you, specifically," I pointed out, since she appeared to need details. "Give me some credit for doing the right thing because it's the right thing, not because I'll die otherwise, please."

Those eyes snapped over to me again, wider, as if she hadn't quite realized what she was doing every time she did the *you're bloodsworn* thing.

Before I could get another apology, I said, "Anyway, that isn't an answer to my question. What're you reading when the candles have burned low that annoyed you so?"

I waited, but she didn't respond. Just reached out and snuffed out the candle.

"Is this another situation like earlier, when I asked you a thing, and you didn't expect me to actually want the answer?" The woman navigated the world with predetermined rules that I didn't understand and wasn't going to learn without clear instruction. Of course we'd misunderstand each other while we figured that all out. "Because I'm just going to offer you a blanket assurance that if I ask you something, I want your response."

Her laugh was nervous. I could still see her in the firelight, huddled low in her nest. "As you will."

I stoked the fire higher. She was definitely acting strangely. "Reading poems that'd make me blush?" She spluttered, and I kind of liked her being off guard. Considering the station she'd been born to, she could talk a good talk, but it felt more like bravado and bluntness than real comfort with the topic of sex. "Yeah, you're right," I agreed, stringing her along just a little longer. "I doubt I'd blush. Perhaps I'd giggle."

"Mayhap you'd weep!" she shot back. "Ugh. The last man who flirted with me while discussing war crimes had to flee this city."

"How's Luca doing, anyway?" I asked since she'd brought him up. "Heard from him?"

She was quiet for a moment. Then, "Why did you guess him?"

"He's the only one brave enough, or ignorant enough, with access to you who would flirt with you. It wasn't hard." Also, he wouldn't know his asshole from his elbow, but I kept that to myself. "Why're you staying up late reading about war crimes, my lady?"

"Oh, so now I'm a lady?"

"You can be a lady until you choose otherwise," I assured her, settling back.

"Well, I'm nothing in particular right now. I don't think you especially want to know about what I'm reading, so mayhap just imagine some poems to make yourself giggle and get some rest." She paused for a moment, then added, "In your bed."

"Chair's comfy." And I didn't feel so alone here. But I probably should go so she could rest properly. Still… "First, tell me what you're reading. You've hedged too hard now. I need to know."

"It's treason," she said, no trace of mirth in her tone. "You don't need to know."

The lingering warmth of sleep vanished. I'd committed my share of treason this year alone, and I was *very* interested in whatever *she* was planning on committing. But I couldn't share all of that. "Audrey," I said slowly, "You do realize you harbor a Matri'sion, don't you?"

"I..." In the gloom, she turned her face toward me. "I suppose. Isn't a single person who lives outside the law a bit less treasonous than fostering ideas, though?"

What a strange leap of logic. "I'm relatively sure treason is just treason. Why are you reading things that'd get you killed?"

"For fun."

"And you weren't going to share?" I asked, pretending to be injured. "I thought we were a team."

In the glow of the fire, I could see her staring at me, unblinking, like some sort of gorgeous owl. As I tracked the wariness and worry flickering over her face, I wondered if she knew how clearly I could make out her features. It felt unfair to keep teasing her, so I reminded her, "I'm sworn to you, Audrey. You can trust me."

"You have to be here," she countered softly. "There's no choice involved."

My stomach knotted. "I have to be in this tower," I agreed, reaching for courage. "I don't have to be in this chair or asking you questions. I don't have to make sure you eat or give your horse treats."

She was silent. Her eyes had gone to the fire. Were they shiny with tears, or had she cried herself dry into her horse's mane? "That's very kind of you," she said in that polite, gentle way that I recognized as a layer of bullshit.

"Not known for my kindness," I said flatly. "Kind would be saying, 'Hey, Audrey, remember those kids I killed a few weeks back? Their blood is on no one's hands but mine.'" She flinched, her jaw tightening. There it was, the festering wound exposed. "That'd be bullshit, though. It was a combination effort. We all did the best we could. Before, during, and after. We all fucked up in different ways." I rubbed my hand across my aching chest and heard her swallow loudly. "Odds are there will be more fuckups," I said, trying to be sensible. "We'll try to learn from them." I felt the weight of the child's body on my blade, and the ache in my chest became a solid weight. "I think." I had to stop for a minute and breathe. "I think I just want to try to forgive the both of us and figure out what happens next. Learn from the past and look to the future. That shit." Kadan would know how to say that better. Wild horses, I missed the man.

"I'm aware there's a lot I don't know," she said, with tears in her voice and a fragile sort of dignity. "I'm trying. And I'm so sorry for the toll it's taken on you."

It was a wonder she didn't *sir* me at the end. "I'm sorry for the toll it's taken on me," I agreed. "And you. And Isolde, and Thomas, and that runner with the wonky haircut who I snarled at after you broke me out of the dungeons." I struggled to figure out how to explain that she wasn't really learning if she was diving head-first into guilt. But I didn't know if that made sense or was true.

She sniffled. "Okay. That's a long speech just to hear about my current project."

Raw as I felt, I still appreciated the lukewarm attempt at a joke. "Did it work?"

She shifted a little, her eyes flickering up to me for less than half a heartbeat before they dropped back down to her hands. In that one moment of connection, my blood heated, and desire flooded my system.

I replayed it quickly in my mind. It hadn't been one-sided, had it? The thought of pulling her into my arms and holding her tight and being this raw and mixed up *with* her made my head swim. I wanted to peel back the layers of polite bullshit and find the ones set by survival, and slowly soak through those. I wanted her to do the same to mine.

"Years ago, Luca visited," she began quietly, and hearing the man's name had the same effect as plunging into the sea in midwinter. "He likes old stories, and I like city planning and how everything fits together. There's actually a lot of crossover."

I didn't care. I thought of how he'd sat there and earnestly told us how she needed to be protected. He'd almost gotten her *accidentally assassinated.*

It was going to be very hard to be nice to him next time I saw him, I realized.

"Makes sense," I managed.

Really, they were nothing alike.

"We visited the library often," she said, pulling the blankets closer. "The weather didn't always suit riding, and neither of us are soiree sort of people, you see."

She'd be a soiree person if she had the right friends. She just thought that socializing had to be superficial. That's what she'd been led to believe. Thanking the One for Kadan teaching me otherwise. But I didn't interrupt, just nodded along.

"Well, La'Angi has been here a very long time." She flicked her eyes toward me. "Since before Barloc."

My mind skipped ahead, and the air caught in my lungs at the implication of what she was saying. She hadn't just found something banned by the King for telling some truths he didn't like. "You've got ancient texts?"

"They aren't *that* old," she objected. Then, sheepishly, "Yes."

I blew out a breath.

"They put the park in a very strange spot, you see. There's this huge tree, and it's just odd. It doesn't make sense from a traffic perspective or in terms of drainage. The rest of the city makes sense. Why would it lead to a *park*?"

"Uh-huh." Mayhap I shouldn't have asked.

"I just wanted to know *why*."

"Did you find out?"

She paused. "Sort of. Did you know the Wife was actually based on an amalgamation of other goddesses who were worshipped? And when Barloc came here, he kind of took on some of the traits of the religion to make it more palatable for locals, so they could keep festival days and such like. That's why we celebrate the birth of the One during the thaw. There was already a rebirth festival then."

That I *had* known, having traveled beyond lands Barloc had reached. What religions hadn't reached the Steppes weren't worth worrying about. "Galeah," I said, then frowned. "Or was that one Irissi? Irissa?" I couldn't remember. I'd heard a *lot* of names prayed to. Seemed to me you prayed to an idea, not a person, but what did I know? It was my job to stick a sword in anyone who got too close, not to think. "Anyway, the park somehow led to you reading treasonous texts."

"There was a rock in the park near the market," she said, unfolding herself. "It was almost as tall as the inner wall. Before Barloc, they prayed to it. The city *was* built around it. It was magical, apparently, but the magic was evil."

"According to Barloc," I clarified dryly. "Who was known for his fair, even-handed assessment of such things."

"Right," she agreed. "Exactly. The people of the time didn't accept it and kept praying to it on the sly. They whipped, tortured, imprisoned, and even killed a lot of worshippers. In the end, they ripped out the stone and threatened to kill anyone who prayed to it. Someone planted a tree where it was removed. They were killed and tossed in the hole, but they've never successfully killed the tree. It's hundreds of years old."

"Fertilized by its believers," I mused. It suited La'Angi, but I didn't tell her that.

She clapped her hands, grinning. "*This is why I'm fascinated!*" She bounced a little as she talked, and it was possibly the most animated I'd seen her. The flush in her cheeks made me burn. I pulled my mind firmly back to trees and ancient city planning. "But the people who hauled the stone *kept dying*, Chay. They would just up and *drop dead*."

A chill went through me. I listened to her talk about how many people's hearts had stopped beating and the lengths the leader at the time went to, trying to shatter or otherwise dispose of this stone. I was skipping ahead, past the details that so fascinated her and made her burn so beautifully.

It was the stone Ylva had named as a meeting place.

"...and the *reason* people prayed to it was because it was protective," she went on. "So after they moved it, there were issues in the city. There was one time when the earth shook, and then a giant wave came and washed away big chunks of land, but it was turned back because of the stone."

My unease grew. "That's no magic I know of." I didn't trust Barloc to have made the best decisions, but the man wouldn't have got rid of it if it was so wonderful. "You just told me all the ways it *killed* people."

She let out a huff. "When it's threatened. We aren't threatening it."

The idea of a rock feeling threatened was just another layer of strange I didn't know I was equipped for. I let her talk it through and tell me all the little pieces of the puzzle she'd been putting together recently. I had no doubt it felt very satisfying to have her focus from all that time ago rewarded so well. And it was really a joy to listen to her after so long in the silence. While I liked her quiet, her passion made my blood heat to witness. She got up, pacing, talking with her hands about how they'd tossed the stone into the sea, and had it haul back out, how a fire had ripped across the land and burned the crops to the ground, and the stone had made them spring back from the ashes. Big, far-reaching disaster stuff.

There was no mention of healing broken bones, prosperity, or births, as you'd often hear folks praying about.

"And I feel like the stone *must* be the same one Ylva mentioned. I looked up the name she said, and I'm *sure* it's almost the same as one of the names in one of the early post-Barloc texts, dated to approximately twenty years before Barloc's arrival."

My head ached. I didn't want to burst her bubble, but the sun was coming up, and though her cheeks were pink with excitement now, I'd seen them deathly pale far too recently. "Embers, that stone isn't magic you can just summon. Or have you been studying magework as well as old city planning?"

"That's the thing," she said excitedly. "It was used by *everyone.* At first, I thought it must be some sort of cultural norm. Everyone might've just studied this magic as part of their day-to-day, so they had the skill to activate the item, the same way we all learn the skill to light a fire, right? But *tiny children* prayed to it."

That didn't prove much. "Tiny children light fires."

"You know what I *mean.*" She let out a huff. "Now I know *where* it is and what it does. I just don't know *how.*"

I shook my head. "You're missing some key points, there. You don't actually know what it does or what it costs. All magic has a cost." I didn't know much about magework, but I knew that.

"What if that mage we fought the other day was using the stone?" she asked, her eyes bright. "What if that's how Ylva knew to go there?"

I shook my head again. I hated being the one to tell her *no.* "There's a lot of types of magics in the world, Audrey. We say they're either mages or they're evil, but it's more complicated than that. To the north over the seas, they use runes to summon their ancestors to advise them from beyond this world, and another group uses magic to transform their shape. Another has it woven into their words so when they speak, they can enthrall you. I've even heard of people raising the dead."

"Blood magic," she said dismissively.

"It works," I reminded her, feeling the bite of steel against my palm. Wasn't blood magic the reason I was here, having this conversation?

She stilled. In the light of dawn, there was so much compassion and grief on her face that it took all I had to stay sprawled in the chair under her gaze. "It's okay," I said, hoping it was true. "We're both here through circumstance. That isn't my point. There's power in it."

She went back to pacing, squeezing her hands rhythmically into fists. "It would make sense if it was elemental magic, though. The storm, the wind, that we saw. The wave it turned back, and the regrowth?"

I didn't think growth was an elemental thing, but she knew more than me, so I let that go. "So how would we activate it?"

"It doesn't say," she said, throwing her hands up. "Anywhere I can find mention of it, it doesn't say how to *actually do it.*"

"Huh." I rubbed my palm against my jaw. "It'd make sense that'd be forbidden information. You thought of asking someone whose family's lived here forever?"

She looked at me like I'd grown a second head. "My line is *unbroken* since Barloc himself terrified my ancestor into allowing him into the keep, and then killed her family and gave her to his General."

That sounded like pretty much what I expected from war, but I didn't tell her that. Expected and acceptable were, after all, different.

"How often would your ancestor have been allowed to visit the stone or tree? Find a family who wasn't so closely watched as your own."

She came to a complete halt, her expression flickering from joy to horror to humiliation and then back to joy. "By the One, it makes so much sense. I'm looking in the entirely wrong direction."

"This direction taught you things," I disagreed. "You exhausted it, so turn elsewhere and keep looking."

She looked at me with so much gratitude that it made me feel a little uncomfortable. All I'd done was tell her she was wrong.

It seemed good things came from saying *no*, too.

CHAPTER FIFTY
THOMAS

"And those that fall upholding the Word of the One will return to his keep in Velkyn, to live in grace and glory forever more."
~ The Book of Bread and Salt

Every bone in my body ached, and I hoped it was because I was exhausted, but I wasn't sure anymore. The stones beneath my feet were icy. I couldn't imagine the keep ever feeling like home. It didn't feel like prosperity, either. It felt like a tomb.

Odds looked good that I'd have company in a common grave, so that was a boon. I didn't think I was cut out for a tomb.

I lifted my hand and rapped on the door. In the quiet that followed, I listened for sounds of stirring inside. The lady rose early. She'd see me.

The sound of dripping water made me glance down. I was soaking wet and filthy.

Wishing I'd changed clothes first, I was considering turning back to the barracks. Was the bathhouse still open? The door opened, though, and Chay met my eyes, his expression turning solemn as he looked at me. I doubted he'd shaved in days, and his hair was a disgrace. His boots, at least, were polished well. Swallowing advice that he didn't want and probably didn't need this moment, I nodded and let myself in.

Immediately, I noticed the lady's pallor and the large pupils that were tell-tale signs of the disease firmly established. And the last hope I had plummeted.

Rose had gotten away, though. I stood away from her rugs, dripping on the stone, and somehow managed to say, "We've set up the hospital in the market square, my lady, as was ordered."

"Thanking you," she said, her eyes big and gentle and worried, like a wobbly-legged calf.

I braced myself and accepted it with a nod. "I need to report, my lady, that we were set upon by a group not wearing any colors. They killed most of the staff and those who fought back, and made off with the food, medicines, our herbalist, and a number of carts." I swallowed around the lump in my throat. "We haven't the men to retrieve them." I'd gone to Kaelson first to confirm what I'd already known. I wanted to be sure before I gave the lady the most accurate account I could. "I'm sorry, my lady. I've failed you."

She was shaking her head firmly. "You did what you could. The failure is mine, not yours."

She wasn't crying. I didn't understand why she wasn't crying, though she'd been so distraught last I'd seen her. I didn't dare ask after Isolde. "Is it your wish that I carry on at the hospital?" I asked.

"Are you willing to, still?"

I thought of the shocked expressions of the survivors who hadn't seen war, the man whose guts had spilled over the road and tangled him up, who'd begged me to put him out of his misery. I thought of the herbalist's sobs and the feel of my spear splintering. And I thought of Rose, safe in the keep I couldn't picture, picking blueberries come the summer.

"Yes, my lady."

"That job is even more important today than it was last week," she said quietly. "If you're willing, Thomas, I'd be grateful if you'd fill that role."

I swallowed around the knot in my throat, bowing. "It may be worth considering turning the bailey or a wing into a hospital, my lady," I said, hoping the suggestion wouldn't offend. "Our numbers are dwindling. We no longer need the large spaces, and keeping a building warm is easier than a tent."

"Kaelson advised we keep our infirmary for injuries," she said with a frown. "But you're right, we have entire wings that are standing empty, or close to empty, now. You're already established in the market, yes?"

"Yes, my lady."

"Then I can get back to you soon? I don't need to address that immediately?"

The knobbly-legged little calf was learning how to walk. My heart ached for the child. "Yes, my lady."

She nodded and blew out a slow breath. "I'm so sorry, Thomas."

"As am I, my lady." I bowed again. "If that's all?"

She hesitated and glanced over my shoulder at where Chay leaned against the fireplace. Beside his spot, I could clearly see a pile of blankets. My grief turned to fury. He could at least protect her and *hide* it.

"Do you know anything about old stones?" the lady asked me.

I tore my eyes away from the knight, struggling with the anger. "No, my lady," I said, hoping it sounded calm.

"Magical cures? The tree in the park?"

I shook my head, my mind on that pile of blankets. I forced my hand to relax from the sword hilt I'd grabbed at some point, feeling the joints click and grind. "The tree, I do, my lady." I struggled with my exhaustion. If Rose had never left that offering, I wouldn't be here, in her service. I couldn't have gotten my family out. There were tears in me at that knowledge. But they were far away. "Some believe it'll grant protection or wishes, if you leave an offering."

She straightened. "What sort of offering? How is it activated?"

"Any sort." I shook my head. "It doesn't work, my lady. I saw it, on the way here. It's not guarded anymore."

"Why was it guarded?" she asked, standing.

"It was often vandalized." I dug for patience. "My lady, people do desperate things. I've seen folks cut off their hair and burn it as an offering to gods that may never have existed. I've seen parents offer themselves up." I bit down over the rest of the examples, clenching my teeth.

"If it worked," Chay offered, from the side. "It sounds like people would know by now."

I managed a nod of agreement.

She nodded, letting out a long breath. "All we know that can help is bathing and heat," she said, sounding as tired as I felt.

"We've been burning what we can, but there's a shortage of fuel." And not enough to build pyres far enough away that the stink didn't clog everyone's lungs. But I didn't explain that to her.

She frowned at me. "Why?"

"Why?" I tried to follow her thoughts but couldn't. I was tired and hollow, and furious at this Raider's Ban wank-rag who'd ruined my lady.

"Fire cleanses," she said excitedly. "That's what you told me. Fire cleanses."

"Yes, milady," I agreed, my head throbbing. "So it's known."

She held her hands to her mouth, her eyes overflowing. "Thomas," I heard her say. "Thanking you."

This didn't make sense. None of it made a lick of sense. I'd taken a knock to the head and didn't know how mangled I was. It was the only explanation. I needed to go and find somewhere to lie down and hope I woke up again. "Is there anything else, my lady?"

"No. No, Thomas. The Son walk with you."

I nodded and bowed on my way out. I had a mighty headache, and I'd forgotten one chap's name, when I'd been listing the dead. I must've copped a blow to the noggin. It made everything make sense.

I made my way back to the barracks, dismissing the entire contents of that conversation from my mind. I'd deal with the cunt-bitten coward later, when everything else was clearer.

CHAPTER FIFTY-ONE

CHAY

"Less information allows easier decision-making. Provide what people truly need to thrive, and they will." ~ Barloc's Wisdom, compiled by F. Bergsoniir

She'd already told Isolde where we were going. I couldn't lock Audrey in, and even if I could, I wouldn't.

The trek with Ylva had almost killed Isolde. Audrey'd told me that, no, the night outdoors in the cold had almost killed her. "I'll wear so many layers you'll think I'm a solstice gift," she'd promised me.

She wasn't only a gift at solstice, though.

I paused in the process of packing a small bag to look at my hands. My sun-browned skin was unusually pale.

I reached for gloves.

She appeared with a scarf wrapped over the lower half of her face and a heavy fur-lined cloak, the same basket she'd borne into the city in her hand. I eyed it, trying to see where the bow she was hiding would fit, but couldn't see an easy place for it. We'd fill it with food, I expected.

"Should I bring a tent and bedroll?" I asked, tugging once on my sword belt to ensure it was secure.

"We'll be back long before dark," she said, pulling the door open with one hand. I wondered if she remembered me making a similar promise. "I—I didn't even…should we bring Thomas, do you think?"

I remembered the way his face had hung slack off his bones. He'd been working long, miserable hours. "He's managing a lot here," I told her. "And we'll attract less attention with just the two of us." And however tired he was, he'd never let her go without him if he knew.

Her gaze skimmed my tabard, all but hidden by the cloak. Did her eyes linger on my chest longer than they needed? Heat spread through me as she turned away as if unsticking her eyes. Mayhap she didn't only enjoy the company of women.

"As you say."

I took a deep breath and shut her door behind me. If I were an honest man, which I was occasionally, I'd admit that the thought of leaving La'Angi was lovely. But as soon as we stepped into the bailey, the wind bit through the clothes I'd layered and cut me to the bone. If she'd felt this way and still come out into the city that day to save us from the ambush…I'd underestimated her determination. And even now, she strode forward, barely flinching at the cold as she headed to the stables.

Piles of sleet had built up in the corners of the stones, and the sight of it surprised me. I hadn't seen the rain or the sleet.

I'd had no attention to spare last night.

Audrey glanced back at me, and my heart squeezed in my chest at the invitation in her eyes. I lengthened my stride to catch up to her as she pried open the door to the stables. We moved together in the gloom, confident in the darkness with the smell of horses and hay. She could prep a horse as fast as any stableboy I knew. "When this is all over," she said to me as we led the animals out into the gray morning, "I want to spend more time on horseback."

When. Not if.

I stepped into the wind ahead of her and closed the door after her. "A noble pastime," I agreed, because I couldn't argue.

"Will you join me?" she asked without a trace of guile.

I glanced over at her as she boosted herself into the saddle and resettled her scarf over her face. Her pupils hid most of the gold that lit her eyes, but she was still in there, and now she was looking at me. Her focus made my blood heat in my veins.

I remembered my early musings about teaching her to ride. I imagined hearing her laugh and talk animatedly as we picked our way through the naked boughs in the winter sun. She'd know strange facts about the orchard that I'd never considered. I wanted them. I wanted the way she'd light up as the information tumbled forth. I wanted to see if she'd spin in the sunlight, whether frost would crunch beneath her nigh-silent feet, and whether she'd leave boot prints in the snow. I wanted to know if she'd have a favorite flower come spring or whether that, too, might be a source of strange and fascinating speculation. Would she spend the time to soak her feet in a stream come summer, or did she prefer to fish, or skip stones? Would she strip down to her leather undergarment the way the Steppe nomads did, and do her hair up in plaits to keep her neck cool, or would little pieces of hair escape her hairstyle to lay against her neck?

"Never mind," she muttered, shaking her head.

My mouth dry, I had to stop myself from grabbing her reins. "Yes," I promised. "Yes, I very much want to join you." She didn't look like she trusted me. I lowered my voice, just a little, refusing to allow that misunderstanding to draw another breath. "You know when all the ideas hit you at once, and you need a moment to sort them?"

Her eyes creased up at the corners a little, with a smile I couldn't see but could feel in my chest. "Oh." That must've made perfect sense because she was suddenly relaxed again. "Well, that's...good, then." She waited for a beat, as if she, too, needed to sort through that, and right there in the deserted La'Angi bailey, my heart turned over in my chest. Then she nodded, appearing content.

I dragged my eyes away from her. If there was some miracle cure, then I'd be very excited to spend expanses of time with her in whatever fashion she found enjoyable. But that explanation felt far too improper to be aired in the bailey of her father's keep. So with need and sadness warring within me, I guided my horse forward.

The city was so quiet and empty that the sound of the horses' hooves echoed along the cobblestone streets. A fat rat peered at us boldly from the front steps of what looked like one of the most affluent houses in the merchants' row. I didn't point it out to Audrey, but I didn't try to hide it, either. We spoke not at all—Audrey gave directions with a pointed finger the few times she needed to. I watched the windows above us as we rode. I marked the ones with shutters that eased open, but none held bowmen intent on killing us this morning.

Almost out of the city and down in a tier slightly closer to what I'd considered the poor quarters than the rich ones—but still an area with glass in the windows and clean, well-maintained sidewalks—we stopped.

A cart stood in the middle of the road. It had been a body cart, clearly, complete with the heavy cloth cover they tossed over and the horrific lumps beneath. But it was left utterly abandoned. A few bodies had been dragged to lay near it. One was wrapped, flowers atop the stained blanket and black feet poking out one end. One looked like someone had done their level best to get the corpse close to the cart but hadn't the strength, and in the end, their friend or family member was left half on the cloth they'd been dragged upon, arm outflung and covered in mud.

"I'll report it," I told Audrey before she could climb down to deal with it herself.

At my voice, a rat popped out from under the cart and peered at us, its muzzle dark.

My stomach rolled.

Audrey turned her head and urged Storm to continue on.

I didn't breathe easily until the castle was out of sight behind us. The apple trees that surrounded La'Angi were naked of leaves. They softened the horses' footfalls and muffled the sound of our passing. Once again, we traced the path Ylva had guided us along.

"It seems the rats can't get it," Audrey said eventually. "I heard the last Ltonan war, the rats got so full they'd pick out the livers of the fallen. Sometimes the eyes, or the brain, but mostly just the livers."

Perhaps I didn't need all of the unusual things she'd learned. I took a deep breath and said, "I bet there were a lot of drunk rats running around." The wind sank talons into my chest, my hips, my legs. The agony of the cold was something I couldn't comprehend. I looked at her, and she was shrunken down in the saddle but seemed undeterred. Faith? Desperation? Or a keen sense of survival tempered by her father's ruthless determination?

She glanced over, taken aback. "I hadn't thought of that."

I didn't know if it was true or not, but before she could start mulling over it, I asked, "What's your plan?"

"I have to get to the stone and activate it."

I shook my head, then had to resettle my cloak to maximize its coverage. The road was utterly deserted behind us, the orchard eerily silent around us. I felt safe to ask, "No. I mean with your father. What's the grand plan?"

Now she sent me a sharp, wary look, but whatever she saw must've reassured her. Deep in the orchard, beneath the naked branches of the apple trees and with the city just a threat on the horizon, she said to me, matter-of-factly, "I'm going to kill him."

There was none of the rage that would've fit that sort of statement and not a shred of the passion that had gripped her this morning. This was the cold woman focused on solving a problem who I'd watched choke a man unconscious and then throw him over the sea wall, and cut the Captain of the guard's throat in front of a hungry crowd. I studied the seriousness of her expression but could see so little of her.

She had one hand braced in the mud, and was doing her best to claw her way back to her feet.

I'd known that, really. I'd seen evidence of it. Over and over again, she'd told me with her actions what was important to her. Finding a way to make things right—trying to protect people, even grumpy road apples like me.

My heart ached for her. For the child she'd never been. I hoped she knew that girl, now, the way I'd gotten to know the boy inside of me.

"It won't undo what he's done," I warned her, in case no one else had.

"No," she agreed, turning her eyes forward again. "It'll put a stop to what he can do. It'll show that there are consequences for everyone's actions, no matter how wealthy and powerful they are. And as I'll be doing it publicly," she continued, as if discussing the weather, "it ought to ensure that the King doesn't try to marry me off to his second-best General, because La'Angi is mine, and I intend to care for it."

There were layers to the plan that I hadn't predicted, a lack of feeling when she spoke of him I couldn't relate to. It made me uneasy. And could a place ever belong to a person?

It would thwart Darrius' plans. If the people followed Audrey, they wouldn't follow Luca or anyone else chosen to climb into her bed.

At that thought, rage rippled under my skin, and I let it out in a hard breath.

"What makes you think you'll make a good Duchess?" I asked her, because I wanted an answer. Because I wanted to defend that hard-won kernel of respect for her.

She glanced over at me again, and I regretted the anger that had crept into my voice. But she asked, "You think I can do it? Kill him?"

That was what she'd heard. That I believed in her. That was how hungry for any spark of hope she was.

"Many things can happen," I said. "That doesn't mean they should."

She looked taken aback by this. "I—well, I don't know why I'd be good," she admitted. "I've the advantage of knowing the city, and I've been lucky enough to be educated. I've got good friends. I try to look at the big picture, and I want to learn. I have half a chance, and that's half a chance more than almost everybody else." She fidgeted with her saddle horn, the first show of unease since she'd started to discuss this treasonous plan. "To be honest, I don't know what else to do but hope that's enough."

Her answer was not the one I'd half-feared she'd utter, but was it a good one? I thought of Kadan, a born leader with his charming, low-pressure way of getting things done. I'd never had to ask if he'd be a good leader. I'd seen him lead. I knew how he worked. But if I'd asked…I suspect he'd have said something similar.

"So." I watched as she ducked under a branch, then avoided the same hazard. "What's the plan, then? An arrow in his heart during a big event?"

"Trial by combat." She didn't look at me as she said it.

I cast my mind back over the times I'd seen her act defensively. Bow, yes. Her shots hadn't missed that day. Knife, perhaps. And then I recalled her standing in front of me, tears on her face and silently pleading with me to train her to use the sword.

My heart sank.

I'd said no.

The wind howled through the trees, but if she felt it, she gave no sign, just lifting a finger to point. "I know these hives. We're about halfway. The terrain gets worse."

I examined the ground. It was safe enough at a walk, but the sun was well into the sky. We'd started much later in the day last time. But we'd also left in a hurry. Who knew how long it would take to attempt to activate this old magic. The cold was surely in my soul by now. I didn't dare take off my gloves to see if my nails, too, were black.

She must've followed my thinking, because she urged her horse to go just a little faster. We rode uphill in silence for a time, and this time I didn't worry about her seat at all. I felt foolish for having considered making her walk Storm last time, which in and of itself was also foolish. She *had* almost come unstuck in the orchard.

She wanted to challenge her father to a trial by combat. She knew he was a swordsman. Even if she could somehow force him to accept the challenge, he'd choose the weapon she was useless with.

She needed me. She knew it.

She hadn't forced it, though. She'd barely even *asked.* And she'd never explained. Not even a hint.

There was an argument that she'd had her hands full, and that was true enough. But despite the crushing urgency of the crises unfolding around us, we'd spent plenty of hours sitting about in her tower, filling time, waiting for situations to unfold. There had been ample opportunities.

"Why didn't you flee?" I asked her before I could think the question through fully. "I'm sorry. You don't need to explain yourself to me, Audrey, I—"

"This is my home," she answered flatly. "I wanted things to get better. Often, it *is* good here, even when he's around. It was so easy to wait just a little longer."

I felt the burn of that hope, deep in my heart. The hopeless, torturous *perhaps* that kept you coming back. I wondered if my mother's ghost still clung to that hope, even now.

"It never does. Get better."

"No." She said it with an acceptance that I didn't know she truly felt. "No, it won't. Not while he's alive. I'd almost come to terms with that, but then the plague came."

And she'd felt obligated to stay. "Seems like another version of the same dangerous hope," I said, though I didn't want to.

"Mayhap," she agreed. "I know the world isn't inherently fair, Chay. But I want to *make* it fair."

And how did a woman who'd grown up warm, fed, educated, and cared for—even if only by her maid and her expensive horse—know what was fair?

I remembered, in detail, the conversation she'd had after I'd killed those children to protect her.

She'd basically put Bernadette and Kaelson in charge of the keep. They only checked in with her out of courtesy and because she showed an interest.

"What if you end up poor and living in a village? Nothing to read. Not even shoes on your feet."

She glanced back over her shoulder at me, frowning. "That feels unlikely. I could get work as a tutor. And anyway, fair isn't everyone having nothing. Fair is people getting what they need."

"What do they need?"

She shot me another look. "I don't know, Chay. I haven't asked yet. What's the point when I've so little to give?" Then, without looking this time, she added, "But I do believe access to food, clean water, somewhere to sleep, healing, and knowledge is the *minimum.* Why is it so few are trained as mages?"

I'd heard Kadan ponder on that same thing. And also plan to kill important men. They were more aligned than even he had known.

I didn't mention to her that she might have allies. I'd need to discuss it first with Kadan. He'd be willing, I was sure.

But it was the older generation we'd need to convince. The ones who looked at Luca and saw a shining example of what nobility *could* be.

"It's a wild dream," she said, hunched down in her saddle. "Isolde says I should retreat to the tribes, learn what I can, and return when I've matured if I still wish to. When I've experience and knowledge."

It was solid advice. "But?"

"People need help *now.*"

And she *was* helping them. Not so much herself, but by adjusting the situation and supporting the people who could make change.

I blew out a long breath. If I could support Luca as King, I could support this woman as Duchess.

"It isn't just revenge," she said, sounding ancient. "There's no way I'll ever really get that. I want it. I want him to look at me and realize he was wrong." My heart sat in my chest like a stone at the conversational way she delivered that truth, and the depth of agony I knew those words could never, ever touch.

I knew that need.

"But I doubt he ever will," she went on, "and my world is greater than the pain he caused. That's a privilege, damn it, but I may as well use it." The end of her sentence lifted up like a question. Her head turned a little, but she didn't look at me, rather, off to the side.

"I'm not hearing a revenge plot," I acknowledged slowly. "It sounds like rebellion."

"Does that scare you?" she asked, turning to me, her eyes full of anger and shadows, and the black, seeping plague.

"Of course it scares me," I said, irritated. "But that's not important. What's important is whether that fear will *stop* me, Embers."

CHAPTER FIFTY-TWO
AUDREY

"In private, it's a fuck up. In public, it's a death sentence." ~ La'Angi saying

The clearing was larger than I remembered it, and quieter.

Storm didn't like it. She danced around, her ears back, her eyes rolling. I stroked her neck, murmuring to her as I looked at the mass in the center. To the side of me, Chay and Bliksem were doing a similar dance, though his beast's stamps were quite a bit more threatening, and also much less regular.

"Give her to me," Chay said impatiently. "I'll walk them until they settle."

"Do you think they remember?"

He looked around, his eyes lingering on the shadows between the trees. I'd already scoped it out and found no one. Still, his attention had me taking the quiver from where I'd looped it on my saddle.

"Could be the wind," he told me. "Feels odd, doesn't it?"

"Old magic," I said, smug about that strange sensation in the bottom of my gut. I'd thought it was the fact I'd been grazed by an arrow last time. He caught my gaze for just a moment, and that shared excitement felt like the first kiss of sun after a long storm.

I turned my attention to the stone. I could see where I'd fallen against it. Some of the moss dangled off, dried and withered, whipped to a strange angle by the wind. I ran my hand up from that gap, knocking more loose.

It was blackened under there. Excitement rippled through me. I wanted to dance, move, or shout, but I did none of those things. Instead, I breathed the need in deep and channeled the energy into brushing more moss free until it formed a big, wide belt of clear stone at the height of my chin. My veins felt like they were full of a million tiny bubbles. I knew that feeling, and I knew the inevitable headache that would come. But for now, I rode the high, running to fetch wood and building a fire on the side furthest from the horses.

Chay appeared as I was almost ready to try to light it. "This wind is bitter. How are you feeling?"

I swallowed the polite answer and had to pause to assess exactly what it was that I felt. Pain. So much pain. I preferred the excited bubbles. "Like my bones are all broken, and my veins are full of old snow."

"That's not what we want." He glanced up at the sky, and I couldn't help but notice the impressive silhouette he made. "Will it take long, do you think?"

Obviously, I had no idea. I didn't bother to remind him of that, assuming it was a rhetorical question. "Could you please stand behind me?" I asked, adjusting my angle.

He did as I asked, his cloak flapping around me.

I looked over my shoulder and had no idea what his expression was. "I'm worried the wind will prevent me from lighting this," I explained, trying not to be annoyed. I hadn't told him, after all. Mayhap he thought I wanted him to shade me from the sun, or watch my technique with flint, or something. "Could you help block it?"

He crouched behind me, his gear chiming softly, close enough that I could smell the scent of beeswax that clung to the leather I'd oiled for him just the other day, and the grass that was crushed beneath his boots. Hiding his tracks would be hard if I needed to. I didn't mind, though.

Skimming through the options in my mind, I steadied my hand and struck the flint. A spark flew true into the small puffs of tinder that started to smolder.

The wind gusted, and I felt Chay shifting beside me, spreading his cloak to better guard against its intrusion.

I hadn't realized quite how horrific the cold was until it eased just a little more, but I didn't linger to thanking him. Focusing my hands on building the fire, my mind danced back over our blunt conversation. Wasn't it odd that he responded so well to directness? Didn't people prefer to talk around and slowly approach most topics, like a horse with a new piece of gear? And Chay was from Raider's Ban. If anyone was horse-like, it ought to be him.

It didn't make sense, and I couldn't change that. So I built the fire until the moss low on the stone was curling and smoldering, falling away in messy, smoking chunks.

To the side, a bird erupted from a nearby tree, squawking. Chay's shield came up in front of me, and I had my bow drawn. But nothing stirred. On the edge of the clearing, the horses hadn't even looked up from the grass they were cropping.

Slowly, I lowered my bow. Slower still did Chay drop his shield. I was sad when he didn't crouch behind me protectively again, which made no sense whatsoever.

"Should we feel something?"

I was confident we would, if it worked. "Fire cleanses," I said.

Nothing.

"*Ceiyemmyah pbettra* awaken," I tried. "Fire cleanses."

Before me, it cleansed the moss off the stone. No more or less.

"*Ceiyemmyah pbettra* cleanse Mysctheras with this fire."

"Mysctheras?" Chay asked from behind me.

"La'Angi before Barloc," I replied, straightening. My body protested, and my joints stuck as I went. I ached, and my head had started to feel the buzz of bees.

He didn't ask more questions, and I was grateful for that. I stood, wrapped tightly in my cloak, and stared at the fire that should've triggered the protective spell set deep into the monolith, but wasn't.

Fire cleanses. Thomas had said it like a mantra. It wasn't unfair to assume it would trigger the spell, was it?

Feeling it all slipping away, I started pulling moss off more aggressively. It *was* blackened. I was on the right path. I had to be. I took the arrow in my hand and, using the steel tip, scraped some of the char off. It flaked away, a thick layer. And there was *more* beneath it.

It had burned. Hot and long.

"Mayhap we need more fire," I said, feeling sick. But I knew that couldn't be right. There wouldn't have been time to assemble a bonfire before a giant wave swallowed the city unless they'd kept it built and ready.

Chay set off to the nearby stand of trees, throwing his shield over his back. I kept working on the moss. If *I* were an old-time person in charge of a magical monolith, I would've engraved instructions on the thing itself.

Chay dragged over wood, and I built the fire slowly around the base of it until I reached where I'd rubbed up against it on the far side.

I'd bled. I'd bled on the stone. And those arrows had stopped.

I'd assumed it had just been the mage's air magic. They'd called a halt, hadn't they? It made sense, if they could control the air, they could control arrows.

My hand shaking, I took the arrowhead and pressed it to my palm. My blood came slowly, thick and black. *Please, work.* I squeezed my eyes closed and pressed my hand to the stone.

Nothing.

"Fire cleanses," I said, but when I got no response, I wasn't surprised.

I looked up to see Chay hauling a big branch in each hand. He was paler than he should've been, given how long he'd been at it and how much he was hauling.

What I could see of the surface was pockmarked and showed signs of flaking, as if some giant hand had shorn off slivers of it. It offered no solutions. I'd run through every single idea I'd had, and a few fresh ones.

Chay dropped the branches and came to stand beside me, hands on his hips, as we both stared at it.

"Wonder if time did what Barloc couldn't," he said softly.

"I think I hate him."

Chay considered it. "That's fair. We won't make it back tonight, you know."

I pushed away the ache in my bones, ignoring the hard stab of hopelessness that made tears prick at my eyes. "Then we'd better keep trying."

CHAPTER FIFTY-THREE

CHAY

"The believers lifted up the Son, and before all his kindness spread. Prosperity and joy like nothing that had come before was experienced. Those who suffered had their pain lifted, if they repented." ~ *The Book of Bread and Salt*

The monotony of the task and the bite of the cold numbed my mind. It was the only thing I could think of to explain why I worked for so long, dragging branches and gathering armloads of twigs. My feet ached. My hips ached. My *fingers* ached.

I'd thought I'd checked in on her often enough. She kept pacing near that damned stone, her eyes on its surface or the ground around it. Sometimes, when I glanced at her, she was warming her hands, and I was glad of it. The color bled from the sky, and the temperature dipped. I'd thought I'd kept track of it.

I'd stopped watching, though. I'd stopped, and when I'd looked around, she was motionless in a pile beside the stone.

My heart froze in my chest. The distance between us was huge, my limbs too cold, too stiff, too ungainly. Leaves slipped beneath my boots and skidded beneath my knees. "Audrey," I said, but the word came out as an explosion of sound as I grabbed her.

Her eyes opened. They were black—but open. "It isn't working," she said, the words full of defeat.

A laugh born of relief bubbled inside me. I locked it deep in my belly, helping her stand only for her legs to collapse.

The laugh burst in my chest. It made my eyes water. I caught her before she fell, picking her up to carry her to the horses. She protested, the words jumbled and slurred.

"Apologies, Embers," I said, holding her in close and hating the necessity of that. "I'll listen to you again as soon as you're capable of standing." There was really no excuse. I should've watched closer. I should've steered her homeward when we'd last spoken. The One, I may as well have been asleep.

At some point, she stopped fighting. I breathed deeply and held her close, willing any shred of warmth from my body into hers. I was damned if I was letting her die out here in the cold, alone. It just wasn't happening. Everything in me refused to let it. I didn't care why. It didn't matter.

Her long legs fit ill beneath her cloak. Bliksem knelt for me as I adjusted the cloth to better cover those vulnerable calves. Layered like a solstice gift she might be, but the afternoon was long, and her illness hadn't been brief.

Patiently, Bliksem waited as I climbed into the saddle, forgiving my own impatient movements as if he knew I was in a chokehold and only barely hanging on.

I just wanted her to complain. She didn't, curling into me when she was jostled in a way I knew damned well would be painful. I wasn't letting her go long enough to tie her to her saddle.

I wasn't letting her go.

Storm willingly followed us down the incline and away from the stone. The beekeeper's hut where Isolde had sheltered. It couldn't be far. I'd spotted its smoke, that day we were set upon. There was none now, but the hut *must* still be there. I breathed through my teeth, my hands white-knuckled where I clutched the reins to her. The icy wind whistled through the trees, stinging my eyes.

It felt like an eon before she moved in my arms. "I've got you," I said, alarmed that she might try to sit up and topple us both. "We're on Bliksem."

She didn't respond, but her arm worked its way around me, and I felt her twist her fingers into my belt. My mouth a desert, I was grimly glad both at this sign of life and for the assistance as I tried to hold her securely and guide both horses on unfamiliar, uneven ground as fast as I could.

We passed a beehive, then a second. The ground leveled out, and I saw a break in the trees ahead, then the stone chimney. "Almost there," I told her. She was still holding me, and I could barely breathe. "Just up here." The little home appeared in the center of a clearing with a small garden. I guided the horses right to the door of the house.

"Stay here," I told Audrey, disentangling myself with difficulty from her claw-like, icy hands. I didn't stop to throw my cloak over her. She needed to be out of the wind.

I unhooked my shield from my saddle and threw it over my shoulder, then strode toward the solid but plain wooden door. Hammering a gloved fist against the wood, I shouted, "Hello?" only for the word to be tossed uselessly into the wind.

There was no response. I tried to pull the door open, but it was barred from within.

My first thought was to raise a leg and kick the damned thing in. Urgency beat at my breast like a drum. But a broken door was a poor windbreak. I ran around the small house and found what I was hoping for—a window on the far side. The shutters were locked, but I managed to force them with the sound of splintering wood. If they were broken, they'd be easier to block than the door.

Climbing in through the narrow gap meant throwing my shield into the darkness first, flicking my cloak back over my shoulders, and twisting my body in a way I knew damned well Audrey would've been able to do far more gracefully. The thought filled me with grim resolve.

The single room reeked of death.

By the thin light I made my way to the door, lifting the bar to let the wind and sun in, such as it was. The place was as cold as a grave anyway. At least the wind carried the scent of soil and salt. I looked back over my shoulder and found the source of the odor.

He'd probably been the beekeeper in his life. In his death, he curled protectively beside the fireplace, skin white, veins black, like roads to one of the old hells we weren't supposed to talk about.

I didn't waste words on him, just grabbed him beneath the arms, dragged him outside, and sat him beside the house. I'd deal with him tomorrow. If we lived that long.

Audrey was already sliding down out of the saddle. She collapsed to the ground with an indrawn breath and a partially muffled sound of pain that escaped from between her teeth. I grabbed the reins in time to stop her from being stepped on, quickly hobbling the horses.

We needed to get back. We wouldn't, not without them. But right now, we both needed warmth.

She gripped my belt again as I put an arm around her to lift her up—she could walk, but it wouldn't have mattered if she couldn't. I would've gotten her in. Determination burned like molten steel through me. Right then, I could've lifted the entire house out of the ground if I'd had to.

Once out of the cold, I pushed her down on the opposite side of the small stone hearth to where I'd found the last resident and threw my cloak over her, reaching for the flint and tinder.

"You should leave," she said, the words thin, reedy. "Before you catch it. Tell Isolde. Tell Thomas."

I'd heard enough last words in my time, and words that the speaker thought were their last, to recognize that tone. Fury writhed in my guts.

She was mine, damn it. That's what we'd both sworn on my blood, sealed by magic older than any of us knew. "Tell them yourself," I demanded impatiently. "Because you swore yourself to me, Embers. Until my heart no longer beats, you swore. That's a magically binding oath, woman. *My* heart. Not yours." The tinder struck, and the flame caught. It wasn't enough warmth. Not yet. "You don't get free while *I'm* alive."

Her lids flickered prettily, but there was no whiskey to be found in her gaze. I wanted to drink deep, but the well was dry.

"That's not…how it works," she murmured. "Not how…the stone works…either."

"Obviously, you did it wrong," I snapped at her, feeding the flame hurriedly. There wasn't much wood, but there was some, and it had to be enough. "Tell me about how that knight used it against those locusts. I bet he has the key."

She didn't move. "I can't, Chay. I'm so cold."

Any other time, and I would've suggested some wonderful ways we could both warm up. And I hated that not even the thought of her in the firelight in this remote little space could shake the threat of death. The reek of it still lingered. "If you die," I told her, without looking, "who's going to stand up to the Butcher? I'll follow you into your rebellion," I told her, willing the flame to burn faster, hotter, higher. "I'll teach you how to use a sword. I'll teach you everything I know. The first thing lesson is now. Move. Fight it."

Tears glittered on her lashes. "It hurts."

"Hasn't it hurt for hours?" I demanded, frustrated. "Days?"

"Weeks," she whispered.

"Well, as your advisor, Embers, I advise you recall that fact and move *despite* it." I tossed a log onto the fire and stood. "I have to get the horses secured, or we won't make it back."

"My bow," she said, stretching her hands out to the flame, the words thick with pain. She was moving her toes in her boots.

I wanted to press a kiss to her head. I had no right to do that. I had no right to ask anything of her at all. But I *had* asked, and I'd damned well keep on asking. She needed someone to tell her no and walk beside her as she braved the lessons that followed.

I shut the window as best I could and strode back out into the wind. Promises made mattered. I settled the horses as fast as I could, then barred the door again. She was sitting up, rotating her head slowly on her neck. I built the fire higher and hoped no one saw the smoke, then went outside to find the wood pile.

With the clouds roiling above us, I put my mediocre woodcutting skills to use, furiously cutting through logs that were still green. He'd used everything.

He'd saved Isolde and then died himself.

Was she alive?

The thought of her retribution if I lost Audrey left me feeling cold. I'd take it.

I needed to get wood into the house. Was I better to ferry it in now, or stack it outside and retrieve it as needed?

I didn't know, but each time I went in, Audrey was still moving. I kept an eye on the sky—the sun was lower than it should've been, the clouds heavier than they had been. We weren't leaving for the keep today. And with that knowledge, I cut yet more wood, stacked it right beside the door, and drew up some buckets of water. The chores felt like they took years. The reverberations of the axe up my arms made them burn. *Until my heart no longer beats.* The words punctuated my thoughts in time with the splintering of wood and the thud of the axe. *Until. My. Heart. No. Longer. Beats.*

When I got back inside, there were still no coals in the fire, and it was still cold as ice. Audrey was lying on her side, wrapped tight in my cloak, but just as I went to curse, she said, "There's honey. Food. East wall."

I gave the place she mentioned a cursory glance. She'd opened cupboards. She'd been up. The relief that flooded through me was dammed up by the way she didn't even shiver, now, before the fire, despite the fact that the edge was barely taken off the air. Or was I too sick to tell? I peeled back the wrist of my glove. The skin there was pale, the veins dark, but not the stark contrast of black and white that I knew I'd find if I looked at her skin. No, I wasn't too far gone.

Moving to the far wall, I grabbed and dragged the beekeeper's pallet closer to the fire, kicking a chair out of the way. "Up off the cold floor," I told Audrey when she looked at me dully.

She moved agonizingly slowly, but move she did. I built the fire higher, hoping again that the cloud cover would be low enough to hide the smoke, that no marauders would venture here, then took out some of the cold meat and cheese from the bags. I sat close to her. She huddled in a little more. I felt every muscle in my body pull taut with the need to drag her into my lap and crush her to me. Rage, impotent and useless, coursed through me. We sat shoulder to shoulder and looked at the flames while we chewed in silence, broken only by the rain that began to lash against the side of the wall. My thoughts went to the horses—there was little I could do for them, though. They had what shelter I could find them.

"I'm sorry," she said, with a few bites of meat still held between gloved fingers.

Without understanding why she felt the need to apologize, I just shrugged and finished my own cold, heavy meal. The wind whistled in the cracks beneath the walls and in the ceiling. I ignored it. There were fewer drafts in here than out there. "Usually, I'd offer straws to see who gets the bed," I said flatly. "But we both need the warmth, so if you don't mind." She turned and looked at me, her expression dull. I waved a hand toward it, and she folded herself down like she was an old woman.

I adjusted the water before the fire. "Isolde said bathing helps," I reminded her.

She didn't open her eyes.

"Probably not when you're wrapped like a solstice gift," I acknowledged, refusing to consider any other alternative for her lack of response as I folded myself down against her back, layering the extra fabric of my cloak over her, then the horse blankets.

She held herself stiffly. I didn't know if it was politeness or her preference, and I didn't have the heart to ask. Exhaustion washed over me like a wave. I didn't expect to sleep. I did, though, within moments, lulled by the sound of rain, wind, and the crackle of the fire.

CHAPTER FIFTY-FOUR
AUDREY

"Should a suitor be found worthy of such, he may, with the blessing of your father, commence courting your family. This will involve spending time with your father and brothers, where you have them, as well as your suitor taking you to visit public attractions, such as gardens. If you attend a ball, attend with your father and brother, and visit with your suitor there." ~ Etiquette in Arcanloc

I drifted in and out of sleep, first because I was too uncomfortable, and then because my brain kept popping strange thoughts into my head, or my dreams did, or because I was worried. I knew I slept, because I didn't remember when he'd put his arm around me.

The stone had been our last hope. Or my last hope. Mayhap there was hope for others.

Lying on my side made the points of my body in contact with the thin mattress hurt so much, I wondered if I mightn't have broken something. I'd probably make it back to La'Angi, but it was just a matter of time now.

I'd often thought about how much Chay must regret swearing that oath. Now I wondered if he felt like he chose the right option, between my father and I.

I wasn't going to ask. I'd never trust his answer. He told me off for being polite, but he didn't always say what he was thinking. None of us did.

Anyway, I wasn't sure that I really wanted to know if time with me and death might be better, or worse, than time with my father and life.

Selfishly, I was glad he'd chosen as he had. But I'd never tell him that. I wanted him to be back in Raider's Ban with that sandy-haired man who told me the enemy of my enemy was my friend, who had made Chay smile and come to his aid.

But he was good and fair. He was easy to be with. He was trustworthy. He *heard* me. And he asked good questions.

I wanted to keep him.

The way his heart had drummed, and his breath had rasped in and out of his lungs as I sank into the void would stick with me forever. That heartbeat, and the heat of him, had held it back.

The fire popped, and he sighed in his sleep, tugging me closer to his chest and nestling his face into my hair.

The sweetness was so complete it made me ache in a different way to the plague, like I was too full, and it had to escape.

I was probably going to die in the next week. I probably needed to see to Isolde. She wouldn't make it, if I wasn't able to bank the fires. I couldn't ask anyone else to.

Chay would. Thomas would. But I didn't want that for them.

I'd known I would need to address the issue once I'd realized I was sick. But I'd selfishly postponed that conversation for just a little while longer.

I must've dozed again because when I woke, the fire was low, and the coals were scattered amongst ash. The wood wasn't good enough to create a lot of coals or burn for long, but it kept the cold at bay.

Outside of the blankets, I wondered if mayhap it wasn't Chay who did that, because the cabin felt icy. Quickly I banked it again and went to return, only to see I'd woken my personal furnace.

He lifted the blanket, and it was the most natural thing in the world to ease back into that spot. But though he settled the covers over us, he didn't put his arm over me, and even stayed a small distance away.

I was confident that he didn't despise my presence. I felt too horrible to worry too much. So I asked, "Where's your arm?" I realized that wasn't all the information, so I added, "Before, it was around me. I just wanted to know if you didn't want to do that anymore, or if it wasn't comfortable, or what other considerations I may have overlooked." All the other things I probably should've explained spun through my head, but I didn't say them because I already had enough regret.

"Do you want my hug?" he asked, and the question stirred the hair over my ear. Heat rolled through me. It would've been a lot less awkward if it was because his breath was hot.

I tried to sift through the possible directions this conversation could go, depending on answers. There were no good options, of course. Because I'd opened my mouth without knowing what was happening.

"When you're offered something, is yes or no harder to say?" he asked me.

"It depends on the situation," I said, relieved there was an easy answer, finally.

"Someone's offering you affection," he said.

My head ached. "It still depends. Will I be punished for saying no, overtly or covertly?"

He sounded sad when he said, "No."

I didn't believe him, and wasn't that a strange thing to realize?

Partly to ease the ache in my hip and partly so he stopped breathing into my ear, I turned onto my back, but then I had to figure out what to do with my hands. "What of you?" I asked him, deciding to clasp them on my belly. They sat there awkwardly.

He rubbed sleep out of his eyes. "Yes is harder," he said around a yawn. "Not by much nowadays."

"Why?" I asked as he shifted to prop his head up on his elbow. I'd had Isolde in my ear since the start telling me I was allowed to say no. "Why is yes hard?"

"Lots of reasons," he replied around a half-muffled yawn. "Enjoying affection is giving someone leverage over you. It can be taken away as punishment or quoted as a favor they've done you. It can be held up like a cube of sugar." My heart ached, and he just yawned again, blinking. "Then there's the back-of-your-brain worry you don't really deserve it, that they'll flee once they understand who you are or what you're doing."

I struggled to draw in breath. He'd summarized it so easily.

"Haven't felt that way myself for a long time," he said, settling in. "But I understand why some might." And he looked at me, not waiting for confirmation or denial, just simply stating facts. "Kadan was probably the first safe person I met."

"And I took you from him." The words were out before I could snatch them back.

He let out a breath. "I chose hope," he said quietly. "Over doom or death, I chose hope. I chose you." Tears sprang into my eyes, and I looked away, my full heart aching in my chest. The reality was he'd ended up with death *and* doom. "This isn't how any of it was supposed to go," he said quietly. "But I'm glad this beekeeper built his home here, and I'm glad you're here with me. I like this bed the best of any I've slept in since I arrived here."

Desperately, I grabbed for the offered distraction in his words, knuckling away tears and trying not to unsettle the blankets in the process. "We haven't slept enough. I ought to let you rest."

"Quality, Embers, not quantity." He shifted a little more. "Can I put my arm around you?" I nodded and then lay still as he did exactly that, no more or less. Exhausted, sick, and far too vulnerable, I shut my eyes to give myself some time to sort through the messy whirlwind inside myself.

"I'm going to point out that if there *is* something you want from me, tonight's probably an excellent time to ask for it," Chay said, the words soft in the darkness.

I'd already reasoned my way to that conclusion, but I'd also circled back to the thought that once he'd been a little boy who'd been made to feel like kindness was a danger. I wanted to lean into him and not entirely for warmth. He didn't seem to mind, so I closed the tiny gap between us, my heart aching.

I knew that child. I tucked my head in beneath his, surrounded by his warmth. "I'm glad you found Kadan."

"I'm glad you found Isolde," he said without hesitation, and there went any shred of doubt that he knew exactly how relevant all his comments were. "I haven't seen much kindness from her, but she's always got your back."

The thought of kindness didn't match well with Isolde. The kindness she showed wasn't what the Wife had taught us it ought to be. She'd sacrifice, but not without limitations. She'd encourage, but not without pointing out flaws, sometimes at length. Her softness was a limited resource.

And perhaps that was why it felt authentic. Because I could trust her to never follow unthinkingly.

"It might've been Luca," I said into the quiet. "For me." I shook my head, though, because he wasn't safe. Not properly. "When I was eleven, I went to Raa'shi to marry him. Obviously that didn't happen, but I still attended a number of parties and feasts." I looked above me and saw the line of his jaw, his eyes on the fire, his expression intent. "I had to dance with him at one of them, and I didn't know the dance. They'd cleared the floor. It was in front of everyone." I felt the echoes of that shame years later. I'd stood there, holding his hand, and felt like someone else steered my skin while I screamed inside. "He told me to stand on his feet. It was the first kind thing I can remember. That sounds ungrateful, and it isn't supposed to."

"It sounds like what it is, which is sad," he told me. "I'm glad he did that."

"For years," I said on a bit of a laugh, "I thought it was the most romantic thing in the world. He'd saved me, in that moment. But then, when I was about his age, we had a delegation from the Citadel attend, including a young cousin of the prince they'd been flaunting under my father's nose. I thought of that child, standing up in front of all the adults, being humiliated, and I would've done the same thing. For a child I didn't know and probably wouldn't even like, I would've done the same."

Chay let out a long breath. "Yeah. It does sound like he gave you some basic decency."

My heart twisted at his tone. I couldn't figure out what it meant, but it wasn't the easy give and take from before. "My apologies. I know he's your friend."

"Acquaintance," Chay said without hesitation. "Ally, certainly. But friend?" He lifted his hand, wavering it back and forth. "I did hear about that time, though, that you went to Raa'shi. He caused quite the stir at court. Apparently, the basic decency of not marrying an eleven-year-old was shocking."

I hated to recall my own disappointment. My life might've been better, had Luca been around. But I didn't want to be shackled to him. "I owe him."

Chay let out a small, hard laugh. "I wouldn't go that far. For someone who's sworn you a Blood Oath, I haven't seen much of him."

Shock rippled through me. I shifted away. "He told you that?" I asked, which was ridiculous because *obviously* he had. "He told you about treason, and you're his *acquaintance*?"

"He and Kadan are close," Chay told me, a little uncomfortable. "Luca thinks they're very close. If you know what I mean."

"Oh." My head ached. Isolde was right about Luca, but it was what it was. "You and Isolde should compare notes someday."

A smile tugged at his mouth. He looked down at me, humor sparking in his eyes. "I expect I'd agree with many of her observations." Then, "What does she say about me?"

He was a brave man to ask such a question. I dug through my mind but couldn't recall very much. "That you're not a total liability," I said slowly. It might've been the highest praise she'd given any man.

He looked pleasantly surprised. "I'd take that to the merchant's guild."

That wasn't the response I'd expected, but for some reason it made affection sweep through me. She would've been amused for a moment to hear him say such, then gone about her day. It was just lovely to feel like he *saw* us.

I had to unclasp my hands and unsettle the covers to reach up and run the pads of my fingers over the short hairs on his jaw. He shut his eyes. I was so close I could feel the slight change in his heartbeat.

He could say no. He'd told me so. It was yes that was hard, right?

Beneath my hand, he remained unmoving. He hadn't been this still when I'd had a knife to his throat all those moons ago.

Whether the stubble on his jaw was classified as a beard yet or not, I was unsure, but the roughness of it made shivers climb up my spine. It rasped against my skin in a soft but spiky way when I smoothed my fingers one way, and gave way entirely when I ran them back the other. It made me feel like my insides were liquid. His jaw had been shadowed when we'd met in the orchard, too. But I hadn't felt it then.

"I wonder what would've happened if we'd run into each other and become friends," I said, thinking out loud.

Before I could explain what I meant, his lips curved. "This, I expect." His eyes had opened, a fact that made my thoughts scatter. His hand had tightened over my waist. As his weight shifted, I brought my knee up and was gripping his shirt before I realized what I was doing.

He'd frozen, his expression one of worry. "Are you okay?" he asked, paused at an awkward angle, leaning somewhat over me, vulnerable to however I wished to ragdoll him.

"My apologies." I released him, my fingers groaning from the tension I'd put them under.

He shook his head a little. "Should I not kiss you? Just to be clear, you understand."

My head spun. I looked up at him, aware of the skewed blankets between us at the same time as I was feeling the heat from his body and thinking about how that beard might feel against my face. He hated politeness and valued honesty. Unsure how my face ought to be arranged, I studied the way his gambeson was tied closed and the way it felt brushing against my belly where it hung ever so slightly away from his. How had he worn his hair before? I could barely picture it now. It was longer. Floppy, against his forehead and the collar of his shirt. Waves of it had picked up in the breeze and drank in the sun.

"You probably shouldn't," I said, trying to breathe. "But I'd be glad if you did." It'd be much faster and more sensible to go up and under his gambeson to feel if his skin elsewhere was as soft as it was on his cheek. Even as a thrill went through me at this idea, my belly twisted with fear. "Wait." I put a hand between us out of reflex again, and he stopped.

Was he doing this out of duty?

He *couldn't* refuse me.

The thought made me feel sick. He'd said he was most comfortable saying no, but *could* he say no to me, regardless of his comfort level?

"What's wrong?" he asked me.

I tried to figure out whether he'd be breaching his oath or not. It was entirely possible he'd know that rejecting my advances, however clumsy, would have hurt. "It'll hurt me a lot more if you kiss me out of duty than if you tell me you'd rather not. In case your oath is guiding your decision-making."

His lips curved in a smile, and his weight settled over me like my favorite combination of blankets. The warmth of his breath stirred the air beside my ear, and my body lit up from toe to brow.

"Noted." I closed my eyes, better to feel the gentle brush of the tip of his nose against the outside of my ear, frozen so as not to end the sensations. "You want to know what's guiding my decision-making?"

A thrill raced up my spine. Without moving my head, I felt his lips brush against my lobe. His cheek skimmed gently against my jaw, and I couldn't help but turn into him, just a little, and rub myself against him. "Yes." That was the right answer. The responsible answer.

He rubbed back, pressing his lips to my temple, quick kisses that dipped once more to my ear. The blankets were far too hot. Why had I banked the fire so high? Could I escape the covers without making him move? If not, I'd just die of heat and be glad of it. His lips closed over my earlobe, and my attention focused almost entirely on that small part of my body as I drank in the sensation.

"I want you to burn for me, Embers." The words were cold against the dampness of my skin and coiled in the valleys of my ear, seeping slowly into my brain.

I had to swallow before I could manage, "I think I'm on the way."

His laughter was silent, but I could feel him shaking, the curve of his lips, the quick exhales. "We'll see." His nose brushed against the point where my jaw met my neck, and I didn't know what to do. I'd thought he'd kiss me, and mayhap we'd shed clothes and—

His fingers skimmed my cheek. I breathed deeply, and he cradled my jaw as his lips skimmed inexorably toward mine. The brush of his thumb distracted me from the occasional rasp of his beard against me. I stayed frozen, waiting for more.

His lips were warm on mine, surprisingly soft. I reached up and fanned my fingers over his cheeks, running the pads of my fingers and palms against the short hairs. The combination of soft lips and biting stubble was almost the perfect balance of sensation, and I struggled to breathe, drunk on the feelings coursing through me. The heat was there, still, and the hunger, but that exquisite balance of *just so* was what consumed my will to move ever again.

When he eased away, the tip of his nose touching the side of mine and his breaths quick, I felt like an arrow drooping away from its notch and the unskilled fingers that might otherwise hold it. I tugged him back down, and he came gladly, his hand between us tugging away the blankets, sending them tumbling to the side.

The rush of cold air against me wasn't enough. The bite of his teeth on my bottom lip was jarring. I held him tighter to me, the balance broken, hungry, and wanting to know all of the sensations now so I could better choose the right ones, in the right combination.

His hand tangled in my skirts. He hadn't known formal skirts from everyday ones. I suspected he'd know how to get into them under normal circumstances, but I'd layered cautiously. He wasn't getting in without an axe and a map.

His teeth scraped against my neck, and the world felt blurry and far away. I wanted it to go even further away. If it never returned, that would be fine.

I need to move. But I didn't want to move. I felt his hand searching through my skirts, and it made me think of myself, my whole life, searching to make it work. And still he kissed, nibbled, and breathed, and I ached the sweetest ache. *I need to move.* His hand coiled around my thigh, right above my knee. It filled his hand, but he gripped me as best he could, breathing like we'd been sparring forever. Breathing like we could continue sparring forever. I parted my legs, and he notched between them, pressed in as close as he could get. Did he feel the way I burned for him?

Was it his lips that begged entry, or mine that begged to be explored? I didn't know. It didn't matter. The world went quiet as his tongue dove deep into my mouth and his body pressed against mine. Sparks flew up my limbs and set fires in my body.

He got my skirts up. I could feel the coolness of the air filtering through my many-layered, stockinged legs and it was like bliss. But his hasty, hungry fingers couldn't find how I'd tucked them into cautious layers.

I wasn't ready to die. But I was quite content to live.

A slight turn was all I needed for him to break away and lean back. My eyes popped open. I tracked him because he was all that was real. Chay, his movements, his touches, the hungry heat in my blood.

There weren't extra words to explain, but I didn't need to. He got out of the way while I wrestled with my clothing, his eyes on me as he stripped off his own layers. The quick movements of his body were like some sort of dance I didn't know the steps to, but I didn't need to follow. I could lie back, untangling myself absently, my attention on the slide and ripple of muscle in his shoulders, and the way the light played over his skin.

He took off his boots. It was real, then.

I didn't stop, though. No one would ever know because we'd never tell them.

Chay knelt before the tangle of clothes I was slowly working through, his expression one of intense focus.

There were many words I could use to describe Chay. Untrustworthy wasn't one of them.

I took in the sight of him before me. An old, faded scar went from the base of his neck across his chest. One of his biceps was puckered at two points where he'd taken arrows. One of his thighs bore a fresher mark, not yet silvered, both wide and puckered. The spots on either side of it showed where his skin had been sewn up.

I wanted to know every story behind every mark.

As I watched, he started rolling up his shirt in a bundle, then layered his gambeson on, too. One of my nails caught on a thread of my stocking and I carefully removed it, but returned my attention to his quick, sure hands as he tightened his belt around the round bundle.

I didn't ask. It was a good size for a pillow, I supposed, though the density of it didn't appeal to me. It was set aside, anyway, as he helped ease one of the freed layers of hose from my body, stopping down near my knees.

I liked the look he cast my boots, full of frustration yet resigned to their necessity. I liked it, but I disagreed with it. Using one toe, I set to work on removing a boot, and he was right there helping me, easing them away from my feet that ached at the protective leather exposing them to the cold.

He'd warm me. I knew he would.

Strong hands coached cloth down my legs, trailing his fingers over my calves and dipping into the valley at the back of my knee and again at the base of my feet. I saw his cock in the shadow between his thighs, hard and ready for me.

What texture would it be? How would it feel in my hand or against my skin? The questions weren't new, but knowing I could have answers momentarily made my head spin, and my fingers hurried to separate the ties of my clothing.

And when the layers grew thinner, his hands lingered longer, his eyes tracking the movement of my hands closely. Tension coiled in my limbs, tightening with every moment of waiting.

The idea of him pouncing on me the moment he saw skin made sparks flurry along my limbs, but he held himself still, poised to assist.

Words clamored in my head, but my tongue wouldn't work. Suddenly, the sound of the wind outside was loud in the boughs of the apple trees, and all I could smell was dust and smoke.

His fingers were on my bare skin, finally, but the sudden unease didn't settle until the last item was removed, leaving me bare from the waist down bar the laces that dangled.

When he came close enough, I slid my hands up his arms. He was cold to the touch and let me pull him into me, arranging the covers over us.

I wanted to warn him against the chill, but when his lips met mine again, slow and lingering, they were warm. And if his thighs were cold, I couldn't tell.

"Do you have a pregnancy charm?" he asked me.

I nodded. It was at the keep, because why would I have brought such an item? But it would work fine even in a number of days.

He went to ask me something else. Something serious. I could see it coming from the darkness in his gaze and the depression between his brows. But I didn't want serious. I had serious baked into my existence, howling at the door, and pumping through my veins. I could feel its aching claws in my skin.

Making sure he had time to withdraw, I took his face again and tugged him back to me, wrapping my legs around his waist. His breath caught, and I traced his lips the way he'd done to mine.

He rumbled something that wasn't quite words and flexed against me. I closed my eyes and soaked in the sensations again, the feel of the fine hairs on his thighs and the weight of him holding me securely, the rasp of his stubble, and the warmth of his kisses. But I couldn't feel his cock.

Reassurances crowded my throat and buzzed through my brain like angry bees. *Don't worry about me,* I wanted to tell him, around his sweet and salty kisses. *I could choke you in five different ways with less than that many moves. I could break either of your elbows before you knew you were in danger.* I didn't know if that would set him at ease. *I won't ask you to lie for me.* But he might need to, at least by omission, if we somehow lived long enough for it to matter.

Breathing quickly, he rested his forehead against mine, his hand skimming down my throat, stroking at the skin above the neck of my overdress.

By way of answer, I ran my hands down his chest, over the firm muscles and smooth skin interspersed with thc occasional patch of hair. I wanted to linger and explore the length of it, the texture and density, but I could feel his questions bubbling, and I didn't want to identify the right words.

He went very still against me as my hands bypassed his hips, following the vee of muscle without lingering overly long. I'm sure it was all nice, and I'd enjoy it all soon. But I needed to *know.*

The first thing I noticed was the resilience of the shaft and the way it sat in my palm, like a well-balanced knife. But his skin was softer than the most buttery leather grip, and the shape of it didn't match a hilt. The way the skin moved over the top of his flesh was strange. And when I ran my fingers over the wonderfully soft, round tip he sucked in a breath.

A quick glance told me that he wasn't in pain, so I settled back and continued with my perusal, keeping my touch feather light as I explored the curve of him, the strange ridge at the base, the little lip around the tip, then the weight of his balls.

I kept returning to the soft glide of that skin, though. The way it shifted and slid given the firmness of his cock was the strangest contrast, and it surprised me how much I enjoyed it.

"Can I return the favor?" he asked me, the words low.

There was no way his hand would comfortably fit between us. I grasped his hips instead, settling him between my thighs.

He made a noise of amusement or something similar, kissing the corner of my mouth and twisting away. My belly ached. "I didn't mean you had to stop," he said, but his thigh pressed firmly into the apex of my thighs, and the words stopped making sense.

I knew he talked to me, and vague impressions came through. Amusement, joy, and sweetness. But it was the sensations that filled me up. The bite of his stubble against my cheek, the still-quick pants of warm air against my ear, the tickle of his hair against my forehead. His hand seared my skin as it skimmed down my body, brushing against my breast. I'd've sworn to the One I could feel the back of his knuckles through half a dozen layers. I arched up, but his teeth just scraped against my lobe, making the air thick and entirely unnecessary. But it was his hand closing over my cunt that shut down my mind.

The weight of him. The warmth. The teasing of his finger and the grind of his palm. If I'd moved, I would've fallen apart. So I stayed stock-still, his hips still held firmly in my hands, struggling to suck in air. Brief, deep pressure, then he was stroking me from the inside and pressing down on my clit all at once.

"Breathe, Embers," he said, and the words clawed up my legs and nestled into my cunt. "Good fires need air."

I drew it in deeply, the heat soaking deep into my bones. The world was quiet, though I could hear us both breathing quickly. I wanted to cut off my remaining clothes and feel his touch on my breasts. I wanted to throw my legs wide and drag him to me. Instead, I stayed still, dazed by the sensations rushing through me.

He nudged in a little closer, and I felt added pressure inside me. I flexed around his finger, and he breathed in quickly, turning his face toward mine.

There was nothing quite so well-timed as his tongue thrusting into my mouth as his hand thrust into me. It was the gasp of his breath over my wet lips and the hungry way he dived back in for more that finally sent me tumbling over the edge, clinging to him as the sensations overtook me, ripping through me in waves that drowned everything out.

And when I could see again, when I could breathe, he was still right there above me, his hand still inside me.

Very much real.

Gently, like I was made of freshly blown glass, he eased his hand from inside me. "There you go," he murmured, and as I gazed up at him, the world was still quiet. His smile was soft and full of shared joy as he pressed a kiss to my cheek, lingering there and making my breath catch. "Now you're ready to burn."

CHAPTER FIFTY-FIVE
CHAY

"A good rider never puts their horse away wet." ~ *Raider's Ban proverb*

Urgency drummed through my veins, and I breathed into it, moved it through my body, felt it burn. Her whiskey eyes were at half-mast, her breathing quick, her hands still locked on my hips.

As I watched, she focused again and found my gaze. My mouth went dry, and the heat swept through me again.

To keep control, I shifted closer, breaking the hold of her eyes and nuzzling gently against the corner of her lips. I could've lit her up again, but she was sick and exhausted. And if I managed to sleep, I was confident I'd wake up with her hand on my cock.

The thought made me smile. "You should sleep," I told her, tugging the fallen covers back over us.

She made a noise of objection, her fingers trying to pull me closer, her lips soft and giving, no longer ravenously seeking.

Wild horses, I could drink from her all day.

"You need rest," I reminded her, and she made another grumpy noise. Pain rushed in when her fingers slowly eased from my flesh. I didn't love the sensation, but the knowledge that she'd held me hard enough to injure me went straight to my head.

Feeling like a starving man politely declining a feast, I steeled myself, breathed deeply, and lifted myself off her. I needed to be responsible, and that meant she needed to rest.

The flushed cheeks and moist, welcoming lips I could've ignored. The thighs urging me closer were tempting as fuck, but they'd be tempting later, too. It was the flicker of confusion, and the early forerunners of doubt that blew away the last traces of my resolve.

She hadn't doubted us earlier. Damned if I'd give her reason to, now.

I wasn't getting at her nipples in a hurry, and I resented that. I wanted to feel them bead against my tongue and see them glisten the way her lips did. But I had other options.

Her eyes went wide as I touched her again, keeping my hand heavy in case she was hypersensitive. Audrey's hands searched my body again, and I knew where they were headed. I had to move fast to avoid her, slipping past her infuriatingly thorough layers to her bare, open thighs.

The skin there was soft and warm. Her legs went on forever, and I gave them only the barest fraction of the appreciation they deserved before settling them over my shoulders, where they belonged.

They fit as well as I'd known they would.

I pressed a kiss to her thigh, and her breath shook, but her legs fell open wider. She was warm, wet, and welcoming. I went in slowly, keeping the pressure heavy again, aware she was still flushed and sensitized. As my tongue glided along her clit slowly, I thought I could still feel her pulsing from her last orgasm. Or was it a new round? The thought of all her rapid gasps and sheer enjoyment made me ache. Careful not to push too hard, I listened to her breathing and read the meaning in every ripple of muscle and twitch of her flesh, forcing myself to reduce the speed of my strokes and suction. I had all night.

She shuddered under my mouth, and I repeated the kisses. Her breath broke, her hands hovering in and above my hair, her legs flexing around me.

Hunger raced through me. I didn't know how long it'd take before those legs locked around my head or whether she'd just lie there, totally trusting, letting me eat my fill. She arched into me, and those fluttering, tentative hands finally settled in my hair.

Satisfied I was where I was supposed to be, I let myself enjoy the way she'd flex and then collapse for a time, flex and then collapse. I breathed in the smell of her, committing it to memory. I savored the taste of her, wanting to draw it out. Her breath broke, and she shuddered. I added in long strokes of my tongue, imagining what it'd be like to have her come against my mouth. How many times could we do this? *Should* didn't matter now. The blood in my veins roared and nothing beyond the now mattered, beyond her.

The hands in my hair gripped tight, and I struggled not to alter my course. She let out a long, low moan, then released me with something that sounded like a mumbled apology. *Don't be sorry.* But I wasn't moving to tell her that unless I had to. Surely, she could tell there was no apology needed.

She tugged gently at me, her hands at my jaw, her body shifting beneath me.

Worry flared, coursing through the veins tangled in lust, a disarming combination that left me powerless when I looked up her body and saw her imploring me with her eyes.

There was something painfully erotic about her top half remaining tightly-laced in her sensible riding habit, with her bare, wide open legs in my hands and cunt glistening for me, her neat plait all but unraveled against the blankets, wisps curling around her face and over her shoulders.

Debauching noble ladies had never been my thing. A moment later, I realized it still wasn't.

Debauching *Audrey*, however…

Wordlessly, she tugged me again, not entirely gently. I turned my face into her palm and pressed a kiss to it, trying to gather my thoughts, wanting to leave them and continue feasting.

She twisted her hips, just a little, as if she knew what I was thinking. I tried to move with her, but she had me under an arm and was levering me up like I was a puppet and she held the strings.

I didn't laugh at the image, just let her lock her legs around my hips again, grabbing the makeshift wedge I'd made before and thanking my own foresight. She rubbed her cheek against mine, breathing quickly still, one hand locked around my neck in a manner that probably should've been threatening, but just made me burn. Before she could find my cock with her other hand, I dropped a kiss on her shoulder, no longer giving a single cuss about the million layers of wool, cotton, and silk.

"Just wait," I told her, wanting just a moment, imagining her expression, the feel of her coming around my cock, the way she'd curl into me afterward.

I straightened, raising up on my knees. I expected she'd raise up, too, keeping her legs locked around me. I knew better than to expect her to lie back and wait, after all.

What I didn't expect was that she'd come with me, stuck like a burr. The woman's determination was simultaneously humbling and the hottest thing I had experienced in my entire life. Her hand fisted in my hair, and she made a needy noise. It was suddenly very difficult to breathe.

If the Wife had appeared at the door in need at that moment, I probably would've kicked it shut.

I yanked the wedge beneath her, praying to every god I'd heard of and any others I might've missed that I'd positioned us right as I lowered her over it, letting her drape back. My feast. My fire.

There was no air in my lungs to reassure her when she made a noise of surprise, and before I could find some, she was leaning back, adjusting the angle where our hips met, trying to fit us together. Her hand reached between us, and my heart about squeezed out of my chest to see her expression of total focus.

Her fingers were strong and sure. I breathed through the hunger, set my weight, and waited for her to guide me into her body, reining in all my instincts and breathing the heat around, feeling her hold on my cock and resisting the urge to pump myself into her hand or her body. I forced myself to focus on her. On the way her breath caught and then rushed out, the delicate furrowing of her brow. The heat of her as she guided me home. The moment of resistance and the quick thought of, *Is she wet enough?* I eased back a little, and her brow furrowed a little more, her long mouth pursed momentarily. I breathed and helped reposition us. She drew me back in and deeper again. Her lips parted, her expression relaxing. My heart might've stopped the same time her lashes gave a tiny flicker. I forced myself to keep breathing anyway. She held us together, sealed tightly, her legs around my hips. And by every deity ever worshipped, it was the most wonderful sensation. It also nearly killed me.

With a long exhale, she lay back, her hips held up by the wedge, and her arms beside her head in graceless, gorgeous disarray. If I'd had anything to spare, I'd have wept at the sight.

I took hold of her thighs and leaned in, separating her labia so her clit rubbed against my pubic mound and keeping my breathing deep and even as she made a hungry noise, flexing against me. Her cunt squeezed me, demanding.

My thoughts fractured. I knew I had to be patient. I had to do this right. I didn't know what wrong was, though. It was *all* so right. I moved, and she started panting. I tried to circle my hips, tried to grind into her. Her cheeks were pink. I remembered the day she'd been riding her pillow. Wild horses, I wanted her to ride me, to grind us together until we collapsed, exhausted. I wanted her on top of me the way she'd been in the orchard, calling the pace, taking what she wanted. I wanted her hand on my cock, and I wanted her to stare at me with those whiskey eyes while I lost myself.

Her back was arched, her hands fisted, her lips open. She flexed around me, and I breathed through the rush of desperation, letting the pleasure burn through every part of me, holding the rhythm without wavering.

The first ripples of her orgasm clutched at my cock, and I held on as she arched up, her eyes unseeing, her expression one of rapture. Before me, she blurred as I struggled to focus or even breathe, feeling the peak coming and struggling to maintain the pattern she needed until the rippling of her muscles turned to a flutter, and I could throw caution to the wind, thrusting hard into her, climbing, and then letting myself fall.

CHAPTER FIFTY-SIX

AUDREY

"Hope can cause you to over-commit. Never hesitate to turn back. Everything is replaceable, except you." ~ *Matri'sion lesson*

My body ached. My hips hurt the worst where they had dug into the hard ground through the thin mattress. My shoulder hurt, too. But *everything* hurt.

The warmth felt good, though, and I knew the pain was only a fraction of what it could be. What it *had* been. I huddled into the pile of makeshift blankets and wished myself back to sleep in the cozy nest he'd re-made around us while I was still trying to recall what world I was in.

Mayhap I drifted in and out of dreams. The pain stayed, though, as I listened to the horses snuffling outside and the rise and fall of Chay's voice as he cared for them. I should've joined him. The sun had been up for some time, and he'd already banked the fire and replaced the water.

But if I moved, then the day was a reality I'd need to face. And I didn't want to. There was nothing good that would come from leaving this bed.

As I was swimming up through a sleepy haze of guilt and hopelessness, the door creaked open, and cold air gusted over me.

I ignored the pain as best I could, wiggling my toes and focusing on my breath. I could've pretended to be asleep, but I didn't. When I saw the worried way Chay was looking at me, the guilt moved to the fore.

"If we wait a little longer, the sun'll burn some of the cold off the air," he offered quietly. "We should head straight back."

There was no point in returning to the stone. Which meant there was no point in returning to La'Angi.

Had Isolde been well enough to bank her own fire? The thought had made my sleep sporadic and kept my belly knotted. And I wouldn't know until I went back.

"We could stay," he said softly, sitting on the ground. "There's wood and some food. Plenty of honey." His eyes went to my lips, just for a moment. "The horses have shelter."

Tears burned my throat, and I swallowed them away. I didn't want to go. I didn't want to stay. I wanted to *fix* this.

"We can't spend another day at the stone," he said slowly. "You know that, right?"

"Yes." That didn't mean I'd accepted it.

He was quiet for a moment, then offered, "I could make the ride to and from. You could wait here. *If* you wait here."

I remembered the time I'd fallen out of a tree Isolde had been teaching me to climb. I hadn't broken anything, but half my body had been bruised. I'd *hurt.* She hadn't been especially gentle or gracious. There had been no additional encouragement or teachings. It was what it was. I healed. I recovered. We tried again.

I didn't know why the memory of such an everyday occurrence made me want to cry. Of all the memories I had of the woman, was that the one that would stay with me at the end? Not the time I'd seen her appear behind a man, cut the artery in his groin, and whisk away the children he'd threatened? Or…or the other things jumbled in my head? Like violently tossed bedsheets, the thoughts layered over one another, jarring. My heart skittered in my chest, and I couldn't slow my breath.

What if she *was* dead?

It was going to happen. I'd known it was. One day, I was going to walk in and find her alone in that big bed, the floor awash, dangling halfway to the floor, bruising around her throat and…

"Storm's happy," Chay said, and the words hit me like as smithy's hammer on hot steel. "She'd prefer her warm stall, of course, but I found some apples that weren't half bad and gave them both some treats." He shifted to sit beside me. "Sun hasn't been up long. I probably woke you cutting the wood a little while ago. The beekeeper must've had chickens, but they've been nabbed by someone hungrier than him. His garden's passable, though." He settled back into his place at my back, and I leaned into him. "I'm sorry about the stone, Audrey. I really am."

Of course he was. He had it, too. I'd effectively ended his life in every single way. "It works," I told him, and my voice creaked from disuse. "I know it does. I just don't know how."

"It might have nothing to do with fire," he said tiredly. "For all we know, it's powered by giant waves."

It wasn't impossible. It had to be fueled by something. "We don't know enough about old magic," I said, wishing I could be angry about that, about everything that had been stolen from us. "Did you know La'Angi used to have potatoes, not apples?"

"No," he said. "Can I hold you?"

"Yes." It was the only answer, really. "I read that fruit was a hot commodity, so the orchards were planted by Barloc's son. The people were worried because trees hide many foes, but they were assured that there would be peace, and they'd prosper more with fruit harvests than common vegetables."

He made a thoughtful noise, holding me close. "They weren't wrong."

"Was it *peace*, though?" I asked him, feeling like I was a million years old.

He shrugged. "For some, it would've been. Few common folk care who wears the crown. If they've got bread in their bellies today, and they know it'll be there tomorrow, things are well enough."

I knew that, but it didn't change the fact that people's definition of *peace* was irritatingly simplistic. I could be silent and not be at peace—and frequently was. "It's either blood magic, or it's a type we don't know of."

"Could be faded after all these years," he said softly.

I shifted, but I couldn't see him properly without craning my head. Even as I moved, he slipped his arm under mine, and it was perhaps the best pillow I'd ever put my head on. "Do Blood Oaths fade?"

"Not as far as I know. But that's one lifetime. We're talking a half-dozen or more. And it's sustained by my life."

Blood magic was so *messy*. "It never made sense to me, needing to kill people to fuel your spells."

"I'm not dead," he said reasonably. "It doesn't all burn through lifeforce."

I turned the idea around in my mind. "Have you seen much of it in your travels?" It was strictly controlled here. What I knew was fragments of a picture I couldn't fathom.

"Fortunately not." He sighed deeply. "I'm sorry. I suspect whatever stopped that arrow the other day is the same thing that stopped the wave, if *either* thing ever happened."

"They happened."

He nodded. "I trust you. I'm not sure what way's up right now. I don't know that I want to, either."

My heart ached. I found his hand and covered it with my own. But there was little I could do to make him feel better, really.

It wasn't an unfair assumption, which is why it'd been mine, earlier. But I'd cut my hand, and it hadn't triggered the stone in any meaningful fashion.

"We could test it again," I said slowly. "I had a cut on my arm that day. It was minor, but I brushed up against the stone. I could blood it, then have you shoot at me."

He clicked his tongue. "My blood'd boil if I did it right. And the arrow would probably go wide and be a useless test. I never did spend enough time practicing the bow. You could shoot at me."

The thought of it failing and leaving him with an arrow lodged *anywhere* made panic flash through me. "No."

"I've a shield," he said mildly.

"Good." I was quietly confident that wouldn't matter. The thought of the man who'd stood in the shadow of curtains, lining Chay up in the rain, waiting for his shot, made me achingly cold. I snuggled back into him. "We could get more blood."

"I could certainly fetch a few people I'd volunteer for that," he agreed. "And why not, if we're all doomed?"

I wasn't sure if he was serious, so I didn't respond to that. I doubted sacrifice was the key. It didn't feel like it'd fit. Lining people up, cutting throats, when you had a giant wave bearing down on you? Too many things could go wrong. A sensible system would be sustainable. And cutting someone's throat didn't involve fire. The monolith had been burned. There was fire involved, somehow.

"I'm sorry I said that," he told me, the words full of sorrow.

"Said what?" I shook my head. "Worry not." They would've kept the area stocked with burnables, I was sure of it. And that would be why drainage didn't include that park. They wouldn't want to extinguish them while they burned. And really, if they were willing to sacrifice *anyone*, that wouldn't be the slowest thing to accomplish, I supposed. But a person took only a short time to bleed out. I'd done it. The memory made my skin crawl. It had felt like an eon but had only been a few moments. Burning blood didn't seem efficient.

Excitement rushed through me. What made sense wasn't to burn *blood*—it was to burn *the whole body*.

"Chay," I said, trying to contain the spurt of hope. "What if it's fueled not by life, but by death? Bone, not blood?"

"Bone magic?" he asked me. "A lesser man than I would make a joke of that, my lady. Tell me more before I decide if I'm a lesser man today."

Laughter bubbled in me. I sat up, searching for my layers. "*If* it's blood magic, and *if* it uses fire, wouldn't it make sense to burn bodies?"

He watched me, no longer laughing. "I know we're in a dire situation, Audrey, but I'm not comfortable setting someone alight. At least, not anyone I can access today."

I dismissed that, focusing a majority of my attention on dressing as swiftly as I could. "Not a *live* person. This is to be used in urgent circumstances. A *smart* people would have a system they could initiate quickly with low variability. You wouldn't want to have to find a sacrifice, then make sure they were sacrificed at the right time in the right place."

He was frowning. "No, you wouldn't."

I didn't look to try to see whether he was laughing at me or not. "It makes sense, doesn't it?" The One, the Wife, and the Son, I hoped I wasn't wrong. "I want to try it."

"I can tell." He sat up. "We can try once, then we return here and warm up."

I nodded, because he was right to be wary, and also because if I had another idea whilst we were there, I was going to try it regardless and he couldn't stop me. "We'll need a body." I should've been more concerned about that. Mayhap it spoke to the levels of loss we'd endured, or mayhap I was not a kind person.

"Got one," he said, straightening. "The owner of our magnificent lodgings."

My heart twisted at the thought. I'd known, of course, but I hadn't really *known*. "It makes sense, though, does it not?"

"It makes sense," he agreed. "It explains why there are no old burial grounds in the city, if you used to burn your dead. I believe it was a very common practice." That bit of information hit me like a match into tinder. My hands started to shake. I couldn't do my laces straight. "I'm going to ready the horses. If Storm'll carry him, it's probably best I tie him to your saddle. Bliksem can carry the both of us, whereas she'll struggle to move me. And I'd rather ride with you than him."

That made sense, too. So many things made sense. And while the thought of tossing the man who'd lived and died in this sweet little home over my horse's saddle made me want to scream at the unfairness of the situation, it was a neat solution. And it had the benefit of Chay's warmth.

And his touch.

I was a monster for thinking such things whilst organizing to transport a person's remains.

"Unless you're not comfortable with that," he added.

"Of course. No. I mean, of course, I'm happy to ride with you."

"I'll see what can be done, then. Don't rush those laces. I'll be checking later."

Delight skimmed over my skin, and I paused for a moment to watch as he let himself back out into the cold. Silhouetted for a moment against the winter sunlight, he looked like the hero I'd always wanted. Strong, long legs, sword riding comfortably at his side, well-worn boots, and shoulders wide enough for even the weight I brought with me.

Then the door closed, and I was jolted from my reverie, guilt rushing into the gap it left behind. He didn't need to carry my weight. No one did. Those wide shoulders had many uses, but that wasn't one of them.

The lace I was tightening snapped under the force of my self-disgust.

It took far too long for me to be ready. By the time I was, both horses were saddled, and Storm was grudgingly permitting Chay to tie the man's remains to her.

He'd tossed a blanket over the body, and I was grateful for the kindness while also feeling like a coward for taking the easy out.

"Did you bank the fire?" he asked me from the other side of Bliksem. "It's worth having somewhere to return to."

I put aside my feelings on the matter and nodded, doing what he recommended and adjusting how he'd set the logs already to slow their burn. If this didn't work, we'd have a safe hidey-hole. At least for another night. If we opted to stay.

Adjusting the scarf around my face, I returned outside to find we were now ready to go. He brought me over, standing behind me, and introduced me to his warhorse, who stood significantly taller than my Storm and looked at me with disapproving eyes.

I wanted to squirm. "I don't believe he approves."

"He's just possessive," Chay told me, taking my hand and offering our joined fingers to his horse. "She's with us, friend," he murmured as the horse snuffled at our fingers. He was a gorgeous beast. I'd expected him to be strong, and he had the deep chest, long legs, and wide back you'd expect from a 'Ban warhorse. But his face was *pretty*. "I wouldn't ask you to carry just any old person, now, would I?"

He snorted at Chay, withdrawing his muzzle. Behind him, Storm nickered at me, and I looked over at her, feeling like a turncoat. "They must be hungry."

"They'd happily have some chaff, but they've grazed well. I'll give you a boost."

I looked up—all the way up—to where I needed to climb, kilting up one side of my skirts quickly.

The loss of those layers increased the chill factor immediately. I didn't dally, and I wasn't proud, letting Chay give me a quick lift to save Bliksem from my attempts. Storm was fine, I knew how to mount her in both saddle types. But this fellow was a different shape, and while I suspected he was a tough old veteran, I didn't want to ask him to use his strength where he didn't need to.

Chay was murmuring to him and Storm both, and I just sat there as he made it all work around me.

The beekeeper's hut looked so small from the outside, so plain. There was a part of me that wanted to climb back in there and curl up under the covers. Except the covers weren't there anymore. They were all in use.

"Coming up," he told me, and I made as much space as I could but had to settle back, practically in his lap.

That probably would've been awkward yesterday. Today, he just flicked his cloak over my right leg where I'd kilted up my skirts.

He didn't kiss me. I sort of expected he might. I didn't know if I wanted it or not. I knew I definitely didn't want to endlessly loop on the topic of the monolith, and I certainly didn't want corpses on my mind. Not the one near us, and definitely not what I might find back at the keep. As we started to move, he murmured encouragement to the horses still. Out of the lee of the beekeeper's home, the wind was bitter and biting. Almost immediately, I ached all the way to my soul.

I huddled back into him, and his arms tightened a little more. One-handed, he adjusted my cloak so my gloved hands were safe beneath it. My heart hurt.

Nothing I'd done for this poor man was good.

I didn't want to think about any of it. So I grabbed onto the first thing I could. "You never asked if I was a virgin," I said.

I couldn't see his expression, but he didn't tense up at all. "None of my business, is it?" he asked me. "You knew what you wanted, and so did I."

It was that simple for him. "Do you still want it?" I realized I'd just referred to intimacy with myself as *it*, but didn't know how to fix my poor wording. Ideas charged through my mind.

"I'd like a bath," he said before I could explain what I meant. "I'm not handling the dead then putting those hands on you, Embers." I wanted to rest my head against his, but Bliksem's gait made that a dangerous idea. My eyes burned. "I don't know what the future holds," he said quietly. "I had a lot of fun, but you need rest and sleep, and somewhere warm."

I did. "You're warm."

Finally, he turned his lips into my hair. "So are you, once I've had a few moments with you," he said, the words a little lower. "If my hands were cleaner and the situation happier, I could warm you up right now."

The thought was so far removed from reality that I had no problem enjoying the fantasy. He probably could, too, the way he'd brought me to my peak with just the pressure of his palm yesterday.

We'd have to get back on a horse eventually. If this didn't work…

"I'm looking forward to it," I told him, and let him shelter me in his arms.

CHAPTER FIFTY-SEVEN
CHAY

"Forgiveness is not earned, it is gifted." ~ *Matri'sion proverb*

Whether it was because I was sick or because my lady had warmed more than just my cock last night, it was harder to dismiss reality and drift in a fantasy. The trip back to the monolith felt like it took all day, but the sun was barely high enough to burn the frost off the ground.

I should've offered to come alone. I should've, but I hadn't wanted to be away from her. Not when she was so vulnerable.

As soon as we arrived, my first task was to remove the poor beekeeper from Audrey's horse. Without prompting, she spent time soothing her unsettled mount.

It gave me the opportunity to arrange some of the branches I'd hauled nearby in a haphazard pyre. The task wasn't one I'd ever done alone. I didn't know how much wood I'd need nor how much tinder to prepare. But I knew I didn't have time to worry about it.

If she was right, it'd have to work fast otherwise it wouldn't have stopped that wave she was so sure had really struck the land.

All I was sure of was that she wouldn't return to somewhere warm until this was done.

She appeared at my side, arms loaded with smaller pieces of kindling that she began to arrange beside me.

"Should've brought some dry wood," I said, just to have something to say.

"You can go get some?" she offered me. "I can continue here. You could empty Storm's bags, and—"

A chill went through me. "No." I shook my head. "Sorry to cut you off." But I wasn't entertaining the idea of separating from her. There was no way she was leaving my sight. The gold in her eyes had shrunk to a small ring of color around her pupils. Already her skin had a gray cast. "I think this'll about do. If it works, we can build it higher."

She accepted that with a nod, looking at the monolith to one side of the pyre. "Do you think he's close enough to it?"

The poor man's hip was bumped up against the rock. "I believe so."

"If this doesn't work, we could bring back some others," she said, fumbling the tinder with her gloves on.

If it didn't work, we were going somewhere as warm as the Steppes in the summer, and I was unwrapping *all* of my solstice gift, then letting her sleep all night in my arms. "Perhaps." I could always trial her ideas while she slept somewhere secure. I stripped the gloves off my hands, taking the flint from her and ignoring the gray cast to my own nails. The pain wasn't too bad yet. I'd be okay to do another trip, if I prepared well.

If this didn't work, I didn't know that it'd be *worth* doing another trip, but hope was important. And I could give her that.

The fire crackled to life, and she crouched down before it, huddled deep in her cloak. I moved around, making sure each point I'd laid was lit to reduce the chance of the whole thing failing due to my knowledge of pyres, then crouched beside her to cut some of the wind.

She leaned into me, and my heart swelled. I took her into my arms, wrapping my cloak around her shoulders. We could've been riding. There was no point waiting and watching the kindling burn. But I didn't try to hasten her out.

"You ever think about all the points in your life you made the wrong turn?" she asked me quietly.

Even in the last season I'd made more mistakes than I could count. "I try not to worry on them, but sometimes, yes." I expected her to respond with some admission or question. When she didn't, and we just sat together watching the fire climbing slowly over the damp kindling, I began to worry. There was one obvious turn she'd made very recently. "Are you rethinking what happened last night?"

She glanced over, eyes wide with shock. The fine veins around her eyes were clear beneath her skin, and I struggled not to react to that.

How many more days did I have being able to serve her?

"No. Somewhat." My heart lurched, but she was frowning. "You mentioned difficulty saying no. I think…I think it's also hard to ask for things?"

Relief rushed through me. "Does it help if I tell you I'd like you to ask for things?"

"No."

I nodded and realized my heart was racing but settling down now. By the One, that was an adrenaline rush I hadn't needed. "Is there a time when it's easier to talk?"

Her eyes were back on the pyre, but I could still make out her shrug. "On the horses was easy. In advance. When—things aren't happening."

The image of her panting breaths and arched back lodged firmly in my brain. She hadn't been talking then, that was for sure. Hunger swept through me, and I turned my attention firmly to the pyre. *You are not getting hard while you burn a man.* "We'll chat on the way back, then." It'd be a good lead-up to unwrapping my gift. "But that's what made it a wrong turn? Not asking for what you wanted?"

"Oh, it wasn't *wrong,* as much as it was *not absolutely everything I've ever had drift through my head.*" She shrugged again. "I didn't mean to confuse you. I've no complaints. Quite the opposite. I had a lot of fun. I just wish I'd done more, experienced more, and slept less."

I was definitely getting hard while I burned a man. I hoped he'd understand. "So that question wasn't prompted by last night?"

"No. No, of course not." She put her hand on my knee. The flames were small, but the smoke billowed mightily. "There've been a lot of times in life I could've walked from the paved road. I never took them. Well, not until very recently, I suppose." Her voice trailed off, and her hand moved off my knee. She hunched down, the picture of failure.

The icy wind crept into the tiny gaps between the threads of my clothes, working its way into my flesh. We sat in a heavy silence that felt right for the side of a pyre.

I should've been with Kadan, complaining about sand and playing darts, helping him recover from his injury and keeping his head whole while he supported a rebellion. I could clearly remember Luca's dismissal as he'd spoken of Ylva's strength, and the moment after Callum and I had spotted Audrey struggling in Mikus' arms.

If I could do it all again, knowing what I did now, I'd need to go back further. I'd grab her in the orchard, kidnap her. She could hate me. She could even kill me. But Luca would have his bride, Kadan would have a suitable replacement king, and she'd be safe.

Her head rested on my shoulder. The thought of delivering her to Luca made my blood boil, and not from the oath. But what was the alternative? Send her to the Matri'sion tribes and never see her?

I was a selfish man.

"We should get back," I told her.

"He isn't burning yet," she objected. "Fire cleanses."

There was no way she could know that. The smoke was too thick, a consequence of the wet, green wood and the leaves that caught and flared. "Regardless," I said, wishing I could feed her hope rather than stifle it, "I'm required to look after you. You are sort of important to me."

She straightened like I'd sworn at her, standing. "You're right. I'm sorry."

My gut twisted. I wanted to snatch her back and hold her close. I stood, too. "I'm not."

She shook her head. "Of course you are. That's only fair. It's okay." But it wasn't. I couldn't see her mouth or her brow. I couldn't hear her breath to judge if it had caught at all, but I knew.

I knew, because her heart was too big to *not* feel horrible about it.

She turned to glance toward the horses, folding her arms hard beneath her breasts. I could see tiny black threads beneath that thin, almost translucent skin. I'd be free soon and the thought left me feeling hollow. "I'm sorry for a lot of things, Audrey. But if we do end up dying here, I won't be sorry to be with you."

When she looked at me, her eyes were almost entirely black and sheened with tears. "I'm sorry you're here. But—I'm glad, too."

My heart felt heavy. I opened my arms, and she came in close, her hands clasped protectively over her chest. She rested her head on my shoulder and shook with silent tears. The answering grief in me burned my throat as I held her.

Circumstances had led us here, but we'd made choices along the way. We always did. And I was proud of a few of mine. I listened to the crackle of the fire, her quick, rasping breaths, and her muffled sobs.

Grand promises crowded in my mouth, but she wasn't the sort to be soothed by make-believe. There was little I could give her except some small joys. There was no future and no hope.

But I did have something. "My pledge to you, freely given," I told her, breathing the words through her scarf and hood. "Is the exact same as the one I gave you under threat of execution, Audrey. You've got me, until my heart no longer beats."

She stiffened in my arms, shaking her head. Rejecting my words. I didn't let myself worry about that hurt. Saying yes was hard. Saying no was hard. But this wasn't a situation where either was needed.

"You don't get to choose what I do with my heart," I told her, injecting some humor into my voice, hoping she might hear it, not the tears. "It's mine to give, and I've chosen to give it to you. You can decide what you do with it, but it's yours, regardless."

She stepped back, wiping her face. Her breath shook. Her hands did, too. "We should go. This isn't helping us." The words were thick with well-earned sorrow. "I don't know if we ought to go to the keep, or…or…" I thought of that cold, foreboding castle that held only pain. "Can you please choose?" she asked, the words wavering, her eyes fixed over my shoulder.

The air didn't want to squeeze into my lungs. I lifted my hand to my chest, pressing it over my heart as I bowed. "Yes, my lady."

"Don't do that," she pleaded, shaking her head violently. "Don't do that, please, Chay. Please."

"Why?" I asked, the ache in my bones mirrored in my heart. I didn't want to die with doubt in my mind. Better to face the truth.

"Are you—" she pressed a hand to her mouth. "This isn't about *you*, Chay. You don't bow to a woman who's failed at *everything*. You don't toss your life away for—"

"You worry about what *you* do," I told her, cutting over her tirade before it could gather momentum. "And trust me to make my own choices."

She fell silent, looking off into the distance with an expression that hurt to try to decipher. Before I could, the wind changed direction. Her cloak flurried toward me, and the smoke came a moment after, burning my eyes and coating my throat.

As I went to move her toward the horses, I caught the whiff of burning fabric. She coughed, her hand on my arm, and dragged me clear. Flames leapt where they hadn't before.

And every ache in my body vanished.

She made a noise like she'd been gut-punched, and I whirled her around, my heart in my throat.

Big, whiskey-colored eyes looked at me. The black lines faded as I watched, and healthy color rushed in. Energy coursed through my limbs, like I'd just had sunlight poured into my very veins. I drew in a deep breath and realized I could breathe *without pain*.

She reached toward me, fresh tears spilling from her eyes. "Chay," she said. "Chay. Your face. Your face. Do you feel it?"

I lifted a hand to my face, disoriented. "You're better."

"*You're* better," she said on a sob. "The One, the Wife, and the Son, Chay—*you're* better!" And she tore the scarf from her face, laughing as she wept. Her fingers were on my jaw like I was a god and she a newly found believer. And I *felt* like one.

My world spun. We were going to be okay. But it had nothing at all to do with Barloc and his deities.

Her hands were on my face, pulling me close. I met her lips, cool from the wind and wet from tears. And our hearts kept beating as I lifted her and spun her around, glorying in our strength.

CHAPTER FIFTY-EIGHT
ISOLDE

"Make sure they're down and *out."* ~ *La'Angi saying*

She danced with frantic energy. The bruises under her eyes were a stark contrast to the smile that didn't leave her face. Though her tears had decreased at the same rate as the cider in her jug, she still bore the red, puffy marks of an extended crying session.

Audrey didn't miss a step. But it had cost her.

Thomas appeared at my elbow, offering me a mulled cider. I hesitated, but took it. After so long craving heat, even with the plague lifted, I was still cold. It was, after all, winter.

"Celebrations are widespread," he said from beside me. "We ought to get her back."

I was less concerned with a drunken party than what came next. Because I had no idea what *next* could be. For all the joy and relief, Audrey had ranted for hours that afternoon about supplies, about how trade was dead, and we would all starve before the crops came in. She'd ranted about the missing Master Steward, and what aid her father might or might not send. She'd ranted about possible repercussions and what might happen with the number of the guard so dramatically drained.

Places where I'd laid too still for too long hurt like the blazes, but my mind spun like a well-oiled wheel. I sipped the warm, spiced cider.

"No one's asking too many questions yet," he said quietly. "But they will, once the initial gratitude wears off."

I didn't know who Thomas had been talking to, but I'd already heard *extensive* questions. And creative answers, too.

So long as she kept her mouth shut and let everyone else answer for her, no one ever needed to know what she'd done. They could all speculate 'til the goats came home, and it wouldn't matter. And if we were staying put, we had time to dig in.

The thought made me feel grimly pleased as I watched the locals celebrate her, as I watched her point them toward Kaelson and Bernadette. She'd already spoken to a few people I recognized, people who'd taken on informal positions of power in pockets of the community.

I was all for saddling up her horse tonight. She wasn't too drunk to ride. But we were staying.

We weren't beaten, and she knew it.

Now was the time to throw off the shackles for good.

EPILOGUE
LUCA

"It's never your enemies who betray you." ~ La'Angi saying

Two of the most powerful mages this side of the Aza Ranges walk into the back room of a middling inn. It was like the start of a joke.

But this poor son of a small fief wasn't about to be the punchline.

I ran the ripples of the short, delicate chain over the side of my finger and sent my friendly smile at the mages. My gut was liquid. I hadn't slept last night. In my palm, the weighted coins settled. They were warm from my pocket, their edges smooth and familiar.

There were five chairs in addition to mine, a platter of baked goods, and a jug with five cups.

"Hello there," the shorter, rounder mage, Amais, said. His smile had shiny teeth and highlighted the flatness of his eyes. "How was your winter, boy?"

I reached out to take a cup, tilting it toward them in offer. My hands were shaking, but they weren't paying me any mind. They shook their heads, Amais waving it away with his bejeweled fingers, Julius snorting and sending me a look laced with suspicion.

Get it together. You've got a job to do.

Arranging my face into what I hoped was the right balance of unbothered and politely interested, I poured a cup for myself and pretended I didn't realize Amais had addressed me.

They caught onto the ploy quickly and, as a countermeasure, simply continued their own conversation about spirits flavored by berries in the west.

Three chairs left. I listened beyond the conversation in front of me for the muted noise of a conversation, made indistinct by the layers of walls, and focused on the task ahead of me. In my palm, the coins' weight shifted comfortably. I ran one between my thumb and forefinger, waiting.

On cue, the door opened again. Unlike the two gray-haired men, this newcomer looked like he'd been shaving only a short time. His hair was perfectly styled, his belt intricately embossed. The embroidery around the throat of his silk shirt screamed *old money.*

Fennix wasn't from old money, or even new money. Fennix was from blood money. He did a good job acting the part, though.

They greeted him as if they didn't have spies in his home, and he greeted them in turn.

Before they could drag out the small talk anymore, I took the floor. "Now that we're all here," I began.

"We aren't," Julius told me. "In case you can't count."

"Amberrick and Desmond won't be making it," I told them, and the words came out like a simple statement. Exactly as if they'd merely been held up. And exactly as I'd practiced. *Just do the job.*

As planned, that made them fall silent, but I wasn't counting on that lasting. But I paused for a moment anyway, because though they didn't speak, there were quite a few pointed looks exchanged. I wondered if I could interrupt that sort of communication, and what impact it may have.

Unsure, I went with the spiel I'd practiced. "Thanking you all for coming today," I told them, returning the coins to my pocket and folding my hands on the table. "I have a variety of news to share with you."

Amais snorted, and Julius' bushy brows rose. But they didn't interrupt.

"First, due to the plague, the flow of information between Council members has slowed. This means some of the plans we'd had in motion have had their timelines shifted."

"What does this mean for us?" Fennix asked, his voice as neutral as mine.

"That's a complex question." I smiled at them. "And it depends on how you feel about some things we must discuss."

"Discuss, then, boy," Amais said. "Your masters know our rates."

My smile turned regretful. I gave them my best *I'm sorry* look. "About that."

Fennix let out a bitter half-laugh, his mouth twisting to the side. His knee propped up on the table. His right hand dipped down below. I didn't try to watch the movements.

Fennix hadn't completed his mage training. He was unregistered, unrestrained, and utterly unrepentant. I'd wondered, for a fleeting time, if we could've been friends. I'd thought he was similar to me.

"One of the things we were to do today was settle outstanding debts." I thought of everything I owed these men.

Thousands and thousands of deaths.

"The Duke is, as you may have noticed, still alive," I pointed out.

"Someone ended the plague," Julius shot back. "Probably him and his mages."

Possibly. The coins weighed heavily in my pocket. Exactly who and how…well, we'd see, wouldn't we? "The deal was, the Duke would die."

"I told you he wouldn't pay," Fennix said to Julius. "You can tell your Council," he sneered the word, which I didn't take offense to. I *had* engaged them without the support of everyone, initially. "We work for coin. We did the work. The integrity of your ploys isn't our responsibility."

"I appreciate that this puts you in a difficult position," I acknowledged. "You *have* received coin."

"Where's Desmond?" Julius demanded gruffly.

I considered the best way to approach the directness of that question. "I can take you to him, if you'd like?" I offered.

"Is he alive?" Julius asked.

I gave him the regretful smile again.

Amais scraped back his chair. "You—"

Fennix shoved him back down. "I think it's time you understood something, *Inky*," he said, sneering my childhood nickname. "I don't take kindly to threats."

"The simple way to resolve this," I said, waving between us with one hand, "is to not require threatening, Fennix." I shrugged. "The next role I have for the three of you—"

"No." Julius slapped his hand on the table. "No more jobs until you pay up, *boy*. You've access to purses deep enough."

"I do," I agreed. The people holding those purse strings hadn't approved the last meeting, though they'd approved this one. And the outcomes I'd predicted. "You aren't going to receive any further coin. You've caused untold damage. You unleashed the plague in the wrong area, refused to attempt to control it, and allowed thousands to die."

"On your orders," Amais snarled.

But I was watching Fennix as he rolled his head on his neck, a small, bitter smile on his mouth. "This isn't how men of honor do business," Julius said stiffly. "I know a few of your Council members, boy. I *know* they didn't approve your actions last time. I *know* they're upset with you."

I shrugged again. I'd managed the situation. And while Amais drew breath, his face red and breaths short, I kept on watching Fennix as he lifted his hand from where it had been concealed by his hip to show a brooch with a clockwork raven on it. It wasn't entirely uncommon. Sometimes, they were even just brooches.

But in Fennix's hand, there was no doubt that it was spelled.

He turned it over in his fingers. Either side of him, the two older mages sat back, and fear coiled in my belly.

I wrapped a hand around the cup I'd poured.

"Luca," he said slowly. "You and I, we're new to this game. I don't know who's tutoring *you*, but I know the person who tutored *me* always advised I never threaten anyone with something I wasn't willing to survive myself."

Considering the things I'd heard Fennix threaten, I doubted anything he'd just said was true. I let him speak, though, because anything else would just drag this out.

"As you know," he went on, "I lost my mother a few years ago."

There it was. The *I have someone in your home.* I felt sick. I'd never wanted it to come to this.

Do the job, Luca.

"This brooch?" He flipped it between his fingers. "Simple make, really, isn't it? If the beak opens…well, ravens eat meat, Inky."

I wished, for a moment, that my parents had given me a less embarrassing pet name. "Fascinating," I said. "Did you want to explain further, Fen?"

He looked at me like I was simple. "Do I need to?" he asked me softly.

I shrugged, digging back into my pocket. "I never understood threatening people's loved ones. So you kill my mother. What about next time? You may as well just torture me. That's a resource that'll deplete much slower." I pulled out the brooch's pair, tossing it onto the table. "That was another point of conversation," I acknowledged, nodding toward it and dipping back into my pocket and taking out the fistful of buckles, earrings, necklaces, and pins I'd taken from their spies, then gently spreading them across the table. "This is your man," I mused, flicking a buckle to Julius. "And this was his partner. She was lovely." The necklace went too. "Amias, your cook was excellent." The pin I flicked over, I did with regret. "All of this I usually would have sent via merchant," I acknowledged, divvying it all up. "But," I laughed a little. "The plague, it had unforeseen impacts, did it not?"

"Some of us aren't afraid of death," Fennix said softly. "You couldn't torture me if you tried, Luca."

"I did consider that," I agreed conversationally. From the bottom of my mind, images swam up of the dead I'd helped carry over the winter. My belly clutched, and for a moment, the shame impaled me.

I shifted and felt the weighted coins in my pocket. "Drink?" He ignored me, so I took my hand from the cup. "Julius, you don't love anyone. Who could I possibly take to ensure your behavior?"

"How do you think we got out of the mage guild?" he demanded, the words icy. "You don't know who you're dealing with."

"You're right, I'm sure," I agreed, injecting humility into my words, the student being incorrectly schooled by their senior. I untied a pouch I'd hoped not to use from my belt. "You don't love anyone, Julius." I set the pouch on the table. The tongue of a little silver bell gave a half-chime. I drew out a piece of parchment, blackened around the edges, and unfortunately crumpled, and slid it over to him. "But you do have such an admirable cheese collection. The experts you pay, and the recipe you use? It's really quite fine. Perfected over years. You couldn't replace that research. Not in this lifetime." I didn't wait for the blood to drain from Julius' face. "And Amais, you don't take pleasure in much."

"I enjoy being paid," he said between his teeth, but his eyes were on the pouch.

I tipped it up, sending the bell onto the table. A sweet little silver bell that made me want to vomit. *Do the job.* "And you enjoy your lovely cat," I agreed. "Such a soft little baby, with her big, round eyes."

He stood, thrusting back his chair. "What sort of monster—"

"Shame if something happened to her," I said softly. "That fuzzy coat of hers, it isn't much protection, is it? She's so delicate." I deliberately didn't look at Fennix. "With her dark, glossy hair. And her new little kitten, too, in the basement next door. Luxuriously outfitted, hidden from view." From the corner of my eye, I saw Fennix's jaw tighten, and I twisted the knife a little more. "She *should* be safe there, shouldn't she?"

Fennix's jaw tightened.

Amais laughed, relief in the sound. "What are you talking about?" he demanded.

I clicked my tongue. My heart was beating too fast in my chest, and I couldn't resist the urge to look toward Fennix any longer. His hand was dipping down again, out of view. "I must be thinking of someone else's pussy—"

His upper body twisted. A silver blur arced through the air toward me, and my heart lurched. The clockwork weapon was small, round, and landed between my hand and my chest with a *click* and the reek of burning hair.

A few sparks came out of it, and then it popped open, silver clockwork pieces, chunks of crystal, and oil falling over the table as if a handful of junk had been dumped from someone's carefully cupped hands.

I picked up a piece and dropped it into the liquid in my cup, which hissed and spat.

They were silent.

"You told me you'd kill the Duke," I reminded them all softly. "I'm not paying for shoddy work. Not in coin. But I am willing to pay you back for my disappointment, unless you improve my mood." I looked at the three of them—Amais' red face, Julius' fixed expression, Fennix's set jaw. I'd made enemies. But at least now they'd go after *me* for their retribution.

We couldn't afford to lose them.

And I couldn't afford to let them go after my loved ones before they went after me.

"I'm a better ally than I am an enemy," I told them all, keeping the words regretful. "So let's work on rebuilding our trust in one another." I looked at Amais pointedly, and he grabbed his chair in a white-knuckled hand and dragged it back under his backside, sitting at the table.

"I have the perfect place to start," I told them all, my smile changing to become welcoming as I drew out a map of Black Borough.

Take La'Angi, take the east. Take the Borough, take the west.

Take the kingdom.

If you have feelings about this book, please share them! Reviews help books find the right readers.

Unchained will be releasing in 2025, and you can follow the author on all the normal places, or find her at elissehay.com

If you'd like more right now, there's a bonus bathhouse scene for all newsletter subscribers. Sign up here:

ACKNOWLEDGMENTS

Amanda, if you're reading this–Lias won't make this iteration of the series, but I hope there are enough green flag characters to make up for it. Your early validation made every difference to the fact this story has survived.

A massive thank you to Sharon, who never stopped asking, "but when's Audrey coming out?" when I would've let her sleep in my drafts forever, and Lynnda, who has always been a cheerleader.

A huge shoutout to Charlene and Holly, whose eyeballs on the (very) rough draft of this helped me see the forest, not the leaves. I can't tell you how grateful I am for the maps you gave me.

Skye, thank you for helping me keep my kitchen clean, and making the best candles I've ever sniffed. I'll never forget you were willing to ride for me, even at school pickup time. That's true friendship. Also, if a fellow Books and Bitches Down Under bitch is snooping in the acknowledgments at the back end of their eBook, you're contractually obligated to make a note in your eReader here and make this one of the most highlighted sentences. I didn't make the rules.

I'm forever grateful to my rescued Owls, and I definitely don't have the word count to express why. Hoot hoot, friendos.

For Sam, from Haus of Fables, whose author services helped me claw my way back from burnout, and whose lessons I hold near and dear, I will forever be grateful.

If you're a fellow author digging for info on editors–you need to now go look up The Fiction Editor. Shelly doesn't list miracle worker in her job description, but she should.

Ols, if you made it here, thank you for being an amazing friend. Also, what the hell are you doing reading romantasy? Just assume I've named you in every book (I do) and read something you enjoy.

And, as always, I have to circle back to Wayne, who has read every iteration of this series I've ever shoved in front of him, which, considering how chonky these are, is probably millions of words. If you're here, this is your Save a Character's Life voucher. Use it wisely. (Don't buy additional books, it only works once.) Thank you for always believing in me. And for the coffee. I love you.

CONTENT NOTES

Family violence (gendered, sexualized)
Death of a parent
War crimes
Plague and plague victims of all ages
Premature childbirth

Turn for detailed information, sorted by topic of:

- Triggers
- Chapters
- The critical contents of that chapter, if you'd like to skip it.

TRIGGER WARNINGS

FAMILY VIOLENCE (GENDERED, SEXUALIZED)

There are frequent, brief mentions of historic abuse throughout the novel. Intergenerational trauma is a core part of the themes of this trilogy. If you are sensitive to this content, please note the below scenes are extended conversations or experiences of abuse, but there are numerous mentions of it not noted here.

Consistent mentions throughout the series of familial abuse.

Prologue: aftermath of physical violence.
Triggers: mentions of physical violence against a child. On-page facilitation of aid in the aftermath. Discussion of escape.
Skipping this chapter? Know Isolde has taken Audrey under her wing, that Luca is betrothed to Audrey and postponed the wedding when young, but didn't sever the betrothal, and he swore a Blood Oath to her.

~

Sporadic mentions of trauma bond.

Triggers: desire to leave but inability to. Walking on eggshells. Acknowledgment of the cycle.

~

Sexual Violence

Chapter 8: On-page, POV character who dissociates.
Triggers: exposure of victim. Body weight of attacker. Threat to loved one. Shame.
Skipping this chapter? Know that the Duke is angry with Audrey for interacting with Raider's Ban men. Isolde is using somatic techniques to ground Audrey and help her process trauma. Luca knows what is happening but does not intervene. Sullivan is the guard the Duke uses, as he's the most controlled.

Chapter 12: Mentions of intent to sexually assault. (see also: war crimes)
Triggers: kidnapping, restraint (primarily off-page). Violent, gendered comments. Physical assault (kidnapping, grabbing).
Skipping this chapter? Know we're introduced to Thomas, a perspective character, father, and veteran of the battle of Wolfswail. He and Chay are forced to swear a magically binding Blood Oath. Chay swears it to Audrey rather than the Duke, and Thomas follows.

~

DEATH OF A PARENT

There are frequent, brief mentions of historic abuse throughout the novel. Audrey's mother was murdered by her father, and this is mentioned throughout the story. If you are sensitive to this content, please be aware it is almost exclusively off-page, but frequently will come up.

Chapter 13: Non-POV character learns Audrey witnessed her mother's death.
Triggers: child witness. Parent's attempt to protect. Blood. Grief. Fear of self.
Skipping this chapter? Know that the tower is a three-level, defensible, self-contained spiral, and that both Chay and Isolde identify Audrey is masking. She is acting cheerful, energetic, and helpful.

~

WAR CRIMES

Semi-frequent mentions of general war crimes.

Chapter 12: POV character experiencing (and dealing with conflict) whilst having flashbacks. (see also, sexual violence.)
Triggers: Nightmares. Blurring of reality and memory. Blood, gore. Grief. Shame. Disassociation.
Skipping this chapter? Know we're introduced to Thomas, a perspective character, father, and veteran of the battle of Wolfswail. He and Chay are forced to swear a magically binding Blood Oath. Chay swears it to Audrey rather than the Duke, and Thomas follows.

Chapter 16: POV character referencing boots full of blood. (See also: premature childbirth.)
Triggers: Blood. Blurring of reality and memory. Disassociation.
Skipping this chapter? Know that Thomas is told his wife has given birth early, that he is struggling with his memories of

war, and that he still gives Chay half an hour to visit Kadan before leaving to be with his wife.

PLAGUE AND PLAGUE VICTIMS OF ALL AGES

The magical plague is a core part of this story. Mentions of illness, pain, slow decline, and death are frequent, especially from chapter 28 onward. If this is sensitive content for you, please enter this book cautiously.

Chapter 23: First on-page plague victims.
Triggers: on page infant, child, and mother death. Grief. Violent death of sick children. Failure of medical intervention.
Skipping this chapter? Know that it's been a moon since the Duke left, that there is unrest in the city due to the illness, and that Audrey attempts to help a family. When a Magework Healer attempts to cure them, the mage dies, as does the child. Older children attack her in their grief. Isolde defends, but Chay is the one who kills them.

PREMATURE CHILDBIRTH

Chapter 16: POV character informed his wife needed medical intervention due to premature birth. (See also: war crimes.)
Triggers: uncertainty. Unable to be present. Hope.
Skipping this chapter? Know that Thomas is told his wife has given birth early, that he is struggling with his memories of war, and that he still gives Chay half an hour to visit Kadan before leaving to be with his wife.

Chapter 18: POV character sees wife and healthy child after a difficult birth.
Triggers: Blood. Uncertainty. Grief. Relief. Healthy infant (boy).
Skipping this chapter? Know that Thomas loves his wife and new child very much, and that he even goes to make an offering at the Bonetree on behalf of his wife.

PRONUNCIATION GUIDE AND GLOSSARY

PLACES

Arcanloc: AR-can-LOCK. *Kingdom story is set in.*
Azashi: AH-zaa-SHE. *Capital of Arcanloc.*
La'Angi: lah-AHN-gee: *setting for the story: capital of the land pre-Barloc.*
Ltona: DE-tonn-AH. *Country to the south of Arcanloc.*
Raa'shi: RAAH-shee. *Small city at the foothills of the primary pass through the Aza Ranges.*
Raider's Ban: RAY-derrs BAN. *Sprawling grasslands city known for its horses.*
Steppes: STEPS. *Primarily open grasslands, extreme weather, northern part of the continent, inhabited by nomadic tribes.*
South (the): SOW-th. *Mountainous region that is to the south of Arcanloc, but north of Ltona.*
Wolfswail: Woolfs-WHAIL. *Larger city in the South, conquered by the Duke of La'Angi in last war.*
Matri'sion Tribal Lands: MAH-tree-SHON try-BULL

lanns. *Area to the far northwest protected by a mountain range. Semi-nomadic women warriors inhabit this region.*

PEOPLE

Audrey: AUH-dree. *Daughter of the Duke of La'Angi and Arabella of La'Angi.*
Chay: CH-ay. *Liegeman of Raider's Ban then bloodsworn to Audrey.*
Darrius: DAH-ree-US. *Count of Raider's Ban.*
Kadan: CAH-dan. *Son of Darrius of Raider's Ban.*
Luca: LOO-cah. *Heir to Raa'shi.*
Rose: ROH-se. *Wife of Thomas.*
Thomas: TOMM-ass. *Veteran of the La'Angi military, bloodsworn to Audrey.*
Victor: VICK-tor. *Duke of La'Angi. Also referred to as the Butcher.*
Wuden: WOO-den. *Son of the leader of the Southern rebels; Worg.*
Ylva: EEL-vah. *Daughter of the leader of the Southern rebels; Worg.*

MISCELLANEOUS

Gaelena: GAAY-len-AH. Southern diety.
Healer: mage who ascertains and attempts to heal physical injuries with magic.
Matri'sion: MAH-tree-SHON. A member of the women-only semi-nomadic tribes.
Sorceress: Southern magic user with she/her or they/she pronouns.
Worg: cursed Southerners. Heightened senses, wear silver.

www.ingramcontent.com/pod-product-compliance
Lightning Source LLC
Chambersburg PA
CBHW010449310726
48979CB00018B/2872/J

* 9 7 8 1 9 2 3 3 4 4 0 2 0 *